Praise for Elizabeth Harris

'Enormously enjoyable...hard to put down. Elizabeth Harris writes with sensitivity and skill and a spine-chilling eye for the sinister'
– Barbara Erksine, author of *Lady of Hay*

'Enigmatic ... the author really captures the imagination'
– Sunday Independent

'A wonderfully descriptive and enjoyable read.'
– Reader's Panel

Other books in The Wilderness Series

A Good Man's Love

Singing in the Wilderness

THE WILDERNESS SERIES, BOOK 3

A Slight Folly

ELIZABETH HARRIS

LUME BOOKS

LUME BOOKS

Published in 2020 by Lume Books
30 Great Guildford Street,
Borough, SE1 0HS

ISBN 978-1-83901-282-2

Typeset using Atomik ePublisher from Easypress Technologies

www.lumebooks.co.uk

For my father

Part One

Follies

Autumn 1990

Chapter 1

Hal

It was a beautiful morning for driving across southern England.

If Hal hadn't had other matters on his mind, he would have admired the bright sunshine on the South Downs and the glimpses of the spangled light on the sea over to the left. The autumn day was one of the best that the season had to offer, and there wasn't even too much traffic.

But he was driving automatically, barely taking in the glories of the day. And it wasn't things on his mind, plural; it was just one huge, solitary, glaring thing.

He shouldn't be there. Shouldn't be driving by himself, on this journey he had no business making. When he had needed to give a reason for his trip he'd muttered vaguely that it was to do with work; that he needed to visit some of the places where Britain's Neolithic inhabitants had lived, apparently thrived, and built their enduring monuments. Avebury, the West Kennet Long Barrow, Stonehenge. It was background, he said, for the new book he was struggling so hard to get on with. When asked how long he'd be away he said, offhandedly, 'Oh, three, maybe four days.' And he'd been swamped with the guilty feeling that, despite all evidence to the contrary, Jo was as suspicious as hell.

But she wasn't. Jo was never suspicious; she believed him to be truthful. Usually, he was.

They had their difficulties – didn't everyone? – but theirs were invariably because Hal found his work far too absorbing to give Jo enough support; to give her and their two sons enough of himself. *Any* of himself, he amended.

Their eldest boy was Edmund, and he was the child of Jo's first marriage to Hal's college friend Ben. Ben had been dead these twelve years. Edmund – Teddy as he'd been in childhood, Ed as he now preferred at the easily-embarrassed age of thirteen (boys who played rugby for the school just weren't called Teddy) – was as much Hal's as Sammie, eight, who was Hal's son with Jo. Hal loved both boys. He just found it hard to remember that they were his responsibility.

He had reached Brighton. Now, abruptly, the traffic was dense, and for some time required his full attention.

But all too soon the congestion cleared again and he was powering up the long slope that circled around behind Hove.

And his guilt seemed to leap up and smack him between the eyes.

He wasn't going to Avebury and the West Kennet Long Barrow. Well, he might do; it depended on whether the true purpose of this journey ended successfully.

He was going to look for someone.

A woman.

A woman called Angela Swayne, whom he had met three years ago in Crete, kissed once, fallen for, left and tried to forget.

He hadn't.

He had been researching his book on the ancient civilisations of the Mediterranean – his 'Minoan Thing', as Jo always called it – and Angela had inspired a long section about Phaestos in which she – or somebody remarkably like her – wandered around with an older guide .

Angela had reddish fair hair, she was tall, curvy, temperamental, with grey eyes that should have been happy and were not. She had been waiting for a man called Rob to join her, and Hal had decided – after hearing only a few throwaway comments about him – that he was a selfish bastard with no imagination and not a lot of intelligence, who was nowhere near good enough for a woman as magnificent as Angela. The temptation to stay in Crete with her and prove this – and that Hal was a much better option – had been all but irresistible.

He had managed to resist. Gone back to the mainland and on to a small, out-of-the-way island, met up with Jo, gone home with her. Picked up his – their – life. Written Angela into his Minoan Thing, put her out of his mind.

Only he hadn't.

He didn't even know her surname when he left Crete. Didn't know in any detail where she lived, other than it was somewhere in the Forest of Dean in Gloucestershire. Didn't know what she did for a living; only that she took photos and had been gathering information for an illustrated article.

Even if he hadn't forgotten her, she was no longer in his life.

But then he'd seen the piece in one of the Sunday supplements. Not an illustrated article, not one of her photos. Just an image of a group of cheerful-looking people standing in front of an attractive old pub in a village near Chichester, one of the five or six photographs in a piece about the decline of the English pub and what measures were being taken by small communities to counteract it.

One of the women was Angela. Angela Swayne, according to the caption, third from the right in the front row next to a fat woman in tight jeans and a floral blouse whose buttons weren't quite up to the job. Angela was smiling and she had what looked like a pint of beer in her hand. Her hair was longer, smoother, centre parted – it suited her, Hal thought – and her jeans and the cool white linen shirt looked much better than her chubby neighbour's efforts.

The name of the pub and the village were both mentioned, more than once. Once would have been enough: Hal knew, even as he skipped through the rest of the article, that this was all the prompting he needed. Was, in fact, what he had been subconsciously waiting for, probably since he'd caught the bus that took him away from Agia Galini three and a half years ago.

He'd set off two days later. This morning – Tuesday – a couple of hours earlier.

And so he was on his way, and his impatience was now so strong that it was all he could do not to let the car have its head and race westwards till he found her.

Chichester was up ahead with its interminable series of roundabouts, off one of which was the exit he had to take. He missed it on the first attempt, had to go on to the next roundabout and turn back. He got into the wrong lane and someone blasted their horn at him. Unthinkingly, he gave the driver the finger, only noticing as he did so that it was a grey-haired elderly woman who, to his surprise, returned the gesture. Then he was out in a maze of increasingly narrow roads until, after too many wrong turns and a fury of frustration made worse by guilt, he was forced to stop and look at the map. Finally, in the early afternoon, he reached the village and the pub that the locals were so determined to keep open.

It was open as Hal screeched to a stop outside.

He went in, ordered a half of bitter. The friendly man behind the bar said it wasn't too late for a sandwich, but Hal, his stomach in knots, declined. The pub was quiet, the man behind the bar inclined to talk.

'I saw the article about you in the Sunday magazine,' Hal said. He was quite surprised at how detached he sounded.

'Oh, great!' the man said with a smile. 'It's attracted quite a lot of attention, of the right sort I might add, and we're starting to think our campaign may at last be getting off the ground, what with …'

Hal, recognising a born chatterer when he found one, interrupted. 'I know Angela, Angela Swayne,' he said, pointing to her in the cutting from the supplement he'd just taken out of the inner pocket of his leather jacket. 'I haven't seen her for ages and I managed to lose her address when she moved down here from Gloucestershire. The Forest of Dean,' he added, going for the nonchalant tone.

'Was that where it was?' the barman said. 'Knew it was Gloucester way.' So far, Hal thought, he didn't seem suspicious.

'She lives right in the village, does she?' he said.

'Just outside,' the barman replied. And, before Hal could risk his luck and try to extract more, added, 'But she won't be there now, of course, she'll be at work.' He stared at Hal, eyes narrowed.

'Of course,' Hal echoed.

The barman, apparently coming to the conclusion that giving away someone's place of work was a lesser sin than their home address, seemed on the point of speaking. As he hesitated, Hal, inspired by something right outside himself, said, 'Is it still that office in Chichester where she works?'

The idea – originating in nothing more than Chichester being the nearest town of any size – seemed to have done the trick. The barman, all doubts now resolved, agreed that it was and provided Hal with chapter and verse.

Angela was apparently a travel agent.

Hal finished his beer, thanked the barman and left.

Chichester was busy with weekday afternoon shoppers, its cathedral rising gracefully amid the crowds and the streets of slow-moving traffic. Hal found a car park, parked the car, paid for his pay-and-display ticket and stuck it on the dashboard. Then, feeling slightly sick, he made his way to what seemed to be the busiest streets and began searching.

He wondered what she was doing working in a travel agency. Maybe that was what she'd done when he met her. He'd never asked. He stared at the shop fronts, anxious now, by turns shivery and suddenly hot. His throat was prickly with nerves.

The he saw it. The not-very-original name – Carrington's Travel Agency – and the wide glass windows either side of the door decorated with travel posters and special offers. Before he could start to feel even worse, he opened the door and went inside.

There were four desks, three manned by men and the fourth by Angela. All four agents were busy with customers, deep in conversation with brochures open on the desks and computer terminals brilliant with photos of blue seas and cloudless skies. Angela's desk was towards the back of the long room, and in front of her a planter containing a large rubber plant and two healthy-looking bamboos provided an illusion of privacy. Hal moved to the other side of the planter.

'I can indeed find a hotel that caters for pets, Mrs Smith-Hammond, but unfortunately it won't be in the village itself because there simply isn't one.'

Angela's voice was achingly familiar. He felt hot again.

The middle-aged woman leaning earnestly towards her across the desk muttered something about needing to be right in the village, because after her operation her knee wasn't up to walking far, and could Angela just make one more check?

Impressed by Angela's courtesy, by her total lack of a single sign of impatience, Hal went on listening. After what seemed like half an hour but was probably far less, the woman was at last satisfied. 'So, the next village along the lake really is equally charming?' she asked, as she rose with evident discomfort to her feet.

'It is,' Angela replied. Although Hal couldn't see her face he could tell from her voice she was smiling.

'And you're certain that Peekoe will truly, genuinely not be made to feel a nuisance?'

'I'm quite sure of it. The hotel's information pack most definitely says pets are welcome.'

'Then I have done the right thing!' the woman said with heartfelt joy.

'You have.' Angela had also got up and was seeing her client to the door, escorting her out. Hal slipped forward and sat down in the chair that the old woman had just vacated.

He sensed Angela coming back. He caught a hint of a well-remembered perfume as she approached her desk. As she sat down he looked up at her and said, 'I want to go to a very tiny inn on the Norfolk Broads with my Pyrenean mountain dog and I hear you're the person to help.'

She sank into her seat. She stared at him. She had gone pale and there was something – some unreadable expression – in her eyes behind the tinted lenses of her glasses.

After a while she said, 'I always wondered if you'd turn up one day.'

He couldn't think how to reply, so he didn't. Simply went on looking at her. Remembering.

'You don't really want to go to the Broads.'

'No. And I don't have a dog, either.'

'Of course you don't.' She nodded. 'I'm working,' she said unnecessarily. 'If you're intending to stay around and you didn't just come in here to wind me up, you can buy me a drink and a pub supper when I knock off. There's a pub called the White Hound, it's in the village where I live, which is …'

'I know where it is,' he interrupted. 'I had half a pint of beer there an hour ago.' She was staring at him, that expression in her eyes again. 'It's how I found you,' he added softly. 'The article in the Sunday supplement about pubs closing. Not closing.'

She nodded, once, slowly. 'And two days later, here you are,' she whispered. Then, with a glimpse of the smile he remembered so faithfully, the one she'd employed when she was poking fun at him, 'What kept you?'

Again, he had no reply.

Eventually he stood up. 'What time?'

'Half six.'

'I'll be there.'

She nodded again.

He turned and strode away.

He had no idea how to fill the time. It was only just three o'clock, so he had three hours until he even needed to think about driving back to her village and the White Hound. He wondered if he should find a hotel. No, a voice in his head answered.

He still felt shivery. His throat hurt when he swallowed. It was nerves, anxiety, stress … Guilt.

He walked on up the high street until he came to a chemist's. He bought a pack of Lemsip and some throat lozenges. It was something to do. Realising, as he emerged onto the street, that Lemsip needed hot water (and Jo always said they were better with a spoonful of runny honey … don't think about Jo), he looked around and spotted a cafe.

He went in, was shown to a table, ordered a pot of tea with extra hot water. The waitress, a middle-aged woman with a weary air and a bad hair-dye job, muttered something to the effect that hot water was always provided and asked if he wanted anything to eat.

'No thanks,' Hal said. He didn't think he could eat now, any more than he'd felt able to in the pub.

The waitress brought the tea, and he waited while she unloaded what seemed to be an endless stream of items from her tray. When she had retreated into the rear of the cafe, he hastily emptied a sachet of Lemsip into his cup and filled the cup half full of hot water. He drank it swiftly, wanting to do so before the waitress came back, and burned his mouth and throat.

After that, it was all he could do to drink a cup of tea.

By a quarter to four he was back in his car. He thought of walking round the town, or alternatively driving off into the West Sussex countryside and finding a place to park and take a stroll. But he was tired. Exhausted. He put it down to the emotions of the day. There was an hour or more still to run on his pay-and-display ticket. He adjusted the rake on his seat, leaned back, put the car rug over himself and closed his eyes. But despite the rug he realised very soon that he was cold; shivering again. He got out of the car and went round to the boot, unzipping his bag, feeling down though the layers. Touching something very soft.

Oh God.

It was the gorgeous, expensive, extravagant pale grey cashmere sweater Jo had just bought him. She'd recently had a surprisingly large cheque from her literary agent – but he really didn't want to think about that particular aspect of Jo – and, typically, had dashed out to buy them all presents. A rugby ball marked with the England logo and this season's replica team jersey for Ed. A monstrous box of Lego for Sammie. The cashmere sweater for him. He didn't want to touch it, to put it on, to think about it even, and he had only included it because she had been in the bedroom when he was packing and said, 'It's too warm today for your new sweater so shall I fold it for you and put it in your bag?'

He'd had no option but to say 'Yeah, thanks.'

Just as he had no option now, for it was the only sweater he'd brought. He took off his jacket, put the beautiful sweater over his shirt and put his jacket on again, then got back in the car and under the blanket.

He hadn't really imagined that he would sleep, but he did.

He had overrun his parking time by thirty-five minutes when he woke up. Flustered, confused, he put the seat back up again, trying to remember how to get out of the town and onto the right road back to Angela's village, all the time full of a desperate urgency to make his escape before a traffic warden spotted his time had elapsed.

He found the correct road, managing to upset just one driver and a pedestrian in the process. He reckoned, under the circumstances, that was pretty good going.

Angela came striding up to the White Hound at thirty-one minutes past six. Couldn't manage to wait any longer, huh? Hal asked her silently as, sitting in his car, he watched her in the rear view mirror.

He was smiling. Didn't seem able to stop. She must have gone home before coming out to the pub because she had changed out of the smart black jacket and skirt and plain white shirt, and into jeans and a baggy jersey in soft cream wool. He remembered her penchant for loose-fitting clothes.

Her hair gleamed, her eyes sparkled. She didn't seem able to stop smiling, either.

Chapter 2

'I thought you lived in Gloucestershire,' he said to her when they had bought pints and packets of crisps – her idea – and were sitting on a sort of pew under a window in the far corner of the bar. The pew had a long padded cushion on the seat, but Hal couldn't get comfortable. His bones hurt.

'I did,' she replied. Then, abruptly, 'I left.'

'You left,' he repeated.

She sighed, a touch of irritation in the sound. 'I finished with Rob. Remember Rob? The man I was waiting for in Crete?'

'I remember Rob.' He was going to leave it there but some devil in him made him go on. 'His shitty wife buggered off with someone else, but he had to go on giving the appearance of being the injured party, which meant nobody must know about you. Moreover, if she decided to divorce him, she'd get half the house.'

She was staring at him in amazement. 'You remembered all that!' she exclaimed softly. 'Bloody hell.'

'I also remember telling you that you were too good to be kept up any man's sleeve.'

She nodded. 'So you did.'

There was a sudden softness in her grey eyes. At the memory of his words? At the thought of this Rob? He didn't like to think.

'So, what happened?' he asked, rather more curtly than he'd intended.

'He came out to Crete. It was all right – good, in fact, most of the time – but then he told me he'd changed his flight so that we didn't arrive at Gatwick together, and certainly wouldn't rock up back home at anything remotely approaching the same time, or even the same day. I agreed – well, he didn't leave me any choice – and then, when we slipped straight back into the old furtive habits – *his* old furtive habits – I decided I'd had enough.' She had been staring down at the round copper-topped table in front of them but now she looked up and met his eyes. 'I told him I wasn't going to be kept up any man's sleeve and if he was so concerned about his wife finding out and, far more importantly from his self-interested point of view, taking half the house, then he'd better try to wean her away from her new bloke and patch it up with her.'

'What did he do?'

She gave a short, harsh laugh. 'After an insultingly brief attempt to make me think again, he agreed. He's now back with the shitty wife and he looks as miserable as sin.'

Hal was on the point of saying that it served him right, but decided it wasn't appropriate. 'So, you saddled up and left town,' he said instead.

'Not being a cowboy, I did no such thing.'

'Figuratively speaking.'

She sighed again. 'I couldn't bear to sell my house. It's not very big and it's nothing special, but I bought it with a small legacy from my grandfather and my own hard-earned savings. I've let it. The tenants are a nice enough couple but …' She paused, and he had the impression that other people living in her house was something she found hard to

21

bear. 'I told them at work I wanted a change and they said there was an opening in the Chichester office – it's the same chain of travel agents – so I got a transfer and found a place to rent here, in the village. It's even smaller than my place – only half a house, really – and to be honest it's pretty dreadful, but it's somewhere to live and the rent is much less than what I'm getting from my tenants, so I'm quids in.'

He took a thoughtful swallow of beer. He'd tried the crisps but the rough edges and the saltiness, not to mention the vinegar, hurt his throat. 'I'm glad you finished with him.'

Even as he spoke the words, he knew he'd made a mistake. Instantly, she rounded on him and said in a low, angry hiss. 'You are, are you? So you can sit in your book-lined study in your marital home in whatever postcard-pretty place it is you live, totally content with your undoubtedly lovely wife and entertaining wild but well-hidden thoughts about the woman you wandered round Crete with?'

'She is lovely,' he said quietly, 'but I'm not totally content. I wouldn't be here if I were.'

'Why *are* you here?' she said after a heavy pause.

I don't know, would have been the honest answer. Instead he reached under the pew and handed her a book. 'I wanted to give you this.'

She took it from him. The jacket illustration was an evening shot of the palace at Phaestos. 'I've already got a copy,' she said tonelessly. 'The paperback, in fact.' She spun round, staring straight into his eyes. 'I wasn't prepared to fork out twenty-five quid on the hardback in case you hadn't put me in it.'

He said, with total honesty, 'I couldn't have left you out.'

She had opened the book, was turning the pages, flipping through until she came to the chapters on Phaestos. 'I read about the signing session in that posh London bookshop.' She hesitated. 'I very nearly came to it.'

22

'I looked out for you,' he said quietly.

She nodded.

In that moment all that might have been between them three years ago and all that might be ahead hung in the balance. He was vaguely aware of thinking, I've given her the book. That could be my excuse for coming to find her. I could finish my beer, say goodbye and must keep in touch, then walk away and get in my car and drive home.

He stayed where he was. Then he reached out and took her hand.

She made a small sound: a sharp intake of breath. Then she leaned against him and said, 'I'm glad you're here.'

The evening took on its own momentum. They had a second drink and she asked if he was hungry. He wasn't. One or two people came in, then some more, and several nodded a greeting to Angela.

After about an hour of fairly staccato conversation, she said, 'Have you booked a hotel?' He shook his head. 'Right.'

He watched as she got up and went over to the bar. She spoke briefly to the barman – it was the same man who had been on duty at lunchtime – and both of them glanced across at Hal. The barman said something and they both laughed.

Angela came back. 'Greg says it's okay to leave your car in the pub car park, and he's pouring us another drink. The lane where I live is too narrow for parking and there's fierce competition among the neighbours for the few off-road spaces,' she added by way of explanation.

'He knows I'll be staying with you, then.' He paused. 'Am I staying with you?'

'Of course you are,' she said, very quietly. Then, in a tone closer to her normal voice, 'I said you're an old friend and we haven't seen each other for ages. He can draw his own conclusions.' Hal went

23

to speak but she didn't let him. She muttered angrily, 'Christ, Hal, what does it matter?'

They finished the last beers. Then she stood up and he did too. She called out goodnight to the barman, and Hal nodded a farewell. Outside, the day's warmth had disappeared at sunset and there was a sparkling of frost. Hal shivered, wrapping his jacket more closely around him. Angela glanced at him. He went to his car and opened the boot, taking out his bag. Then she led the way up a narrow lane leading out of the village. Overhung with trees bearing the last of their leaves, it was dark, dank and gloomy.

He wondered what on earth he was doing.

He felt awful. His throat ached, his neck hurt – he had surreptitiously felt for raised glands earlier and found hard lumps under his ears and either side of his larynx – and he longed for the comfort of another Lemsip. With a spoonful of runny honey.

But then, as if she felt his mood, suddenly she was closer, leaning into him, and he put his arm around her. He smelt that well-remembered perfume, felt the smooth hair brush against his cheek. 'You had curly hair,' he murmured, kissing the top of her head.

'I'd had what they call a soft perm,' she replied. 'Didn't like it, so I let it grow out. This is the natural me.'

He kissed her again, and she turned her head so that this time he kissed her cheek. 'I like the natural you.'

It wasn't far to her house. It was tiny – part of a little cottage, ruthlessly bisected by a new dividing wall – and the door opened straight into the living room. There was a very basic kitchen against the far wall, a cubby-hole of a utility area to one side. A partly-open door on the other side led to the bathroom; there was no window and a definite smell of damp. A flight of open stairs led up to a platform on which there was a double bed and a small calico-covered hanging space. The remainder of the ground floor contained a table and two chairs, a huge sofa in front of a wood-burning stove. The place was shabby and had an unloved air.

But the stove had been carefully banked down, was ticking over nicely and giving out such a wonderful, welcome warmth that Hal groaned.

She was watching him. 'Sit down.' She indicated the sofa, and he dropped his bag and sank down.

She went over to the kitchen and he heard her fill a kettle and switch it on. He leaned his head back and closed his eyes. His eyes hurt. His chest hurt. His throat hurt. And he had the worst headache he could remember.

After a while – he wondered if he had briefly slept – she was beside him. She had a mug in her hand, and she held it out to him.

'It's lemon, honey and ginger,' she said. 'It's not too hot, I added a bit of cold water.'

He took the mug and tried a sip. The hot liquid was delicious, soothing. She held out her hand again. 'Paracetamol,' she said. 'You'd better take a couple.'

He did so. He finished the drink and leaned back again.

'You're not well,' she said.

'No,' he agreed. Then, 'I'm sorry, Angela. I'm really sorry.'

What, he wondered, was he apologising for? For being ill? For coming here to seek her out when she was doing just fine without him?

But she was looking at him, such an expression of tenderness on her face that his heart melted. 'Oh, Hal,' she breathed. Then she leaned towards him and gave him a gentle kiss.

'You're very hot,' she said with a frown as she straightened up. 'I think you may have flu.'

'Of course I haven't,' he said.

But he was afraid she could be right. Someone in the village back home had flu, there was talk of an autumn outbreak, and people were saying surely it was too soon, the authorities hadn't even got the flu vaccination programme properly organised yet …

Flu.

His eyes had drooped closed again but suddenly he opened them. 'God, Angela, I shouldn't be here! If I have got flu I'll give it to you, and …'

To his vague surprise, she burst out laughing. 'And that's the only reason why you shouldn't be here? Never mind all the others, which we won't even try to list, you shouldn't be here in case you give me whatever it is you've got?' Mutely, he shook his head. She reached for his hand. 'No need to worry,' she said. 'I've had a flu jab.'

'I thought they were only for the elderly and the vulnerable,' he muttered.

'I have asthma.'

He went on staring at her. 'I didn't know.'

'Why would you?' Suddenly she seemed upset. 'We met three years ago, we spent some time together, something happened between us, only nothing did really except you kissed me and I never forgot it, and there wasn't the opportunity to discover much about each other. Anything, really …' She looked sad. 'And now here you are, and it's wonderful, except you're ill, and I don't know whether I feel devastated or relieved.'

He knew exactly what she meant.

His eyelids were drooping again and he didn't know how much longer he could go on sitting there. She must have realised, for she stood up and got him to his feet and across to the small bathroom. She put his bag on the floor, closed the door and said, 'Call me when you're ready. I'm going to put a hottie in your bed.'

Your bed, he thought as he fumbled in the bag for the tee shirt and cotton drawstring trousers that served as pyjamas. *Your* bed, not *our* bed. Of course she's not going to sleep with me, he told himself angrily, I'm virtually a stranger. And – he was staring at the ghastly apparition that faced him in the mirror over the basin – I seem to have flu.

He used the lavatory, washed his hands, cleaned his teeth. The water felt like ice on his hot skin and his shivering was now so violent that it hurt. Along with everything else.

He emerged from the bathroom, trying to carry his bag and his discarded clothes and dropping both. His hands seemed to have no strength. She uttered a soft exclamation of distress and came to help. She supported him as they stumbled across to the stairs, and her arms were round him as they went up on to the platform. She turned back the duvet and he got into bed. Parts of it were warm and welcoming – the hot water bottle doing its job – and parts were like frozen ground. He moaned, in pain, in distress, regretting things he barely comprehended.

She was leaning over him, her cool hand on his burning forehead. 'Go to sleep,' she said. She kissed the place where her hand had rested.

'What about you?' he managed to say.

'Sofa,' she said shortly. 'Don't worry, it's a futon. It's very comfortable, and I have plenty of spare bedding. Sleep,' she repeated.

His eyes closed and he couldn't find the strength or the will to open them again. He nestled into the soft pillows – they smelled faintly of her perfume – and felt the duvet settle around him.

He felt all resistance leave him. In a very short time, he was asleep.

He was dreaming.

Violent, horrible dreams. People in danger, people threatened by fire, a statue-still screaming figure on a pyre, flames roaring as if in a furnace. He cried out.

Someone was beside him, someone with cool hands and a quiet voice. The someone held a cup to his lips and he drank greedily, gulp after gulp of cold water. Then, a hot drink that soothed his burning throat, and the quiet voice said – ordered – 'Take these,' and gave him a couple of pills. He started to cough, and his chest, his whole upper body, was shot through with such pain, only it was just a faint echo of the agony in his head. He whispered something – a name, perhaps – and then he was being helped to lie down again. Sleep took him once more, and he returned to the hellish dreams.

He didn't know how long it went on. She was there – Angela – when he woke. Not that he truly felt awake, for he couldn't work out where he was, why he wasn't at home, only then of course he could, and that was worse. At one point – it was dark, or at least dusk – and he was struggling to get up, to abandon the sweaty bed, find some clothes, leave, go somewhere … home, probably. With increasing desperation a woman's voice told him to stay where he was, and then some unknown time later there was a big man there too, someone who had wide shoulders and a lived-in face with a bent nose, and he held Hal down forcibly, told him not to be a bloody idiot and that there was no question of him getting up, that he'd punch him to make him lie down if he had to. He'd become part of the nightmare world, only then Hal heard Angela laughing, making some comment that punching patients wasn't what the NHS normally advocated, and he realised the big man must be a doctor.

Sleep returned, and this time he had the impression that it went on for a long time.

* * *

He woke up. It was late afternoon, or at least he thought it was. He wondered vaguely how he knew, but after some time he heard a church clock somewhere quite close strike the quarter hour. Presumably, then, he reasoned – very slowly – he must have heard it strike the hour, and the hour had been three, or four; a time, anyway, that if it were the small hours would have meant darkness.

It wasn't by any means dark. A low sun was making golden light outside, and he lay for some time watching the play of leaves in the gentle breeze. He turned his head and realised he could see over the balustrade and down into the room below, where Angela sat at the table, a laptop open before her. She was typing swiftly.

Angela.

Then he thought: Oh, God. Jo.

He tried to get out of bed, stumbled, tried again. Angela heard him, leapt to her feet and flew up the stairs. 'Careful!' she cried. 'Don't even think about trying to go downstairs.'

He took no notice. He'd seen what he wanted: there was a telephone on a small table beside the bed. He grabbed it, dialled his home number.

'Hello?' Jo said.

'It's me.' His voice was rough and much deeper than usual.

After a brief pause she said 'Hal?' in a tone of disbelief.

'I'm sorry I'm not back yet,' he said, his voice coming and going. 'I've been ill. Flu, I think.'

'Yes, I can hear,' she said. 'You do sound rough.' He tried to say something, but she was still talking. 'But what do you mean, not back yet? You said three days, maybe four, and that was the day before yesterday, the morning you left.'

29

'What day is it?' he demanded. He was talking to Jo, but he was looking at Angela. Just as Angela mouthed Thursday, Jo said it. 'So – you're not expecting me? You're not worried because I'm not there?'

Jo laughed. 'No to both.' Then, suddenly not laughing, she said, 'But I am a bit worried that you've been ill. Are you any better? Is there anything I can do? I could come and fetch you, only that would be two cars to get back home, unless I caught the train and …'

'No,' he said, far too forcefully. 'I mean, it's not worth it, I'll be fine. I'm better, I'll be okay to drive in a few days.'

'Are you sure?'

'Yeah.'

'Stay over the weekend,' she urged. 'You won't have got much work done if you've been poorly, I'm sure, and you'll only have to go back again if you don't get whatever it is done now.'

'Work.' He managed not to make it into a question.

'Work, Hal,' Jo repeated. 'Researching ancient places for your articles and books, remember?'

She was laughing again, and he managed a brief laugh too, although it sounded more like a cough. 'You're sure?' he said.

'Of course, why shouldn't I be? I wasn't expecting you till tomorrow at the earliest and probably Saturday or even Sunday, so Monday will be fine. There's not much on – Ed's playing on Saturday, but the match is at home, so Sammie and I thought we'd go in to watch and then we'll all grab a burger and go to the cinema in the afternoon.'

She'd stopped talking, obviously waiting for him to respond, and for an awful few seconds he could think of nothing to say. Eventually, he said huskily, 'Give them my love, and to you.'

'I will. See you some time on Monday. Oh, and Hal?'

'Yeah?'

'Take care, won't you? Plenty of rest, and keep up the liquids.'

'Yeah, right.'

'Could you find a doctor, if you needed one?'

He almost said he'd already seen one – or one had seen him, for he'd been pretty much an inert partner in the exchange – but bit it back. 'Of course,' he said instead, 'I'm in West Sussex, not Antarctica.'

She laughed again. 'Right. Hope you'll be okay. Love you.'

'Love you.'

He hung up.

He sank down on the bed, panting, jelly legs shaking. Angela had retreated down the stairs as he'd begun to speak, and now she came back up again. She was watching him, her grey eyes wide. 'Are you really feeling better?'

He thought about it. 'Slightly less terrible describes it more accurately.'

She came to sit beside him. She put her hand on his forehead. 'You don't feel nearly so hot. You were burning, late yesterday, and I was worried because you kept trying to get up.'

'That was when the doctor came?'

'Yes.'

'You still get house calls here?'

'Hardly ever. Mick's a friend, he's with the save-the-pub group.'

'What did he say?'

'That you were unlikely to die, which frankly was a huge relief, and that there was nothing more to do other than make you stay in bed, keep you warm and hydrated and feed you painkillers, and that you ought to start improving …' she glanced at her watch 'round about now.'

'So precise and so accurate.'

She smiled. 'He's a good bloke.'

Hal lay back against the pillows, and Angela pulled up the duvet. She watched him for a few moments, then said, 'Do you want a cup of tea?'

He thought about it. Then he said, 'Yes, please.'

He continued to improve. He managed to stay awake for several hours that afternoon and evening, during which time Angela told him that she'd been reluctant to leave him and had gone into work the previous day only to fetch her laptop and some reports she had to type up. 'But I'll go in tomorrow,' she added. 'If you'll be all right?'

'I will.'

He slept that night without any dreams that he could afterwards recall. He was awake early in the morning, and felt strong enough to go downstairs. Angela ran a bath for him, and with enormous relief he washed off the stench of sickness and began to feel more human.

She had put a bath robe out for him and he put it on, emerging from the bathroom towelling his hair.

'I've put fresh sheets on the bed,' she told him, 'and I've put a wash on that includes your pyjamas.'

'Five star service,' he remarked.

She looked at her watch. 'I'm off now, but I'll try to get back soon after lunch. Try to rest till then – you still look a bit pale.'

I still feel a bit pale, he thought. 'Okay.' Then, as an afterthought, 'Is it all right if I … that I'm still here?'

She looked at him for what seemed like a long moment. Then she said, 'Yes.' Turning, she hurried away, closing the door behind her.

He slept again – taking a bath had been far more tiring than he'd expected – but woke up knowing he was better.

He got up, straightened the bed, took the wash out of the machine and, stepping outside, found a small walled garden with a washing line, where he hung out the damp clothes and bedding. That took its toll, but not as severely as he'd anticipated.

He managed some bread and cheese for lunch and made some coffee.

He kept checking the time.

He felt sick again, but it wasn't a relapse of his flu.

He heard a car stopping outside; heard it reverse. Heard a door close. Heard her footsteps, watched the door opening.

Watched her as she stepped into the room, turning to close the door. She glanced briefly at him, and then she locked the door.

She knows too, he thought.

He moved towards her, put his arms round her and held her the way he'd wanted to for so long. He put a firm hand to her chin, turning her face up so he could kiss her. She was kissing him back, her fervour matching his. They stumbled for the stairs and up to the platform, flinging off garments as they went, and then he pushed her down onto the bed and lay on top of her.

Forcefully blanking from his mind thoughts of anything but her, he breathed her in, trying to sense all of her body with all of his. His hands on her, her hands on him, and it was as if they had at last reached a destination for which they'd long ago set out. Moving inside her – she was ready for him, welcoming, eager – at long last, they were one.

Chapter 3

Jo

Jo wasn't unduly worried about Hal. She was quite glad she didn't have to rush off to Avebury or wherever he was to bring him home. She'd taken him at his word when he said there was no need, and she was quite sure he'd let her know if he changed his mind. If, heaven forbid, he got worse and couldn't drive himself.

She had enough to do without unscheduled journeys halfway across the south of England. While it was true that she and the boys hadn't much on over the weekend, the following week was another matter. Next Friday was the last day before the autumn half term, and both boys were going away. Ed was off to rugby training camp, and Jo would need to have everything ready for him on Thursday morning because he'd be staying that night with his friend George, who lived close to the school, and George's mother was going to drop both boys off on Friday morning. The coach would be leaving after lunch, and the boys would be away until the Sunday of the following week.

It was the first time Ed had been away to rugby training camp. While knowing that the school – renowned for its prowess at most sports and rugby in particular – took good care of the boys, nevertheless Ed was only thirteen, and …

He'll be fine, said Ben's voice in her head.

She smiled. She quite often heard Ben speaking to her. She knew it was her imagination, but it was lovely just the same.

'Our boy, Ben,' she said softly to him now.

Don't worry, Ben replied.

Her smile widened.

Sammie was also going away, and a great deal further that his half-brother: Sammie and Hal were flying to the west coast of America on Thursday evening and would be spending the following week with Sam, who was Hal's father and Sammie's beloved grandfather. The boys did well for grandfathers, Jo reflected now as she went through the clothes she'd laid out for Sammie, for they both regarded their respective father's fathers as common property and they had Jo's father, Paul Daniel, as well. They only had the standard two grandmothers, however, Ben's mother and Jo's, for Sam was a widower of many years' standing and had loved Hal's mother too much ever to think of replacing her.

Sam had once shown Jo a picture of Ruth, in advanced pregnancy with Hal's little sister. Only Ruth had died, and the baby too. Hal hadn't been told about the baby, either back then or at any time since. Jo wasn't sure what she felt about sharing such a secret with Sam.

'Stop it,' she said aloud to herself.

To distract her, she thought about the conversation she'd had with the headmaster of Sammie's school. Jo had written a fairly brief letter asking permission for her young son to miss the last day of school before the half term break, assuming it was a mere formality. But the Head had telephoned, asking for details, and Jo, unable at short notice to dress the trip up as anything remotely educational, had told the bare truth: that Sammie didn't see much of his grandfather or of the country where half his genetic inheritance originated, and it had seemed a good idea to redress this.

'Thank you for being honest, Mrs Dillon,' the Head had said disarmingly. 'Most people try to mention as many museums, art galleries and other places of supposed academic merit as they possibly can, and one ends up feeling the child in question would probably have preferred to be at school.'

'Sammie's father would wear the child out traipsing round museums if he had his way,' she replied. 'His grandfather, on the other hand, will probably insist on taking him sailing.'

'I'm sure he'll enjoy it.'

Jo was just thinking that she – and Sammie – had got away with it when the Head added firmly, 'We shall expect a proper "What I did on My Half-Term" essay, Mrs Dillon,' and she replied hastily, 'Of course!'

The week jogged cheerfully enough on to its end. On Saturday morning Ed played rugby (and won 15–7; three tries for Ed's side but none of then converted because their usual fullback was off games with a hamstring injury) and both boys loved *Back to the Future III*. Sammie spent the rest of Saturday and quite a lot of Sunday trying to build a DeLorean out of Lego.

The weekend was quietly winding down with the usual Sunday evening flurry of last-minute homework and the regular hunt for bits of games kit that had to be washed, aired and back in the sports bags before school the next day, when Ed looked up from his geometry exercise book and said, 'There's a car outside.'

'Is it Daddy?' Sammie's face was alive with excitement; he seemed to think he couldn't begin to look forward to the thrilling trip to the west coast until Hal was safely home, despite Jo's frequent assurances that Hal was fine, he'd be back in good time and there was absolutely nothing to worry about.

'It could be,' Jo said, getting up and heading towards the hall and the front door. 'Only he said it'd probably be after the weekend, and …'

'It's not,' Ed said. He had gone ahead of her and had the door open already. 'It's a black BMW, but …'

'Then it is Daddy!' Sammie shouted, rushing at his brother and elbowing him out of the way.

'It's NOT!' yelled Ed. 'It's got two doors, which means it's a coupé, and Dad's is a four-door, thickhead.' Or, possibly, dickhead.

The boys shot down the well-greased slope into furious quarrelling, one or two words were muttered that Jo had hoped they didn't know yet, especially Sammie, and there was a swift mêlée of shoving, pushing and punching. Reaching out two practised arms, Jo prised them apart. Then, peering out at the slightly apprehensive-looking man approaching up the drive, she said, 'Sorry about my sons, they …' Then, as he came into the light, 'Oh, hi!'

He was in his late thirties, early forties, broad, quite tall, with short brown hair, a regular-featured face and very light-coloured eyes that were creased in a smile and went down slightly at the outer corners. He was dressed in jeans and a white linen shirt under a very well-tailored black jacket, and wore glasses. Taking them off, he held out his hands to Jo and said, 'Hi, I'm sorry I'm so late.'

And Hal's cousin Max stepped forward to give her a hug.

Jo returned the hug and said cautiously, 'It's lovely to see you, Max, but …' She stopped.

'But?' His smile began to fade. 'I know I said mid-afternoon but

I hadn't anticipated so much traffic on a Sunday, which was probably pretty stupid, but you are expecting me?'

Jo shook her head. 'I'm really sorry, but I'm not.' She tried to take the sting out of the words by smiling at him, which wasn't hard because she was very fond of him.

The boys liked him, too. They had started to treat him like family very soon after meeting him for the first time a year or so ago, which was hardly surprising since he *was* family: Hal's second cousin once removed, since their fathers were first cousins. Now Sammie had grabbed Max's arm and was trying to pull him inside the house and Ed was strolling round Max's new car doing that male thing of kicking the tyres, trying to look nonchalant and unimpressed.

But Max was backing away, despite Sammie's best efforts. 'I'm so sorry, Jo. Hal and I spoke on the phone a few days back and when I told him I'd be heading for Portsmouth this coming week he said, why not call in on the way and stay for a few days, and I said I would.' He spoke very quickly, his embarrassment almost tangible.

'Oh, Max, it should be me who's apologising,' Jo said, wondering wildly if it should have been I who's apologising, 'because as I'm quite sure you've worked out by now, Hal totally forgot to tell me – he's not here, by the way, he's down in Wiltshire looking at stone circles and old barrows – and right now I'd quite like to kick him.'

'Old barrows?' Sammie said, puzzled. 'Wheelbarrows?'

'No, barrows as in ancient burial mounds,' Jo said, hoping she sounded as if she knew what she was talking about. Max was probably even more of an intellectual heavyweight than Hal, and currently running some research project at Cambridge. 'Come in, come in,' she added, beckoning with stupidly exaggerated gestures as if all of a sudden Max had lost the ability to understand what come in meant.

She stood back, pushing the door fully open. 'Honestly, it's fine!'

Max hadn't moved. 'No, I won't stay,' he said firmly. 'Hal's away, you're not prepared for an unexpected visitor and I have no wish to disturb your evening. I'll ring in a couple of days and …'

'Don't go!' Jo exclaimed. 'Really, don't!'

He came a step closer, and Sammie grabbed his arm again, looking hopeful. In the light spilling out of the hall, she could see Max's face more clearly and it struck her anew that he didn't look much like Hal – at all like Hal, in fact – but she'd always thought there was a definite resemblance to Sam. 'I'll come in just long enough to fix up a hotel somewhere,' Max said, stepping inside, 'then …'

But Jo had rather forcefully closed the front door behind him. Silly, she thought, since he'll have to go out again to fetch his bag, but maybe he'll take it for the welcoming gesture it is.

'Stay,' she said firmly. 'I'm about to have a drink …' She glanced at her watch. 'Well, in a bit, and once I've fed the boys I've got smoked salmon for supper which I'm going to do in scrambled egg with brown bread.'

'I like smoked salmon!' Sammie piped up.

'You hate it,' she said repressively, 'and anyway you're having that wonderful shepherd's pie I made earlier and yes, you can have ketchup. So,' she turned back to Max, who was still standing hesitantly in the hall, 'you're not putting us out, there's plenty of supper, I can make up the spare bed in about three minutes and I'll feel so much better about Hal having forgotten all about you if you don't head off into the night.'

He was smiling. He had a really nice smile, which increased the resemblance to Hal's father. 'Really?'

'Really,' said three voices together.

'In that case, thank you,' Max said, 'and is it possible you can re-open that very firmly-closed door so I can fetch my overnight bag?'

* * *

Jo rushed around the kitchen trying not to make it apparent since if Max picked up that she was the least bit harassed, he'd feel guilty all over again at having interrupted her evening. He was very good at picking things up. She was trying to think if she had any salad ingredients that were anywhere near fresh enough to serve with the scrambled eggs, and a brief glimpse at the limp green things in the trough at the bottom of the fridge quickly answered that. Putting the oven on to re-heat the boys' shepherd's pie, she hoped Max wasn't wondering where she'd got to with the promised drinks.

Sam had been so happy when Hal and Max had finally got in touch, she reflected as she hunted for a tin of peas. Although they'd both been living in England, it had been years since they'd seen each other; not since boyhood, in fact. There was a family story, that Hal had told her, about a Christmas get-together when Hal, the older of the two small cousins, had been commanded to play with Max and had carried him on his new bike and Max fell off and tore his jeans. The family didn't appear to have been close, and the occasional Christmas or Thanksgiving get-together, usually at Sam's elder brother Thomas's house, had, according to Hal, been somewhat stiffly formal affairs since Thomas and his wife had no children and didn't seem to enjoy the company of people under fifty.

She had found the peas and now they were in a pan on the stove. She set out plates and cutlery and then, aware that she'd already left Max on his own with the boys for too long – she could hear Sammie giggling uncontrollably, always a warning sign that things were heading rapidly towards the vulgar – she abandoned the kitchen and went to the rescue.

'So, Hal phoned you in the week?' Jo said to Max.

She was sitting on the older and more battered of the two sofas, having insisted Max have the one that didn't face the telly, hence its relative state of newness. She had mixed gin and tonics for them, found a plastic container of Japanese crackers that hadn't been opened and emptied them into a pretty dish. The boys were eating shepherd's pie and peas at the kitchen table.

'Well, I phoned him,' Max replied. He took a sip of his drink and winced slightly.

'More tonic?' Jo asked anxiously.

'Please.'

She fetched the bottle and put it on the low table between them.

'Thanks.' He smiled, and Jo reflected how much she liked his disarming smile; it made him look like a boy planning mischief. Perhaps she should have left him and Sammie being vulgar after all.

'Sam's so pleased that we're all in contact,' she remarked.

'Yes, I know,' he agreed. 'I have a lot of time for Sam. He's a good man, warm, full of affection. Perceptive, too.' He paused, helping himself to a handful of crackers. 'When Hal and I were kids and the family met up now and then, Sam picked up that I'd noticed the other grown-ups didn't like my mother much – to be fair, she could be bossy, but she'd been a nurse and didn't seem capable of breaking the people-managing habit – and he understood it was hard for me. He went out of his way to make me feel better.'

'Sounds like Sam,' Jo murmured.

'Right.'

Jo delved in the bowl of crackers. Max must be starving, she reflected, since he'd absent-mindedly eaten most of them and now only the boring ones that didn't taste of anything were left. She thought back to the occasion when she and Hal had gone up to London to meet Max for lunch: the cousins' first meeting since childhood, and only arranged because Sam kept insisting it was wrong for the two of them to be living so close yet not be in contact. Sam, clearly, had no concept of the distance between Cambridge and the rural depths of Kent, even less of the perpetually congested state of British roads.

There had been something of a misunderstanding over lunch. Hal, fairly typically, hadn't really explained very much and Jo thought Max had only just arrived in England, and that Sam had told him to look up Hal and his family so that they could help him get settled. But Max, it transpired, hadn't required any such help, having been born in Cambridge – Jo, to her own discomfiture, thought it was Cambridge, Massachusetts, not Cambridge, England – and he'd lived in England on and off all his life.

In the course of that initial meeting, she had tried to place his accent. 'I didn't realise I had one,' he'd replied when she asked him; it had been the first time she'd noticed his nice smile. 'You do,' she'd said, emboldened by then by a large glass of white wine. 'It's very faint, and it's not American, and ...'

'Canadian,' he said. 'My mother was from Vancouver.'

Since that London lunch there had been regular meetings, with Max coming to Copse Hill House for weekends and Hal and Jo visiting him in Cambridge, sometimes with the boys. Max had a jewel of a house in a Victorian terrace that formed part of a square, and he had opened up much of the ground floor so that it was airy, spacious and light. One reason for not taking Ed and Sammie every time was that they were fascinated by the dark, spooky cellar, reached by a perilously steep flight of steps, and once Ed had frightened his little brother so thoroughly with ghost stories that subsequently Sammie had disturbed the entire household – and probably Max's neighbours, too – with his screams as he shot into terrified wakefulness from a nightmare of a burned house and a sinister figure in a red hood who had leered at him.

'It's a while since Sam's been over to stay with us,' Jo observed presently. Her glass, she noticed, was empty. 'He doesn't seem so keen to endure the flight these days and …'

A shout from the kitchen interrupted her: Sammie. 'Mummy, MUM, can I have a yogurt *and* a banana? Ed says it's one or the other!'

'Yes,' she yelled back. 'Yes, you can have both,' she elaborated. Ed was going through an extremely irritating pedantic phase and would undoubtedly have informed his brother that her quick yes could equally mean he was right and it was indeed one or the other. She glanced at Max, grinning. 'Sorry. Another drink?'

'No! Thank you,' he added hastily. She must really have been heavy-handed with the gin.

'I'd better go and make sure the boys are okay, and set the seemingly endless process of bedtime up and running,' she said, getting to her feet.

He stood up too. 'Of course. Anything I can do to help?'

'No, everything's under control!' she said brightly.

If only, she thought silently as she went into the kitchen and set about the mess around Sammie's plate. He seemed to have been flicking peas at his brother again. She sighed and picked up the sink cloth.

It was all going very well, she thought, about an hour later. Sammie was in the bath and she was waiting for him to call down that he was out, dry, in his pyjamas and ready for tucking-up and a story. He had absolutely no need of stories anymore, being more than capable of reading to himself, without moving his lips, and having been able to for well over two years if not more. But he liked the moments alone with her, and so did she. Ed was in the small sitting room where the old telly was, to which was attached the video player. Prompted by *Back to the Future III* the previous afternoon, he was re-watching the first in the franchise. Jo thought she'd probably have a minor skirmish on her hands when it was time for bed and she had to prise him away from it.

The kitchen was now reasonably clean and tidy, two plates were warming in the top oven, she'd set out cutlery and napkins, pepper and salt, the brown loaf and the butter. She'd also found two very nice crystal glasses and put a bottle of white wine in the coldest part of the fridge. She had beaten the eggs and shredded the smoked salmon, and had just poured the eggs into the hot butter in the pan when Sammie called down.

She hurried upstairs, and a few minutes later she and her younger son were deep in *The Hobbit*.

Jo came slowly down the stairs, smiling softly, the imprint of Sammie's warm, slightly damp mouth still on her cheek from his final, fervent good-night kiss. She glanced in on Ed, but he was enthralled and anyway, at thirteen, he really didn't have to go to bed just yet.

What was I doing before Sammie called out? she wondered.

Eggs.

Bugger.

She ran into the kitchen. Max stood by the stove, calmly stirring, and the eggs were a beautiful, creamy froth in the copper pan.

'Thank you so much,' she said.

'My pleasure. They haven't been on the heat all this time,' he added quickly, 'I guessed you'd be a while and I came in and turned the plate off. I have to admit I was listening in, and when I realised you were getting to the end of the chapter, I came back, put the heat up again …' he paused, stirring more briskly. 'And I've just added the salmon.'

She reached round him for the warmed plates, putting them on the worktop beside the cooker. 'You star.'

He waved the spatula in acknowledgement.

She sliced and buttered the bread – neatly, quickly; there were *some* things she could do in the kitchen – and arranged the bisected slices on a plate, putting the plate on a large tray with the glasses and the cold wine. Max dished out the eggs and salmon mixture, and they took their meal back to the living room.

They ate in silence for a while. Jo hadn't realised how hungry she was, and Max had done a great job with the scrambled eggs. They had a glass of wine each, and as they finished the food, she reached out and topped up their glasses.

'Sorry about the gin,' she said. She reflected vaguely on how relaxed she always felt with him. 'I think I accidentally poured you a belter.'

He smiled. 'You did, but it was fine once I'd added more tonic. This is good.' He held up his wine glass.

'Yes. It was a present, from someone who I think was trying to impress me.'

He turned the bottle so that he could read the label. 'They certainly were.'

She realised that her remark might have sounded smug and self-congratulatory. 'People hardly ever have the slightest desire to do that. Impress me.'

He waited, smiling gently. 'No?'

'No. Far from it. But recently …' She paused. Did she really want to tell him what was making her both thrillingly excited but also sad and a bit guilty? What it was that seemed somehow to have come between her and Hal, for all that she wasn't entirely sure why – only she was sure really and she didn't like it, not at all.

It seemed that was exactly what she did want – well, he was Max, and he was so easy to talk to – because she heard herself start to speak.

'I wrote a story,' she began. 'In fact, I wrote quite a few stories, around the time I met Ben. Ed's father?' Max nodded. Yes, of course, he'd know about Ben; Sam would have told him. 'Much later, when Hal and I were married, I wrote some novels, too – sort of historical mystery things with a present-day setting and a bit of the supernatural thrown in. But one story, that I wrote soon after Ben died, was different.' She stopped. This was hard to speak of, because after all the years, still stating aloud that stark fact – Ben died – had the power to stop her in her tracks, make her throat clam up and the tears start in her eyes. 'It – the story – was inspired by a dream I had about him,' she hurried on, 'and in the dream Ben looked like an angel, and so beautiful, and the image stuck with me and I came up with this little tale about a father returning from the dead to be his little son's guardian angel.'

Max said softly, 'It sounds beautiful. Like a tribute.'

She nodded, momentarily quite unable to speak. Max would understand, she thought, because he'd lost his wife. He'd also had a little sister who hadn't survived early childhood. Jo was well aware that he, of all people, wouldn't feel awkward at her wet eyes; that she didn't have to apologise or even try to explain.

'Yes,' she agreed after a moment.

She took one or two deep breaths. Then, continuing, she said, 'A few years ago, a small film company became interested in the angel story. Did I ever tell you?'

'You mentioned something about a film – it was during the lunch when we met, as far as I recall – but Hal cleared his throat rather loudly and we started talking out something else.'

Yes, she reflected glumly, that sounded about right. 'Well, then I heard nothing for ages, and I thought it had been relegated to a forgotten filing cabinet. Only it hadn't, and right at the end of last year – annoyingly, it was just before everything came to a total halt for Christmas and New Year – they got in touch again and said it was all going ahead. I haven't told many people about it – well, nobody really – because I've kept thinking they'll change their minds and it'll all come to nothing. But they haven't, it's all going ahead, and they've found this brilliant artist called Flavia McGinty – she's sixty-five, seventy, wild grey hair, long skirts, smells of patchouli, eccentric as they come but really brilliant – and she's expanding on the original illustrations for the animated bits of the film, and there's going to be some live-action sections as well, and there's a Celtic band called Finnegan's Pig doing the music, and this lovely song called 'I See You in the Half-Light', which is so moving, and the whole thing's almost finished now and it's going to be on telly at Christmas, and somehow Hal's incredibly hacked off about the whole fucking thing and I don't know what to do.'

She stopped. The echo of her last words, spoken far too loudly and with a great deal too much emotion, faded and died.

From two rooms away the *Back to the Future* music filled the abrupt silence.

'I'm so sorry,' she whispered. 'A large gin and half a bottle of this apparently hugely impressive and probably wildly expensive wine seem to have gone to my head.'

Max didn't say anything for some moments. Then, thoughtfully, as unperturbed as if women made a habit of spilling their souls to him with a smattering of rude words, he said, 'The story is about Ben, you said, so isn't it likely Hal's jealous?'

47

She gave a snort of laughter. 'Jealous? Hal? Max, you obviously don't know him. Well, you do, of course you do, he's your cousin and we've all seen quite a lot of each other over the past eighteen months or so. But ...' She paused briefly then plunged on. 'For someone to be jealous presupposes they have profound feelings for the person involved, that they need them, depend on them, want to be with them and can't bear the thought of losing them.' Hearing what she'd said, abruptly she stopped.

'Hm,' Max said. Then, calmly, 'And that doesn't apply to Hal?'

'No. Yes. Oh, probably. It's just that ...' She baulked at the enormity of explaining Hal to someone who hadn't seen all that much of him since childhood, and even then hadn't been close. 'He's detached. Well, I expect you've noticed. He likes his own company. He doesn't really commit much.'

'He sounds rather like Sam,' Max said.

'But Sam's warm, loving, big-hearted!' she protested.

'He's also been on his own for decades and he likes his own company as much, if not more than, anyone I know.'

'As I just said, you don't know Hal.'

She wished she hadn't spoken quite so harshly; it wasn't fair on Max to involve him, to be so frank. But then, glancing at him – he was looking at her as if he understood quite a lot more than she was saying, although as she turned to him he quickly looked away – she had the feeling he didn't mind. It was all right.

Silence fell once more.

After a while, Jo got up. 'I should suggest to Ed that it's bedtime,' she said. 'Back in a minute.'

He nodded.

She went through to the small living room. Ed looked up. 'Are you okay, Mum? I thought I heard you yelling.'

'I was,' she admitted, 'but I'm okay.'

'Not stressed out by Dad's cousin Max out there?' He smiled, looking so like Ben that her heart did a flip.

'Not in the least. I'm very fond of him, as you know perfectly well. I've been telling him about the Angel film and all that.'

Ed nodded. 'And that made you yell.'

She wondered if he'd heard the bit about Hal being hacked off about the whole thing. The whole fucking thing, in fact. He probably had, because she'd really been yelling by then. She met his eyes. 'Well, you know.'

'Dad.'

'Dad,' she agreed. Not Ed's real dad, but Dad as in Hal, who had fulfilled the role for virtually as long as Ed could remember.

Ed muttered something. It sounded very like 'He needs to grow up and get over it and stop being a knob and spoiling it for you.' Jo grinned, for that was precisely what she thought, too.

But since she knew full well she shouldn't encourage such opinions, especially as Ed just seemed to have called his stepfather a knob, she pretended she hadn't heard.

She went to stand right behind him, a hand on each shoulder, and bent to drop a kiss on the top of his head. 'Is it nearly over?'

'Nearly. Five minutes, ten at most.'

'Then bed?'

'Okay.'

'Come and say goodnight as you go up?'

''kay.'

Back in the main living room, she found Max calmly looking at one of the Sunday magazines. It was definitely time to shift the mood towards something less high-octane. As she sat down and shared out the last couple of inches of wine, Max abandoned the magazine and said, 'You're expecting Hal back some time tomorrow, I believe you said?'

'Yes. He said Monday when we spoke on the phone on Thursday.'

'Right.'

'He's off researching the ancient settlements along the Marlborough Downs – Avebury mainly, I think, but he told me he's been unwell,' she went on. 'From what he said, and what he sounded like, it was probably one of those twenty-four-hour flu bugs – virulent and pretty uncomfortable for a while, then gone again.'

'Even more unpleasant to be ill when you're away from home,' Max commented. 'Was he being looked after okay?'

'He said so.' She grinned, remembering. 'I asked if there would be a doctor available if he needed one, and he said of course, it was West Sussex not Antarctica.'

'But …' Max began. He stopped, and almost immediately said, 'I'm sure there are doctors in Antarctica. All those research stations, there are bound to be medical facilities.'

'Yes,' she agreed. She wondered why he was bothering, when it had been a throwaway remark. Recalling how the exchange had begun, she said, 'Why do you ask? About when Hal's getting back?'

'Oh … because when we spoke on the phone I said I'd be on my way to Portsmouth this week, and that was when he invited me to come and stay, and I wanted to check that I wasn't going to miss him.'

'When are you going to Portsmouth?'

'Thursday.'

'Then no, you won't miss him. If he wasn't coming home tomorrow he'd have let me know by now. Probably.' Not wanting to dwell on that she added, 'Why are you going to Portsmouth?'

'I'm booked on the night ferry to St Malo.'

'Holiday?'

'Sort of.' He paused, then went on. 'My mother came from Vancouver, as I think I once told you, and her parents emigrated to Canada from France not long before she was born. I know very little about my French ancestry, apart from a few dates and the name of some tiny place in the middle of Brittany where the family lived. So, I'm going to see whether I can find out a few more details.'

His mother was dead, Jo recalled – as indeed was his father – so the obvious solution of asking her to fill in the gaps wasn't an option. 'Quite a challenge,' she said, 'but an interesting one. Best of luck – I hope you discover something; well, lots of things. Do you speak French?'

'No.'

'Oh.'

'Oh indeed.'

Ed appeared in the doorway. 'I've come to say goodnight.'

Max stood up, went over to him and shook his hand; he seemed to know that thirteen-year-old boys didn't like being embraced, or, even worse, having their hair ruffled in a jovial way, by older male relations. 'Goodnight, Ed.'

Ed mumbled something. Then he came to stand beside Jo, bending down to give her a swift kiss. 'Sleep well,' she said. 'Don't read for too long.'

He muttered something else, then they heard him pounding up the stairs. 'You'd think he was trying to smash his way through the treads,' Jo said resignedly.

Max smiled. 'They don't do quiet at that age. Too little control over suddenly long limbs and big feet.'

Jo suppressed a yawn. Getting up, hoping he hadn't noticed, she gathered up the plates, glasses and cutlery and stacked them on the tray. Max stood up too, clearly intending to help, but she said, 'No, honestly, there's not much and I won't bother to dry up anyway.'

Taking the hint – he really was the most tactful man – he sat down again. She handed him the television remote. 'We might just catch the end of 'Antiques Roadshow',' she said.

'Oh, good,' he said.

And she couldn't decide for the life of her whether or not he was being ironic.

Chapter 4

When Jo saw Hal getting out of his car in the mid-afternoon of the next day – Monday – her first thought was that it had been stupid and irresponsible of him to drive home because he really didn't look at all well.

She hurried out to meet him.

'Are you all right?' she asked, trying to hug him while he was still only half-out. Not very successfully; he pulled away, extracting himself from the seat belt.

'I'm fine,' he said.

'I don't agree,' she said. 'You don't look fine, you're so pale you're almost grey and you're clearly exhausted.'

'It was a frustrating drive. Crash on the M25, one of those crazy hold-ups which keep you stationary for an hour then when you get to the spot, there's nothing to see but some shards of rear light covering and a stray wheel trim.'

'No blood and guts all over the tarmac,' she said coolly. 'Always such a disappointment.'

He gave her a sharp look, then went round to the boot to fetch his bag.

'Max is here,' she said.

He spun round. 'What?' Then his expression changed and he looked furtive; guilty, almost. 'Christ, Jo, I'm sorry. I forgot.'

'You forgot,' she echoed.

'Where is he?'

'He's gone into Tunbridge Wells. He's looking for a detailed map of Brittany, so I suggested Waterstones and that's where he is, I imagine.'

Hal nodded. He had his bag in his hand and he slammed down the boot lid. He leaned towards her, his arm going round her, and she closed in towards him. 'Good to have you home,' she said.

'Good to be here.'

Once more as if you mean it, Hal, she thought.

They went into the house. 'Boys not back?' he said, chucking down his bag.

'Sammie's gone to his friend Alex's house for tea, Ed's on the late bus. Rugby.'

'Right.' He sat down at the kitchen table and she put the kettle on.

'Cup of tea?'

'Please.' Then: 'Max all right?'

'Fine.' She glanced at him. He was looking preoccupied, and very tired. 'If you had to impose someone on me without any warning, Hal, I'm quite glad it was him.'

He grinned faintly. 'He tell you what he's up to at the moment?'

'No, not really. He didn't mention any plans to go away, other than his trip over to Brittany.'

When Hal had first said they'd be meeting Max, he'd added casually that sometimes he travelled about and stayed in places for a year or two, and Jo had thought he meant Max was some sort of explorer and envisaged Ray Mears, or a younger David Attenborough. Hal had grinned and told her no, Max was a professor of psychology.

'Brittany?' Hal said, yawning. 'Yeah, he said he'd be on his way to Portsmouth for the ferry.'

'We talked about lots of other things, though,' she went on, trying not to be cross all over again at Hal having forgotten to tell her Max would be coming. She paused in the act of putting a couple of tea bags in their mugs. 'I always feel comfortable with him. He's such easy company.'

Hal didn't answer. When she turned to look at him, he was rubbing his face with his hands, quite hard, as if he was washing it.

'He's going off again on Thursday morning. The day you go,' she said.

'Who?' He removed his hands, stared at her for a split-second as if he'd forgotten she was there.

'Max, of course. The person we were just talking about?'

'Sorry, kid, I'm beat.'

She passed him his tea. 'Go and have a lie-down,' she said. 'Take your tea with you. Have a sleep if you can, then you'll be in a better state to greet the boys when they get in, not to mention your cousin Max. Leave that,' she added as he bent down to pick up his bag. 'I'll sort it, and put your dirty stuff in the wash.'

He stood up, the action infinitely weary, and managed a thin smile. 'What have I done to deserve you?' he asked softly.

'I have absolutely no idea,' she replied, hardly softly at all.

She could hear Hal upstairs as she unloaded his laundry. She put the items not requiring washing back in the bag, for transportation upstairs and putting away in the bedroom and bathroom cupboards. His tee shirt and pyjama trousers, she noticed, smelled of a different fabric softener from the one she used, and she registered absently that he must have had them laundered in the hotel.

Something was missing. She went through the bag again, checked the stuff she'd put in the washing machine, then went out to the hall cupboard, where he'd hung up his jacket, and checked there. No, still missing … Had he been wearing it? No. Definitely not.

She went upstairs, his bag in her hand, and into the bedroom. Hal was standing with his back to her looking out of the window. 'Where's your new grey jumper?' she asked. 'I can't find it – did you leave it in the car?'

He gave her that weird look again. As if he didn't know who she was, or perhaps as if he'd been expecting her to be someone else … But all he said, in pretty much his normal voice, was, 'I'll have a look.'

She put his wash bag, jeans and an unused hand towel away. She waited. He came back.

'Sorry, Jo, I seem to have lost it.'

She looked at him in dismay. 'But it was new! I only gave it to you a couple of weeks ago!'

He shook his head. 'I can't think what can have happened. I must have left it somewhere.'

'Oh, Hal! Your new sweater!' She was torn between exasperation at his carelessness, irritation that he hadn't taken better care of her expensive present, and pity, because he looked devastated.

'Maybe it was when I was sick,' he muttered. 'I remember being very hot, and not really aware of where I was, so perhaps I took it off and forgot I even had it. Sorry,' he said again.

'You were that ill?' She went over to him, putting her arms round him. 'Don't worry about it. I'll buy you another.' She paused. 'I'm just relieved you made it home in one piece.'

Footsteps sounded, coming up the stairs. Max's voice called out, 'Is that my second cousin Hal in there?' and he came into the room.

Hal stepped forward, shook his hand, said, 'I'm sorry I forgot you were coming.'

'It's your day for apologies,' Max said easily. 'Couldn't help hearing, as I came upstairs.' He was smiling at Hal, but Jo could see that Hal didn't take the remark too well.

'The sweater really doesn't matter!' she said briskly. God, it was bad enough having Hal back home looking as if he'd had a near-run thing with dengue fever without him and Max getting off on the wrong foot. 'It was a present – from me, actually – and grey cashmere, so Hal's going to have to make amends by cooking supper tonight and serving the drinks at six on the dot.'

'But I ...' Hal began.

'I'll do supper if you like,' Max offered. 'I like cooking. Hal can still do the drinks, though.'

Hal managed a smile. 'Fine.'

Jo took Max by the arm, turning him round and walking with him out of the bedroom. 'I promised Hal a bit of feet-up time before the boys get back,' she said cheerfully, 'so why don't you and I go down to the living room and you can show me your map of Brittany. Assuming Waterstones came up trumps.'

'Indeed they did,' he said as they went downstairs, 'although I still have no idea where this place is I need to locate.'

Behind them, Jo heard the bedroom door close with such finality that, had there been a lock, she was quite sure Hal would have employed it.

Following Max into the living room, she wondered miserably what else, besides residual flu symptoms, Hal had brought home with him.

The rest of the day passed in reasonable harmony. Max cooked liver and bacon with mashed potato for supper – Jo had forgotten to remind him she didn't eat meat, and obligingly he made her the standby of every person unexpectedly cooking for a non-meat-eater, an omelette, except his was really nice and had herbs and just the right amount of cheese – and the boys (and Max) had seconds. Hal ate a bit but soon ran out of appetite, explaining that he was still off his food after the flu. He excused himself shortly after they'd finished, saying he was exhausted and was going to bed.

Sammie, watching his father with wide eyes, said, 'Daddy's going to bed before me!', and kept on saying it until Jo told him to go and finish his spellings homework.

When the boys had also gone up, she and Max sat together in the living room.

'D'you think Hal will be feeling better in the morning?' Max asked after quite a long silence.

Jo shrugged. 'Possibly.'

Max said 'Ah,' quite quietly.

'Why?'

'Oh … well, because although we've seen quite a bit of each other recently, we've still got some catching-up to do and I'd been hoping these few days would give us the chance for a few good long talks about our mutual relations and our common history. As well as spending some time with you,' he added with swift diplomacy.

'Yes, of course,' Jo said, 'and thank you for the gallant last remark, although I promise you it wasn't necessary.' They exchanged a grin. 'As to whether or not Hal will perk up, I have no idea.' She paused. 'He's not usually like this, Max,' she said, with an effort. 'Well,' she amended, 'not very often.'

'Maybe I could take you both out for a pub lunch tomorrow or Wednesday?' he suggested. 'I'd like to do something to thank you for putting me up.'

'Oh, it's really nice of you, but Hal doesn't really do pubs.'

There was a sight pause. 'What about *you*, though, Jo? It's you who took me in, and you who have looked after me so hospitably since I arrived.'

She laughed again. 'Not really. You saved the scrambled eggs last night, and you did supper this evening.'

He gave her his lovely small-boy's smile. 'That's true, but you made me feel welcome, and that's a far greater and more important talent than being able to knock up a quick supper.'

'Thank you,' she said gravely. 'You were welcome – you *are*.' Then, lowering her voice, 'As I blurted out to you yesterday after the gin and the wine, Hal's not at his best just now. It's fine – it's nothing I can't handle – but I find when he's like this it's best to let him decide what we do and don't do.'

Max looked at her. 'Is that right?'

There was, she thought, either the quick answer or the very, very long one. She didn't think she knew Max quite well enough to go for the long one – although she couldn't help thinking that it would be nice if she did, because he was a good listener and a wise sort of man and might even give her good advice (Lord, where did that come from?). So she just said, 'Yes, it is.'

Max smiled at her again. As if he'd picked up her thought, he said, 'Well, let's just hope he'll be at his best next time we all meet up.' His smile widening, he added, 'Or as near to anyone else's definition of best as he's likely to get.'

She laughed out loud. Then she said, meaning it, 'I hope so too.'

She was busy for most of Tuesday, and Wednesday went by in much the same way. She spent far too long chasing up the last-minute items on Ed's and Sammie's seemingly endless lists of what they'd need for their trips, including having to go into Tunbridge Wells twice on successive days because she'd misunderstood Ed's instructions about his new gum shield. Max came with her the second time, which made the excursion a lot more enjoyable since they went for the pub lunch Max had suggested, just the two of them, took their time over the meal, talking the whole time and laughing quite a lot, and Jo drove them home the long way so that she could show him some more of the local countryside.

Hal and Max went out for an early evening drink on Wednesday evening which, from the expressions on both their faces when they came back after quite a short time, hadn't been an unmitigated success. Jo steadfastly refused both their offers of help, Max's because she could see he was already thinking about setting off on his own trip, Hal's because he was frowning, clearly not happy about something.

She'd have known that, even without the frown.

There had been a weird moment on Tuesday night: she had got up to go for a wee and as she'd crept back into bed, Hal had suddenly opened his eyes and stared at her. He'd had a smile full of love on his face, but then as he focused his slowly-closing eyes on her it had faded. He had turned away and very soon begun softly snoring, deeply asleep again.

She attributed it to the disorientation of someone on his way back from the brink of exhaustion and still recovering from a brief but severe bout of flu. She could see, however, that he was making a very obvious effort to seem upbeat and cheerful so as not to alarm Sammie and make him think the trip might be called off at the last moment. She admired him for his fortitude, because it was all too obvious that he was still not himself.

* * *

Now it was Thursday, the Big Day, and everyone except her was about to leave. She drove Ed in to school with his sports bag and his travel bag, leaving in good time to allow for the morning traffic congestion. She dropped him off as near the school gates as she could, but since quite a lot of parents were doing the same thing for all the other overloaded boys going on the rugby training week, this wasn't in fact very close.

'Have a great time,' she said as he leaned over to give her a hug and a kiss.

'I will. Don't get out of the car, Mum, I've just seen George so I'm going to run and catch him up.'

'No, right, okay,' she said. 'Take care, won't you? No tackling boys who are more than three stone heavier than you.'

It was an old joke, but he was kind enough to laugh.

'You take care too,' he said, quite surprising her. 'Enjoy the peace and quiet, and don't worry.'

'I won't!' she said brightly. I probably will, she thought.

Don't, she thought she heard Ben say. She smiled.

She watched Ed race away. The she drove home.

She was still concerned about Hal. She'd spotted him out by his car just before lunch; he'd said something about looking for his sunglasses because he needed them for the California sunshine. Then he'd suddenly leapt into the driving seat and shot off up the lane in the direction of the village, returning quite shortly afterwards with a face like five miles of bad road, as her decorator friend Reggie Pickett was wont to say about his sister-in-law. The mood of ill humour had persisted as he came into the house for the scratch lunch of bread, cheese and pickle that she was setting out for the two of them and Max, although he seemed to be doing his best to hide it. She wondered if someone had carelessly opened a door into his bodywork and left a dink. Knowing him, he wouldn't be content until he'd made arrangements to have the damage put right.

Then, as she was putting the lunch things away, she saw Hal and Max out on the path that led into the garden. Hal was leaning towards his cousin, alternating between giving him what looked like a somewhat ingratiating smile and glaring at him. He was speaking earnestly to Max – *at* him, in fact – and Max stepped back slightly, away from Hal's intent face. She wondered what they were talking about. Then Hal noticed her at the window, and, taking Max's arm, took him round the corner of the house to where the cars were. Maybe Max knows about repairing cars, she thought. She went back to trying to shove the cheese onto an over-full shelf in the fridge and forgot about it.

'Thank you, Jo, for being so generous to an unexpected guest,' Max said. They were standing beside his car, the three of them, and he was about to set off for Portsmouth. He put his hands on her shoulders and kissed her on the cheek. 'I meant what I said about meeting up again soon. Come up to Cambridge, just you or the pair of you,' he turned to include Hal, 'or the boys as well. It's always good to see you.'

Hal muttered something uncharacteristically mundane about the perpetual charms of Cambridge and Jo said quickly, 'We'd like that. Thanks, Max.'

'I'll be away for just under a week,' he said as he opened the car door. 'But we'll keep in touch, yeah?'

'Of course!' Jo said. Hal muttered something else. He was looking down at the ground, and Jo wondered if he was feeling unwell again;

worried, perhaps, because pretty soon he was going to have to adopt the role of cheerfully eager father who just couldn't wait to embark on his holiday with his eight-year-old son. Poor Hal, she thought, he probably just wants to go and have a sleep, and here we are standing on the drive being polite.

Max called out goodbye, they both echoed him, and then he was away, tyres sending up gravel, a hand waving from the open window.

Right on cue, Hal said, 'Okay if I go up to bed for a while before Sammie gets home?'

'Of course,' she said, putting her arm round his waist as they went inside. 'I'll make sure he keeps the noise down when he gets in.' And that'll be a walk in the park, she thought ruefully, remembering how Sammie had been this morning: so excited that he couldn't eat his breakfast and totally unable to stop talking. 'Sleep as long as you can. While you can,' she added, 'since I don't suppose you'll get much tonight on the plane.'

He gave her a look which, once again, she couldn't quite interpret.

In the late afternoon, she took Hal and Sammie to Gatwick.

Sammie had gone far beyond excitement now and Jo didn't envy Hal, having to keep the lid on his son's exuberance for the endless time before the plane took off and the many hours of the flight. 'Good luck,' she muttered to him.

He grinned, and for the first time looked like himself. 'I'll need it,' he muttered back. 'I'll call you from Dad's, okay?'

'Fine, yes, do that,' she said, all in a rush.

Then they were at the check-in, and there seemed little to be gained by hanging around. She gave Sammie a huge hug and two kisses, then did the same for Hal. 'I'm off!' she said cheerfully to them both. 'Have a wonderful time!'

Then, before Sammie's suspiciously wet and glistening eyes could undermine her, she turned and hurried away.

The house felt very, very empty.

She passed the remainder of Thursday evening in a whirl of tidying, cleaning, washing and ironing. She treated herself to fresh sheets on the bed, white and crisp with starch, and found herself quoting Desdemona's sorrowful words to her maid; 'Lay on my bed my wedding sheets.'

She wondered why that poignant line came into her mind right now, when she was going to be spending the next few nights on her own.

She had supper on a tray in front of the telly and went to bed early with a Val McDermid novel. She read for hours, luxuriating in having nobody drop heavy hints about putting the light off.

She woke the next morning soon after five, wondered for an instant why the bed – the room, the house – felt different, then remembered. It's Friday, she thought, and I have a week and two days before anyone comes back. On the heels of that she had another thought: I don't really need to be here. My husband and my boys are away, there's nobody I need to look after till they come home again.

She thought for a few moments. Fetched a cup of tea, had a quick shower. Found herself packing a small bag: toiletries, a couple of changes of underwear, one of the long tee shirts she wore as a nightdress, a white cotton shirt and a navy linen one, a newish pair of jeans and a sweater. She dressed in tee shirt, her comfy old jeans and a fleece, then packed her walking boots and waxed jacket and slipped on her favourite trainers.

She had decided to do something she'd always wanted to do: drive right up the Great North Road to the region where England gave way to Scotland. The urge to get away was strong and growing stronger, and she saw no reason to resist. She knew she was not happy but she didn't dare delve too deep and find out why. It was to do with Hal, of course it was, and why he was being an arse about her angel story and film, and what on earth had got into him since he'd come home from his Avebury trip.

'I'm going,' she said aloud. 'Now.'

But then she remembered that Hal had said he'd phone once he and Sammie had arrived at his father's house. 'Bugger,' she said softly.

California was eight hours behind England, so it would be ... she glanced at her watch ... about ten in the evening for Sam. She hurried to the phone, grabbed it, dialled Sam's number.

'Hi Sam, sorry it's late, nothing to worry about, everyone's fine and Hal and Sammie are on their way,' she said in a rush.

'Hi, Jo,' said Sam's warm and affectionate voice. 'Glad to hear it. What can I do for you?'

'Hal was going to call when he and Sammie get to you,' she said, 'only I've decided to go away myself for a few days, so if he phones I won't be here and I didn't want him to worry.'

'I don't think he'd have worried, exactly,' Sam said thoughtfully, 'although he'd probably have wondered where you'd got to.'

'I'm not sure yet – I thought I'd drive up to the north east of England, maybe on into Scotland.' Now that she was putting it into words, it seemed an absurd idea, and she wondered what on earth Sam must be thinking, and if he ...

But, 'Don't blame you,' Sam replied. 'It always gives a wonderful sense of freedom, I find, setting off by yourself and with no specific destination. Make the most of it, my dear girl.'

She felt a rush of love for him. 'I don't know where I'll be – I haven't had time to book anything – but please would you tell Hal that I'll ring when I have a contact number?'

'Of course. And don't worry, they'll be fine. I'm setting out to meet them shortly – I've checked, and the fight's on time. And before you say it, no, I'm not too tired, I had a good long sleep this afternoon.'

'That's good, Sam. I'm glad. Give them my love, and to you, of course.'

'Will do. Bye, lovely Jo.'

She put the phone down. Then, before she could change her mind, she rushed through the house doing the security checks, turned off everything that needed to be turned off, stuck a note in an empty bottle for the milkman and, slamming the front door behind her and making sure it was locked, hurried out to her car.

Her old Range Rover had finally given up the unequal struggle, and now Jo had a dark blue Discovery. She loved it. Hal had been inclined to be scathing about her choice until the snowy morning when, late for an appointment, he had edged his BMW out onto the lane and found he could go no further. The postman and a passing dog walker, discovering him spinning his tyres on a patch of ice and unable to progress forwards or backwards because his back wheels were in a hollow, had kindly given him a push back into the drive and Jo had driven him to the station just in time for his train.

Since then, he hadn't been scathing at all.

Now, she patted the steering wheel affectionately and said, 'Come on, Blue, we're driving north.'

It was still early, and she was able to indulge her need for speed on quiet and, at first, all but empty roads. Then she reached the A21 and the rest of the world began to join in. The M25 was pretty much as it always was, so she stuck a tape into the music system and let her impatience flow away.

By mid-morning she was on the A1M.

And, increasingly, she had the strong sense that she was off on an adventure.

Chapter 5

Max

The previous afternoon, Max had set off for Portsmouth in bright sunshine, spending the first part of his journey trying to rid himself of his irritation at his second cousin once removed.

Something quite bizarre had happened shortly before Max left Copse Hill House. Hal had taken him by the arm and marched him round the side of the house – and for a moment Max had suspected he was going to show off his garden, although even at the time he had reflected that taking a pride in his garden didn't sound much like Hal.

Hal had come to an abrupt stop and turned to frown at Max. He had something in his hand: a package roughly the size of a man's palm, with Hal's distinctive writing on the address label.

'I need to ask you a favour.' He made himself smile, but Max sensed it was an effort. 'It's valuable, and it's urgent, and it has to go by registered post.' He paused, glancing quickly back at the house, then edged Max back towards the drive. 'I tried to get it in the post myself but I'd forgotten our local post office is "closed for essential maintenance", according to the notice on the door, and I've run out of time. Too much to do before I – Sammie and I – set off.' He was keeping his voice low, as if he didn't want to be overheard.

'Yes, sure,' Max replied. 'Presumably I'll pass one or two post offices between here and Portsmouth.'

Hal made a sound of impatience, which Max thought was strange for a man asking someone a favour. 'Naturally,' he said shortly.

Max had meant his remark as a joke, feeling the need to lighten the atmosphere. He felt uneasy; unwilling to comply, although he had no idea why. The reaction was unreasonable since it was not an arduous request, and besides, he'd just spent the last four nights under Hal's roof.

Hal leaned in closer and the frown intensified. 'I'll give you the money,' he muttered, and handed Max a five-pound note.

'No, don't worry,' Max said, but Hal thrust the note at him and he had to take it. 'Okay, then, thanks,' he said. But why, he would have liked to add, are we having this conversation outside in the garden?

Hal, not being totally without perception, must have picked up his reluctance.

'Of course, if it's too much trouble you must say so. I can ask Jo, although she's got enough to do.'

'It's no trouble.' Max held out his hand for the package, and Hal gave it to him.

Then Hal's hard, tense expression relaxed and he very nearly smiled. 'Thanks,' he said gruffly. 'Appreciate it.'

The winding and busy nature of the road through Uckfield, Lewes and on to Brighton absorbed most of Max's attention, and when at last he got onto a decent stretch of dual carriageway as he sped away from Hove, he put his foot down and opened up the car's powerful engine. He put a tape in the cassette player and he felt himself start to relax as the mathematically satisfying pattens of Bach flowed out into the car. He hadn't really appreciated until this moment that staying in Copse Hill House had been pretty tense; once Hal was home, anyway. Now, as he turned his mind to the night crossing ahead, his thoughts filled with pleasurable anticipation of his Breton holiday and he ran over in his mind the various avenues he hoped to explore.

It was on the third of the roundabouts on the Chichester bypass that he remembered Hal's package.

Max cursed softly.

There seemed no chance of coming across a post office any time soon, and even if he did spot one, there was nowhere even to pull off the road, let alone park for the length of time it would take to go inside, register the package, buy the necessary stamps and put it in the post. He'd have to look out for the distinctive red sign in Portsmouth, on the way to the ferry terminal.

Damn.

He saw a line of brake lights ahead at the approach to yet another roundabout and slowed down. As the car came gently to a stop, he glanced across at the package.

It was addressed to A. Swayne, c/o Carrington's Travel Agency, and the town was Chichester.

Albert? Alan? Andrew? Augustus? Alexander? He let his mind turn over the possibilities as the traffic eased and the car moved forward. And then he thought: Chichester. I'm going round Chichester – very slowly – right this moment.

At the roundabout he took the turning to the town centre. There was no need to post the package; he would deliver it to this Swayne person at the travel agency by hand.

* * *

A plump young man in a lurid tie and a sharp suit that looked as if it had been made for someone slightly smaller greeted him warmly as he entered Carrington's Travel Agency, although the warmth faded rapidly when Max explained he wasn't there to enquire after a holiday.

'I wonder if I might give this to A. Swayne?' Max asked politely, indicating the name on the package.

'She's not here,' the young man said offhandedly.

'Do you know when she'll be back?'

Without answering, the young man turned to an older man sitting at a desk behind him. 'Rodge? Angela Swayne's off sick, right?' The older man muttered something that sounded like an assent. 'She coming back?' The older man shrugged indifferently.

'She's off sick,' the young man said, turning back to Max. Then, perhaps recognising he was being less than helpful – perhaps even belatedly hoping Max might change his mind and decide he wanted a week in Ibiza after all – he added, 'I'll take it if you like, hand it to her if and when she turns up?'

Max hesitated. It was tempting to accept the offer, for if he did he could be on his way to Portsmouth and have time for a leisurely beer or two before embarkation began. He could even read his way right through the *Times*, something he rarely found the occasion to do in a habitually busy life. On the other hand, Hal had said that the package was urgent and contained something valuable, and Max wasn't at all sure it was right to leave such an object in the dubious hands of the youth with the sharp suit ...

'Does she – Miss Swayne? Mrs? – live nearby?' he asked. 'If so, I could drop the package off at her house.'

The youth stared at him through narrowed eyes as if assessing him. Then he said, 'I can check if she's okay with that. Bear with me.' Picking up a phone, he dialled a number. After quite a long pause, it was answered and he said, 'Hi, it's Terry. Terry from work? Yeah. There's someone here with a registered package for you wants to deliver it to your house, since you're not here. That okay?' He waited, listening, said a curt, 'Righto,' and put the phone down.

Then he went to a filing cabinet behind the desk, pulled out a drawer and extracted a buff file. He licked a forefinger and flicked rapidly through the small number of pages inside it, then fetched a pencil and a scrap of paper and wrote out a few lines.

Turning back to Max, he said, 'She says it's the little lane that branches off the bigger lane just after a pub called the White Hound, in the middle of the village.' Then he shoved the piece of paper across the desk.

'Thanks,' Max said shortly. He didn't think more effusive gratitude was appropriate.

He found the village and the pub called the White Hound without too much difficulty. There proved, however, to be several narrow lanes overhung with chestnut trees leading out of the pretty little place, and he decided not to waste more time but ask someone if they knew where Angela Swayne lived. There was a harassed-looking woman stacking crates of empties in the yard beside the pub, and she helpfully pointed out the lane that Max needed.

'Not sure if she'll be at home, mind,' she added, 'although, come to think of it, she hasn't been in the pub for quite a few days and someone said they thought she might be under the weather. Had a friend come look her up and apparently he went down with that nasty flu bug, so maybe she's got that. She ...'

But Max felt obliged to interrupt. Thanking her, thinking (amongst far more insistent matters) of his boat and its eight-thirty departure, he nodded a farewell and drove off up the lane.

He was trying very hard to hold on to a charitable interpretation of what was unfolding. A. Swayne wasn't Albert, Anthony or Art, she was Angela. And Hal had been staying with her and very possibly given her his flu.

She could very well be some creaky, fusty old spinster archaeologist with whom Hal had been discussing standing stones and burial mounds. She probably was, and she'd left some personal possession in Hal's car during one of their excursions and it was this that had to be returned to her, that was in the package on the passenger seat of Max's car.

But why, the uncharitable voice in his head asked relentlessly, would an elderly archaeologist be working in a Chichester travel agency?

He found what must be the right place, and drew the car off the road onto a short length of lay-by. He was about to get out and go to knock on the door of the end house in the row when it crashed open and a woman came flying across the lane towards him.

She was about thirty, thirty-five. She was tall, her shoulders and upper body well developed and shapely. She had smooth reddish-fair hair cut in a long bob and she wore large-framed glasses with tinted lenses. She was pale, she looked as if she had been crying – her nose was red and swollen – but as she ran towards his car her face was alight with joy.

As Max got out and walked to meet her, smiling nervously, her expression changed so abruptly that it was as if she had put on a tragic mask.

She stopped dead in the middle of the lane.

'You're not ...'

Not Hal, Max thought. It was very obvious that the word had been on her lips.

'No,' he said gently.

'But the car, your car ...'

Max turned round to look at his car and saw what she had seen. From the front and before you made out that Max's car was a coupé, it looked very similar to Hal's. Same colour – black – and same distinctive blue and white insignia on the bonnet above the equally distinctive radiator grill.

He was about to speak, about to explain what he was doing there, when she seemed to sway and he thought she was going to faint. He hurried towards her, put an arm round her waist and took hold of her hand, and supported her back along the short stretch of lane to her door. He helped her inside – there was a step down – and lowered her onto a sofa.

The house felt dank, the furnishings were worn and slightly battered and the paintwork needed refreshing.

'I'll make you a cup of tea,' he said easily. 'It's … er, it's cold outside and warm in here, so I expect the change of temperature made you feel weak suddenly.'

The day, in fact, was quite mild. And, other than the red nose and bleary eyes, she looked as strong as a horse.

She said mechanically, 'Thank you, you're very kind.'

Had she not been still in shock, Max thought, she'd demand to know what I wanted and at the same time start to get irate about my being in her house, putting her kettle on to boil and setting out a cup and a tea bag.

'My name's Max Dillon,' he said before she could do so. 'I'm Hal's cousin and I've just been staying with him and his family. He found something that apparently belongs to you in his car,' he reached in his inside pocket and held out the package, 'and he asked me to put this in the post. He had to go to the airport.' He had no idea whether or not she knew what he was talking about but from her dazed expression he thought not. They both looked at the package. 'I forgot to post it until I was just outside Chichester, so I decided I'd deliver it instead. It's addressed to your work. Apparently, he doesn't have your home address.'

'No,' she said dully. 'No, I don't think he has.'

He moved over to her and handed her the package. She had taken off her glasses and he saw that her eyes, like her nose, were red and puffy. As if she had a cold. As if she had been weeping. Slowly, she tore open the stiff paper of the envelope and withdrew an elegant black leather wallet.

The kettle had boiled and Max made the tea, going over to the fridge for milk. 'Sugar?' he asked.

'No thanks.'

He gave her the mug. She nodded, and took a sip.

He noticed that there was a pale grey sweater folded on top of the cushion at one end of the sofa. It was wet with tears, dark with streaks of mascara.

Ah, he thought.

He perched on a stool beside the kitchen counter. 'I'm sorry I distressed you,' he said quietly. 'I didn't ...'

'I'm not distressed!' she said sharply and in contradiction of every scrap of evidence. 'I ... just ... I just ...' Then, clearly unable to think of a single thing to excuse her reaction to his arrival, she went on the offensive. 'What are you doing here?' she demanded. 'You were in the area – you said you were outside Chichester. What for?'

'I'm on my way to Portsmouth for the night ferry to St Malo,' he said shortly. 'Which means, as I'm sure you're about to point out, that this place where you live is more than a little out of my way.'

'Sorry,' she muttered. 'I should have said thank you for returning my wallet. I am grateful, very. Losing it on top of everything ...' She pulled herself up. 'Thanks,' she said instead.

'You're welcome.'

There was a short, awkward silence. Then she said, 'Going on holiday?'

'The ferry? Not really. Five-day return trip. I'm doing some research into my matriarchal line – my mother's family.'

'I know what it means,' she said curtly. 'I do quite a lot of genealogy for people doing what you're doing.'

'Oh?' he queried politely. 'Well, I have quite a task ahead of me, since I don't know Brittany, or indeed any part of France, the place I need to find is so small that it isn't on the large-scale map I bought and I don't speak French.'

'That will be a problem, since not many people speak English in the depths of rural Brittany,' she remarked.

He glanced at her. 'You know the area?'

'I do.'

'I don't suppose you've heard of Les Forges de Paimpont, or a tiny hamlet called St-Yves-les-Forges?'

She frowned. 'Paimpont's in the middle,' she said. 'It's in the ancient stretch of forest they used to call the Broceliande.'

'And do you speak French?'

She nodded, sipping her tea.

He stared at her, quickly looking away when she looked up and noticed.

He'd just had an idea. Probably a rash, foolish one, but he was moved by the state of her. Hal seemed to have left her and she had been crying. For days, perhaps.

It wasn't for Max to feel guilty, and he didn't.

But something about the brave way she was trying so hard to pull herself together, to make conversation, to appear normal when she must be feeling so awful, touched him profoundly.

He managed a short and not very convincing laugh. 'I don't suppose you could take a few days of holiday?'

'I'm on leave,' she replied swiftly. 'I'm ... never mind.'

He met her wide grey eyes. 'I was just thinking how much better my chances would be of finding out what I want to know if I had somebody like you to help. To show me what to do. Not somebody *like* you,' he corrected himself. 'You.'

'*What?*' She gave an incredulous laugh. 'God, you have to be joking!'

He shrugged.

'I mean ...' She stopped, clearly wondering which to select out of all the reasons to turn down this wild and absurd proposition. 'I don't know you! Well, I know who you are, but we've only just met! You're leaving on tonight's boat, which means I'd need to make up my mind in about ten minutes flat, never mind having to pack a bag and find my passport and see if I've got any francs from the last trip I made. If there was any likelihood of my saying yes, that is, which I can assure you there isn't.'

'It was just an idea,' he said quietly. 'I apologise if I've offended you.'

'Offended ...' She shook her head as if giving up on trying to guess the limits of his folly. 'I'm not offended, and in fact I've done trips like yours with other people, especially to France. But ... but ...' She gave up. She stared at him, half smiling, and shrugged.

'Fine,' he said. 'I'd better be off.'

Suddenly she stood up.

'Will you be footing the bill?'

'Naturally.' He felt a flash of optimism. 'I'll pay you for your time, as well. What do you usually charge?'

'Eighty quid a day plus expenses normally, but ...' She didn't compete the sentence. 'You pay for my hotel, the ferry, and things like that.'

'Fine,' he said again, but this time it took on a very different meaning. 'May I use your phone?'

'What for?' she demanded, looking at him suspiciously.

'While you pack a bag, I'd better call Brittany Ferries and see if they have another cabin available.'

'But …' She was scowling at him thunderously, as if she could hardly believe what he was doing. What she appeared to have just agreed to. Then, grinning very briefly – it really was there and gone in a moment and he almost missed it – she muttered, 'What the hell?' and pointed to the phone.

It was difficult, Max thought, as they drove on to Portsmouth, to hit the right conversational note. Angela, he sensed, would perhaps have preferred silence, but that didn't seem right as the atmosphere in the car tended to darken alarmingly when neither of them spoke for any length of time.

So they talked trivialities. The weather. The state of the traffic. The eternal problem of roadworks. Max would have liked to ask her the questions that were foremost in his mind, such as, how long did the affair with Hal go on? Why did he finish it? Did he finish it, or was it you?

He didn't. It was none of his business.

Except, said a censorious voice in his head, Hal made it your business by asking you to post that package.

But Hal had no choice. He would have realised Angela really needed to have her wallet back because no doubt, like everyone else's, it was full of credit cards, membership cards and maybe even a driving licence, not to mention cash. He'd tried to put it in the post as soon as he discovered it, but his local post office was shut.

So he gave it to me to post, Max thought, and I forgot. I could have found a post office in Portsmouth; I had plenty of time. It was my decision to deliver it in person.

And now look what's happened …

Max thought about that while with the rest of his mind he kept up a stream of banal remarks about contraflows on motorways and Sunday shopping.

He risked a quick look at Angela while they waited for an inexplicable hold-up in the traffic to resolve itself. She hadn't taken long to pack her bag and be ready to leave, but he noticed she'd washed her face, put on some makeup, tidied her beautiful hair and changed out of her tatty jeans and baggy sweater into a smart pair of narrow, well-fitting black trousers, boots and a chestnut-coloured leather jacket over a soft amber-coloured jumper. A silk scarf united the outfit effectively and enhanced the colour of her hair.

He was struck again by how courageous she was. She'd put on a brave face, accepted his invitation to accompany him to Brittany – and they'd only just met! – and now here she was, keeping up her end of the conversation as if this were just another job, and he hadn't just seen her in floods of tears because his cousin Hal had treated her badly.

Perhaps, he thought, as the road ahead cleared and he accelerated smoothly up through the gears, anything was better than sitting by herself in that dismal little house. Even setting off to Brittany with a stranger.

They were in good time for the night boat.

The loading process began shortly after they drew up, and presently they found themselves in a second queue, this one on the far side of the customs check. Another forty minutes and they were driving across the ramp and onto the car deck of a huge ferry. They were handed a card with the deck and staircase number, to enable them to find the car again the next morning, then they climbed a few sets of steps and emerged into the main reception area.

Max's cabin was on the highest accommodation deck, and on the outside; there were two bunks side by side and a large window in between them, at present filled with a view of the ferry terminal and the Royal Navy dockyard beyond. Angela's was a deck down and on the inside, with bunk beds and no window.

'I'll have this one,' Max said as they entered the second cabin, and he dumped his bag down on the lower bunk. 'You take the one with the view.'

She shook her head. 'No, that's not fair.' Then, as if she was quite unused to men making gallant gestures, she said, 'Why would you make the offer?'

He opened his bag and removed his sponge bag, moving her out of the way so he could put it in the tiny shower room. 'It's not an offer, I mean it,' he said shortly. He handed her the slip of card that acted as a key to the better cabin. 'Go on. I'll meet you in the bar in ten minutes.'

She eyed him suspiciously, as if she sensed he was feeling sorry for her and didn't like it. 'I'm all right,' she said sharply.

'I know.' He grinned at her. 'Hurry up. Last one in the bar pays for the drinks.'

They sat at a small table in the dimly-lit bar, watching the Portsmouth waterfront slide by. The ships of the Royal Navy, the passenger ferry to the Isle of Wight, the very tops of HMS *Victory*'s masts, the old vessel – still a ship of the line, he'd read somewhere – tiny in comparison with her later sister ships, the beautiful lines of HMS *Warrior*. The funfair at

Southsea, the pier. Then they were turning into the Solent, and slowly passing the first of the forts.

Angela, perhaps wanting to make him aware that she was taking her new job seriously, had extracted a notebook and pen from her bag and asked him what information he had concerning the place in Brittany where his family had originated. Max would have far rather gone on staring out at the stupendous view, but it seemed unkind not to go along with what was evidently a way of distracting her from her sadness.

He told her the few details he had, and handed her the half-page of rough notes he'd made on the places in the middle of the forest. She nodded, then, writing busily, fell silent.

After a while he said, 'I'm ready to eat. Shall we make our way along to the restaurant?'

She looked up. 'I'm not hungry,' she replied. 'I'm going back to my cabin' – she smiled very briefly – 'your cabin, and I'll finish making up my notes. I've got a guide to Brittany in my bag which has a very detailed map in the back, and I'll try to locate those places you mentioned: Les Forges de Paimpont and St Yves-les-Forges. I think that's right?'

'It is.' He was very surprised she'd recalled the names so precisely, considering the state she was in. 'But don't you want any supper? You …'

'No,' she said, with a distinct air of finality. She got up. 'See you in the morning.'

Then she strode away.

Max had a very good dinner: buffet hors d'oeuvre, heavy on the seafood and the oysters a tantalising hint at the joys to come once they were in Brittany; a main course of salt-raised lamb in a stew dark with red wine and fragrant with garlic. Then, back to a different part of the buffet for a selection of desserts. He drank half a bottle of wine and was tempted to have a glass of brandy with his coffee. He gave in.

He was by no means the only person eating alone.

But it crossed his mind to wonder whether any of his fellow lone diners also had an intriguing and good-looking travelling companion only a deck below, whose presence would have made the meal so much more enjoyable.

He drained his brandy, drank a glass of water, then paid his bill and went to bed.

Chapter 6

Dawn was lightening the sky as the ferry sailed into St Malo. Max was sitting at a table for two and halfway through a very good breakfast when Angela strode into the restaurant and sat down beside him, a book in her hand.

'We're going to need a better map,' she said after they had exchange brief good mornings. 'The one in the back of this book doesn't show the little village we'll be looking for, although it's fine for familiarising ourselves with the general picture, and you said the large-scale you bought in England didn't show it either, so we'll have to find one of those walkers' maps that show all the contours and every kink in every stream.'

'Okay,' he said easily. 'Coffee?' A waiter was hovering.

She looked up from her notebook. 'Yes, please.'

'It's a serve yourself buffet.' He pointed.

'Yes, right.'

She got up, fetched cereal, fresh fruit and a pot of yoghurt, swiftly, efficiently. Studying her, he thought that the transformation from deeply distressed abandoned mistress – if that was what she had been – to hard-working researcher and guide was now complete. She had swept her hair up into a neat bun and was again dressed in the smart trousers and leather jacket, although today she wore a white silk shirt and a different scarf, this one in tones of silver that echoed the small silver earrings and picked up the colour of her eyes. Her expression was serious and determined.

She returned to the table and sat down. She ate quickly, and he had the impression that taking on food was like putting petrol in your car: necessary in order to keep going but without any element of pleasure or enjoyment for the recipient. He smiled wryly, bending his head so that she wouldn't see. It wasn't funny at all, merely poignant, considering what it was that had robbed her of her pleasure in food.

She had unfolded the map from the back of the book. 'I have managed to find Les Forges,' she said, 'here.' She pointed. 'We leave St Malo and head for Dinan, and then take the road for somewhere called Caulnes, and then St Méen le Grand and Paimpont, and that's in the middle of the Broceliande forest and from there it's only a short hop on to Les Forges.'

'Great,' he said. 'And you're happy to be navigator?'

'Perfectly happy.'

She folded away the map and finished her breakfast.

The strengthening sun was dissipating the mist as they drove away from the port. St Malo was a maze of roundabouts, crossroads and early morning traffic, but Angela was a good map-reader and calmly told him which lane to get into where there was a choice, and which signs to look out for when half a dozen place names appeared all together at junctions. Soon they were out of the congestion and on their way.

Dinan, over to their left, was a beautiful image of tall spires reaching up out of the vestiges of the mist. Seeing him glancing that way, Angela said, 'Dinan's a lovely town. I've been there several times and on each visit I find an interesting new corner.' She paused, then added in a rush,

'There's an ancient stone bench beside one of the gates in the town walls and it's called the banc de la critique – I've no idea what its original purpose was but it could serve nowadays for watching passers-by and muttering, "Not that tee shirt with that muffin top", or, 'White trousers? Really?" or even "Wow, that's a great outfit".'

He smiled, pleased that she had ventured a comment that wasn't strictly to do with their purpose. 'Maybe we could call there on the way back,' he said. 'I'll make sure I'm wearing toning colours and buff up my shoes,' he added.

She made a non-committal noise that he hoped might mean yes.

On the far side of Dinan they encountered a series of huge rounda-bouts, and on the final one Angela only spotted the sign for Caulnes when it was almost too late to take it, and it felt as if he negotiated the exit on two wheels. Then they were on a road with little traffic that widened to dual carriageway here and there, usually on an uphill slope and twice, obligingly, when there happened to be a tractor to overtake. Looking to left and right at wide fields, woodland, farms and little settlements in the shallow valleys, Max realised this was a region of traditional agriculture, where the huge farms typical of America and, to some extent, Britain, still had not taken over.

He began to relax. He had the sense that he was going to enjoy this trip.

They had left the main road about half an hour ago, at a place called Gaël. As they did so, the signs appeared to have given out.

'I think this is right,' Angela said, without a lot of conviction. They had just retraced the last five miles, since she had become increasingly certain they had gone wrong. 'We ought to be going south, and to judge by the sun, this road is more south than the last one. Sorry,' she added curtly.

'It's not your fault,' he replied.

'Well, I'm navigating, so it is, actually.'

He smiled. 'It's difficult to navigate in the absence of signposts.'

Suddenly, making him jump, she yelled, 'Paimpont!'

'Great! Are we there?' Then, dubiously, 'Is this it?'

They were at a junction with a scattering of about half a dozen houses and a boarded-up café, in front of which a large ginger cat sat washing itself in a shaft of sunlight.

'No, of course not, but there was a sign, over there.' She reached behind her and pointed. 'It's okay, we're going the right way. I think it said eight kilometres, so that's five miles.'

He nodded.

The road straightened out from its winding course and forest rose up on either side. Here and there wide rides and narrower tracks led off into the darkness beneath the trees; there was a lot of pine. There were also stretches of deciduous trees, the leaves turning to gorgeous shades of tan, orange, yellow and gold, shining in the soft rays of the low autumn sunshine. He opened the window a few inches, relieved to discover that the stench of pig excrement that had frequently filled the air as they drove through the farm lands had now been replaced by cool, sharp air as fresh as a glass of cold water.

Presently they came to a small town, and a sign beside the road said Paimpont. Looking briefly at Angela, Max saw that she was smiling. 'Well done, navigator,' he said.

She made a small bow.

They passed a campsite on the left, which appeared to be closed. Then a lake appeared on the right, a stretch of dark water overshadowed by trees. It opened out into the misty distance, and an abbey rose up on the left shore. The road went over the lake's end, and Max slowed almost to a standstill so they could have a proper look.

'It's lovely,' Angela said. 'There should be an arm clad in white samite, the hand holding up a sword.'

'Right,' he agreed. 'It's that sort of place.'

He drove on, into the little town. On the right a row of houses was cut thorough by an archway, and a street led away past more houses and a few shops. On the left there was a restaurant called Le Relais.

Max drew up in front of it. Angela turned, giving him a questioning look.

'It's half past twelve,' he said. 'This is the first settlement of any size we've come to for ages, and the only place where we can get something to eat, apart from that café that looked as if it closed some time around 1945. How far is it to Les Forges?'

'A few miles.'

'Then we'll have lunch here, and head on out this afternoon,' he said, firmly. He had the clear impression she would have rather gone on but after all, who, he asked himself, was paying?

They had the *menu du jour*, in the company of a party of four hikers and several groups of men in suits or shirts, trousers and jerseys, who looked as if this was their normal lunch stop. The food was simple but good, and Max could hardly believe how little it cost.

He had a look around while Angela went to find the lavatory. The place appeared to be a hotel, and the man behind the bar that doubled as a reception desk was friendly and welcoming. When Angela came to join him he said, 'What do you think about booking ourselves in here for two or three nights? If Les Forges is just down the road, then we're unlikely to find anywhere nearer, and I like this place.'

'Fine, good idea,' she said. 'Want me to ask if they have rooms available?'

'Please.'

She addressed the man behind the bar, who nodded vigorously and backed up the affirming gesture by several repeats of *oui*, *oui*, *oui*, only it sounded more like *ooWAh*. Smiling, she turned back to Max. 'He's got two en suite rooms we can have in this main building, or there are cheaper rooms in the annexe at the back that have a shared bathroom, only they're usually for students and hikers.'

'Then we'll be in here with the posh folk,' he said.

The man got out a block of forms, filled in a couple and asked for a look at their passports. Angela glanced at Max's, his name in the inset on the front showing clearly.

'You're a professor!' she said.

'Yup.'

'Of what?'

'Psychology.'

She gave him a long look, an eyebrow raised. He didn't know what the expression signified and wasn't sure he wanted to guess.

Les Forges de Paimpont proved to be a collection of deserted houses, some large, semi-ruined buildings that suggested heavy industry, a chapel and a nineteenth-century metal cross, elaborately decorated, on a stone plinth. The little settlement was set beside a lake, or perhaps a series of lakes, deep in the midst of the forest. There was an old wooden sign – which could also have been nineteenth century – announcing the name, without which they probably would have driven straight past.

'There's nobody here,' Max observed. He had parked the car beneath the trees by the old chapel. No other vehicles were in sight. Apart from the distant drone of a tractor, there wasn't a sound. 'Shall we take a look?'

'I'm not sure what we're looking for, but yes,' Angela said.

A beaten earth road ran between the two rows of houses. It led down a gentle slope, at the end of which there was a structure that looked like an enormous fireplace. Other buildings stood nearby: a truncated tower, monster-sized walls that could have been part of almost anything. Water ran nearby: its sound was loud in the silence, and they discovered various man-made channels beneath the undergrowth, clearly diverted from the lakes opposite.

'Well, it could easily have been a forge,' Max said, breaking quite a long silence.

'Mmm.' Angela was staring at the rising ground beyond the enormous fireplace. 'There's a house on top of the bank. Maybe somebody there can tell us something.'

'Right. Let's go and see.'

He set off, eager now, moving quickly, and she kept pace with him. They climbed up out of the shallow valley and on to the road between the settlement and the lakes, then turned up to the right, rounding a corner beneath trees – everywhere there were trees – to find a long, low house made of reddish granite, slate-roofed, green-painted woodwork in fairly urgent need of attention. A few metal tables and a stack of plastic chairs on the forecourt suggested that it might be a bar in the high season, but now it was as deserted as the settlement below.

Max felt a stab of disappointment. He wasn't sure what he'd expected – in fact he had worked hard at not expecting anything but waiting to see what happened – but to discover nothing but unidentifiable ruins and an absolute dearth of people, information or even a helpful sign or two was quite a blow.

Angela must have picked up his mood. Coming to stand beside him, she said, 'It's daunting, I know, but it's by no means the end of the road.

In fact, we've only just started, and it's a good enough start since we've found one of the places you mentioned.'

'Yes, but it doesn't teach us anything,' he said dully.

'Not yet, no,' she agreed, 'but there's a great deal we can find out once we know where to look.'

'But …'

'Max, didn't I tell you I've done this sort of thing before?'

'Yes.' It was the first time she'd called him by his first name; called him anything, come to that, and he found he liked it. 'You did.'

'This isn't really the way to start,' she went on, her kindly tone removing any sense that this was a reprimand. 'What I'd usually do is sit down with someone, look at every bit of information they have on the person, or people, they're trying to trace, ask a lot of questions and then come up with a list of steps to take.'

'Such as?'

'Such as looking in census records – well, I'd do that in the UK, I'm not sure about Brittany – and parish records. In England, there's been a form of recording the population for nearly two hundred years, and it's been the law since 1837, when Victoria came to the throne,for births, marriages and deaths to be officially noted, not only in the church records but also the civil ones. We've had a census approximately every decade for slightly longer – since 1801. From the small amount of work I've done in France I'm pretty sure it's the same here.'

'There doesn't seem to be a church here, just that chapel where we parked.'

'True, but there was a huge abbey back in Paimpont, and I'm sure we can pick up a lot of helpful information there. We might even find a tourist office or a museum!'

He thought that was optimistic, but didn't say so.

'What now?' he asked instead.

'Now?' She turned in a slow circle, frowning. 'Honestly, I don't think we can do any more here until we know what we're looking at, and, indeed, for, if you see what I mean.'

'Yeah.'

'So we'll go back to Paimpont, check into our posh accommodation, then meet up in the bar, where there will no doubt be a welcoming roaring fire as soon as the sun sets and the temperature drops, and you can bring all the notes and information that you have on your mother's family.'

Her enthusiasm was infectious. Feeling considerably more optimistic, he reached in his pocket for his car key and they returned to the car park.

'My mother was born in Canada,' he began an hour or so later.

They were in the bar, the fire had indeed been lit, and they had already established themselves in their rooms. They had discovered the accommodation to be basic but clean, furnished in French country style with at least two wallpaper patterns in each room, dado rails with brown gloss paint on the woodwork, and an enormous wardrobe in the corner of Angela's room that she said was large enough for several bodies. Max's room had a chaise longue upholstered in scarlet and pink brocade. It looked like something out of a brothel.

'Canada,' Angela said, writing it down.

'Vancouver,' he added.

'Date of birth?'

He told her.

'Maiden name?'

'Ledanose.' He spelt it for her.

'Parents' names?'

'Her mother was called Tilde – Matilda, I suppose, or probably Mathilde, since she was French – and her father was Einar.'

'Their dates?'

'I only have the years.' He showed her his own notes, and she copied them down.

'And your mother's still alive?'

She asked the question as if she expected him to say yes, which was reasonable given his mother's year of birth: she would only have been in her late sixties, which wasn't old by any means for nowadays.

'No,' he said quietly. 'My father was killed in a car accident when I was twenty-two. My mother never really got used to living without him, and she died a few months later.'

Angela had put down her pen, her expression stricken. 'I'm so sorry,' she said. 'I had no idea, I just assumed …'

'Perfectly reasonably,' he interrupted. 'Please, don't worry.' He smiled briefly. 'It was a long time ago,' he added gently.

She went on watching him for a few moments, a troubled expression in her eyes. Then she picked up her pen and said, 'So, if I'm right in guessing that your interest in finding out about your mother's side of the family began when it was too late to ask the questions you wish you had asked – which is most people's experience, to be honest – then this,' she indicated his notes, 'is all we've got?'

'It is.'

'And you have no other living relatives who might be able to add some facts and figures?'

'Er …' Had she forgotten that he was related to Hal? 'No, I don't believe so,' he said quickly before she could remember. 'It's not a very close family.'

She had bent her head over her notebook, so he couldn't detect if the reference to his family had distressed her. He found himself hoping very much that it hadn't.

'So,' she said, finishing the note she was making, 'your late mother's parents went to Vancouver from here?'

He explained that his mother's parents had emigrated to Canada shortly before she was born. 'She went to England during the war as a nurse,' he went on, 'and she was based near Cambridge. My father was called Robert and he was in the USAAF, and he and my mother – her middle name was Olive, which was what my dad called her, but her family called her Dora because her first name was Teodora – met, fell in love and married, and I came along while they were still in Cambridge after the war ended.'

She was nodding as she wrote.

'My father loved Cambridge,' he went on. 'He got to know some people there who were very kind to him; they welcomed the stranger in an alien land, as he used to say, into their home during and after the war. It was a real family home – parents and three grown-up children, all busy on war work, and the parents went on living here after the war, although their children had all left home by then. My father used to take me there to see them sometimes. They were lovely people.'

He was about to say something else but, as if she'd heard enough concerning a matter not strictly to do with their current research, she interrupted him.

'Then later you went back to Vancouver?' she prompted.

'Yes. We lived there till I was in my late teens, then I came back to England to study.'

She wrote for some time. Then: 'Back up a little. Did you get to know your mother's parents in Canada?'

'My grandmother Tilde lived near us. She was widowed and getting old and infirm, and I wouldn't say I really knew her. When she died, my parents took us to live for a while near Dad's relatives in California.' Among them Hal's father Sam Dillon, he could have said. Who, it appeared, was a more honourable man than his son. 'I'd finished my first degree not long before my parents died,' he hurried on, 'for which I studied in England. With them gone, there wasn't any point in returning to Canada, so I stayed in England.'

'And do you have family there?' She had stopped writing and was looking at him, an expectant expression in her eyes as if she was waiting for the details of a cosy domestic setup and a family house full of kids, dogs, muddy boots and a slew of toys.

'I live on my own.' Then, taking a run at it because it was less painful that way, 'I was married. My wife was called Billie Mallory, we were married for six years and she died of a rare sort of brain tumour.'

Once again, her face fell into distress. 'That's dreadful,' she said very softly. 'I shouldn't have asked.'

He shrugged. 'You're helping me with my family story,' he said reasonably. 'No point not giving you the full picture.'

'I'm glad you told me,' she said. 'Now I know, I won't mention it again.'

But *I* might, he thought. Of the few people I've told about Billie, you, Angela, are one of perhaps two or three with whom I could even think about sharing more than the basic harsh fact of her death.

She had turned to a new page and now said briskly, 'So, your mother's parents were French – Breton, I suppose – and lived near Les Forges. We could start our research tomorrow by finding out exactly what sort of industry went on there, and first, before we go back to that house behind the ruined village, we'll locate the mairie here and see what they can tell us.'

'Mairie has to be where the mayor hangs out?'

'Yes. Unlike in England – and I have no idea what happens in Canada – here in France every community has its own mayor, which means that the mairie is involved right at the basic local level. It seems to work all right, but apparently there's a vast amount of bureaucracy.'

'Which could work in our favour, if the records are kept and go back far enough,' he said.

'To …' She flipped back a few pages. 'To 1920, when your grandparents left, and before that 1893 when your grandmother was born, 1886 for your grandfather.'

He felt a sense of deflation. 'Is it really likely?'

'That the records will be there for us to find? Highly likely! We're talking under a hundred years, which is nothing in genealogical terms. I've followed one branch of my family back to 1470.'

'Good grief.' He was amazed. Her wanted to ask about her family. He hesitated, then thought, she asked about mine. 'Do you have brothers and sisters?'

'No. And my father's dead.'

'I'm sorry.'

She stared into the fire. 'He buggered off when I was five and married someone else. She was awful, and my mother's attempts to keep me in contact with my father ended very suddenly when, during a visit to him and his new family, I threw a plate of porridge over my stepmother's head and ruined her new hairdo.'

'Oh.' He tried to keep a straight face, but knew he was failing.

She too was grinning. 'It was magnificent,' she said. 'She sat there, porridge dripping off her fringe and landing in splatters on her huge bust, and she was making these little squeaking noises. My father tried to make me apologise but I refused, then I ran upstairs and packed my case and stormed out. I didn't have any money and it took me most of the day to walk home.'

'How old were you?'

'Seven.'

'What did your mother say? Wasn't she worried about you?'

'Well, no, because she had no idea I was walking home till I arrived, and by then there was nothing to worry about because I was home.'

He shook his head. 'Good for you,' he said admiringly.

She chuckled. 'It made my mother realise that trying to make me go and stay with my father really wasn't on, so it was well worth the blisters.'

For the third time since meeting her, Max was struck by her courage. And also by the thought that he could appreciate what Hal had seen in her, and that it couldn't have been easy to walk away.

Chapter 7

The next morning, Max and Angela were out straight after breakfast and headed for the mairie, which they had learned was in a small square to the left of the abbey. Beside the mairie, however, there was an office which offered information for visitors to the region, and without waiting to see if Max agreed, Angela opened the door and went inside.

Her request for anything on Les Forges – that was what Max presumed she'd said, although in truth he only isolated those two words from her flurry of rapid French – was met with an encouraging response. The stout, bespectacled woman with the aggressively short hair who was sitting at the desk talked for about five minutes with hardly a pause, then got up and fetched a leaflet from a stand behind the door. She handed it to Angela, pointing to photographs and to several dense blocks of print. When Angela managed to get a word in – a short string of words, in fact, which began with merci beaucoup – the woman seemed all set to resume her outpouring, undeterred by Angela slowly but firmly backing towards the door.

When they were finally outside in the sunshine again, she turned to Max with a grin and said, 'I had an idea we'd be there all day.'

'Me too,' he agreed. 'Perhaps she doesn't get too many enquiries.'

They walked across the stretch of grass in front of the abbey and went to sit on a wall overlooking the lake. Then Max said, 'Go on, then. What did she tell you?'

'Right. The site at Les Forges was an obvious place for iron ore extraction because the presence of the mineral deposits was accompanied by both water for power and wood for combustion. That's this bit.' She pointed to the opening paragraph of the leaflet. 'They got through seven and a half thousand cordes of wood a year, which would be a much more impressive statistic if I had any idea of how much a corde was.'

'It's the same word in English but without the e,' he said, looking over her shoulder. 'It's a wood stack that's four foot deep, four foot high and eight foot wide.'

She turned to him. 'How did you know that?'

'Backwoods living,' he said nonchalantly.

Her expression suggested she knew he was fibbing.

'In 1820,' she continued, returning to the leaflet, 'the state ordered a modernisation scheme that included the construction of two blast furnaces which can still be seen today – that must be the big things at the far end, although I only recall seeing one – as well as a foundry and a rolling mill, whatever that is.' She looked at him. 'Does backwoods living offer any clue?'

He grinned. 'It's for rolling out metal to make it a uniform thickness.'

'Right. Of course it is. Anyway, the site down the road there utilised water power – oh, I suppose that must be water-driven – copying the method already being used by the English. That'd be our industrial revolution,' she remarked. 'We were world leaders in all sorts of processes back then. At Les Forges they did something to the water levels in the ponds in 1836 to increase the efficiency of the power – sorry, I have no idea what the French word means – and bumped it up to a hundred horsepower. But although the forges flourished for a while, it became increasingly difficult to compete with the great modern installations of the north.' She studied the leaflet for a few moments, frowning. 'I'm not sure of this next bit but I think it's saying that here was a trade treaty with England in 1860 that did away with the import duty on smelted iron and that was the death knell for the Paimpont forges. There was a brief resurgence in 1870, but the blast furnaces went out for ever in the 1880s.'

She turned to him again. 'Do you think that's why your grandparents emigrated to Canada? Because your grandfather worked in the forges and the work dried up?'

He shook his head. 'No. The timing's wrong, because they didn't go to Canada till around 1920.'

'Perhaps he didn't work at the forges, then.'

'But he was a blacksmith. Or so my mother said.'

'Blacksmiths don't necessarily work in foundries,' she observed. 'A smith has his own forge, and he makes hinges and plough-shares and railings. Domestic items and suchlike. And he shoes horses, obviously. That would be the major part of the work before the age of the internal combustion engine.'

Max slipped down off the wall. 'We have to find this village, this St-Yves-les-Forges,' he said decisively. 'Until we do, we're guessing.'

'Okay.' She jumped down beside him. 'Where do we begin?'

'Back at Les Forges,' he said with more conviction than he felt. 'We'll see if we can raise anyone in that house behind the site and take it from there.'

On the way back to the hotel to collect the car, Angela suggested that they stop at the little supermarket and buy something for lunch. It made sense, Max agreed, given the dearth of cafes, restaurants or any other signs of life in the place they were heading for. They bought two baguettes, still warm from the oven, a round of Camembert in a little wooden box with a gingham-patterned paper lining, tomatoes, a couple of pears and two bottles of Perrier. The man behind the till chatted to Angela and, as they left, Max, thinking it was time he tried out some French, added a couple of words. The man looked faintly surprised, and Max wondered if his pronunciation was at fault.

As they walked back up the street Angela was trying not to smile.

'What?' he demanded.

'I'm just wondering why you wished the bloke in the shop good luck.'

'I didn't! I said have a nice day, or the French equivalent, like they all seem to do.'

She was laughing now, and he noticed how much it changed her face. 'Have a nice day is bon journée. But you said bon chance, which means good luck.'

'Did I?' He started laughing too. 'Lucky it wasn't worse really. When I was trying to think of the words, what initially came into my head was bon voyage.'

This time they were in luck at the house behind the deserted foundry.

The cafe was as firmly closed for business as it had been the day before, but now a door was open at the far end of the long building and the sound of voices came floating out: a man's and at least one woman's. The woman's voice was high-pitched and shrill.

'I think it's Kate Bush,' Angela murmured.

Max smiled. 'Shall we go and have a word?'

'What's this "we"?' Angela replied, striding towards the open door. Leaning inside the dark interior, she called out, 'Bonjour! Il y a quelqu'un?'

A short, stocky man in his late sixties or early seventies appeared in the doorway. He returned Angela's greeting, and then shook his head, saying something about café and fermé. Non, non, Angela said, and Max guessed she was saying they weren't after food or drinks. Then there was a long exchange, at the end of which the man said, 'Attendez, madame, je vais chercher ma femme et sa mère.'

'He says what the woman in the information office said, that the forges closed down at the end of the last century,' she said as Max went to stand beside her. 'I asked what became of the workforce, and he said he didn't know but thought probably they'd gone to find other foundries in the north. But he's gone to fetch his wife and her mother since they're much better at remembering the ins and outs of local history than he is.'

'His wife's mother?' Max said. 'Good God, how old must she be?'

'Old enough to remember when the forges closed down?' Angela said hopefully.

'Probably not, as she'd have to be over a hundred, but she could be old enough to remember what became of the people who used to work there. If so …'

But the man had come back, accompanied by two women, and with a swift, excited smile, Angela turned to greet them.

The women, the man and Angela talked for what seemed to Max, listening and catching no more than a word or a phrase here and there, a good half hour. There was a lot of repetition of forgeron and maréchal-ferrant, and Max thought – hoped – he heard mention of St-Yves-les-Forges, and at one point Angela suddenly beamed and said, 'Ah, oui! Je comprends!' and even Max knew what *that* meant.

The old woman came to have a closer look at Max. She was tiny, skinny and wiry, dressed in black with a long skirt over which she wore a starched white apron. Her thin white hair was drawn back in a very small bun, her face was like a walnut and her dark eyes as bright and alert as a robin's. She said something to him, a long stream of words, but he shrugged in apology. Shaking her head at his obtuseness, she said, 'Nom. Nom. NOM! Comment vouz appelez-vous?'

'Max Dillon,' he said.

'Not your name!' Angela said. 'The name of the people who lived here. What was it again?'

'Ledanose,' he said. 'Mathilde and Einar.'

The old woman looked doubtfully at him. The, turning to her daughter – who looked like a taller, rounder version of her mother and was dressed in tan crimplene trousers and an emerald and mauve shell suit top – she spoke for several minutes, waving one hand and pointing inside the room where the three of them had been working. She seemed to be persuading – bullying – her daughter to do something she didn't want to.

With a sigh the younger woman gave in. Angela, catching her eye, shrugged and said with a smile, 'Je suis desolée!'

'What's happening?' Max demanded in a hiss.

'The old girl seems to recall the name Ledanose, but she says it's not right, or it wasn't how they were called when they came here – sorry, that's the closest I can get. Her accent's incredibly strong and lots of the words aren't familiar. Anyway, there's an old accounts book or something – this place used to be a little shop, a bakery that did basic supplies as well, and the people in the forges used to put things on the slate and pay when payday came. I think that's the general gist,' she added.

But Max hardly took in the last words. 'A book with names?' It seemed too good to be true.

'Yes, but the old woman only has a vague idea where it's been stowed away and her daughter, understandably, isn't too keen on going through a hundred years of accumulated junk till it turns up.'

They waited. The old woman was muttering to her son-in-law, turning repeatedly to stare at Angela and Max. At Max, mainly, and it made him uncomfortable.

'What's she saying?' he whispered to Angela.

'Can't hear,' she hissed back.

Presently the daughter returned. Empty handed. The old woman must have noticed Max's expression, because she grabbed hold of his arm and let out a barrage of words. Angela, trying not to laugh, translated.

'She says her daughter's an idiot and couldn't find her foot to put her shoe on, and *she* knows where this book is, only it'll take her a while to find it so we can come back tomorrow if we want and she'll have it for us by then.'

The daughter, clearly put out at having her mother call her an idiot, had flung both hands up and uttered a loud 'Bouf!', then gone back inside. The man, looking both intrigued and slightly apprehensive, grinned nervously.

Angela, smiling warmly, said something to the old woman, taking both her hands, and then added 'Au revoir! À demain,' and turned away.

Max, after saying his own goodbyes, hurried after her. 'Should I have given them something for their trouble?'

'Maybe tomorrow,' she replied. Then, with a grin 'If that accounts book turns up.'

Then, because he couldn't bear to wait any longer, he said, 'Did they know about St-Yves-les-Forges?'

'They might have done,' she said, straight-faced. Then, laughing, 'Yes. You heard, I saw you react. The old woman said some of the men from here found work there in the forge – they were blacksmiths by trade. The man gave me some pretty vague directions and they all said nobody's lived here for years, but there's a bigger village nearby and that has a church, and they can't be sure but they think it's probably where the people of St Yves went to worship because their own village – hamlet, I suppose, they called it a hameau – didn't have its own church.'

Before he could think about what he was doing, Max threw his arm round her shoulders, pulled her close and kissed her cheek. 'You're amazing,' he said warmly. 'I don't know what I'd do without you.'

She slipped out from his embrace, but when she replied — she said fairly repressively, 'You wouldn't have understood any of that, for starters' – she was smiling.

It took them more than an hour to find St-Yves-les-Forges, even though it was not far away. It was nearly one o'clock by then and they stopped to eat their picnic before going to explore. Not that there was much to see: a long, low building whose windows were broken and which had a huge chain and a heavy padlock holding the double doors closed, and a couple of rows of very small houses. Max parked on a low rise above the settlement so that they were looking down on the buildings while they ate.

Then they got out of the car and, slowly, thoughtfully, walked the length of the row of houses.

'This is the place that my mother mentioned,' Max said, stopping before one of the dwellings in the middle of the row. It was single-storied, although the dormer window in the roof suggested an attic room. The doorway was low and the ancient door had worn pale green paint, as did the small window beside it.

Peering in, Max saw a hearth, a chimney, some rusted old cooking implements. At the other end of the room was a stone sink. There was no furniture, apart from a broken stool. 'This could have been her parents' house.'

'You said your grandfather was a blacksmith,' Angela said, her voice soft as if she didn't want to break the spell. 'It could easily be that he was one of the men who came here to work in the smithy when the forges closed for good.'

He turned, giving her a grateful smile. 'It could, couldn't it?' Then, swiftly, for there was suddenly something very tender in the mood between them, 'We'd better find this nearby village with the church, and see if we'll be permitted a browse through the parish records.'

The village was less than a mile up the lane, the church stood vast and dominant, seeming to be far too large for the community it had been built for, but as Angela remarked, the Bretons had always been renowned for their piety and the church would have served the outlying hamlets as well as the village itself.

They went inside.

Max found his palms were sweating.

A young priest wished them a courteous good day, and Angela explained what they wanted. He seemed to take it in his stride, Max thought, watching him closely, and when Angela made a remark about being désolée about dérangeing him for something that strictly speaking wasn't his proper métier, he shrugged, smiled and said, 'Aujourd'hui, c'est comme ça. C'est normale.'

He led the way into a small, dark and damp-smelling room set off a corridor leading away from the church itself, opened a cupboard and drew out a large ledger. 'Servez-vous,' he said. Then he went out again.

'I said I was sorry to bother him with something that wasn't really his job, and he said everyone's doing it nowadays, it's no big deal,' Angela said as they stood looking down at the ledger; she seemed as nervous about opening it as Max was.

He nodded absently. Then he flung the vast book open.

They didn't find anyone called Ledanose.

Trying to deal with the crushing disappointment, Max went over and over the pages covering births, marriages and deaths between 1880 and 1900, then went over to the cupboard and helped himself to the earlier volume and the later one. Nothing.

But Angela pointed out an entry for June 1919: someone called Einar had married a woman by the name of Tilde Muller. The man's surname was indistinct; it looked as if a previous entry had been erased, and another name put in its place. Neither looked much like Ledanose, but then, as Angela pointed out, they didn't look like anything else, either.

'That could easily be Le at the beginning,' she said.

'But that's an N,' Max countered. 'There's a sort of shadow beneath the later letters that looks like Nico.'

'Nicolas? Is that a French surname?'

He shrugged. 'I guess so.' Then he said, 'The marriage was in 1919, so we'd be looking, what, twenty, thirty years before that for the baptisms?'

Eager now, Angela stared going back through the pages. They were both concentrating hard but it was she, perhaps more used to interpreting old handwriting, who found what they were looking for.

Tilde Muller was born in November 1887, Einar Nicholas in May 1886.

Max, writing furiously, copied out all the relevant entries. He wasn't sure why he was hurrying; it wasn't as if the young priest was standing beside him impatient to put the ledgers back in the cupboard and lock them away.

When he had finished, Angela said, 'Do you want to go further back? See if we can find Einar and Tilde's parents' births, marriages and deaths?'

He looked at his watch. It was earlier than he'd thought; the dark little room gave no clue as to the passage of time in the world outside. 'Yes,' he said.

But their luck had all but run out. There was a marriage in 1880 that could have been between someone recorded as K. Nicolasson and a woman called Cilla Jaspers, but the handwriting was awful and neither Max nor the more experienced Angela were confident that the names were relevant to their search.

'But we've done so well,' Max said as they put the final ledger back in its place on the shelf. 'Much better than I'd thought we would, and all because of you.' He smiled at her.

'I've enjoyed it, I really have,' she replied. She grinned. 'But I won't object if you offer to buy me the best dinner that our hotel can offer and a bottle of fizz to celebrate.'

As they went off to locate and thank the young priest, Max reckoned that was the least he could do.

The old lady, on her own today, greeted them the following morning with a beaming, gap-toothed smile and a cry of 'Je l'ai trouvé!'

She led them inside the room at the end of the building, switched on a couple of lights and sat them down at a small table. Then she thumped down in front of them a big book with loose pages and faded ink, the corners of the pages brown with finger marks and the cover worn and blotched with what looked like red wine stains. She opened it, licked a finger and flipped through several pages, muttering under her breath. Then she spotted the marker sticking out between two pages, and with a shout of delight spread the book open.

And there, at last, in a neat and decorative hand, was written K. Le Danose, Mme Le Danose, Cille, followed by a brief list of food and small household items.

Max, hardly able to take it in, stared down at the brownish ink that recorded his great-grandparents' purchases in a little shop that had ceased trading over a hundred years ago. He tried to say something, but no words came.

And why, he was wondering, was the name Le Danose and not Nicolas or Nicolasson?

The old woman hadn't finished. Turning the page, she pointed to another entry. This one said A. Muller, Mme Muller, F. She stabbed her finger repeatedly on the names, as if demanding Angela and Max's attention. 'Copains!' she cried. 'Amis, tout les quatre! Ils sont arrivés tout ensemble, et les deux hommes ont travaillé aux forges!'

Angela turned to Max, frowning. 'She's saying the two couples were friends, mates, and that they arrived together, and the blokes worked in the forges.'

And he said very quietly, 'Muller was Tilde's maiden name.'

'Yes!' Angela exclaimed. 'One couple had a son, one had a daughter, and they got married and their daughter was your mother. But what does she mean, they all arrived here together? Where from?'

'Elsewhere in Brittany, probably,' he said. 'Looking for work, which they found here. For a while, anyway, then they went on to work at the smithy when the forges shut down.'

Angela was still looking doubtful. 'Wait, I'll she if she knows.'

There was a brief, dramatic conversation. Max, watching intently, heard the old woman say several times, 'Attendez, il vous faut attendez!' and Angela looked increasingly puzzled.

The old woman hurried out of the door and stood staring up the road. Her impatience was tangible.

Angela said unnecessarily, 'She's waiting for someone.'

And, after perhaps ten minutes, she returned. A very old man shuffled in behind her, and he sank down gratefully on the chair she pushed forward for him.

Max's sense of unreality grew.

He listened as the old man spoke, as Angela asked questions, as the old woman butted in and the old man tried with increasing frustration to finish his tale.

Finally he was done. He sat back in his chair, wiped his forehead with a spotted handkerchief and gave Max a gentle smile. 'Mais, ils étaient très gentils quand même, vous savez?'

Max, with absolutely no idea what had just transpired, just nodded.

Then, surprisingly, the man leaned closer and patted Max's hand. 'C'est les yeux,' he said with another smile. 'Je vous ai vu, et tout à fait, immédiatement, je vous ai connu.' He nodded. 'Vous êtes bienvenu.'

Max smiled, said merci several times, listened as Angela made the right remarks and, finally, they were able to leave. She nudged him, and he put the envelope into which he'd slipped some francs onto the table. The old woman scooped it up.

Both of the old people stood in the doorway to wave them off.

Angela didn't say anything until they were back in the car. Then she said, 'Don't drive off yet.'

He shot her a look. 'As if,' he replied.

'I needed to wait till you were sitting down,' she went on, 'because it's quite a story.'

He felt a quiver of nerves somewhere in his stomach. 'Go on.'

'Both of them recall your family,' she began. 'The old man knew Einar, who was a friend of his father's, but he stated very firmly that not a lot of people were privy to what brought the four of them, your great-grandparents, to Les Forges. He was only prepared to tell me – us – because he said he knew you were who I said you were because of your eyes.'

'My eyes.'

'Pale eyes like yours run in your family, apparently.'

'They do. My mother's were the same as mine, and so were my grandmother Tilde's.' His nervousness was growing more pronounced.

'They arrived here in the late 1870s, maybe early 1880s,' she said, speaking quickly as if she had realised that he really needed to hear the tale. 'They were running away – had run away, in fact. Your great-grandfather, who was actually called Kai and not K, wanted to marry your great-grandmother Cille, only her father – who was a minister – had ordered her to marry someone else. This other man was a bully and Cille hated him and wanted to marry Kai, but her father put his foot down. The other man was a drunkard and he attacked Kai with a knife, but Kai had his friend Aksel with him and they fought back, and in the struggle the other man fell and hit his head and they thought he was dead. He wasn't in fact, but they didn't find that out till much later. They fled, Muller with his wife, who was called Freja, and Kai with Cille. They – Kai and Cille – were married as soon as they were settled here.'

'In the church down the road,' Max murmured. 'K. Nicolasson and

110

Cille Jaspers.' He shook his head in puzzlement. 'So how come they were recorded here as Ledanose?'

She reached out and very gently touched his hand. 'They thought they'd killed a man and they were fugitives,' she said. 'They needed to fudge their real identities, or at least Kai did. I'm guessing it was he who struck what they believed was the killer blow.'

'Le Danose,' he muttered. 'Two words. It was written that way in the old woman's account book.'

Angela paused, and he had the impression she was plucking up her courage. 'Have a think,' she said. 'About where they might have fled from.' She glanced at him and he shrugged. 'Where there was a minister, not a priest. Where they had names like Nicolasson and Muller. Where people had light-coloured eyes.' She gave a small sound of impatience. 'Max, it wasn't France, was it?'

'Not ... But my mother said her family came from Brittany. From right here!' He thumped the steering wheel for emphasis.

'It's undoubtedly what her parents and her grandparents wanted her to believe!' Angela cried. 'Even if they did find out later that the bullying drunkard hadn't died, they'd still have wanted to cover it up! Still have been quite happy to perpetrate the myth that they'd been French – Breton – all along.'

'Ye-es,' he said slowly.

But he was thinking, very hard. Thinking about Nicolasson, which was probably Nicolajsen, and Muller, which was probably Møller. Even Jaspers, which could really have been Jesperson. He had a memory, somewhere in the recesses of his mind, of once having seen all those names written down. And another memory, about a great friend of his mother who had been called Anja. About some of the Christmas traditions his mother had loved. About the very name Ledanose. Le Danose. Le Danois.

Now Angela was holding his hand. Tightly, as if she wanted to give him strength. Her hand was warm and strong.

'You're not half French after all,' she said very softly. 'You're half Danish.'

Chapter 8

Jo

The drive up the A1M, known more evocatively in earlier years as the Great North Road, wasn't quite as romantic as Jo had anticipated. Her very early start meant that traffic was only moderately thick for the first hour or so, but the M25 came to a complete standstill for a quarter of an hour just before the A1M exit, on a particularly uninspiring not to say downright ugly stretch of road, and she had to try very hard to remember why she was doing the trip at all.

But a sense of anticipation started to creep over her as she ploughed on north. Stevenage, Peterborough, then Grantham, Newark (and a vague memory that King John died near there) and the flat, dark, fertile lands of Lincolnshire. She stopped for her sandwich lunch in a service area just north of Doncaster with around 200 miles on the trip clock, and thought, with a certain amount of self-congratulation, that she was doing well. She was, she reckoned, roughly half way.

The driving began to feel tedious round about Stockton-on-Tees, and as she pulled into yet another service area for a wee and a cup of tea, she checked her watch and saw she'd been driving for not far short of seven hours. Tiredness kills! and Take a break!, the signs on the motorway's overhead gantries had been shouting at her with righteous bossiness, so she took her time over her tea.

Then back into the car for the last leg.

And soon the road – degraded now to simply the A1 – was running close to the sea, and she could see the grey-blue mass of it over to her right, late sun sparking orange lights off the waves that went on endlessly as far as … She tried to picture a map of the British Isles and their near neighbours in her head and after some moments of thought decided it was probably Denmark.

She was driving more slowly now, aware that she was tired and that the afternoon light was starting to fade. She passed a sign to Alnwick, and there was a big hoarding beside the road advertising the natural beauty of the Farne Islands. She liked the idea of being on an island, and wondered about heading for Holy Island. But there was no access at high tide, she remembered reading, and she had absolutely no idea when that would be, so maybe going to Holy Island would be better left for the morning, when she would very likely be in explorer mode.

Another sign loomed up, pointing once again to the right, and the coast, and to yet another town, or perhaps village, whose name she didn't fully take in, other than to note it ended in -wick. There was a big, colourful poster beside it advertising a pub called The Farne View, and another, smaller one offering the services offered in the village which – bliss to her tired eyes – included accommodation.

She took the turning, and a narrow road led with only a few twists and turns down to the shore, following the course of a little river. She spotted the pub – you couldn't really miss it – and there was a chalk board outside listing the day's specialities (fish featured strongly) and announcing there was to be live music and karaoke that evening.

She drove on slowly along the narrow main street. It was pretty much the only street, although one or two alleys turned off it on either side and ahead the tarmac turned into a track that led to a small harbour. On a low rise above the water was a stout brick-built building quite out of keeping with the stone houses of the rest of the village, but a sign swinging from a post read 'GANNET COVE HOTEL', and beneath the letters there were three stars. A further legend read 'Rooms'.

Jo pulled into the small car park, slotted the Discovery into a space between a Metro and a small Ford, then reached behind her for her bag and got out. Knowing – hoping – that she was done with driving for the day, she stretched her stiff back luxuriously and for some time, then, limber once again, went in through the lowering porch and strode up to the reception desk.

A man of around fifty was bent over a large book. He was bald, with flabby, red-veined cheeks and dressed in a tweed jacket over a checked shirt with a carefully knotted tie. There was absolutely no possibility of his not knowing she was there, but nevertheless he ignored her for a good half minute.

She was on the point of asking if the hotel really was open or if the sign advertising rooms was just a dubious joke to confound weary travellers. But with an audible sigh he put his pen down and, staring at her with a vaguely accusing expression, said curtly, 'Yes?'

'I would like a room, with a bath or shower,' Jo said courteously.

'All our rooms are en suite,' he said crushingly.

She smiled. 'Good for you. May I have one?'

He grunted, turning a page and staring down at the single entry for that day's date. 'How long for?' he demanded.

She was about to say she wasn't sure, since she was on holiday and it depended on what she decided to do tomorrow, but then she thought, why should I explain? This is a hotel, he has rooms available and I wish to occupy one.

'It may just be tonight, or possibly another day or two,' she said coolly.

He raised his head and glared at her. 'Can't you be more definite?'

Several answers flipped through her head. But she just said, 'No.'

Life with Hal had taught her, among quite a lot of other disparate things, that there was no need for anybody to be guiltily apologetic in the face of other people's rudeness.

He muttered something, then turned to stare at the rows of room keys hanging up behind the desk. He handed her one – it had a large wooden fob with '4' painted on it – and said, as if it were an enormous concession, 'I can let you have Room 4. Do you want dinner?'

Not if it's going to be cooked or served by you, she thought. 'No thank you.'

'Up the stairs to the first floor, down the corridor on the right and it's at the end.' The very determined way in which he returned his attention to his book suggested he wasn't going to help her with her luggage, so it was as well she only had her satchel-like handbag and the one small holdall.

She turned and headed for the stairs.

Room 4 was, confounding her expectations, very pleasant. The decor was simple, the bed was large and bouncy with white linen, plenty of pillows and a duvet, the little shower room was perfectly adequate and there was a breath-taking view over the harbour to the wide sea beyond.

She sank down on the end of the bed, and for some time just stared out at the water. She wasn't actively thinking – she really didn't want to think – and it was pleasant, simply sitting there, allowing the languor to flow through her, her mind and her tired body relaxing.

After some time she got up, unpacked her tee shirt and pyjama trousers, put her wash bag in the bathroom and, stripping, had a long, hot shower. The towel rail was warm enough to heat the little room, so she washed out her underwear and today's shirt, carefully hanging them in the shower so they didn't drip on the floor. She dressed in jeans and a fresh jumper, dried her hair, put on some makeup and then picked up her bag and went out to have a look round.

There was a phone box at the end of the road. She took the hotel's card and a stack of change out of her jeans pocket and then dialled Sam's number. Sam answered. 'Hi, it's Jo,' she said, and, even as he began to speak, went on, 'Sam, I'm sorry but I'm in a call box so I have to make this quick. Please will you tell Hal that I'm staying in the Gannet Cove Hotel in Edeswick, Northumberland, and this is the phone number.' She read out the numbers slowly and clearly.

'Got that, Jo,' Sam said. He chuckled. 'I'd have got it even if I'd been deaf and daft.'

She laughed. 'Everyone all right?'

'Everyone's fine. Go on, enjoy your freedom.'

'Love to all of you.'

'Ours back to you.'

She put the phone down. Knowing that now Hal could contact her if he needed to made her feel much better.

Made her feel, if she permitted the sentiment, that she had done her duty and was off the hook …

Darkness was falling as she wandered round the harbour. The lights outside the Farne View had come on and she saw people going into the pub, talking and laughing. She looked at her watch and was quite surprised to see it was almost seven o'clock.

She went into the pub, ordered half a pint of bitter and asked the pleasant young woman who served her if it was too early to eat. 'No, course not,' the woman said cheerfully. 'Best to order now because we'll get really busy once the band start, not to mention the karaoke!'

'Right, okay, then I'll have the fish pie with peas.'

'Good choice,' the woman observed. 'Where will you be?'

Jo pointed. 'In that corner.'

'I'll bring it over.'

The fish pie was indeed a good choice. Jo ate all of what had seemed on its arrival to be a huge portion, not having appreciated how hungry she was. She had another half pint, watching a group of four men and three women bringing their instruments inside and setting up at the far end of the bar. Their ages ranged from about nineteen to maybe seventy. They obviously knew each other very well, and there was a lot of laughter.

Jo's thoughts went straight to Finnegan's Pig, and their beautiful song, and the angel story being made into a film, and how much she had enjoyed the summer in Cornwall and working with Flavia McGinty, and the musicians, and the animators, and showing the man who was the driving force behind the film the places she'd had in mind as she drew the original images of the angel.

Ben.

Then she thought, despite her efforts not to, about how Hal had been all summer. How at first they'd all gone down, Hal and herself, Ed and Sammie, and the excitement had got to them all. Or so she had believed. They had stayed at Jo's parents' house, and Ed and her mother Elowyn had resumed their quiet pleasure in each other's company. Jo's father had been there too, but only for some of the time; he had passed the management of his financial business in Zurich over to his sons, but he still couldn't stop himself making fairly frequent visits there. Jo's presence had been required again, and again, and yet again, and Hal had made it plain he had better things to do than trail around Cornwall with her. She had taken to going just with the boys, sometimes just with Ed. She'd found it hard to admit it, but it was so much better without Hal.

He trivialises it, she thought now, gazing blank-eyed down at her nearly empty glass. He manages to make it seem I'm earning a lot of money for something that I wrote in five minutes and that's not worth all this vast effort of turning it into a film. Not worth all the attention I'm getting …

Then, hard on the heels of that, she thought, I don't like the way he's behaving. Don't like the way he assumes it's fine for him to go away for days, weeks sometimes, to research his books – his academic, worthy bloody books – and we all have to accept it because he's him, and that's what he does, but when I get the opportunity to do something similar, he doesn't like it one bit.

I don't like *him* just now.

But that was a dangerous thought.

She drank the last inch of bitter, stood up and headed for the door. She edged round the fiddle player, busy tuning up, and he turned to give her a smile of apology for being in her way.

The pub was filling up rapidly and in the doorway she bumped into a man coming in. He took hold of her shoulders – he'd trodden on her toe and she had almost fallen – and said, 'Sorry! Did I hurt you?'

'No, not at all!' she said brightly.

'You're not leaving?' he asked.

'Well, that's what people are usually doing when they're heading out through the door.'

He laughed, a generous, smiling mouth in the midst of a tidy beard. Brown hair, dark blue eyes. He was around her own age, a little taller than her, broad-shouldered. He was dressed in jeans, shirt and a heavy navy-blue sweater. The foot that had trodden on hers wore a Timberland boot.

'The band'll be starting up very soon,' he said, still standing in the doorway and blocking her way.

'Yes,' she said. 'And there's karaoke, I gather.'

'And that's why you're going?' He smiled again. 'Stay. It's not what you think.'

'No?'

'No. More folk than 'My Way'.'

'Folk,' she repeated. 'Do they stick one finger in their ears and hum dubious experimental harmonies?'

'It has been known.'

All at once she wanted to stay. Room 4 awaited her, it was true, with its wonderful view and its comfy bed, but she'd have to get past the angry hotelier and she was in no mood to be polite. Besides, the thought of music – even karaoke – was appealing, and the man standing in front of her was looking at her in a way nobody had done for ages.

'Okay,' she said casually. 'You've talked me round.'

His face lit up. 'Great! Come back inside, then, and I'll forge a way past the band and through the crowd to the bar and buy you a drink.'

'I'm Silas Gerritt,' he said when they were seated on a couple of bar stools he'd purloined for them and each had a drink, his a pint and hers another half. Lots of the people in the pub seemed to know him; he'd exchanged some vague insults with the band, and the young woman behind the bar clearly fancied him.

'Jo Dillon.'

He was looking at her, straight into her eyes. The intensity of his gaze was disconcerting. 'On holiday?'

'Yes. My husband's taken my younger son to visit his grandfather in California, my elder son's away on a rugby training week with the school.' Best to state that straight away, she thought. 'So, I thought I'd get away too.'

He nodded. He was still staring at her. Then, as if he sensed she had noticed, and perhaps also the disconcerting effect it was having, he said, 'I'm a painter. I'm doing a big mural for a place on a small island just off the shore, and it's a depiction of the spirit of the sea. I need to include an image of a sea being, and you are almost exactly what I've been carrying in my head. Will you sit for me? I'll pay,' he added.

She was astonished.

Was it a chat-up line? No, she dismissed that thought, for she was under no illusions whatsoever that she only had to walk into a bar for every man there to want to sleep with her. Was it ...

As if he sensed her consternation, he said, 'I really am a painter.' He pointed to where a group of small, framed paintings hung in an alcove behind the door. They were oils, and all of them showed the sea, and the shore, and waves and clouds so vibrant with the illusion of movement that she could almost feel the wind. If he had painted them then he was indeed a painter, and a very good one.

And a rebellious voice in her head said, why not?

She turned to him from her contemplation of his paintings. 'What would it entail?'

Eagerness filled his face. 'I live on the island where the place is that I'm doing the mural. It – the place – is called Old Harbour and it's a sort of retreat, a sanctuary, for people who need a break from their lives.'

Like me. The thought sprang into her head in an instant. It surprised her very much.

121

'It's run by a man called Archie Sutherland, it's very peaceful and beautiful, and my house is separate, not part of the sanctuary. I have some old outbuildings that I converted into accommodation, and Archie uses them when he has too many guests for the rooms within the retreat. My studio's there, which would be where we'd work, and I could offer you one of the converted units to stay in. I'd pay you, too. Did I say that?'

'Yes. But if you're offering free accommodation, I should think that would do.' Especially on an island that people retreat to because they need a break from their lives.

'I'll throw in food and drink too,' he said. He was smiling at her again.

'How long would it take?'

'How long have you got?'

'A week.'

'Then I'll have to work quickly.' He held her eyes, and she didn't try to look away. 'What do you say?'

She held out her hand. 'Yes.'

Solemnly they shook hands.

Then the band crashed into a loud and lively version of 'The Rocky Road to Dublin', and further conversation became impossible.

Later, at the end of a loud and very entertaining evening that she had loved, and into the mood of which she'd flung herself without reservation – she'd even sung, for heaven's sake, singing along with the old guy in the band and Silas in an old Pogues number, although she'd managed not to harmonise – Silas insisted on walking back to her hotel with her.

'Bet you really regret staying on,' he remarked.

'God, yes,' she replied. 'For one thing, I could have spent a solitary evening up in Room 4 trying to avoid Mr Grumpy on the front desk.

For another, I wouldn't now be hoarse from singing and laughing. For a third, I wouldn't have found myself agreeing to sit for a painter I've only just met.'

He smiled slightly, but then, frowning, he said, 'You can change your mind about sitting for me.'

'But we shook hands on it,' she reminded him. 'In any case, I want to.'

'Really?'

'Really.'

Now his smile was no longer tentative. 'Great.' Abruptly he came to stand beside her, pointing back towards the pub and the quay. 'See where that road goes up the slope beyond the pub?'

'I see it, but it's not a road, it's a dirt track.'

'If you drive along there for a mile or so, you come to a gateway on the right. Go through it and drive on down to the shore – it's about a hundred metres or so – and you'll find a car park. I'll wait for you there at half past nine. Unless that's too early?'

'No, it's fine.' She hesitated. 'Er ... should I book out of here?' She inclined her head towards the hotel.

'For heaven's sake, yes,' Silas replied. 'The sooner the better.' Apparently he shared her opinion of the proprietor. Then he looked straight at her for a moment, nodded, said, 'See you tomorrow,' and strode away.

There was nobody behind the reception desk, although Jo could hear the sound of a television through an open door on the other side of the hall. She hurried across to the stairs and up to her room.

She undressed and got into bed. She closed her eyes, and the images of the long day flew through her mind. Traffic, congestion, an open road. The sea. The little village, the pub. Silas Gerritt's paintings. Silas Gerritt. Herself, singing. Agreeing to become an artist's model. Agreeing to check out of this hotel, which was actually rather nice despite its irascible owner, and take up lodgings next door to a retreat.

'I'm going to take a break from my life,' she said softly aloud. And on that thought, she went to sleep.

Chapter 9

The hotel proprietor was even more grumpy when she told him after breakfast that she would be checking out.

'But you said you were staying several days,' he protested, scowling at her.

'I said one night, possibly two or three,' she replied firmly.

'In fact you said it might just be one night, with the definite implication that it could be more.'

She looked at his angry face. 'In the absence of a recording of our conversation, we'll never know, will we?' she said as pleasantly as she could manage.

He humphed several times, but made up her bill. She checked it carefully, but the room rate was what he had quoted yesterday plus the addition for breakfast. It was more than reasonable, and she paid in cash.

'I'm going to stay on the island.' What was the name? 'At the Old Harbour.'

His head flew up and he glowered at her. 'You've booked? I hope you have, young lady, they're *very* exclusive.' He said it with a very obvious sneer.

Deciding that her future accommodation was really none of his business, she didn't answer but said instead, 'I have given the phone number of this hotel to my father-in-law, and should anyone call me here, would you kindly tell them where I have gone?'

She watched with secret amusement while he fought the desire to say not bloody likely, or what do you think I am, an answering service? The duty of courtesy owed by a hotelier to his guests won – by a whisker, she thought – and he gave a curt nod.

Then she picked up her bag, thanked him in as neutral a tone as she could manage, and left.

The Discovery climbed the narrow, bumpy dirt track with ease. Jo rounded the top of the rise up out of the village, and the wonderful sight of the long coastline stretched out before her. The bulk of Holy Island lay some five or six miles away to the north, the distinctive profile of Lindisfarne Castle a dark silhouette. She drove on, found the gateway on the right and was soon drawing up in the car park. There was one other vehicle, a mud-splattered black Toyota pickup truck. Silas was standing beside it.

'You still haven't changed your mind, then,' he said as Jo scooped up her bag, locked the Discovery and went to join him.

'No. Will my car be okay here?'

'Yes. This bit of land is private and belongs to Old Harbour. Also, people are reasonably honest round here. In small communities most people are known to each other.'

'Okay.' The car is insured, in any case, she thought.

He took her bag from her and led the way down a path that seemed to be leading straight into the sea. 'We're going to wade to this island?' she asked, half-amused, half-anxious.

He stopped, putting down her bag. 'Wait,' he said. 'Keep looking, just there.' He pointed to the little waves rippling up over the end of the path.

She looked.

And within perhaps five minutes, perhaps less – time was becoming rather elastic, she thought – as if by magic, a raised track seemed to float up out of the water. Her logic told her what was happening – the tide was going out – but in that moment, standing on a beautiful, wild shore with someone who was kind, who laughed and made her laugh, who looked at her as if he really saw her, who was going to paint her, for heaven's sake, she decided to go with the magic.

Presently he looked down at her feet. 'Good,' he said. 'You're wearing boots.'

Then, he picked up her bag again and stepped down onto the narrow causeway to the island.

It wasn't a long walk: around a quarter of a mile, she reckoned, maybe a little more. As they climbed up onto the shore at the far end she said, 'No cars, then, unless there's another access?'

'No cars,' he confirmed.

'What happens if someone's ill?'

'There's a launch and a speed boat. Archie has been muttering about a helicopter pad, but everyone who comes here is trying to talk him out of it.'

They were walking quickly, and now a large white-painted stone building appeared on the left, much of it hidden behind a wall. Through the open gates she glimpsed a big house with a couple of extensions. 'That's Old Harbour,' Silas said. 'The house is situated above the quay. It was just the big house originally, and the other buildings have been added over the years. There's a seawater pool now, in that glass-roofed structure over to the left. That was added a couple of years ago.'

She nodded. There were few people about. Someone was raking up leaves on the lawn in front of the main house, and a couple walked purposefully out through the gates, wished her and Silas good morning and strode on towards the shore.

'This way,' Silas said.

They walked for another quarter of a mile or so, and another stone building came into view ahead. This one had not had the white paint treatment, and the golds and greys of the natural stone were pleasingly set off by pale blue-grey paint. The structure had been placed across the neck of a narrow promontory stretching out south-eastwards into the sea, and the extensions on either side gave the overall impression of a shallow curve, as if the house was rounding its shoulders to protect what lay between it and the sea from the eyes of the world. Silas turned right, round the north end of the house and, following close behind him, Jo saw what the house was protecting.

She turned round in a slow circle, trying to take it in.

The northern extension of the house was single-storey, with large windows set in the slate roof. The main building was square and solid, with a door in the middle and regularly-spaced windows like those in a child's drawing, one on each side of the door and two dormers set into the steeply-pitched roof. To the south, joined to the house by a short covered way, was a row of four cottages. The structures surrounded a cobblestoned courtyard, with a series of low outbuildings on the far side.

The view out over the sea was, however, totally uninterrupted.

'What a place!' Jo murmured.

'You're seeing it at its best,' Silas said. 'It's bleak in the winter and when there's a storm you feel like you're at sea.'

'I hope there's a storm,' she said.

He smiled. 'I thought you'd like the cottage at the far end,' he said, leading her along to it. 'It's tiny but it's got the best views.'

Thinking that they'd be pretty astounding from all four cottages, Jo followed him. The row was in good order, the pointing on the stonework clean and fresh, as was the paint on the woodwork, the same blue-grey shade as on the main house. The names of the cottages were hung over the doors on slabs of slate: Fulmar, Kittiwake, Puffin and Tern. Silas opened the door to Tern and stood back to let her go in.

It was small, simply decorated – mainly in white, with touches of blue – and minimally furnished. There was one main room with a wood-burning stove, off it a kitchen and a little bathroom. Up a narrow staircase was a bedroom with a double bed, opposite it a large cupboard full of spare blankets.

'The room looks out over the sea,' he said, pushing the door fully open to demonstrate.

And what more could I want? she thought.

She was overwhelmed.

Then, feeling that she should start giving something back in return for this unexpected bounty, she said, 'Your studio's at the north end of the house, right?'

'Yes?' He turned it into a question.

'Give me ten minutes to settle in, then I'll come and find you.'

He looked as if he might protest – for politeness's sake, she thought with a smile – but he didn't. Excitement filled his face and he said, 'Right.'

Then he was out of the cottage and running off towards the house.

'I know I've seen you somewhere before,' Silas said.

It was about half an hour later, Jo was perched on a stool in his studio, and she was just beginning to lose her self-consciousness at having someone draw her. The room was warm – another wood-burning stove – and there was a soft, thick blanket on the stool in case she needed it.

'I can't think where,' she replied.

He drew in silence for a few minutes. 'Have you been on the telly?'

'No.'

He paused, frowning. 'I think I saw a photo of you.' He looked at her, then back at the drawing. 'I didn't say so last night because I thought I'd probably freaked you out enough already, but it was this photo that I'm sure I've seen somewhere that convinced me you were right for the Sea Room.'

She thought about how someone who lived in Northumberland could have seen a photo of her.

And all at once she knew.

'This photo couldn't have been in a shop window?' she asked. She felt embarrassed; awkward at having to mention it because it made her feel that she was being big-headed.

Silas worked on for a moment or two, but she knew he wasn't ignoring the question. Then he said, 'A book shop. Yes. There was a stack of books – children's books – and one was featured in particular. It had an image of an angel on the jacket and there was a photo of the author.' He looked straight at her. 'You.'

'The publishers were pushing it earlier this year,' she said. 'I did one or two signing sessions, which I hated, although they were mainly in and around London.'

He nodded, perhaps quite used to southerners believing Britain stopped at the northern perimeter of the M25. 'The angel image was very moving,' he said. 'Did you do it?'

'Yes. I used to illustrate children's books, then I wrote a few myself and illustrated them too, then I wrote one about a man who died and came back as an angel.' She didn't want to think about Ben, not just then. 'I wrote some novels – adult books – too,' she hurried on.

'Your name was different,' he said.

'I'd started to write before I was married, so I used my maiden name. Daniel.'

'Jo Daniel,' he said quietly. 'Yes. That was it.' He looked at her briefly. 'I wish I'd bought a copy.'

'It's being made into a film,' she blurted out.

'That's terrific! Congratulations!'

'Thank you.'

After some time he said, 'Your face – all of you – has changed.'

'Oh. Sorry.' She tried to resume her former pose, but couldn't really think how to.

'No need to be sorry. But I'm wondering how having a book you wrote and illustrated being made into a film is an occasion for sadness.'

She didn't – couldn't – answer. Then he said, very gently, 'The man who died?'

'Yes,' she whispered. 'He was called Ben, and we hadn't been married very long, and Ed – my elder son – wasn't much more than a baby. Ben went to work on a wreck – he worked for a salvage outfit – and there was an accident, and he was killed.'

She paused, trying to keep hold of herself. 'I had a dream about him one night in which he seemed to be an angel, and later that day I drew him, just as he'd been in the dream. Teddy – my son Ed, I called him Teddy when he was little – came and saw what I was doing, and recognised who it was, and he said angels stopped you falling over. At his nursery school they had that old picture of the angel saving the little children from the river, or the cliff edge or whatever it is. He said, "Is Daddy my angel?" and the story grew from there.'

Silas didn't speak for some minutes. Then he said, 'So you've been working on the film and it's brought everything back.'

'No. Yes, of course it has – I've been down in Cornwall much of the summer, it's where the story's set, because Ben and I lived there – and the memories just flooded in, but in the main they were happy memories. Good memories.' She waited to see if she was going to go on and tell him about Hal.

It appeared she wasn't.

Silas went on working, but she saw from his face that he had taken it all in. 'I'm not surprised you are sad,' he said.

Yes I am sad, she thought. Max said Hal was being an arse because he was jealous, but I don't believe he is sufficiently engaged with me for my enduring feelings for Ben to trouble him much. Besides, Hal was Ben's friend.

'How did you know I'm sad?' she asked very quietly.

'Because your whole self – your face, your body, your soul – shouts out that you are unloved.'

'Ben loved me!' The words – she'd virtually sobbed them – had shot out of her before she could stop them.

But Silas just smiled. 'Of course he did,' he said. 'He does. That's why you perceived him as present with you when you dreamt of him as an angel. He's with you right now.'

'Don't!' she said with a shudder.

He put down his pencil. 'Why not? Love hangs around, Jo. I'm not saying he's a ghostly presence, or that he's in heaven looking down. I don't believe either of those things, although I have no quarrel with people who do and who derive comfort from them. But your love for him is still a part of you, and it always will be. So it's natural – or so it seems to me – that something so vibrant and strong can sometimes take a tangible form.'

She felt as if she was retreating into herself. Ben felt very close, and possibly for the first time since she'd lost him she simply opened herself and waited to see what would happen.

She heard him laughing.

She gasped.

And she wanted to laugh too.

Sometime later, Silas said, 'You don't look sad anymore.'

After that, it was very peaceful in Silas's studio.

He worked in silence, and she watched with vague interest as he put sheet after sheet of paper on his easel, drawing image after image.

She was warm, comfortable, serene. Serene, she thought, that's something I haven't felt in a very long time. She let her mind wander. Ben was there, with her, in her. It felt good. She thought about Hal. About how he had been all summer, and, if she was honest, for a long time before that. She had said to him once that he was impenetrable. That it was always his mood that set the atmosphere between the two of them, or in the family, never anyone else's. When you're preoccupied or tired or fed up, she'd said, you never think that perhaps you could make an effort for my sake, for all our sakes.

That hadn't changed. She'd thought it was going to, after she'd said those words to him. But it hadn't. He hadn't. He had spent the summer just past spoiling her pleasure and then when they all went home again he set off on that research trip to Wiltshire and he was ill and then he came home again and he was even worse.

She thought about that.

Something was bugging her: something he'd said – on the phone, she seemed to remember – that had vaguely nagged at her at the time, but that she'd soon forgotten.

She thought about it now.

And it came to her.

She'd asked if he would be able to find a doctor if he needed one and he'd said of course, this is West Sussex not Antarctica.

But he'd said he was going to Wiltshire.

They took a break at lunchtime. Brown bread that tasted home-baked, with cheese and pickles, sweet little tomatoes and a Cox's apple to finish. Jo had thought they'd go straight back to work, but Silas said they needed to get out and move. They put on boots and jackets and set off, going first to the end of the finger of land that arrowed out into the sea beyond the last of the cottages. Right at the point, where there was nothing between the land and the waves crashing several meters below but a few widely-spaced outcrops of rock, large stones had been laid out in a maze.

Jo walked carefully around the perimeter of the maze and stood looking out to sea, feeling the wind blow strong in her face. 'There's no sign of the modern world in sight,' she said.

Silas came to stand beside her. 'No. No sign, either, of the island's long history.'

'Was it a religious centre, like Lindisfarne?'

'If it was, those who lived here left no trace. But for centuries the fishing boats used it. Up beyond the main house there's a perfect little harbour, naturally sheltered from the sea and the worst of the winds and the storms. It was a base for the herring boats that fished up and down the coast.'

'So, the old harbour was how the island got its name.'

'Right. If it was ever called anything else, people have forgotten.'

Jo was feeling awkward about having revealed so much of herself during the morning's session, and it was a relief to discuss a far less emotive subject.

'How did you come to be here?'

'My grandfather and Archie's grandfather owned a small fleet of fishing boats, and in the good times both of them built houses on the island. Through a variety of circumstances, Archie and I are the sole heirs of our respective families. Archie spoke of setting up Old Harbour as a retreat before I left England. When I returned, three years ago, the place was thriving, and he asked if I'd consider turning some of the old outbuildings alongside my house into accommodation. At first I said no, but he changed my mind. He can be very persuasive.' He turned to look at her. 'We'll call in on him before we go back. You ought to meet him.'

'Okay.'

They set off back along the path leading up the promontory.

Then she said, 'Where did you go? You said you left England.'

'Yes.' He paused, and she sensed he was reluctant to speak. 'I went to Greece,' he said eventually. 'I was engaged to restore some frescoes in a monastery halfway up a mountain. It was a very long process, and I discovered I really liked living there. I stayed for seven years.'

She couldn't think of anything to say. She wanted to ask if he'd become a monk, but it seemed too intimate a question.

But he must have known what was in her mind. 'I didn't take any vows,' he said. 'I don't know what my faith amounts to – not for want of thinking about it – but I have yet to find an organised religion that feels right.' He paused. 'It sometimes seems to me, that

135

whatever we think of as God is much bigger than any man-made system of worship.'

She thought about that. She felt as if she was on the verge of understanding, then it was gone. 'And ... er, and the monks didn't mind you living among them when you weren't one of them?'

He smiled. 'No. But then they were very keen on having their frescoes restored, and that meant me.'

'For seven years? How big were these frescoes?'

His smile widened. 'You're right. I stayed on because I was happy there.' He hesitated. 'I think probably only someone who has lived in a religious community can appreciate how incredible it is.'

'But a life of poverty can't be easy.'

'It's not, but it's made tolerable – or at least it was for me – because the monks believe there is a purpose to it. And living with a band of people who always put themselves last and everyone else first has a certain charm.' He shot her a glance. 'What surprised me the most was how much laughter there was. I don't know if it's typical of such communities, but it was certainly a feature of the place where I was.' He shrugged. 'To be honest, though, I don't really know why I stayed there so long.'

'Maybe you just didn't want to be anywhere else.'

Very gently he reached out and touched her shoulder. 'That's about it.'

The island wasn't large, perhaps half a mile deep and three quarters of a mile from its north western to its south eastern extremities. Walking quickly, they were soon outside the big dwelling they had passed on the way to Silas's house earlier. Silas strode ahead, ignoring the imposing front entrance under its porch, and headed around the left side of the building to the glass-roofed structure that housed the pool. He opened a door and they went inside.

The pool was not large – doing breaststroke, Jo thought, ten good pulls would do a length – and its base sloped gently, from steps leading down into the shallow end to a deep end where the water turned from turquoise to navy. There were two viewing windows set into the side wall, and Jo realised that an underground passage, or a room, had been dug out alongside the pool. It reminded her of the aquarium she and the boys had visited, when you could walk along a glass-walled tunnel right through the water.

'It's used for therapy,' Silas said. 'A lot of people live unnatural lives - the sort of lives our bodies weren't designed for - and their joints and muscles become stiff and painful from too long sitting at a desk. Exercising in a pool is good because the body's weight is supported.'

She nodded. 'And the therapists need to see the muscles in action.'

'Right.' Then he said, 'I was hoping you would swim while I draw you.'

'That I'd … Oh, I see! The sea spirit in action.'

His face lit up. 'Yes! What do you think? Could you do it?'

'I'd love to.'

They went into the house through an open back door and Silas called out, 'Archie?'

A voice from deeper inside the house answered, and they went towards it. They entered a large room lined with books, with a desk set before the window, and leather-covered armchairs and a small sofa placed around a fireplace. The room had an atmosphere of calm contentment.

A man stood up from behind the desk and came to greet them. His expression was one of friendliness and warmth, and the look he exchanged with Silas spoke of long-held affection.

'This is Jo, Archie,' Silas said. 'She's going to be my model for the Sea Spirit. Jo, this is Archie Sutherland.'

The man shook her hand. He was a robust, fit-looking man of seventy or so, thinning brown hair around a bald pate, a weather beaten face and a pair of light brown eyes that crinkled at the corners. He smiled at Jo.

'So, he's found you at last,' he said. 'I always knew he would.' He had a soft Scottish accent and his voice was one she felt she could listen to all day. 'Welcome to Old Harbour.'

Part Two

Consequences
Autumn–Winter 1990

Chapter 10

Hal

Being in California was like a restorative, relaxing holiday, marred for Hal only by the feeling that he didn't really deserve it.

When guilt threatened to blacken the bright, sunny October days, he would make himself concentrate on Sammie's happiness. The boy loved his grandfather, threw himself into life in Sam's casually comfortable house on the edge of the ocean, and, if they'd let him, would have been on Sam's boat the whole time, day and night, whether they were sailing in the bay or the boat was moored in its place along the wooden pontoon. Sammie's total absorption in the boat, the sea and the shore gave Hal and his father quite a lot of time together. Once or twice, Hal sensed that Sam was ... not anxious about him, exactly, but certainly unquiet.

Late on the Sunday afternoon, as the sun began to set, they sat together on Sam's porch. Both of them kept an eye on Sammie, who was busy sluicing down the deck of Sam's boat. It didn't need sluicing, but Sammie loved doing it. They talked about Hal's work, and he held forth at length on the early agrarian civilisations of the Wiltshire downlands until Sam's eyes glazed over.

'Reckon it'll have the appeal of your Minoan thing?' Sam asked, when Hal at last wound to a conclusion.

Hal shrugged. 'Time will tell.'

'Nearly done, are you?'

'Getting there.'

'Any ideas what to do next?'

'Oh …' Hal thought. 'Perhaps something on the Basque lands of the Pyrenees and north west Spain.' He paused. 'Or maybe Central America.'

He had no idea where the latter thought had come from.

While Sam burbled on about some article he'd read about Andorra – which Hal could have said but didn't was indeed in the Pyrenees, but nowhere near the Basque country – Hal wondered why he should suddenly be considering writing about Central America.

It was where his writing career had begun.

After the horrific suicide of a fellow student that he and Ben had witnessed, both of them had taken off to travel. Ben had gone to Cyprus and met Jo. Hal had gone to Mexico, fallen deeply in love with a beautiful woman he couldn't have, and set off down into South America when she married someone else. He had produced a long series of articles based on his travels, and the restrained but generally enthusiastic reception they had received in academic circles had opened the door to his subsequent career.

When he went back to find the beautiful woman, she was dead.

He had avoided thinking about Central America for years: all the long years of pain after losing Magdalena, the happiness of meeting and marrying Jo, the hard work of being a husband and a father. And the unlikely and extraordinary turn his life had taken when he met Angela, then discovered he couldn't forget her – and what he had done about it.

I should have left her alone, he thought now. Selfish bastard.

Sam had got up to fetch a couple of beers from the cooler.

Hal kept seeing Angela's face as they made love. He thought this was the main source of his guilt: that she'd been living quite happily without him, had probably put him firmly in her past, and then he'd gone and sought her out. With thought for nobody but himself, he had revived the feelings that had sprung up so unexpectedly and so strongly between them when they met in Crete.

I went to look for her out and then I left her, he thought. Six days together. For half of them I was so unwell I didn't know where I was. The other three were like a spell of time in a different place, filled with warmth and a lot of laughter, with hands that automatically reached to clasp, with beer and sandwiches in out-of-the-way country pubs, with long coastal walks, with talking, always talking.

And making love with passion so fierce and fiery it had burned them up ...

He shut the door of memory, very firmly, on those other three days.

Especially on how they ended. How he'd slunk away, not answering her questions about whether he'd be back. Leaving her to realise for herself that he'd gone for good; that he deeply regretted having searched her out in the first place.

Then, he'd found the damned wallet.

He'd packed it up and scorched up to the post office in a panic. The damn place had been shut and, no time left, he'd given the package to Max to post for him.

Max wasn't stupid. He was very far from being stupid. Just how long would it have taken him to begin to wonder? To ask himself why Hal had taken him outside, just to ask him to post a package. To wonder why he couldn't get Jo to do it. He'd told Max he'd do so if Max couldn't or wouldn't, but he'd have put money on Max spotting that for the bluff it was.

How long before Max suspected that something had happened?

Hal told himself, repeatedly, that he was worrying about nothing. That Max would have done precisely as he'd been asked: put the package into the hands of some efficient postmaster or postmistress and thought no more about it.

But he had a chilling suspicion that it might not have been like that at all …

Sam's voice broke into his uncomfortable thoughts: his father was calling out from the kitchen. '… reckon it's time we fetched that boy of yours in for a shower and his supper.'

'I'll go, Dad.'

But Sam, coming into the room, pushed him back in his seat. 'No, stay there. I need to check he's locked up properly, although I don't know why, since he's more efficient than I am.'

Sam ambled off, calling out to his grandson as he went. And Hal, perhaps in expiation of his shame concerning people who were far away – for Angela was by no means the only woman he was feeling guilty about – roused himself from his self-indulgent indolence and hurried inside to Sam's kitchen to set about putting a meal together.

They had a visit from Mary MacAllister. Bernard didn't accompany her. He was showing his age now, and, as Mary calmly said, preferred to be within his own four walls.

Hal had so many memories of his old friend Ben's mother. Mary had been kind to him over the years, and she loved Jo and the boys. She plied him with questions about how they were all doing, what they'd been up to over the summer, exclaiming over Jo's film. 'Oh, boy,' she said excitedly, 'I can't tell you how thrilled we all are! The book was wonderful, but we've known it and loved it for a long time now, and having it turn into a film is something else! We just can't wait to see it when it's released! Christmas time, isn't it? And maybe we'll be sent a video, if it's not shown over here?'

'I'll make sure Jo keeps you informed,' Hal said.

Mary gave him a puzzled look. 'But Hal, she already does!' She frowned as if she couldn't believe he didn't know. Then, with rather too obvious diplomacy, she turned to Sam and asked him how his new hip was doing.

Sammie made up for Hal's taciturnity by talking virtually non-stop to Mary, filling her in on every last detail of life back home until even her abiding interest in Hal and Jo and the family began to lessen a little. Turning cheerful chatter into positive action, however, Sammie willingly gave up the room he was using to his 'sort-of-grandmother', as he called her, and slept on the sofa in the main room.

'So, Teddy's playing rugby football!' Mary said over one of their long drawn-out meals out on the porch in the autumn sun. 'My, that must be tough!'

'He's Ed now,' Sammie said, not for the first time.

On several occasions Hal was aware of her eyes on him. Kind eyes, compassionate eyes, as if she knew he wasn't easy in his mind. He wondered if she would still look at him like that if she knew.

Although he was glad to see her, nevertheless he was relieved when her two-night stay came to an end.

The following day, Sammie was invited to go sailing with Sam's friends, who had a catamaran. They also had two children, a boy of about Ed's age and a girl a year older than Sammie. Sammie was desperate to go, and Sam said quietly to Hal that he'd be perfectly safe.

'Dirk – that's the father – has sailed the seven oceans in that cat of his,' he said as Sammie stared up at his father with beseeching eyes. 'He runs the boat as if it's a naval vessel, and nobody's allowed to twitch an eyelash unless he says so.' Sammie suppressed a giggle. 'Oh, don't you go laughing, my young lad, I mean it!'

Hal and Sam went to see Sammie safely into the care of his new friends, then returned to Sam's house. 'They'll be out all day,' Sam remarked. 'I have chores to do, and then I'm having a finger food lunch with my bridge club. Finger food!' he repeated, with a derisive chuckle. 'Then we'll play a few rubbers. Why don't you take the car and go for a drive?'

It was exactly what Hal wanted to do. 'Aren't there some things around here I could be doing for you?' he made himself ask.

Sam spread his hands as if to display his cluttered but clean and orderly home. 'Such as what? If you try and tidy up I'll never forgive you, and I like the front porch paintwork looking weathered.'

Hal grinned. 'I'll stop at the store on my way home and pick up a load of groceries.'

'Now that,' Sam said, 'would truly be helpful.'

Hal left Sam to his pottering, and set off.

Until he was in the car, alone, driving out of Morro Bay and turning up into the hills, he hadn't realised how much he had been longing for some time in his own company. He knew that was something he had to think about – it had been preying on his mind for a long time now – but he told himself he wasn't going to tackle it today.

Today was a perfect Californian autumn day. The sky was deep blue and clear of cloud. The ocean was calm, with only a light breeze lifting the skirts of the waves. Thinking of Sammie, Hal hoped they were finding some wind further out to sea.

But, if he was honest with himself, he wasn't bothered.

'I am a selfish man,' he told himself solemnly. 'But, hell, what can I do about the wind?'

Then he shut his mind to everything else and let the pleasure of his outing take him over.

He drove north to Harmony, turned inland to Paso Robles, then took a long southern leg down to San Luis Obispo. He used the lesser roads whenever he could, ambling along, in no hurry, the window down and a selection of Sam's music playing on the car stereo. Sam appeared to have discovered – or maybe rediscovered – Richard Strauss. Hal was entertained by 'Till Eulenspiegel' and a selection from 'Der Rosenkavalier', he renewed acquaintance with 'Don Quixote' and found himself surprisingly moved by the 'Four Last Songs', especially 'Beim Schlafengehen'. He let the music wash through him. He wasn't really aware of thinking about anything. I'm having some down time, he reflected.

He stopped at a small country store to buy food. Bread, ham, some fruit. He ate it sitting on a wooden bridge over a stream. There was nobody about and the air smelt of pine trees.

He got lost on the way back to Morro Bay. His desire to travel the smallest roads had its culmination in what was in fact more of a track than a road, full of potholes that threatened the suspension on Sam's car. But he wasn't worried. For the car's sake, he slowed right down to a crawl, patiently waiting until the track emerged onto a road. He knew he was going in the right direction – or he hoped so – and if he got lost, he'd simply be late home.

It didn't matter. On that day, nothing mattered.

In time, he found himself on a road again, a narrow, winding country road. Suddenly, the ocean appeared down to his left, and, drawing off into a passing place, he got out of the car and went to see if he could work out where he was. Standing behind the car, looking back the way he had come, the humped rock in the middle of Morro Bay was ahead and slightly to the right. Far from being lost, he was exactly where he'd reckoned on being. He murmured aloud, 'Lewis and Clark, eat your hearts out.'

He got back in the car and drove on.

He soon realised that the expected road turning down to the left towards the coast wasn't going to materialise as soon as he'd hoped. Unfazed, he continued. And, just as he had suspected, some five or six miles further on a lane zigzagged its way steeply downhill. He was about to take it, but something made him go straight on.

The road wound up through a belt of trees. One or two dwellings were visible on either side. It would, he thought, be a marvellous place to live. Isolated, trees on the hillside behind to shelter you, the ocean visible in front of you. He followed the numerous bends in the road. Gradually, the houses petered out.

At the point where the road began to slope downwards again, he saw ahead of him a small house all by itself, up to the right. It was set into the hillside, a stand of pines to the right and some deciduous trees to the left. It was single-storey and a long deck ran all the way along the front, protected by the downward slope of the overhanging roof. The front wall of the house was made of glass.

There was nobody about, and the house had an air of having been deserted for some time. Parking the car at the end of the driveway, Hal got out.

The gate was closed but not locked. He opened it, went through, headed up the gentle rise towards the house. He noticed there was a garage tucked away behind the pine trees. Silently, he applauded the unknown architect for his – her – desire to hide away this reminder of the ubiquitous automobile.

He wandered right round the house. It really was small: almost more a cabin than a house, and, in keeping with the cabin tradition, incorporating a lot of wood. It had the air of a fairly recent build yet, belying this, the wood was old and weathered. To his eyes, it seemed to blend the old with the ultra-modern in a strangely pleasing way.

He stepped up onto the deck.

He turned, and took in the view.

He stood quite still, simply looking, for a long time. It was utterly quiet, totally isolated, and he felt completely at peace.

The ocean was visible a long way below, although close enough to be a constant presence. Settlements were dotted among the vegetation of the hillside, and some large coastal town sprawled over to the right. To the left he could see the Morro Bay rock. He'd once said to Jo, in a letter, that it looked as if a camel was walking along the sea bed with just its hump showing.

Jo.

He thought of her for a few moments.

Then he returned to the view.

Over where the deciduous trees stood in their clump, someone had affixed a rope with a short length of wood on the end to a stout lower branch. Holding onto the length of wood, you'd be able to swing out into the air and feel you were flying. It was safe, however: the flying would be an illusion, since the ground didn't fall away until some distance from the trees. Even if you let go, the worst you'd suffer would probably be a sprained ankle.

He could imagine Ed and Sammie playing there.

He let them fill his mind for a while.

Presently he spun round and, holding up a hand against the light, peered in through the glass front wall of the house.

There wasn't much in the room that ran the width of the place. A vast stone fireplace to the left, a large leather sofa along the back wall, sagging, the leather well-worn and cracked here and there, a thick blanket neatly folded and laid over the back. The floor was wood, the walls stone with wood cladding here and there.

He imagined sitting on the sofa, totally relaxed, a glass of beer in his hand, watching the sun set. Watching the stars come out. In silence, with no clamour of voices, nobody asking him to advise, to comment, to contribute on matters that he kept forgetting were his concern; matters which, being brutally frank with himself, he didn't much care about. His mind free to stay where it wanted to be, deep within whatever he was working on, planning what he'd write the next morning.

Alone.

He'd be alone.

He leaned forward until his folded arms rested on the porch rail. He dropped his head onto his arms.

After a while he straightened up, walked back down the drive and carefully closed the gate. Then he drove back to Sam's house.

Then it was Friday, and the week was drawing to its close.

There was something Hal wanted to do, but he wanted to do it by himself.

Aware that he was being devious – but it's in a good cause, he told himself firmly – he suggested to his father and Sammie that, since Bernard MacAllister hadn't been up to visiting them, they could drive up to San Francisco and see him.

150

'It's a long drive, son,' Sam said dubiously. 'Must be five hundred miles, round trip. It's a heck of a distance to do in a day, unless you're planning for us all to stay the night?'

'No.'

'I don't really want to go,' Sammie said. Then, instantly and more emphatically, 'I *really* don't want to go.'

Hal glanced at him. Sammie, he remembered all too vividly, tended to get car sick.

Sam seemed to pick up that his and Sammie's lack of enthusiasm might be disappointing. 'Why don't you go on your own?' he suggested. 'If you get tired on the way back, you can always check into a motel.'

'You wouldn't mind?' Hal glanced from one to the other.

'No!' they chorused, far too enthusiastically for Hal's liking.

But then he thought, this trip is for me, so why should I expect them to agree to having their pleasant daily routines interrupted? Why should they mind if I set off alone?

'Okay,' he said easily. 'I'll go tomorrow.'

He arrived at the MacAllister house in the late morning. Uncomfortably aware that he'd be walking through the door not long before lunchtime, he had stopped and purchased some items from a delicatessen, as well as autumn flowers and a box of chocolates.

Even as he went up to the door, his mind was in the past. He remembered going there to collect Jo, during her summer visit. He could recall the very moment when he had understood that he was falling for his dead friend's wife. And that brought the further past into focus, and all at once he was there with Ben, and they were laughing about something. Ben had always made him laugh.

The door opened and Mary looked up at him, her face full of delight.

151

'Now I know just why you're here, you nice man!' she said, hugging him warmly. Hal felt himself give a start of surprise, but it was all right: 'Bernard's through there, in the day room – oh, he'll be so pleased to see you!'

The visit was as much a pleasure to Hal as to Bernard and Mary. Ben's death was still an ache for all of them, but he had died well over a decade ago and, as Mary said through tears that were both sad and happy at the same time, 'You just have to move on.' And there was much more laughter than grief. Ben had lightened the mood wherever he went and it seemed he still did.

Hal got up to leave, aware that Bernard was looking tired. They shook hands, and Hal promised to come back when he could. Mary showed him to the door.

He said quietly to her, 'I'm going to pay one more call before I go back to Dad's.'

She understood; she hadn't needed to peer inside Sam's car and see the second bouquet of flowers on the back seat.

'That'd be nice,' she said. She stared at him, a slight frown on her face, and, after a brief hesitation, said, 'Everything okay, Hal?'

For an instant he wanted to pour out his heart to his old friend's wise, kindly mother.

But he didn't. With a smile he said, 'Everything's fine. Bye, Mary – we'll keep in touch.'

Hal walked beneath an arch set in a wall into a quiet, secluded area bordered by cypress hedges. He passed a few rows, counting silently. But in fact he had no need to keep count: he knew exactly where it was.

Ben's grave was marked out in stone, with a plain white tablet at the head. The short turf had been recently clipped, and the pot for flowers held some chrysanthemums, beginning to go over. Hal didn't think Mary – he was sure it was Mary – would mind if he replaced them.

He did so, working quickly and efficiently, putting the dying flowers in a bin and drawing fresh water for the replacements.

Then he stood above the grave and read the words on the headstone.

BENJAMIN CHARLES MACALLISTER
3rd June 1948–5 August 1978
Beloved son, husband and father
'Many waters cannot quench love,
Neither can the floods drown it.'

Hal stayed there for a long time. The words he would have said to Mary sounded loud in his head. He hadn't said them to her, but now he told his old friend everything, and felt as awful as he'd expected to. He realised he was asking Ben what he thought; what he felt Hal should do.

But if Ben heard, he found no way of answering.

Chapter 11

Max

Angela was withdrawn and quiet in the way back to Paimpont. Max had an idea that she was backtracking from the moment of closeness when they had made their discovery; the moment when he had hugged her and kissed her cheek and she had briefly held his hand.

He didn't try to talk to her. When he had parked in the hotel's car park he said, 'Shall we meet in the bar around seven?', deliberately avoiding any reference to her comment yesterday about him buying her a slap-up dinner and a bottle of fizz. They'd both forgotten about it the previous evening, and now it no longer felt appropriate, for the mood between them had changed.

'All right,' she said as she got out of the car. She strode off across to the hotel and disappeared inside.

Max looked at his watch. A quarter to five. Two and a quarter hours till he could do what he so wanted to do and ask her what he should do next. To ask her if she happened to speak Danish as well as French.

Of course she won't, he thought. And, judging by how she's been on the way back here, the chances of her agreeing to go on helping me in this unexpectedly dramatic journey to trace my mother's roots are less than nil.

He locked the car and then, not in the least wanting to go up to his room, set out up the road to the lake. He went over the bridge that crossed it at its extremity, then took a path off to the left that ran parallel to the shore.

The lake waters were still and dark, there were few people about, and the path led beneath trees that grew right down to the shore. It was an atmospheric place. He wished Angela was with him.

After about half a mile, the path turned away from the lake and led through the trees to an open area where a stream ran through on its way to the lake, crossed here and there by little bridges. There was a small shrine at the far side, with a statue of the Virgin and china plaques expressing deep gratitude for prayers answered. A raised area reached by wooden steps had a wide stone altar, presumably used for open-air services. The sense of peace and serenity deepened.

Max found a bench and sat down. He found himself thinking about Angela. I like her, he thought. I enjoy her company. I wish I knew more about her, but I am afraid she'll react badly if I start asking questions.

Only one way to find out, came the reply in his head.

Presently, he got up and walked back the way he had come. He crossed the bridge, but instead of going into the hotel, he turned right beneath the arch and walked on down the main street of the little town.

It was narrow, the houses built in two continuous rows, facing each other. There were one or two shops, a hairdresser and the small supermarket they had patronised earlier. He spotted an enamel plaque on the wall, but this was no thank you for favours granted by a deity: the wording mentioned Madame de Gaulle, and there was a date, and something about her son making a broadcast from London to occupied France. Piecing it together, and with a bit of guesswork, Max decided that the plaque marked the house where de Gaulle's mother had listened to her son speaking from London, addressing his countrymen as they suffered under German occupation. Not suffering with them, Max reflected, but instead accepting the hospitality of a country and a people he was well known to have deeply disliked.

He strolled on and went to have a look at the abbey. He stopped for a beer at a lively little cafe on the corner at the end of the street. Then he set off back to the hotel.

A shop on the right caught his attention. It was called Le Fil Rouge, and gentle harp music and the scent of joss sticks issued through its open door. There was a display of books that appeared to be about myths of the Broceliande Forest; about pixies, faeries and King Arthur. They all seemed to be in French. There was a shelf of pewter chalices and model swords and beyond it a display case of crystals and jewellery. One piece caught his eye: it was a clear crystal, delicately faceted so that it caught the light and gave off sparkles. It was set in silver and suspended on a fine silver chain.

He recalled that Angela had been wearing a small gold pendant of some sort when he first saw her. But she had apparently left it behind; certainly, she hadn't been wearing it since they set out.

He called out to the dreadlocked young man sitting behind the counter and indicated that he'd like to buy the pendant. With a smile, the man got up to unlock the case and extract the pendant. 'C'est comme cadeau, oui?' he asked. 'It is present?'

'It's a present, yes.'

The young man put it in a box and wrapped the box neatly in dark blue paper, adding a decorative silver foil bow. Max thanked him and paid, slipping the box into his pocket. Wondering quite why he had just bought Angela quite an expensive present, and what her reaction would be when he gave it to her, he went back to the hotel.

He had a quick shower and put on a fresh shirt, and he'd been in the bar only a few minutes when she joined him. She had changed out of her smart business-like clothes and wore a black top with a vee neck over a full black skirt. She had put on fine dark tights and shoes with a heel, and he noticed how good her legs were. Perhaps she'd remembered about the celebratory evening after all. He was pleased that he'd made an effort, too.

They each had a kir, and the man behind the bar put out a small dish of salted nuts. 'You'd better have some while the going's good,' Angela said, pushing the dish over to him. 'I'm starving.'

'Me too. Shall we see how soon we can eat?'

Straight away, was the response. They took their kirs into the dining room, where they were shown to a table. A waiter gave them menus. Angela translated one or two items for Max, and then they ordered.

'Et comme vin?' the waiter asked.

Even Max knew what that meant. 'Champagne,' he said.

Nodding, the waiter turned a page of the wine list and indicated with his pencil. Max pointed, the man nodded again and disappeared.

Max risked a glance at Angela. She wasn't exactly smiling, but she didn't look as shut-in as she had done earlier. Max wondered if alcohol would help; he picked up his kir and finished it, and was pleased to see that she did the same.

The champagne arrived, quickly followed by their starters. The food was plain but very well prepared and both of them cleared their plates, making no more than a few brief efforts at conversation. The main course was equally good. Max ordered a second bottle of champagne.

The cheese board featured a variety of excellent local cheeses, and they both tried most of them. Then, pushing herself away a little from the table, Angela said, 'Do you mind if we wait a bit before pudding?'

'Not in the least,' he replied. 'It'll give us a chance to finish the wine.'

She held out her glass.

'I'm glad we made such good progress today,' she said, raising her glass to him.

'Me too,' he said. 'Thanks to you,' he added. 'It's extraordinary to have made such a discovery.'

'I imagine so,' she said.

'I can't leave it there,' he went on. 'Now I have to think how I go about finding the family's roots in Denmark, and that'll …' He stopped, having realised even as he spoke that his remark could be taken to suggest he would appreciate her ongoing involvement. Quickly, he added, 'But that's for another day,' and she nodded.

There was a brief silence. 'What about your family?' he asked. 'You mentioned following one line in your own ancestry back a long way, I wondered if you'd found anything interesting.'

She sighed. 'Not very. Both of my parents were only children, and my father had dutifully traced back both lines on his side for a few generations, shortly before he died. Since then I've done the same for my mother's side. Rather a mundane set of upper middle class men and women, with not a black sheep or even a modest rebel among them.'

'Your father must have died young,' Max said. 'I'm sorry.'

She shrugged. 'He wasn't that young. He was much older than my mother. And anyway, like I told you, he left when I was little.'

'And married a woman with a huge bust over whose new hairdo you tipped a plate of porridge.'

'Yes.' She grinned.

'What about your mother? You said she tried to ensure you kept up contact with your father, so she ...'

'Don't go assuming that was for my sake,' Angela interrupted. 'The only reason she was so desperate to make me go and stay with him was to give her some time off, so that she didn't always have to have a child dragging along after her.' Her expression hardened. 'And because it allowed her to bask in her friends' admiration for her selflessness, for having any consideration whatsoever for the bastard who'd left her for someone else.'

She sounded very bitter.

'I see. And did she ...'

'She lives in Cheltenham with my stepfather,' Angela went on as if she hadn't heard. 'He was in the City, something Very Important in Finance – my mother always says that in a way that suggests capital letters – and when he retired, he instantly barged his way onto the committees of the golf club, the residents' association and every other damned organisation not determined enough to keep him out. Because he's the sort of man who just loves the sound of his own voice and can't possibly be happy unless he's telling other people what to do. I loathe him and keep well away.' She paused. 'So I don't see much of her. My mother.'

The cloud of fury that had hovered over them as she spoke slowly dissipated. Max glanced at her, but she was staring down into her almost empty glass and didn't notice.

He thought of her life in the sordid little rented house.

It struck him how lonely she must be.

On impulse, he reached in his jacket pocket and took out the little box. Handing it to her, he said, 'I saw this in a shop in the street across the road. It's to say thank you for coming with me and to recognise that I wouldn't have got much further than St Malo on my own.'

She nodded but didn't answer. She was staring at the box as if it was a hand grenade.

'Open it,' he said quietly.

With an impatient gesture she did.

She picked up the crystal, held it up to the light. 'It's lovely,' she said, so quietly that he hardly heard. She went on looking at it, making no move to put it on. Then, raising her eyes to look at him, she whispered, 'You saw, didn't you? The pendant I used to wear, that I was wearing when we first met?'

He knew exactly what she meant. He didn't think it was a moment for anything but honesty. 'Yes. Something small, on a gold chain.'

'It was a Cretan axe. I believe it's called a labrys and it's where the word labyrinth comes from, because the axe was the symbol of the Minoans and found throughout their buildings.' She paused, drew a rather shaky breath and went on. 'Hal brought it for me. Crete was where we met, where we fell quite heavily for each other, but did nothing about it because he was married and I was waiting for a man called Rob to join me. Hal left the axe as a parting gift at the place where I was staying. ' She paused, then added in a bitter voice, 'He was no better at goodbyes back then than he is now.'

Max said nothing. He hoped she would go on, and soon she did.

Glaring at him challengingly, she said, 'You know something happened, don't you?'

'Yes,' he said again. 'It was the way you looked when you heard my car draw up – you thought I was Hal, and I wasn't. I'm sorry I wasn't,' he added. She shrugged that away. 'Also, I was staying at Hal's house when he got home – he'd forgotten I was coming. Jo – that's his wife – was unpacking his bag for him and asked where his new grey cashmere sweater was. I saw it on your sofa.'

'And your sharp eyes also spotted I'd been crying into it,' she said harshly. 'Well done. Ten out of ten for observation.'

'He found your wallet in his car and he asked me to drop it in the post for him,' Max hurried on. 'I was heading off on the night ferry. But you know that, of course.'

'You didn't post it,' she muttered.

'No,' he agreed.

'And neither did he?'

It sounded like a question. 'He didn't have time. As I believe I mentioned, he was about to fly to California. His father lives there and he's taken his son to visit him.'

'Oh, good,' Angela said ironically. Then, very softly but extremely vehemently, '*Fuck* Hal.'

He echoed the sentiment.

After a moment he leaned closer to her and said, 'Angela, it's good that we can talk about it. Isn't it?' She gave a reluctant nod. 'For what it's worth, I believe he's to blame.'

'Oh, I didn't turn him away.'

'No, but I don't think you went searching him out.'

'I didn't!' Her head shot up. 'I might have done if I'd known where he lived, but probably I wouldn't, because I knew he was married.'

'His wife's lovely,' Max said.

'Of course she is,' Angela replied instantly.

161

He smiled briefly. 'Really. And I don't think she finds him easy.'

Angela was holding up the pendant, swinging it gently so that the crystal reflected the candle flame. 'It was because he was ill,' she murmured. 'I was holding out, keeping my distance, then he got bloody flu and I looked after him, and then when he was better ...' She stopped.

'And after that, he went home,' Max finished for her.

'After that he went home,' she echoed. 'I was all but sure he wasn't coming back. Then you drew up outside, and ...'

Abruptly her eyes filled with tears. She put the crystal pendant very carefully into its box – the action went straight to his heart – and briefly buried her face in her napkin.

He gave her a moment. Then he said, 'What about the man you were meeting in Crete?'

She lowered the napkin. 'He's a shit, too. His wife left him and he discovered he quite liked being the wronged husband – lots of sympathy from lots of women that went a long way beyond bringing him casseroles and batches of scones; right up to his bedroom in fact, which I didn't realise when he and I were together – and he didn't want to let it be known that he had someone special. Only I can see now that I wasn't as special as I thought I was.'

Max leaned both elbows on the table. Or tried to: he missed the edge with his right one at the first attempt and it occurred to him that he was more than a little drunk. Good, he thought. We wouldn't be talking like this if I hadn't ordered the second bottle.

'Angela,' he said quietly, 'not all men are like Rob and like Hal.' He felt an irrational urge to defend his cousin. 'In fact, I don't think Hal's like that really, but I quite understand that you might not agree.' Her mouth twitched in a swift smile. 'It seems to me that you've had bad luck. Or maybe what happened with Rob made you undervalue yourself.' Stop, he told himself. He reached out for her hand. Several quite pertinent remarks ran through his head but every last one sounded patronising or corny or both. So he just said, 'Why don't you put the pendant on?'

She looked at him, surprised; clearly she had been expecting something else. Then she smiled, and the smile developed into a laugh. She unfastened the clasp on the silver chain, put it round her neck and did it up. The crystal lay on the smooth flesh of her chest, just above the hollow between her breasts.

'It looks wonderful,' he said.

She held his eyes. 'Thank you. And thank you too for such a beautiful present.'

She went on looking at him, and for a moment he thought she was going to add more. But then, still smiling, she said, 'What about one of those huge ice cream sundaes for pudding?'

They finished the champagne, then had coffee. They were talking easily now, relaxed with each other – which Max attributed to the champagne – and the mood between them was warm with affection.

She stumbled a little when finally they got up, and he didn't feel any too steady either. 'Shall we meet for breakfast a bit later in the morning?' she suggested as they made their way carefully up the stairs.

'Definitely,' he agreed. 'And we can have a holiday day tomorrow. We've got what we came for, so shall we simply enjoy being here?'

'Okay.' She paused outside her room, her hand on the door handle. 'Thanks for this evening. The meal and the fizz. This.' She touched a finger to the crystal pendant. 'For listening,' she added, so softly that he only just heard.

'You're welcome,' he replied. Then, before he could do what he badly wanted to and lean forward to kiss her, he said, a soft new version of her name slipping into his mind all by itself, 'Night, Anja,' and walked away to his own room.

Chapter 12

The bright, clear weather continued the next day. They looked at a stand of leaflets in the hotel's foyer, advertising local attractions. Quite a few had an Arthurian theme.

'Shall we go for it?' Angela suggested.

'Fine by me,' Max replied.

'What about this? We can incorporate a magic fountain and a golden tree, and neither is more than a few miles away.'

'We'll call in at the shop before we set off and I'll treat us to another magnificent picnic.'

She smiled. 'Baguette and a hunk of cheese is the only thing to have for a picnic lunch in France.'

It took them a long time to find the fountain. They followed some fairly unobtrusive signs and managed to locate the car park, hidden away at the end of a track that wound between low, red granite buildings, then set off along a succession of branching tracks through woodland. It was very peaceful; they had the place to themselves.

'I think,' Angela panted as they reached the summit of a long ride between two wooded areas whose slope had looked deceptively unchallenging, 'we may have misinterpreted their use of "fountain".'

Max stopped, bending forward with his hands on his hips. 'So I shouldn't be looking out for something like you'd find in the gardens of Versailles, or made of Italian stone with a huge statue of Oceanus in a chariot shaped like a shell?'

'No.'

'How reassuring,' he remarked. 'Then being out in the middle of a forest with absolutely no signs of human habitation needn't be discouraging after all.'

'Come on. Where's your explorer spirit?' She was setting off again. 'I have a feeling it's up here.'

Presently they came to a lively stream winding its way down the hillside. It had cut itself a narrow channel, and the noise of merrily rushing water was loud in the silence. Angela, spurred to fresh efforts by this encouraging sign, led the way up a muddy track full of rock outcrops, and after five or ten minutes they emerged into a clearing at the summit.

The centre of the clearing was marked by a huge, flat slab of rock. It hung out over a steep-sided depression in the ground; a natural basin filled with clear water with a sightly reddish tinge.

'Iron,' Angela said.

'Like at Les Forges.'

She looked up, meeting his eyes. 'Your ancestors feel very close,' she said softly.

They knelt down either side of the basin. After a moment, Max said, 'Look.' He pointed. 'There's a gas of some sort, coming up out of the ground. There!'

She watched, fascinated. 'Do you know what it is?'

'No idea. You?'

'No. I had to give up chemistry when I got eighteen per cent and failed the exam in the third year.'

Max had put the leaflet from the hotel in his pocket. Drawing it out, he put on his glasses and read aloud. 'If you stamp three times on the big rock, it causes a sudden and very violent tempest.'

'Then we'd better not.' After a second she said, 'Wow! Your French is coming on!'

He held out the leaflet, silently pointing to the English translation.

They found their way to the closest village to the next attraction, which was called Tréhorenteuc. 'Before you ask,' Angela said, 'I have no idea how you pronounce it.' Once again, there was a sign for the car park, but after that the only further direction was to something called the Val Sans Retour. In the absence of any other signs, they went that way.

'Valley of No Return sounds Arthurian,' Angela said as they set off from the car. 'I think Viviane used to lure her unfaithful lovers to it, then abandoned them.'

Max didn't reply. Since the woman who had just raised the matter had recently suffered in a very similar way at the hands of two unfaithful lovers, he sensed that any comment would amount to entering a conversational minefield. And Angela seemed cheerful today.

But after a moment she said, 'I could summon up Rob and Hal, couldn't I? I don't think anyone would miss bloody Rob if I managed to mislay him in a magical valley in the wilds of central Brittany, but from what you say the same thing doesn't seem to apply to Hal.'

'It doesn't,' Max said. Then, for he sensed she was sad suddenly, 'Maybe just leave him there for a week or two?'

And, to his relief, she smiled.

They turned up to the left, past a second car park. A French family in a camper van were settling down to an elaborate late lunch – Max and Angela had eaten their picnic some time ago – and responded with smiles and waves when Angela wished them bon appétit.

'Bon chance? Bon voyage?' Max said.

She laughed.

After a few hundred yards they came to a lake. The water was very dark, overshadowed by trees. The track around the shore was littered with fallen leaves, most of them gold and amber.

'It's really …' Angela began.

But Max, who had been looking round, touched her hand and raised his arm, pointing to the left.

Set amid a thicket of granite stones, placed upright in the earth like a bristling barrier, was a dead tree. Its trunk and branches were totally bare: it appeared to be the victim of a forest fire, and its shape was symmetrical and stark, and strangely beautiful.

It had been covered in gold.

'The Golden Tree!' She hurried over to it, stopping on the far side of the deep cleft that kept the tree isolated from those who came to look at it. 'Is this part of the Arthurian legends? If so, it must be a Breton variant, because I've never heard of it.'

Max was consulting the leaflet again. 'No. It was done after a devastating forest fire, basically as a way of telling people to be more careful and have more respect for nature.'

They stood looking at the tree for some time. Then the camper family, clearly having finished their lunch, came chattering, laughing and yelling up the track from the car park.

The spell was broken.

Max and Angela turned and left.

* * *

The next day they left the forest and went north to Dinan.

They parked in a big central square, near a huge statue of a spectacularly ugly man sitting on a horse, chest swelling with a victor's pride and a combative expression on his face. 'That's Du Guesclin,' Angela said, consulting a guide book she'd fished out of her bag. 'So ugly as a child that his mother gave him away, and he grew up to be a great soldier, a marshal of France, and he beat the Duke of Canterbury in single combat right here.'

'In the car park? Dodging all the Renaults, Peugeots and deux chevaux?'

'Absolutely.'

They turned off the busy main road through the town and found a delightful medieval city. The timber-framed buildings leaned out over the narrow streets and the sunlight struck sparkles of light from the granite. 'It wouldn't look so entrancing in the rain,' Max remarked.

Wandering back in the general direction of the big square, they passed the tourist office, a compact theatre and, just opposite, a hotel sharing a small open courtyard with a little church. The hotel looked inviting; Angela said it would be nice to be right in the heart of the old town. They went in and booked rooms.

They had galettes and crêpes for lunch, accompanied by a jug of local cider that was served in pottery vessels like handle-less tea cups. As they waited for the food, Angela said, 'Professor of psychology, eh?'

'Er ... yes.' He wondered what was coming next.

'What does that mean?'

'Right now it means a year-long research project into an aspect of human behaviour.'

She waited, and when he didn't continue said with some impatience, 'Go on, then!'

He said, after a moment, 'What are you good at doing? So good that you can almost do it without thinking about it?'

She caught on straight away, which was more than most people did. 'I can touch type, I love driving, I used to knit.'

He nodded. 'Any sports?'

'Riding. You couldn't get me away from the stables when I was young.'

'Good. Well, I don't ride but I do drive, so let's use that as the example. On a long drive, have you ever experienced the sense that all at once you're driving better than you ever do normally? Smoothly, able to predict exactly what's going to happen on the road ahead, feeling that you're riding a wave and every action you take is precisely the correct one?'

She thought about it. 'Yes, I think so. But I've certainly felt it when I've been on a horse. A sudden sort of… knowing, I suppose, that you're completely in tune with the horse and with your surroundings, that your body is working just as it should, that you're not even having to think about what to do because all at once it's coming automatically, and you're doing it better that ever before.'

'You're not even having to think,' he repeated. 'Yes, that's it. That's what the research project is investigating: what subjects say they feel, and what's happening in the brain when they're experiencing it. We haven't thought up a way of testing people when they're riding a horse, and we're still working on the driving example, but we've had people touch-typing and achieved some results that are certainly worth following up.'

The food arrived. She didn't speak for a while, but he was quite sure she was thinking about what he'd just told her. Then, looking up from her egg and cheese galette, she said, 'Thank you for telling me. I hope you don't think I was being nosy.'

'Not in the least.' You can ask me anything, he added silently.

They finished the meal and, both feeling bloated, retired to their rooms for a rest. Then they explored the rest of Dinan.

'You can't do it justice in a day,' Angela said over dinner.

And Max had to fight the impulse to say, Then we'll come again.

They had asked for an early call in the morning, and had eaten breakfast and checked out soon after eight o'clock. Angela got her map out again and they made their way back to St Malo. The roads were busy with Monday morning rush hour traffic, and it took them some time. The check-in booths had already opened by the time they reached the ferry terminal, and within half an hour they were waiting in the final queue before boarding.

The sea was calm, the boat wasn't crowded and they had a comfortable, if long, crossing.

They had lunch in the self-service restaurant, then found reclining seats in one of the lounges.

Angela read a book. Max sat, thinking.

I have to speak up, he thought. I only met her six days ago, and in very awkward circumstances, and in addition I know – partly because I saw it with my own eyes, partly because she told me – that she's suffered recently; in the case of my cousin Hal, very recently. She's not in the least likely to be open to the idea of a new relationship.

But set against that is the fact that we've enjoyed our time together. I have, anyway, and she certainly seems to have done so. She's bright, sparky, very attractive and ...

He wondered why he was thinking and not speaking.

He heard himself say, 'Angela, I don't want to take you back to your house in the village near Chichester.'

She put down her book, looked faintly surprised - hurt? - but swiftly recovered. 'No need, I can take the train and then the bus,' she said, and he thought he detected a chilly, defensive tone in her voice.

'No, I didn't mean ...' he began.

But she spoke over him. 'I don't blame you,' she went on. 'It's a hole, isn't it? I hate it, but it's not actually mine, I'm renting it. In fact I have a very nice house in Gloucestershire, in the Forest of Dean. I left the area because of the bust-up with Rob – in a fit of pique, really, which hurt me a lot more than it did him – and my house now has tenants in it.'

The air between them seemed to crackle with her emotion.

'That wasn't really what I meant,' he said quietly.

'What wasn't?' she said curtly.

'I didn't mean I didn't want to drop you off there because it was horrible – which I agree it is,' he added. God, why was this so difficult? Just go for it, he told himself. 'I don't want to drop you off anywhere, Anja. This week with you has been so good – not just what we found out about my grandparents and the family, but the fact that we were doing it together. Being together, getting to know you, that's what I've really enjoyed.'

She was watching him very intently, he noticed, but she didn't interrupt. He ploughed on. 'I live in Cambridge. It was the only place I wanted to be, when I settled in England.' He paused briefly, then continued. 'I bought the house where my dad's friends used to live – the ones I told you about, the family who made him so welcome during the war?' Her eyes widened and she nodded. 'Cambridge is where I work, too. Come back there with me. Come and stay – I have two spare rooms – and we could just see how it goes.'

She said slowly, 'But I work in Chichester.'

'Yes, I know. I've been there, remember?' She nodded again. 'Is it a job you like a lot?'

'Not much.'

'You hate your rented house, you don't much like your job. Why not come with me and see if life in Cambridge is better?'

She made a non-committal sound.

'This probably sounds spur-of-the-moment and poorly thought out,' he went on, 'but the thought's been growing in my mind for a couple of days that I don't want to say goodbye to you. Will you come home with me when we reach England? See the house, have a look round the city, walk along the Backs and go out to Grantchester to have tea, and ...'

She had been smiling, the expression gradually brightening her whole face, and now, suddenly, she laughed. 'Stop, Max,' she said softly.

'You're not coming?' He felt a crushing disappointment.

But she bunched up her hand into a fist and very gently punched his arm. 'I *am* coming,' she corrected him. 'I was just enjoying listening to you trying to win me round.' She grinned at him. 'You had me at "I don't want to drop you off anywhere."'

They were off the ferry soon after half past six, and quickly on the road and heading for Cambridge. The journey took over three hours.

He noticed her staring about her as he drove slowly into the square where his house was. 'We'll drop the bags, then I'm afraid we have to go a bit further. Or if you're tired, I'll let you into the house and take the car on my own. As you'll see, there's nowhere to park here.'

'I'll come with you.'

He felt obscurely pleased.

Getting out, he went up to the house and unlocked the door. She already had the boot open and was hauling out their bags. He took them from her, dumped them in the hall and they got back in the car. He drove the short distance to the house of the friend who allowed him to use his garage, where he put the car away. There were lights on, but now wasn't the time to go visiting.

They walked back to his house side by side, in step. He felt close to her. The old brass letter box gave its familiar little rattle as he pushed the door open. He stood back to let her go inside first, then shut the door on the night.

He gave her a quick tour. His study to the left of the hall, the big, open living room beyond, the kitchen at the back of the house to the right. Upstairs, three bedrooms and the bathroom. His room had an en suite shower; he reflected that he'd have got it ready for her had he known she would be with him.

She chose the smaller of the two guest rooms. It had the original Victorian fireplace, and he had furnished it in a style to match. There was a brass bedstead and a vintage patchwork eiderdown on top of the duvet. Down in the cellar he had found a beautiful old button box, still full of buttons. It stood on the chest of drawers.

Angela stood in the doorway. 'I love it,' she said.

He managed not to ask her a single question until the following Friday.

The week had been a joy.

They had walked all over Cambridge. The colleges, the Backs, King's College Chapel, Heiffers, the river, the market. They had gone out on the bus to some of the outlying places, visited the American Cemetery at Madingley and stood on the bridge over the long, straight scar of the east coast railway line to watch the InterCity trains thundering past below. They had gone round to take tea with Max's friend Gus – Augustus

Lansdowne-More, to give him his full, grand, name – whose garage Max used, and Gus had been his outgoing, warm, friendly self, and Angela was enchanted.

On hearing that Angela was thinking about a longer stay in Cambridge, Gus said, 'You must stay. I'd love you to meet my partner Kieran, but he's away until next month.' Angela opened her mouth to reply, but Gus was on a roll. 'If you'll be requiring a job – of course you will, everybody does – then perhaps I can make a suggestion. The small museum where I work is in urgent need of someone to help with a vast, and much overdue, cataloguing project.'

'I don't …' Angela began faintly.

Gus leaned towards her and put a hand on hers. 'Don't answer now, dear girl. Just bear it in mind.'

On Friday, Max cooked pasta with scallops in a cream and mushroom sauce and opened a bottle of Sancerre he'd been saving for a special occasion. As he and Angela sat down to eat, he said, 'What do you think?'

There was a long pause, during which he imagined her coming up with all sort of responses, each one saying more or less the same thing: it has been lovely, but I'm not staying.

She took a sip of wine, carefully put down her glass and turned to him.

'I'll have to return to Chichester to hand in my notice and give up my tenancy,' she said.

'And then?'

'Then, I'd very much like to come back.'

He felt an unstoppable smile spreading across his face. Tentatively, he reached out and took her hand. She didn't take it away. He said, 'Is it okay if I go with you?'

With a grin, she said, 'Of course. In fact, in the absence of my own car, I was hoping you'd drive me.'

He felt that something momentous was happening. To lighten the mood he said, 'I feel I ought to. You might change your mind and decide to stay there otherwise.'

He was looking down, rubbing absently at a sauce stain on the tablecloth. When she didn't answer, he looked up.

She was staring straight at him, and her face wore a soft expression he hadn't seen before.

'I won't,' she said. 'I've been happier these last few days than I've been since – oh, I can't remember, and I don't want to try. That's the past, and it's gone.' She hesitated, then went on quietly. 'We've only just met, but since we did we've spent almost all our time together. I feel … easy with you.'

He nodded. 'I know what you mean.'

He wanted to say more: that her undertaking to stay on didn't mean she'd be under any pressure to take their relationship anywhere else, that for the time being it was good enough just to be together, that …

But the thoughts got no further.

For at that moment she got up, came round the table to him and, bending down, took his face between her hands and kissed him.

Chapter 13

Jo

Old Harbour cast its spell on Jo right from the start.

Archie acted as though he'd always known she would turn up, sooner or later. He welcomed her with warmth, took her arm in a fatherly way as he showed her around the main building of Old Harbour and introduced her to his staff, and insisted she must feel free to join in any of the classes, since by agreeing to act as Silas's model she was doing everyone at the sanctuary, staff and guests alike, a huge favour.

Jo was aware of Silas following them as Archie led her round the house. Glancing at him briefly once or twice, she noticed he was smiling.

As they continued on their progression, a short, comfortable-looking woman of around fifty emerged from what looked like an office, a sheaf of forms in her hand. Her greying brown hair was bundled up in a loose bun, into which she had stuck a pencil. She wore a black long-sleeved tee shirt and trousers, and over them a white overall, unbuttoned.

'Archie, we need to ...' Noticing Jo, she stopped. 'Hello!' she said. The preoccupied expression on her round face turned into a smile.

Archie introduced them. 'Helly, this is Jo. She's going to sit for Silas, for ...'

'For the Sea Room fresco. Yes, I can see.' She stared at Jo more intently.

'Jo, this is Helly Dunbar,' Archie went on. 'She is the mother ship of Old Harbour, she is intuitive and kind, and one of the most sensitive yet constructive healers of the troubled that I have ever met.'

Helly raised an eyebrow. 'Bloody hell, Arch, give me a totally unrealistic build-up, why don't you? Nice to meet you, Jo. Hope you can swim. I'll bring the forms round later, Archie. I can see you're busy just now.'

She spun round and dived back into the office.

'Come along, Jo,' Archie said, 'there's the yoga room, the physio unit and the meditation hall to show you yet!'

There seemed to be quite a few guests in residence, engaged in various activities, for some of the rooms that Archie wanted to show her had their doors firmly closed. From behind one of them floated out soft, wandering notes of music; instruments that made strange sounds blended with human voices, and there was a deep, repeated humming note underneath it all that seemed to come right up through the ground. 'Tibetan meditation,' Archie whispered.

They emerged into a long narrow hallway that ran along the far end of the house and appeared to be the junction between the original building and a new extension. The sound of the sea was suddenly loud. Archie pointed along the passage to where a door stood open a crack. He stopped, took both of Jo's hands and said, 'That's the last room, but I'll leave Silas to show it to you.' He turned to Silas. 'Coming over for dinner?'

'Yes please, Archie.'

Archie nodded. 'Then I shall see you both later.'

As he strode away, Silas said, 'Come on,' and, turning right, led the way down the hall to the partly-open door on the left .

He pushed it open, bent to take his boots off – Jo did the same – and they stepped into the room.

It was huge, and the impression of size was increased by the fact that there was virtually nothing in it. The floor was light oak; wide boards that shone with the soft sheen only decades of soft-soled or bare-footed traffic could bestow. The walls and ceiling were very pale – either white or off-white. There was an amazing sense of space.

The largest wall faced east, and it was made almost entirely of glass. Padding over to it, Jo was astonished to discover that she was immediately above the water; the sea washed right up to the base of the wall some way below, and its movement made constant bright reflections that played against the white walls and ceiling.

She stood entranced; hypnotised, almost, by the sea's rhythms.

After a moment, she sensed Silas beside her.

He said quietly, 'You see why it's called the Sea Room.'

'Of course,' she murmured.

He pointed to the wall opposite the glass. 'The fresco's going there,' he said. 'It'll be a deep band, about a third of the way down.' She followed his pointing hand. 'The band will narrow as it turns the corner onto the two adjoining walls, gradually fading away to ripples, or ribbons of seaweed – I haven't decided yet – then to nothing.'

She nodded. She could see what he meant. In a strange split second, she thought she could see the design, spreading across the white walls, bright emerald, turquoise, and a soft, greenish-blue so pale that it was hardly there at all.

179

'The figure will be faint, hinted at rather than clearly defined,' he went on. 'I want to make it so that the viewer sometimes sees it, sometimes can't find it, so that they wonder if it's an illusion.'

'You like a challenge,' she observed.

He smiled. 'I do.'

She was entranced.

And she felt very slightly afraid, although she didn't know why.

'When do we start at the pool?' she asked. Her voice was too brisk, too business-like, and she wished she could recall the words and try again.

But perhaps he too had sensed the presence of danger, for he answered in the same tone. 'Tomorrow, if you're happy with that?'

'Yes.'

'I've checked with Helly, and we can have the pool for most of the morning.'

'Okay.'

They went back out into the hall. As they put their boots on, Jo said, 'Helly?'

'Her name's Helga, but she's always called Helly.'

'And she's one of the – healers? Practitioners? What do you call them?'

'Archie just calls them his people, but I suppose practitioners describes them best.'

'They'll be there at dinner?'

'Some of them, yes, as well as the guests who choose to eat in the refectory this evening.'

'Refectory?'

He glanced at her, chuckling. 'Don't look so worried,' he said. 'I have the feeling you still half believe I've lured you into some weird cult that's secretly an enclosed order, but you have my solemn word that Old Harbour is just what I told you it was.' He paused, adding softly, 'Jo, it's a *good* place.'

The frisson of alarm was back, but ruthlessly she suppressed it. Determined to control whatever element of her mind was threatening to run away, she said brightly, 'Do we have to dress for dinner?'

The answer had been no, definitely not, which was just as well, Jo thought later in her room in Tern Cottage, because the only alternative to jeans and a sweater was another pair of jeans and a different top. She smoothed out her navy linen shirt on her bed and decided that it had survived her packing pretty well. She put on a necklace of jade beads that a member of her father's far-flung family had sent home from Hong Kong, and the bright green lifted the dark shade of the shirt. She brushed her hair, put on some lipstick, then wiped it off again. Lipstick, she thought, was probably too frivolous for Old Harbour.

She was just wondering if dinner in the refectory would be all earnest conversations and deeply correct food, when she heard the door to the cottage open and Silas's voice calling up the stairs.

Dinner was a revelation.

Silas had said they didn't dress for dinner, but a more accurate answer would have been didn't *have* to dress for dinner. Most people hadn't bothered; one young woman who'd been introduced to Jo as an art therapist seemed to have come straight from one of her classes, with paint on her hands and wearing a garment that looked like a hessian smock. But in contrast there were many who had changed into something a good deal smarter. An intense-looking man with a shock of white hair and badly bitten fingernails wore a dark grey suit that must have cost four figures; a large woman with red-rimmed eyes wore a long-skirted, rose-coloured taffeta gown that was so well cut it made you overlook the fact that she was considerably overweight; two women

181

in their twenties, who held hands unless eating made it impractical, wore identical outfits that undoubtedly bore designer labels; a painfully thin man of around thirty wore a Chinese-style tunic made of heavy, glossy black silk.

The food was delicious. Some of the twenty or so people round the long table were vegetarian; some, like Jo, didn't eat meat but ate fish; a couple were vegan; many ate the roast lamb served up as the main course. And to her relief there was wine: a choice of red or white, and the white was, she found, very good.

The conversation swelled as people ate and drank, and there was much laughter. A man sitting up at Archie's end of the table told a joke, and as the appreciation died away Silas leaned close to her and said, 'And there were you, imagining we'd sit in silence while someone stood at a lectern reading improving literature from an ancient leather-bound book with thin pages and very small print.'

She laughed. It was pretty much what she had imagined.

The meal ended with coffee, and everyone got up and, carrying their cups, began to circulate. Jo found herself next to the large woman in the rose taffeta gown.

'You're new, aren't you?' the woman said, with a faint note of accusation.

Having no idea whether or not it was all right to say what she was there for, Jo just said, 'Yes. I arrived this morning.' Good grief, was it only this morning?

The woman's expression had eased into something friendlier. 'I thought so!' She patted Jo's hand. 'I have problems with my short term memory,' she added disarmingly. 'I do this exercise where I make myself remember everyone's faces and do a sort of mental check regarding who I've seen already and who's new, so I'm so glad I was right about you, and that you haven't been here for ages!' She laughed. 'Do you like it?'

'I do,' Jo said with total honesty.

The large woman was studying her. 'They'll help you, if you let them,' she said kindly.

'But …' But I don't need help, she had almost said.

I do, she thought. I need a break from my life, and it seems I'm going to get it.

She and the large woman had been joined by a thin man in jeans and a loose-fitting checked shirt. 'I'm Phil,' he said, holding out a hand to Jo. 'I know who you are,' he murmured quietly to her. 'I do aromatherapy,' he went on aloud, 'and …'

'And he's marvellous!' the large woman interrupted. 'I used to think it was pure indulgence, but I was wrong.'

'So kind,' Phil murmured.

Phil and the large woman got into a fairly intense conversation about the benefits of jasmine oil, and Jo wandered away. She put down her empty coffee cup and staggered slightly. It made her realise how tired she was.

'You can leave whenever you want,' Silas said, appearing beside her.

'Now?' she said with a smile.

'Yes.' He looked over the intervening heads to Archie, over by the fireplace with the two young women in designer outfits, and Archie, understanding, waved a casual hand in farewell.

Then they were outside in the night air, and it was as cold, as fresh and as exhilarating as icy champagne.

Silas walked down to Tern Cottage with her, waiting while she put on a couple of lights. 'You'll be okay?' he asked.

'I'll be fine.'

'There's tea and coffee and some breakfast cereals in the kitchen cupboard and a pint of milk in the fridge,' he said. 'I'll come and knock on the door at half past nine, if that's all right?'

'Okay.'

'Night, Jo.'

'Night, Silas.'

In a daze – or maybe it was a trance, for Old Harbour seemed to be that sort of place – she undressed, paid a perfunctory visit to the bathroom and then went upstairs to bed. Through the open window right beside her, she could hear the sea.

A dozen strands of thought ran through her head.

One by one she imagined herself gently winding them up and carefully laying them aside. Don't think, she told herself.

Quite soon she was falling into sleep.

The water in the pool was blue and inviting. It was also, Jo found to her relief the next morning when she dipped her hand in it, quite warm.

She and Silas stood on the pool's edge.

'What do you want me to do?' she asked eventually; he seemed to be somewhere deep in his imagination, and he hadn't yet given her much idea of her purpose.

He turned to look at her. 'I've brought a wet suit,' he said. 'It's in the changing room over there.' He pointed across the pool. 'The pool's warm, as you've just found out'–- he must have seen her bend down to test it – 'but you'll be in there quite a while, and not moving as vigorously as you would be if you were swimming hard. You're okay with a wet suit?'

'Yes.' She hesitated. 'Ben and I used to go diving.'

He made no comment, but the look he gave her suggested he understood. 'Good,' he said. 'That's good. Also I need to see how fabric behaves under water when you move around, so there's a long garment made of long strips of thin silk, and if you could put that on somehow, that'd be great.'

'A wet suit and a floaty garment?' she said.

'I want to give the impression that your body's made of silver,' he replied. 'I don't think there's any such thing as a silver wet suit, but the outline – the silhouette – is more important than the colour.'

'Okay.' She walked off towards the changing room.

It had been a long time since she last put on a wet suit. Ben was vivid in her mind. She thought of yesterday, and Silas saying love hangs around. She smiled, and whispered, 'Hi, Ben.'

She reached over her shoulder and zipped herself up. There was a long mirror on the wall; she glanced at herself. Her shoulders were very square – too square, she always thought – and surely not very much like a sea spirit. Her waist was still apparent, even after two children, and she'd come to terms with the slight bulge of her stomach that all the post-natal exercises in the world hadn't got rid of.

Turning away, she picked up the swirl of pale green and deep blue silk that lay across the bench along the wall. She flung it up over her head and watched it float gently down. She began to get an idea of what Silas had in mind.

Eager suddenly, she went out to join him.

At first, it was difficult.

He had gone down into the room whose windows looked out into the depths of the pool. Although she could see him quite well – her eyes had stung fiercely at first as she opened them to the salt water, but she was over it now – he was blurred, and she couldn't read his expression. After quite a lot of trial and error, they evolved a system of signals, and then everything was much better.

It only occurred to her afterwards that they had worked out their sign language without words: he had remained where he was, in the room with the windows, and she had stayed in the water.

She found she could hold her breath for longer and longer intervals, making her lungs work hard and pushing out every breath in a slowly diminishing stream of bubbles. Self-conscious to begin with, soon the simple joy of being in the water, of having it support her while she twisted and turned in increasingly ambitious shapes, took her over. She did forward rolls, back flips, and invented a long, sinuous movement where she went over in a backwards roll while simultaneously going from being on her back to being on her front. Silas liked that one, so she went to the surface for a short breather and then did it again. As she turned, she caught glimpses of the silk, floating and twisting behind her as if it was alive.

Sometime later she swam to the side of the pool, laid her arms on the stone surround and rested her head on them. She was exhausted. The fine silk hanging from her shoulders was waterlogged and felt heavy now, and she reached down to haul it out of the water.

He was there, helping her. He took the fabric out of her hands and bundled it up, squeezing out the water. 'Thank you,' he said. 'You were amazing.'

'Oh, good,' she gasped.

'Coming out?'

She looked up at him. 'I'm not sure I've got the energy to swim to the steps.'

So he reached down, put his hands on her ribs and lifted her out.

'Crikey, you're stronger than you look!' she said. 'I'm no lightweight.'

'You're perfect,' he replied. 'Perfect for a sea spirit,' he went on quickly. 'I didn't want a thin, insubstantial body. I imagine beings of the sea are strong and lithe, and for sure they don't look like fashion models.'

She had been sitting on the pool's edge, and now she stood up. Her legs were shaky. Noticing, he took her arm. 'Are you okay?'

'Yup.'

The air seemed to thrum with something she didn't understand. She needed to get away. 'I'm going to get dressed,' she said.

'Right.'

She turned back as she went over to the changing room.

He was staring right at her.

The days took on a pattern. They had more sessions at the pool, none as long as the first one. But there was a certain movement that Silas was trying to capture – where she came out of a dive and swam straight towards him, arms wide open, back bent and her hips and legs curving up behind her – and he drew it over and over again.

They also spent long mornings in his studio, and as he worked they talked.

It was almost like talking to yourself, she thought. Sitting on her stool, sometimes with the soft blanket over her legs, she could almost forget there was another person the other side of the easel; another human mind thinking, remembering, feeling.

Almost.

He talked about himself. With extreme reluctance, and only after she had pointed out that it was his turn now since she had pretty much taken him through the entire story of her life. She'd left quite a lot out, but she had the strange sense that he was well aware of it and knew why.

He came from a family of five children. His parents were hard working, almost rigidly conventional, and she sensed they had neither understood nor appreciated their middle child. His two older brothers had gone for what he called parent-appeasing jobs, one a finance clerk in a hotel chain, the other following the parental example and becoming a salesman in the same company that employed his father. Silas's sisters were both married with children, housewives like their mother before them. Silas had joined the army at eighteen, worked his way up to a commission and then gone into some branch that he referred to only obliquely and that Jo guessed must be intelligence.

Whatever happened during those years in the service had led him to a total life change when he came out, when he had turned a hobby into a job and become a painter.

'I went travelling,' his quiet voice went on, 'and when I was in the wilds of Greece I heard about the monastery with the decaying frescoes.'

'Where you stayed for seven years,' she said.

He smiled. 'I did.' A brief pause, then: 'I came home to Old Harbour and Archie said my grandfather's house needed a bit of attention – which was an understatement if ever there was one – and I've been here ever since.'

'Do you see your family?' She wasn't sure if she should have asked, but he didn't seem to mind.

'Oh, yes. My father died a couple of years ago, but we'd made our peace some time before. I used to go and sit by his bed, reading. My mother hasn't much time for me, neither have my brothers, but my sisters keep in touch and the younger one – she's called Rosie – sometimes brings her kids and comes to stay.' He looked up, studied her for a few moments and then looked down at his canvas. 'She's divorced and bringing up her two children on her own, so she's done me a favour by replacing me as the outcast child in our mother's eyes.'

Jo watched his face as he talked. Neither his tone nor his expression showed any sign of bitterness; if anything, his mother's intransigence seemed to be a cause of gentle amusement.

She said impulsively, 'I'm sure she loves you, both of you, really. She wouldn't bother to make her disapproval so obvious if she didn't.'

He smiled. 'How perceptive,' he murmured.

Late the next day they had another pool session. Silas had almost got the image he wanted but he asked her to perform the move several more times, quite clearly focussing on it to the exclusion of everything else.

When at last he was satisfied, she swam to the side of the pool, breathless, tired and slightly dizzy. Coming up from the viewing room to find her, he was instantly apologetic.

'Jo, I should have noticed!' he said. 'Are you all right?'

'Yes! Stop fussing.' She clambered out and took off the silk rags, and he wrapped her in a huge towel. Beneath it she stripped off the wet suit, handing it to him.

'Go and have a hot shower while I deal with this,' he said, 'then come along to the house and I'll have tea ready and fix you something to eat.'

It sounded good. She nodded, then hurried off to Tern Cottage. She had a very hot shower, washed the salt water out of her hair then quickly dried it and dressed in jeans, tee shirt and fleece.

She went into Silas's kitchen. A big mug of tea stood ready on the old pine table, and as she sat down he put a plate of marmite toast in front of her.

She always did marmite toast for Ed and Sammie when they got home from swimming.

The sight and the smell of it took her straight home. Her sons leapt out at her, hugging her, Ed's stern expression and sudden illuminating smile, Sammie's sticky buttery kiss on her cheek, and she put her hands over her face to hold back the emotion.

She was aware of Silas coming to sit beside her. He put an arm round her, holding her close. After a while he said, 'What is it?'

She thought, it's Hal, and how he's such hard bloody work, and how he's there in our lives, the boys' and mine, but *not* there, because he's not really engaged with us, his mind only sparks alive when he's working, or off travelling to research something; so that home, and the whole package that contains two boys and a wife, and domesticity, comes a very poor second.

And, just as she had done with Max, she thought despairingly, how do you explain Hal to someone who doesn't know him?

She did her best. She told Silas how she and Hal had met, how she'd fallen deeply in love with him, how they'd got married and set off to travel together, the two of them and Ed the little boy who was still called Teddy, how she'd found she was pregnant when they'd only got as far as Rhodes and everything had changed.

Silas didn't say anything. He went on holding her, and his warm presence was both very comforting and somehow familiar.

After puzzling over this sense of familiarity for a while, she suddenly thought, he reminds me of Ben.

And in the same instant she felt that flash of warning that she'd sensed before, only now it was accompanied by a huge surge of joyful relief.

He gave her a hug, then stood up and moved away, going to sit down on the opposite side of the table. A quiet peace seemed to fill the kitchen. Into it he said, 'Stay here a while. Be in the serenity. Treat it as a break from reality.'

Then, so softly she wasn't sure she'd heard right, 'Be with me.'

Chapter 14

She didn't pause to consider if it was sensible, or right, or wise; or if she should be packing her bag and running across the causeway from Old Harbour as swiftly as she could, leaping into her car and flooring the accelerator until she was far away.

She stayed.

Two more days, she thought that Wednesday night as she lay in her bed in Tern Cottage. Then on Saturday I'll go home.

She wasn't going to think about that until Saturday came.

Silas knew she'd soon be gone and he worked flat out at capturing her while he could. Then, late on Thursday, he said, 'I'm done. I've got all I need, and next week I'll start putting the images on the Sea Room wall.'

I won't be here, she thought dismally. I won't see it.

He picked up her thought. He always seemed to know when she was sad.

He came over to her, took her hand and helped her stand up; sitting still for so long at a time made her stiff. 'We'll go over to the refectory for dinner, we'll be polite, friendly, sociable. Then we'll return to our respective beds and tomorrow we'll be on our own. No work, no other people, just us. All day.'

She looked up into his eyes. Just for a moment, his expression was unguarded, and she saw how much it meant to him. And to me, she thought wildly. Oh God, and to me.

It's just a day, she thought, just one day.

She said huskily, 'Yes.'

He was waiting for her outside Tern Cottage early the next morning. He wore walking boots, a waxed jacket over jeans and a sweater, and carried a rucksack. She looked at the rucksack as she laced up her boots.

'Are we going far?' she asked.

'We're going over there.' He pointed north to Lindisfarne, steadily materialising out of the early morning mist. 'We'll walk over as soon as the walkers' way is clear of water, like the pilgrims have done for centuries, then wait for this evening's low tide and come back again.'

'It's quite a long way.'

'It's the mist, it's deceptive. Come on.' He held out his hand.

She took it and stood up.

They discovered within about half a mile that they walked well together. It makes for harmony, Jo thought, when you fall naturally in step with someone and they walk at exactly the pace you'd have chosen if you were on your own.

They reached the car park on the mainland – her Discovery was still there, precisely as she had left it, but she didn't want to look at it, didn't want to think about getting into it the next day and driving away – and turned along the coastal track towards the north. After two or three miles they came to the Pilgrims' Crossing, and the beginning of the pedestrians' path was already visible. They waited, and presently another couple joined them, then a young man on his own. But all of them seemed to understand that this wasn't a time for casual chatter or remarks about the weather.

Jo looked out across the stretch of water that was still keeping Lindisfarne an island. She looked at the road, a short distance away and still under water, bare of traffic. There were some refuges set out along it, set up high on stilts. Silas was still holding her hand. She leaned her shoulder against his.

The Pilgrims' Crossing to Lindisfarne took hours. But the going was easy, apart from frequently having to splash through muddy water. Jo got her second wind about a third of the way across, and she and Silas increased their pace. They'd had frequent drinks from the water bottles in Silas's rucksack, and now and then he'd given her a sweetie 'to keep you going'. By the time they climbed up onto the island, she was ravenous.

They sat on a rocky outcrop and ate a huge picnic. They heard seals, and they saw so many different types of sea birds that Jo lost count. She let her eyes run back over the crossing.

He said, 'We'll catch the bus back.'

'I can walk!' she protested.

He smiled. 'I'm sure, but if we have to allow the time, we won't be able to look round the island.'

'Oh, well, in that case …'

He laughed and gave her a chocolate biscuit.

They went to the priory and paid their respects to St Aidan, the torch of peace in his hand. They went up to the castle, wandering round almost in silence, very aware of each other. They had a cup of tea and a scone in a little tea room. Then it was time to catch the bus back to the mainland. Sitting beside Silas, feeling as close to him, as familiar with him as if she'd known him for ever, Jo had no idea how she was going to leave him.

They walked back across the path to Old Harbour as the waters of the rising tide began to lap across it. By unspoken agreement, they didn't go to the refectory for dinner, instead eating a simple meal in Silas's kitchen. Neither of them had much appetite.

'I don't want you to go,' he said at one point.

'I know. But you know I am going.'

'Of course I do.'

They sat on opposite sides of the table, eyes intent on each other's. 'I …' she began.

But he shook his head. 'Don't say it,' he said swiftly. Then, because he sensed she was hurt, 'There's no need.'

It was dark now, and the wind was rising outside. Presently rain began to hurl itself against the windows, and the noise of the sea grew very loud.

Silas got up and put pillows and blankets on the big sofa by the fire, drawing it out so that it made a bed. Then he came over to her, his hand resting lightly on top of her head.

He said, 'I've been celibate for years, so when I say I can sleep on the sofa beside you without making love, please believe that I mean it. I know you're married, that you have a husband and two children whom you love very much, and that anything physical between us is not possible.' He stopped abruptly, but she had already heard the pain in his voice. 'But I don't think I can bear to be apart from you tonight.'

She didn't say a word. She simply stood up, hugged him and moved across to the sofa.

She barely slept, and she didn't think he did either. They talked for hours, about anything that came into their heads. They tried not to

195

speak about the extraordinary thing that had happened between them, and in the main they succeeded.

She woke as it was getting light, from a sleep that, from the scratchy-eyed way she now felt, was deeply inadequate as a preparation for the long drive home. But I have to go, she thought. It would be unbearable to stay.

She was lying in front of him, and his body was curled round hers. They were both still almost fully dressed. One of his hands was twisted in her hair. Carefully, she moved out of his arms and stood up. Her legs felt weak. She bent down to him, and, as he stirred, whispered, 'I'm going along to the cottage to have a shower and pack.

He didn't speak, but simply nodded.

She felt she had to hurry; dragging out this awful goodbye would be far too painful. He was waiting for her when she came out of Tern Cottage, and together they walked across the island, past the main house and over the path. It wasn't quite clear of water but it would do.

'Will you say goodbye to Archie and the others for me?' she said as they splashed up onto the shore.

'Yes.'

She unlocked the Discovery and put her bag in the back. She turned to him. He had tears in his eyes. She blinked away her own.

'I don't know what to say,' she said, her voice breaking.

He shook his head. 'Say nothing.' He leaned forward and, very gently, for the first and only time, he kissed her.

Then she got into the car, started the engine, drove away.

She looked back, just once.

The sight of him standing there alone was almost too much.

She put the radio on and tuned in to a music station. She drove with the window partly open. She made herself focus on the road, ruthlessly concentrating and blocking out everything else.

She stopped at noon for a cup of coffee and tried to eat a sandwich. It made her feel sick.

She took a turning she hadn't intended to and got onto the M11 instead of the A1M, but it didn't matter, they both led south.

By early afternoon she knew she was going to have to stop for a while. Her eyes were prickling with fatigue, with the after images of a thousand cars coming towards her. Tiredness kills, the signs on the gantries reminded her. She smiled grimly. I might feel at rock bottom, she thought, but I don't want to die.

She started seeing signs to Cambridge. She knew her way to Max's house; would it be okay to call in and beg a cup of tea and an hour or so's break from the drive? He might even ask her to stay the night, which would be fine provided she made an early start in the morning. Ed was coming home in the afternoon, and she had to fetch Sammie and Hal – oh, Hal – from Gatwick at midday.

Heartened at the thought of seeing Max, she signalled and left the motorway.

She drove in busy stop-start traffic through the outskirts of the city, turning into the square between Midsummer Common and an open space quaintly called Christ's Pieces.

She drove past his house. There was no sign of his car, but the little street was a no parking zone. She drove on and found a multi storey in a nearby shopping centre. She paid for a ticket up until the time that parking was free, then, thinking optimistically that it wasn't far to come back for her bag if he insisted she stay the night, went off to find him.

His house was in a terrace, the houses well-kept and prosperous-looking. Each had a tiny front garden separated from the pavement by a low brick wall topped with black-painted iron railings, and each had a door with a window beside it and two more windows above. The doors were different colours, and Max's was yellow.

She raised the knocker and let it fall with a thump.

She heard footsteps and he opened the door. His expression on seeing her was at first delighted, then something else flashed across his face. He said, surely too loudly, 'Jo! What a nice surprise!' and then, after an almost imperceptible pause, he stood back and invited her in.

'I'm driving home from the north east but I got on the M11 by mistake, and as I was passing I thought I'd call in,' she said as he showed her along the hall and into the minimally furnished, sunny room that looked out over a walled garden. 'I'm ...'

He wasn't alone.

There was a woman sitting on the sofa. She was around Jo's age, with reddish fair hair cut in a long, glossy bob. She wore glasses, behind which her eyes were grey and clear. She was dressed in a silky shirt and well-cut trousers, and she was looking up at Jo with the residue of horror on her face.

She quickly smoothed her expression, stood up and held out her hand. 'Hello, I'm Angela,' she said brightly.

'Jo,' Jo responded.

'Jo's my cousin's wife,' Max said, standing close beside her. 'You remember, I was staying with them before the trip to Brittany?'

Angela said 'Hal! Yes!' quite loudly, just as Max turned back to Jo.

'Angela came to France with me,' he went on. 'She's been a great help in finding out about my forebears, and we've made a lot of progress in a few days.'

198

'Oh!' Jo said. 'Do you live in Cambridge?' she asked Angela. She was puzzled, wondering why Max hadn't mentioned he'd have company on his trip.

And, adding to the puzzlement, Angela didn't seem to know if she lived in Cambridge or not. 'Er ...' she said, staring frantically at Max as if for help.

Slowly a deep flush was spreading up her throat and into her cheeks. She was biting her lip.

'She's about to move here,' Max said. He had what looked to Jo like rather a fixed smile on his face.

'I see. Where from?' Jo asked.

Max said 'West Sussex' at exactly the same moment that Angela said 'Gloucestershire.' Then Max embarked on a complicated explanation about Angela having moved into rented accommodation in West Sussex but having a house of her own in the Forest of Dean, looking hopefully at Jo as if desperate for her to say 'I see' and drop it.

'I see,' she said, managing a smile.

West Sussex.

I'm in West Sussex, not Antarctica.

And just now, when Max had said Jo was Hal's wife, this woman had said, Hal! Yes! as if she knew him.

But Max didn't mention Hal's name, so how did she know?

Did she know Hal?

In a series of flashes like images illuminated by a strobe light Jo saw Hal when he'd come back from Wiltshire. No, not Wiltshire, West Sussex. Not Antarctica either. She saw Hal looking sick, disconsolate, deeply distressed. Hal turning to stare at her as if he'd forgotten she was there; forgotten who she was. Hal half-awake in the middle of the night and looking at her with his face full of love, only to turn away when he saw who she was.

199

Hal standing in the garden at Copse Hill House speaking intently to Max - Max - about something he clearly didn't want her to overhear.

And now here was Max with a woman called Angela who had said Hal! Yes!

Suddenly Jo felt sick and light-headed. Her knees felt odd.

Max was looking at her anxiously, clearly waiting for her to respond to whatever he'd just said, only she had no idea what it had been. She tried to think back to what it was she'd last said … I see.

And then she rather thought she did see.

Don't think about it now, she told herself silently. You can't stay here, not even for a cup of tea, not now. You've probably got it all wrong and everything's fine, but you must leave. You have to get home, and there's still a long way to go.

Don't think.

She turned to Max and said politely, 'I won't stay, I'm clearly disturbing you, and …'

'You're not!' they both insisted. Max's eyes on her held embarrassment, but she also saw profound sympathy. Don't be kind, she thought. If you are, I can't do this. For an instant his face merged with Silas's as he'd stood there in the car park, watching her drive away. She swallowed a sob, and it came out sounding like a burp. She giggled. She was close to … hysteria? Breakdown?

She pulled herself firmly under control.

'Nice to meet you, Angela,' she said. 'Max, I'm sure we'll be seeing you soon.'

He came with her to the front door. 'I wish you'd stay, Jo,' he said quietly. 'You look all in.'

'I'll be fine!' she said.

He looked at her anxiously. 'Call me when you get in?'

'Okay! Bye, Max.'

She hurried away. She stumbled at the corner, then ran on in case he'd seen and came after her. She ran all the way to the multi storey, then got into her car and drove away.

The journey back to Copse Hill House was horrible. It was Saturday, which was about the only good thing because traffic was lighter than on a weekday late in the afternoon.

She adopted the same method of fierce concentration on the road that she'd used all the way from Old Harbour to Cambridge. Now it wasn't leaving Silas she was trying to button up – he was a welcome relief now and she turned to him as if he could come to her through the medium of her thoughts and hold her hand – but Hal.

She found herself muttering, over and over again, 'You bastard, Hal.'

But then the other part of her mind would remind her repressively that he might not be – probably wasn't, almost certainly wasn't – a bastard at all.

Innocent until proven guilty, she thought as she went through the Dartford Tunnel. Heaps of women live in West Sussex, and there's no sensible reason to leap to the conclusion that Hal went to see the one who now seems to be staying with Max. Who went to Brittany with Max. Who said 'Hal! Yes!' when his name was mentioned and flushed a deep, awkward red. But how did Max meet her? Had he arranged all along for her to go with him? He'd have mentioned it, surely he would.

So what happened?

As she got onto the A21 she thought again about Hal and Max out in the garden, just before Max left. She'd thought Hal looked quite fierce.

What if he'd been telling Max to go to see Angela? What if Max had had no intention of taking anyone away with him but Hal told him he had to?

But that made no sense, because if Hal was involved with her, why on earth would he send Max to look her up and persuade her to go to Brittany with him?

How did Hal know Angela? If he did. He might not!

That was such a good thought, such a reassuring, sensible thought, that she said it aloud. 'He might not!'

But if he did know her, maybe she was just an acquaintance, and Hal had simply remarked casually to Max that he might look her up if he was nearby, and then Max and Angela had liked the look of each other and they decided they'd go to Brittany together.

She wished she could believe it, but she had to admit to herself that as a comfortable, comforting theory it was full of holes. For one thing, there was just far too much awkwardness and secrecy hanging about. Max and Angela had looked aghast at having Jo suddenly arrive, Angela in particular. And even if there had been an explanation for that – maybe they'd been in the middle of a particularly earnest conversation – there was the huge obstacle of Hal. Who, however Jo looked at it and tried to explain away the oddities of his recent behaviour, was simply not himself.

So what was she to think?

She was nearly home now. Flimwell, and the slowest traffic lights in the known world, then a few more miles, and at last she'd be able to stop driving.

Did Hal know Angela? Had he known her for years? Had he slipped away specifically to go and see her? To stay with her in her house in West Sussex or Gloucestershire – West Sussex, he'd been in West Sussex, damn it, he bloody well said so! – and was this just the latest of many visits?

Her mind couldn't take in the implications of that. She was exhausted, her shoulders ached, she longed to lie down in a dark bedroom and go to sleep, but she didn't think sleep would come easily tonight.

She was angry, she was full of wildly conflicting emotions, all of them painful, and she had no idea what was happening to her world.

Had Hal been with Angela? Her mind shied away from a more potent verb.

Had he?

'I don't know!' she cried aloud. 'I don't bloody know!'

The echo of her furious words bounced around the car, but nobody answered the question.

Chapter 15

Hal

He knew, from the moment he saw her waiting at Gatwick arrivals, that something had happened.

She was pale, her eyes were sunk in dark circles and, even in the week or so since he'd seen her, she looked thinner. She'd made an effort, though; her long fair hair shone in the garish light, and she wore her new jeans and a black leather jacket over a green shirt that picked up the colour of her eyes. Seeing Sammie rushing towards her, she gave a cry and hurried to meet him, her face alight with love. She'd only given Hal the swiftest of glances, as if simply verifying his presence.

'Hi, kid,' he said to her, putting a hand on her arm.

She looked up from her intense concentration on Sammie, who was attempting to tell her about Sam's boat, the friends' catamaran and Sort-of-Grandma Mary's chocolate fudge cheesecake all at once, and her eyes stared intently into his. She said neutrally, 'Hal. Hello. Good flight?'

'It was a flight,' he replied. Then, to Sammie, 'Come on, Sammie, let's get out of here.'

Sammie chattered all the way from the terminal to the car park, and when Jo spoke it was to exclaim at something he was telling her. She unlocked the car and waited while Hal unloaded the luggage. She got into the driver's seat, drumming her fingers on the steering wheel, and he realised with a drop of the heart that she wasn't doing what she usually did at airports, which was to take the trolley back while he stowed the bags. So he did it himself.

It unnerved him.

'You can take the front seat, son,' he said to Sammie as the boy ran to meet him, still talking. 'You have a deal to tell your mother, and it'll be easier if you're sitting next to her.'

Sammie gave a whoop of delight, front seat privileges being rare and hardly ever happening when his father was in the car.

Hal made himself comfortable in the back. Jo set off, negotiating the carpark and the airport roads with her usual efficiency, and presently they were on the M3, heading for the M25 and home. He glanced over her shoulder at the speedometer and noticed she was driving faster than usual.

He wondered if it was significant.

He wished he could go to sleep. He was worn out, and this tension was making him edgy. But she'd agreed to meet them, he ought to show his gratitude by being civil and joining in the conversation. Straining forward against the seatbelt, he picked up on what Sammie was currently talking about and raked through his mind for an interesting and pertinent contribution.

'We're home,' said Jo's voice.

Hal rocketed awake. His mouth was open and unpleasantly dry and he guessed he'd been snoring. His neck was stiff. He unfolded his long legs and got out of the car. 'Right. Sorry. Have I been asleep long?'

'All the way, practically.' Then, her voice changing – thawing – 'Come on inside, Sammie, I'll see to your bag and you can take your souvenirs up to your room and start thinking how you're going to display them.'

'Cool! Will you come and help me?'

'Yes, soon as I've got a wash on. Ed's due home soon and he'll have a mountain of sweaty rugby kit to be done.'

'Can I help?' Hal asked, following her through to the utility room, his bag in his hand.

'Yup. Sort out what's for the wash and stick it in with Sammie's.'

'Do we have to go and pick Ed up? I could ...'

'No, George's mother's dropping him off.'

She was pouring soap powder in the tray, and as he reached out and put a last pair of dirty socks in the drum, she almost slammed the door on his hand.

Oh, boy, he thought.

The remainder of the day went by. Ed was as full of his week as Sammie was his, although in a relatively restrained thirteen-year -old way rather than as an excited and slightly over-tired child of eight. But the boys had done Hal a favour by being so keen to talk about what they'd been doing since, unable to get a word in, he hadn't had to join the ongoing conversation.

As they had a six o'clock supper – Jo was insistent that it was a school day tomorrow so everyone was having an early night – Ed turned to her and said, 'What did you do, Mum? Did you have a nice week?'

'Bet you missed us!' Sammie said.

'Of course I missed you,' she said. 'But not that much, to be honest, because I didn't stay here pining for you, I went on a trip of my own.'

'I knew that!' Sammie said, looking at his brother smugly. 'You phoned Grandpa Sam and said you were in a hotel by the sea!'

'It was managed by a very bad-tempered and unwelcoming man with a red face and a big nose that looked as if someone had punched him,' she said – Hal listened with secret admiration as with such ease she turned a bald account into a story – 'who really would rather not have had guests at all, which was pretty silly for a hotelier, so I decided I would only stay for one night, and then I discovered an island that wasn't an island.' Her eyes were fixed on Sammie, who was obviously trying to work out her remark.

'Tidal,' Ed said in a superior tone. 'It was an island at low tide and not one at high tide.'

'Ten out of ten,' Jo said, grinning at him. Her face under the smile looked tense, Hal observed. 'You'll never guess what happened next.'

The boys suggested several fairly unlikely scenarios, ranging from the road to the island flooding under a particularly high tide so that she got stuck there (Ed) to a mist rolling in from the sea that concealed an alien space ship (Sammie). Jo laughed with them as the suggestions rapidly ran out of control, then she said, 'I said you'd never guess, which is obviously about right, so I'll have to tell you.' There was a tiny pause and then she announced, the smile firmly in place, 'I became an artist's model!'

'You?' Sammie gasped, and Ed, shooting her quick little glances as if trying to disguise the fact that he was looking at her, appeared to be even more amazed than if she said she'd done a parachute jump, which had been one of Sammie's other suggestions.

'Me,' she confirmed. 'The island settlement was called Old Harbour, and there was once a fleet of herring boats based there. There was a big house where people go who are recovering from an illness, or need some time to think, or just want a bit of peace and quiet. They do things like aromatherapy, massage, yoga and meditation, and they have this beautiful room with big windows right above the water that they call the Sea Room, and they're doing a fresco on the walls – that's a special sort of painting, Sammie, where you slap the paint onto wet plaster – and there was to be a sea spirit, and the person doing the painting said I looked right for it, and so before I knew where I was, I was sitting on a stool and swimming in a pool and being sketched for the preliminary drawings!'

She had made it sound like something pleasurable, light-hearted, an entertaining novelty. But Hal, who had been watching her face, saw something else in her eyes.

So what was it? Had she sat in on a meditation class and realised a few things? Confronted one or two facts about her own life – her life with him – that had needed distance and a quiet mind to emerge?

He hadn't thought he could be more apprehensive about what was going to happen when the boys went off to bed. He discovered he was wrong.

She took a long time. He heard bathwater running, then, later, running away. He heard voices, laughter, a snatch of song as Sammie began on one of the time-honoured bedtime favourites, its words considerably changed from when the boys were little and now quite a lot ruder.

Then everything went quiet.

He glanced at his watch.

Twenty-five minutes later he glanced at it again, just as Jo came down the stairs and into the living room. She closed the door.

'You took a while,' he remarked easily. 'Kids difficult to settle?'

'No, Sammie went out like a light and Ed was doing one continuous yawn. He - Ed - has got bruises all up his ribs but he says not to worry, they're just stud marks. He's actually quite proud of them.'

'Like a drink?'

She sank down onto the sofa, glancing at his gin and tonic. 'Yes, all right. Thanks, I'll have one of those.'

He went into the kitchen, returning with her drink. 'Cheers,' he said as she took a sip. A big sip, he noticed.

'Cheers.'

He had returned to the chair beside the fireplace, where he had been sitting. They were facing each other. He was about to ask some pretty meaningless question about this island sanctuary she'd found, when she spoke.

'I called in to see Max on the way back. I was tired and I got onto the M11 instead of the A1M, so as I was going right past I thought he might give me a restorative cup of tea to get me the rest of the way home.'

Okay, he thought. Talking about Max was okay.

'How did his trip to Brittany go?'

She was staring at him, her eyes narrowed slightly. 'It went well. He took somebody with him. A very striking woman called Angela. She was there with him.'

'She ... there at his house?' Shocked, his heart thumping furiously, he said the first thing that came into his head.

'At his house.'

'She ... who is she, a friend of his?'

Jo shrugged. 'I presume so, since she's just been to France for five days with him.' She went on boring into him with her eyes. 'I was quite surprised, though, that he hadn't mentioned he was taking someone with him while he was staying here. In fact,' – she put on a puzzled face, but he knew it was an act – 'I clearly recall him saying me and I when he was telling me what he planned to do.' Now the eyes were like two sharpened points of jade. 'Isn't that odd? Perhaps they met on the ferry, or at some interesting tourist site they both happened to be wandering round?'

He was thinking as hard as he'd ever done, trying to work out what she suspected, what she knew. He was also fervently hoping that the remark about meeting at a tourist site was no more than a lucky guess: it was precisely how Hal had first encountered Angela, at the Palace of Knossos on Crete. Later, his writer's imagination fired both by the other famous palace at Phaistos and Angela's presence there with him, he'd turned the relevant chapter of his book – his Minoan Thing – into an account of a sad and lonely woman walking round the Phaistos site in the company of an older and better-informed man.

He shrugged, muttered, 'Maybe.'

There was a silence, bristling and crackling with tension.

Then Jo said, 'Angela lives in West Sussex.'

He knew what was coming, even before she said it.

'That's where you were.' Her voice was low but perfectly audible. 'You said you were going to Wiltshire – the Marlborough Downs, Avebury, West Kennet, I believe you mentioned – but when I asked you on the phone if there was a doctor you could consult over your flu, you said you were in West Sussex not Antarctica.'

He made himself meet her eyes. 'Did I?'

'Yes.' She paused, still staring straight at him. 'And it was weird, because when Max introduced me as his cousin's wife she said "Hal! Yes!" as if she knew you.'

After a long pause, he sighed. I could lie to her, he thought, but it would mean bringing something into our life that hasn't been there before, something I'd have to stand by and maintain for ever. Even given that she believed me.

Or I could tell her the truth.

'I do know her,' he heard himself say. 'I met her when I went to Crete to research the Minoan Thing. We visited a few places, we enjoyed each other's company.' He drew a breath. 'Nothing happened. I think I kissed her once.'

'You *think* you kissed her,' she repeated. 'And these few visits to places, this enjoyment of her company, led to that odd chapter in the book. The one the critics said was unworthy of you, since near-fantasy had no place in a work of scholarship.'

'Fortunately for me, the opinion of the critics didn't stop the reading public from buying the book in their thousands,' he said caustically.

'Yes, how lucky was that?' she agreed.

He realised with a sudden chill that he had no idea what she was thinking.

'So, have you kept in touch with her since?' she asked.

'No. I saw something in one of the Sunday supplements – a piece about saving rural pubs – and her photo was in it. So that's how I found out where she lived, or, more accurately, where her local pub was.'

'And so you sought her out.'

'I wanted to give her a copy of the book!' he protested. Was that true? Had that been all he'd had in mind?

Her withering look told him she didn't believe him any more than he believed himself.

'So, you got ill, she nursed you, you started to feel better, you spent some convalescent days together and then, what, you came home?'

There was a spark of hope in her tone. He wished he could say, yes, that's how it happened.

He shook his head. 'I slept with her.'

He thought Jo gasped. Her hand had flown to cover her mouth. 'You – *Hal*.'

He went to get up, to go to her, take her in his arms, but she held out both her hands in a stop gesture. 'Stay there.' Her voice was icy.

'I've never …' he began, but she shook her head violently and wouldn't let him speak.

'So then what happened? Why the fuck did you send Max – Max! Clever, sensitive, astute Max – to seek her out?'

'I didn't.' His voice was suddenly loud. Then: 'Don't swear,' he added coldly.

Very clearly she said, 'Fuck, fuck, fuck, fuck.'

He glared at her. 'She left her wallet in my car. It had credit cards, cash, and I packed it up and went to post it the day I left for Dad's, but the damned post office was closed so I asked Max to post it for me. It had to go by registered post,' he added, as if it mattered now.

'So … what? He didn't post it but decided to deliver it himself?'

'I have no idea,' Hal said wearily. 'I guess so, yes.'

She nodded very slowly several times.

'And she – this Angela – looked out of her window and saw Max draw up, and so the woman you'd just shagged and left probably had the sudden optimistic hope that you'd changed your mind and were going back to her.'

He winced at her language. She saw – of course she saw, she was Jo – and murmured, 'Oh, dear, have I offended you?'

He knew he had to say something. Explain, apologise.

No words would come.

But then, in some awful sort of retaliatory gesture, he made the remarkably stupid decision to go on the attack.

'So what about you?' he said quietly. 'This island paradise, and posing for someone painting sea nymphs? Did you get your kit off, and did he like what he saw?'

He knew from her face that he'd hurt her, but at that moment he didn't understand how.

'When I was swimming in the pool I wore a wet suit. When we were in the studio I was in my ordinary clothes, quite often under a blanket, since sitting still tends to make you feel cold.'

'Yeah, okay, but …'

She raised her deathly white face and once more fixed her eyes on him. 'I liked him a lot. He was kind and sympathetic, and it would have been very easy to make love with him. But I didn't. We didn't. He kissed me goodbye' – her eyes filled with tears – 'just once, and I left.'

He knew she was telling him the truth.

He put his hands up over his face, rubbing hard at his eyes, sore and tired from long hours in the dry air of a plane. 'Jo, I shouldn't have slept with Angela,' he said. 'It's the first time, the only time, I've been unfaithful to you, and …'

'*First*! *Only*!' she shouted. 'You say that as if it's a good thing!'

She stood up, began furiously pacing up and down the room. Then, coming to a halt in front of him, she spun round and faced him. 'I used to think you and I were uniquely each other's – that you

213

were mine, and I was yours, and what we had was special, and both of us recognised it. But then … then you started to go away on your own – yes, okay, I'm sure you're going to say you were doing exactly what you said you were doing, and researching for your blasted books – and slowly I realised that you liked it. You liked being on your own, travelling without the complications of having your family with you, without the need to talk to me, to listen to me rattling on and when I stopped and waited expectantly for you to reply, you'd have no idea whatsoever of what I'd just been saying and you'd stand staring at me, looking slightly cross and I'd be furious with myself because I'd just interrupted something you wanted to think about, something that absorbed you so deeply that anything else – anybody else – was just a distraction.' She paused. Then, softly: 'I came to understand just how hard it was for you when you had to come home.'

'Not just hard,' he protested. 'It was good, too.'

She stared at him for a long moment. 'I think I've known for some time that what I thought we had doesn't really exist,' she said, and her voice was infinitely sad. 'I was fooling myself, really.'

'No, you're right, we do have something special,' he said, quickly, urgently, 'and it'll get easier as the boys grow older and you have more time, more freedom, and can come with me, and …'

'Come with you,' she echoed. 'Tag along, going where you want to go, finding out about the things you need to find out about, and maybe, if I prove my efficiency and my staying power, you might let me make notes for you and take a few photos.'

It was only then that he understood how angry she was. How the resentment of years was bursting out of her.

'Jo, don't, we need to talk about this, work out how we deal with it, where we go from here, sort out how to put matters right and …'

Now she leaned down over him, her hands on the padded sides of the chair making him a prisoner between her arms. 'Mend it? Fix it up? Don't make promises you can't keep, Hal, and don't give the impression that you might change when I know you won't, because how you are is all there is.' She drew a long, shaky breath and said bitterly, 'You've broken it, Hal. You've fucking well broken it.'

Then she straightened up, crossed the room and let herself out, closing the door very firmly behind her.

He went on sitting there. He couldn't find the energy to move, to think.

After some time – he didn't know how long – the door opened again. Ed stood there, hair tousled, face crumpled from sleep. His eyes on Hal were hard, and blue just like his father's.

'What's happened?' he asked gruffly. 'I heard Mum getting shouty.'

'Ask her,' Hal said shortly.

'She's in the bath. I'm asking you.'

'We were talking. She – she's cross with me.'

'No shit, Sherlock,' Ed muttered. Then, before Hal could remonstrate, 'Is it about her film again, and you not liking all the attention she's been getting? Because you ...'

'It's nothing whatever to do with the film,' Hal said wearily, even as he thought, oh, Christ, the film, and yet another flash point between us. Then, trying to arrange his face into something pleasant and friendly, he added, 'Sorry if we disturbed you, Ed. We're all tired, I guess, and need a good night's sleep.'

Ed went on looking at him for a moment, his expression suspicious. 'She always seems tough, and like she's able to deal with stuff, but it's not all of what she is,' he said. 'She ... things hurt her, and you think she's not reacting but actually she is, she's quietly working out how she's going to deal with it.' Hal thought he'd finished – it was perceptive for a thirteen-year-old boy, and he was surprised Ed had been so outspoken – but then, turning to go, Ed said, 'She found out years ago that she's stronger than she thought.'

And, as he padded away towards the stairs, Hal had the uncomfortable realisation that he'd meant his last words as a warning.

Chapter 16

Max

Max watched as Jo hurried off along the pavement. Even the way she moved seemed to cry out her pain and he very nearly went after her. But then, all at once, even staring at her seemed too intrusive when she was so clearly showing she wanted to be alone, and abruptly he went inside and closed the door.

Angela turned to him as he went back to the bright living room. She was standing by the window and her expression was one of deep distress. 'Max, that was awful!' she said. 'She – when she asked where I was moving from and you said West Sussex, and her face! I think she knew – I really think she did!'

He went over to her, taking hold of her hand. 'I do too,' he agreed. There was no point in denying it. 'Hal told her he was in West Sussex. And …' He'd been about to add something else – something undoubtedly worse – but stopped.

'What?' Angela said anxiously. 'What were you going to say?'

'Oh – just that when I said she was Hal's wife you said "Hal! Yes!"' And your face lit up for a split second and I know she saw, he thought.

217

Jo wasn't the only person in the room who had been affected by that split second.

'Oh, no!' Angela whispered. 'Oh, I'm so, so sorry.' She met Max's eyes, and, aware that she was regretting what she'd made him feel as well, he felt suddenly better. 'She looked …' Angela gave a shrug, as if she couldn't find the words. 'And she's got to drive home!'

'Yes, I know,' Max said. 'I asked her to phone when she gets there, but I doubt she will.'

Angela took her hand out of his and went to sit on the sofa.

He looked at her. He wondered what this meant, this sudden re-eruption of his bloody cousin into the fragile happiness of their new relationship.

He knew that he had to ask her. That they must discuss the implications.

He went to sit beside her, leaving a gap between them.

'Anja, I said before that I believe what happened between you and Hal was far more down to him than to you,' he began. He sensed her stiffen and felt quite sure she didn't want him to go on, but he knew he had to. 'I don't know much about their life – Jo and Hal's – but for sure it hasn't been a bed of roses just recently. Jo's had, or maybe is having, a big success with some story she's written that's being made into an animated film, and it seems it's brought a lot of matters out into the open.'

'But that's no …'

'He came to find you,' he said firmly. 'Ask yourself if he'd have done so if he was fully content in a loving, happy marriage.'

'So that makes it all right?' Now she sounded angry.

'No, it doesn't. But it's happened, it's having consequences, but it can't *un*happen. And we have to find a way round it.'

'Is that the professional you talking?' she said, and she sounded scathing. 'The calm, detached counsellor to the unhappy and the unfulfilled? The psychologist?'

The emphasis on the final word made it sound like something despicable.

He paused, determined not to answer in the same tone. 'No,' he said calmly. 'I don't do counselling.' He glanced at her. 'I told you, currently I'm doing research. The study into what's happening in the brain when we go into automatic mode?'

She met his eyes. She nodded. Then she muttered, 'Sorry.'

They sat without speaking for a while. Then, when the need to know finally overrode the fear of how she might reply, he said, 'So, what shall we do?'

She came out of whatever thoughts had been holding her. 'What do you mean?'

'We'd made plans,' he said softly. 'We were going to go down to your house and stay there, together, for as long as it takes for you to quit your job and terminate your tenancy. Then we'd thought we might come back here, and see how it goes.'

She'd kissed him, yesterday. It had been a joy, but it had been just a kiss. They had retired to their separate rooms, just as they'd done all week.

He tried not to think about that. Tried not to think about anything, but simply waited.

He felt her fingers touch his. She slid them beneath his palm and grasped his hand. She said, 'Max, I feel awkward because only a couple of weeks ago I slept with Hal, and now I'm here with you, and it's where I really want to be.' He felt something inside his head begin to sing. 'But I'm thinking how it must seem to you, and I'm wondering if you're assuming that I'm ... that I sleep with blokes I fancy the moment I've

219

met them, that I go from relationship to relationship without a lot of thought, and …' She stopped.

'I don't think any of those things,' he said quietly.

She made a muffled sound that might have been a nervous laugh, or equally well a sob.

Presently she said, 'Max?'

'Still right here.'

'Do you know what I think we ought to do?'

'No. What?'

He raised his eyes to look at her. There was a soft smile on her face.

'Precisely what we said we would.' She seemed to steel herself, then went on, 'As you just said, what happened with me and Hal can't be undone. But something so good came out of it – you, turning up on my doorstep – and I'm not about to let it go.'

He went on looking at her. After a moment he simply said, 'Okay.'

They spent a week in Angela's rented house while she wrapped up her former life. Displaying a forceful side to her nature that Max had sensed was there but hadn't yet experienced, she informed both the letting agency and her employer that a week was quite enough notice under the terms of her arrangements with them, and refused to budge to pressure to make her change her mind.

She was at work for all of each day, and Max got on with the multiplicity of tasks at the house that didn't need her direct supervision. The days were busy, and he found himself looking forward very much to her return each evening. The letting agent would be coming round while she was at work to check the inventory; the little house was a furnished let, and the inventory was several pages long. Angela, however, went through her own copy with Max, and between them they laid out everything for inspection, correct to the last teaspoon.

'Lots of the owner's stuff has stayed in the cupboards,' she said to Max as they worked. 'The sheets had suspicious stains and the blankets stank of mould, or it could be cat piss, so if the agent tries to say that's my fault, please put him or her right.'

She also arranged for the disposition of the items she'd bought but didn't want to keep. As she and Max went through them she kept repeating, 'Chuck.'

'You're sure?' He held up a set of four colourful mugs.

'I'm sure. They didn't cost a lot, but the charity shop might make a couple of quid.'

He surmised from her expression – from her mood – as they went through the house that it held few, if any, happy memories.

She put a card up in the pub advertising her car for sale. As Max had pointed out, one car was more than enough in Cambridge, and hers was some way past its best.

While she worked, Max took on the task of taking bin bags of rubbish to the tip and cardboard boxes of items too good to throw away to the charity shops of Chichester. He took over the shopping and the cooking, and even cleaned the kitchen from top to bottom the day before the letting agent was due to give it the once over.

There was a quiet satisfaction when the large young woman from the agency could not come up a single reason for withholding any of the deposit that Angela had paid when she took the house. Especially when her expression, not to mention the vaguely insulting way she had of peering right into the corners and inspecting the results when she ran a finger along the shelves, suggested that she was quite determined to find one.

Angela finished work at lunchtime on Friday.

Max was there to meet her. Her car had been picked up by its new owner the previous evening. Max had already handed in the door keys at the letting agent's office.

Neither of them felt like eating. They got on the road straight away and he drove fast. He sensed her beginning to relax as the miles between them and her former home steadily increased.

He was very relieved to be leaving, for the week in her house had been unsettling. He sensed that it would not be long before they became lovers and it was troubling that, during the days in her house, she seemed to withdraw from him. She slept in her bed upstairs, he on the sofa bed in the living room. At times, lying awake, he'd felt she was much further away than a flight of stairs.

But as the journey progressed, he sensed her returning to him. She broke quite a long silence by telling him how her former colleagues had given her a card and a book token, and how she'd been touched at how much the token was worth, and her voice sounded warm and easy. Responding in kind, he described how the large young woman in the letting agency had grabbed the key from him and how he'd seen the house already being advertised in the window as a very rare chance to live in a quintessentially English village, quite eye-catching except that they'd mis-spelt quintessentially.

It wasn't what Angela said that steadily began to reassure him, for they spoke of trivialities, and quite often she made him laugh. It was … He couldn't come up with an answer. And, in the end, he decided it was simply her relief at having made a decision and stuck to it. If he was right, then it was a sentiment he wholeheartedly shared.

They stopped at a supermarket and bought some special things for supper. In addition he bought champagne, and the Bendicks bitter chocolate mints he knew she loved. He wanted to buy flowers, but maybe that was going too far. Then they drove to the house, unloaded the car and went on to Gus's to leave it in his garage, walking back arm in arm.

She seemed as happy to be back as he was. He lit the fire, for the place was chilly; they were halfway through November now, and Cambridge felt several degrees colder than Chichester. He prepared supper while she went upstairs to unpack and put away the clothes and the small number of items she'd brought from the house. He heard her moving about, and the thought that soon she'd be downstairs with him, sitting by the fire and raising a glass to celebrate their return, gave him a glow of happiness.

They ate the meal, finished the champagne and returned to the sofa with coffee. They had been talking for hours, most recently about where to go next in their quest to trace his family's Danish roots. She had clearly been giving it a lot of thought, and he watched her as she explained at length the various paths they might take.

'Anja,' he said softly.

She was deep in describing a method someone had told her about for tracing foreign census records on line and barely seemed to register his voice.

'Anja,' he repeated more loudly.

'... and it seems there's often no problem with not speaking the language because ... what?'

He reached out and touched her hair, tenderly pushing a long strand away from her face. 'You're beautiful, and I'm very, very glad you're here.'

She looked at first surprised, then pleased, then her expression grew soft with happiness. 'Me too,' she whispered.

They leaned towards each other, and he put his arms round her. For a moment he looked down into her eyes, then he kissed her.

And later, when they disentangled enough to go upstairs, it was to his room, his bed, that they went.

One evening at the start of December, Max had a call from Jo. As soon as he heard her voice, he realised how pleased he was to hear from her. He also felt extremely guilty because of what had happened the last time they'd met, and because his total absorption with Angela had pushed almost everything else out of his mind, including whether Jo had got home all right that day and what had been going on since.

'It's good to hear you,' he said. 'How are things?'

'Oh, okay.' She sounded infinitely weary. Then very quietly she said, 'I know, Max. He told me.'

'Ah.'

After a moment she went on in a brittle sort of voice, 'Hal and I are being really nice to each other. Both of us know we have to make it work. But ...' Whatever she'd been about to say, she changed her mind. 'I'm so sorry I crashed in on you and Angela that day. It must have been awful for you.'

'It really wasn't your fault, Jo. How were you to know she was here?'

There was a brief pause. 'She's still staying with you?'

'She is.'

'I'm glad. For you, I mean. You're obviously happy with her, or at least I assume you are.'

'I am,' he said simply.

Then Jo said abruptly, 'Max, remember the animated film I told you about? The one based on my book about the father coming back to be his little son's guardian angel?'

'Yes, of course. How's it going?'

'It's done. It's all ready, and it's being shown on telly on Boxing Day.'

'That's amazing! I'm so pleased for you.'

'Thank you. But that – when it's being shown on telly - isn't why I'm phoning – well, it is, sort of, because before that there's a charity showing on the fourteenth of December, and I'm allowed to say who I want to be sent tickets, and I'm sorry that it's short notice but I wondered if you'd like to come?'

'Very much.' Max hoped she didn't pick up the *but* in his voice.

She did. 'This is really difficult because of Angela, and quite honestly I don't much want to see her, but I'd really like you to be there.'

He thought he detected a slight questioning note in her voice.

'I'd very much like to be there too, Jo,' he said. He thought for a few moments. 'Anja – Angela – and I are together, living together, and it's all quite new and tender.' And I'm so happy I could sing, he could have added. 'It would be quite awkward if she didn't come with me, but I'm sure she'd understand, and for sure I do, and I …'

But Jo, interrupting, said gently, 'Max, I wasn't saying she couldn't come, only that I don't want to see her, but there will be heaps of other people there and we won't have to talk to each other or seek each other out.'

He let out a long, silent sigh of relief. 'That's very kind of you, Jo,' he said. 'Extremely tolerant, too.' He paused. 'Will, er …'

She understood.

'Hal won't be there,' she said quickly. 'And before you jump to the perfectly reasonable conclusion that he's taken the hump because I'm getting all the attention, actually it's not that. Sam had a fall and he broke his tibia, and he's going to be coming out of hospital around the time of the charity do. He's doing his utmost to deter Hal from going over – he doesn't know about the do, he just keeps saying he'll be fine and there's no need for Hal to fly out so close to Christmas – but Hal says he's going and that's that.'

'I'm sorry to hear about Sam. I think Hal's right to go,' Max said.

'Oh, so do I! It's not really because of the broken tibia. Sam's been having some tests to see if there's a reason for why he fell over, and Hal just needs to be there.'

'Of course he does.'

'So, if you and Angela would like to come, there won't be any risk of embarrassing encounters.'

'We'll all four have to meet up some time,' Max said gently. 'I have no intention of allowing you and your family to slip away.'

'That's nice, and I agree,' she said. 'I'd just rather we didn't do it on my special evening.'

Max laughed. 'Fair enough. I'll check with Angela, Jo, but I should think she'd like to go.'

'I promise I won't throw a trifle at her,' Jo said lightly.

He thought it was probably better to pretend he hadn't heard.

'What's the charity?' he asked into the slightly awkward silence.

'It's a new one, to help bereaved children.'

'Good choice.'

'Nothing to do with me,' she said disarmingly, 'the film company selected it.'

'Is Hal there?' Max asked, sensing she was winding up to say goodbye.

'No, he's in London, but he'll be back soon – oh, he's here now, I can hear the car. Do you want to speak to him?'

'Yes. I'd like to send my best to Sam.'

'Of course. Hang on, I'll call him. Bye, Max.'

He heard the clatter as she put the receiver down. A murmur of voices, hers calling out, Hal's replying. Then Hal said, 'Max.' No greeting; just his name.

'Jo may have told you that she called in to see me and Angela was here,' Max said without preamble; if Hal was going to be terse and barely courteous, then so was he. 'I took the package to the place where she works and she wasn't there, so I went on to her house and she thought my car was yours. She was distressed. I won't bore you with the details – which in fact aren't really any of your business – but she agreed to come to Brittany with me in her professional capacity. Her presence there proved to be invaluable as well as a great pleasure, and she came back to stay in Cambridge with me when we returned to England. Staying has turned to living, and we are now what people seem coyly to refer to nowadays as *together*.'

Hal didn't reply.

After a moment, Max said, 'Are you still there?'

'Yep.'

'Jo just told me about your father. I'm sorry to hear about the fall, and the tests.'

This time, Hal spoke up. 'He tells me he's fine,' he said. 'I reckon I have to see for myself, though.'

'I'd feel the same,' Max said. 'Please give him my best wishes when you see him.'

'Sure.'

'And will you keep me informed?'

Hal muttered something that was probably yes, and then said he had to go. After a fairly perfunctory exchange of goodbyes, he put the phone down.

Max looked up to find Angela watching him. She'd been in the bath when the phone rang, and she was wrapped in a thick towelling robe and smelled delicious. He went to take her in his arms. 'That was Jo. Well, in that it was she who phoned, although just then it was Hal I was speaking to.' He gave her an outline of the two conversations.

'It's a shame about his dad,' she said. 'I hope he'll be okay.'

Max kissed the top of her head. 'They don't sound too worried. He's old, though. It makes a difference.' Then: 'What do you think about the charity event?'

She didn't answer for a few moments. Then, with a faint sigh, she said, 'You don't have much in the way of family.'

It sounded like a statement, not a question, but he said 'No' anyway.

'Then I think perhaps you should cling on to what you have, which means I think that yes, we ought to go.'

Now he kissed her properly, at first because he was glad she'd seen it the way he did, then because of a more urgent emotion. While he could still remember what they'd been talking about, he said, 'Thank you.'

Chapter 17

Hal

The California winter was cold, foggy and damp, but the conditions didn't affect Hal's pleasure in being there. He had flown out on the Monday before Jo's charity event, saying with perfect truthfulness that he needed to get the house warm and aired before Sam came out of hospital on Wednesday.

'Yes, I know,' Jo had said. 'Sam will have been lying in bed for quite a while, and if he were to return to a cold, damp atmosphere it could lead to pneumonia.' She gave him an odd, assessing look. 'It's okay, Hal,' she said tonelessly. 'I do realise you have no choice.'

When she'd seen him off at Gatwick he had taken her in his arms and for a moment they had just stood there, silently hugging. Then she said, 'Take good care of Sam and give him my love.'

'I will.'

'Call me when you get the results of the tests?'

'Of course.'

Then, his heart heavy, he had left her.

* * *

His father's house was indeed cold and damp when he arrived around midday on Tuesday. He was tired and fed up, and having to make his own way to Morro Bay made him realise what a luxury it was to have had Sam come to collect him over the years.

He slung his bag in the spare room, glancing into Sam's room in passing to make sure all was well, which it was. Sam's cello stood in its case in the corner. It was some time since Hal had heard him play, and he'd concluded that nowadays Sam didn't reckon his playing was fit for anyone's ears but his own. He knew, however, that his father would go on playing till he died; it was a part of him.

He then set about firing up the boiler and hunting out kindling and firewood for the wood burning stove. He kept his heavy coat on while he worked, and vacuumed and dusted the entire house while the temperature slowly rose. When the place was warm enough to remove a layer or two, he realised suddenly that he was starving.

Braving the dank chill outside once more, he went out to Sam's car, got it started and drove to the local store. He'd forgotten to check before setting out what supplies Sam had in the house, so to save a return trip, bought everything he could think of, including a pack of fat red candles and a large red-flowered pot plant, whose identity he didn't know, to brighten up the main living room.

It was, after all, not far short of Christmas.

Back at the house he put the provisions away, discovered quite a lot of still-edible food in the fridge and the freezer, tended the fire. He made himself a huge club sandwich and cracked a couple of beers, then lay down on Sam's special chair and had a short sleep.

A sudden and violently disturbing dream shot him awake. Disoriented, he looked around, recognising the familiar room with relief.

'Keep busy,' he said aloud, getting up.

Struck with an idea, he went out to the garage and rummaged through the neatly-labelled boxes on the shelves. He found what he was looking for.

There was no need to drive back to the store, for he had seen somewhere just up the road advertising what he wanted. He togged up once more and, on foot this time, trudged the half-mile or so and then returned to the warm, welcoming house. Evening was drawing on now, and he pulled the curtains and lit a couple of the red candles.

Then he stuck the Christmas tree he'd just bought into the tub he'd prepared before he went out, and set about arraying it with the wonderful assortment of baubles, bells, stars and little figures that Sam had amassed over the years. Some of them took Hal straight back to his childhood; one reminded him poignantly of his mother, although he didn't know why.

He held it up.

It was the figure of a little old woman. She was dressed in a long dark gown, over which she wore a brightly-coloured apron. She was holding a red-painted heart in her hands. A white cloth covered her head and her face was wreathed in a huge smile that made her cheeks bunch up. The cheeks had been painted apple-red. He knew just by looking at the figure that it was old, and that it had been made a long way from California.

He had found it at the bottom of the box, wrapped carefully in layers of tissue paper crumbly with age. He studied it, turning it upside down, and saw something etched lightly across the woman's right foot.

He smiled. He'd been right; it had originated with his mother, perhaps given to her by a grandmother; Ruth's maternal ancestors had come from Hungary.

He said aloud, 'Time you saw the light of day again, old woman,' and hung the little figure at the front of the tree, towards the top.

* * *

Sam returned to his own home with very obvious pleasure and a measure of relief: the results of his tests had been revealed to him that morning, and the doctors had been able to find nothing abnormal in any of them.

'Told the damned fool lot of them that I tripped!' Sam had grumbled most of the way home. 'Don't you ever trip, I asked one young girl who looked as if she should still be in braids and knee socks!'

'They were looking after you, Dad,' Hal said for perhaps the fourth or fifth time. 'It's their duty, they …'

'They're terrified in case they miss something and I sue them!' Sam fumed. He was still sore at the initial couple of days of his hospital stay, when the nursing staff had refused to let him out of bed and he'd had to use a portable urinal and, even worse, a bed pan. One of the nurses had confided to Hal that they'd suggested a catheter, but Sam was so angry that they feared for his blood pressure. 'It was only because he was in pain!' she'd said, distress in her eyes. 'We thought it would be easier for him.'

'Sure, I can see that,' Hal had replied, thinking with a private smile, You don't know my father.

Sam was delighted with the Christmas tree. 'You shouldn't have bothered, son,' he said. 'I haven't had one for years.'

'Then it's high time you did.'

'And you found the box of decorations, and you made the lights work!'

'Eventually, yeah.'

'And you …'

Sam stopped.

Looking up, Hal saw that he had seen the little old woman with the red heart. Sam was standing very still.

After a moment Hal said, 'That was Mom's, wasn't it?'

'It was.' Sam's voice wasn't quite his own.

232

'I thought it might be time to let her come and join us,' Hal went on.

This time the silence went on for longer.

With a sigh, Sam said eventually, 'You're right.'

He touched a finger to the little figure – a gentle gesture, a caress – then limped out of the room. Soon he was back, and he had a photo frame in his hand. He put it on the shelf beside the Christmas tree.

Hal studied it. He recognised the photo: his mother in her twenties. It usually stood in Sam's bedroom.

'That's good, Dad,' he said quietly. 'Good to have her in here with us, and …'

But Sam had taken a brown envelope out from under his arm, and now he opened it. He hesitated briefly, then handed another photo to Hal.

His mother was laughing, her expression so vivid, so full of joy, that Hal thought he could hear her. She was turning to look at the camera, her face rounder, fuller, and her body in profile was …

'She's pregnant,' Hal said.

And Sam said, 'She was. But she lost the baby – she was a little girl – and it left her so down that she couldn't fight the pneumonia as she should have done.'

Hal heard the pain in his father's voice. He knew he should have said something to try to give comfort. But he said, 'Why did you never tell me?'

'When she died, when we lost her, you were too sad and puzzled, and I didn't want you to have to cope with anything else. After that …' He shrugged. 'I guess it was easier not to deal with your reaction.'

Hal nodded. He wasn't the only one, then, to duck away from the imperfectly-understood challenge of profoundly emotional issues. Perhaps his inability was hereditary.

'I told Jo, that early summer visit you paid me when you'd moved back here,' Sam said.

'You did?' Why her and not me? was on the tip of his tongue, but he held it back. He knew, anyway. Jo didn't run away from the dangers of sharing what was deep in your heart. He just said, 'Yeah.'

Sam nodded. He held put his hand, and Hal gave him back the photo. Sam looked at him for a moment, then his eyes slid away. 'Do you … Should we …' he began. Then he shook his head.

'We'll have it framed, Dad. We'll take it to that place in town, have a proper job done.'

And, after a moment, Sam said softly, 'Yes.'

Having the Christmas tree in the window, lit up and visible to passers-by as soon as the sky began to darken, had the effect of announcing to the neighbours that Sam Dillon was celebrating the festive season rather more enthusiastically this year. Cards instantly began to drop through the door, and the family who had taken Sammie out on their catamaran in the autumn called by and asked what Sam was doing on Christmas Day. When it transpired that he had been planning a quiet day with his music, his books and his favourite things to eat and drink – a day which Hal, watching with amusement, knew full well was no hardship at all but in fact his father's preference – the neighbours insisted that wouldn't do, and told Sam he was going to share the festive meal with them.

'Damned tree,' Sam grumbled when the deputation – father and the two children – had gone. 'It's your fault, son.'

'Bah, humbug,' Hal replied.

He remembered he'd been meant to phone Jo. He did a rapid calculation and phoned in the early evening, catching her at home when it was morning for her. He told her what the doctors had concluded.

'I'm so glad,' she said. 'He's really all right?'

'He really is. He's limping, and I guess he's in pain at times, but he's not letting on.'

'You're taking good care of him?'

'It's what I'm here for.'

There was a pause, then she said, 'Hal, I'd better go, the charity showing's the day after tomorrow and I have a list of things I still haven't done.'

'Sure,' he said quickly. Probably, with hindsight, too quickly. 'Good luck. Hope it all goes well.'

'Tell Sam and Mary too, if you see her, I'll get copies of the film for both of them as soon as I can,' she said.

'I'll be seeing her. She's coming down tomorrow for a couple of days, probably loaded with apple pies and casseroles for Dad.'

'Don't knock it, it'll save you having to cook,' she replied.

He laughed. 'I can cook a casserole.'

There was a stiff silence. He could have kicked himself. It was forbearing of her, he thought after they had said goodbye and he'd put the phone down, not to say Then why the hell don't you ever offer to do so?

Mary came to stay for a couple of nights, and Sam probably uttered at least twice a day some variation on the themes that she shouldn't have made the road trip in winter weather, it wasn't comfortable for her stuck in the little spare room, and it was a shame to leave old Bernard on his own so near to Christmas.

'He's not alone, Sam dear, or he won't be from noon today,' Mary replied calmly – this particular conversation took place at breakfast time on her second day – 'because Emily and the kids are arriving, and Dean'll be joining us Christmas Eve.'

'Well, all right, but …'

235

'Have some more toast,' Mary said, and both Hal and, he was sure, Sam, heard the unspoken addition *and let's hear no more about it.*

It was good to see her, Hal reflected. She had confided in him that Bernard wasn't too well. 'Nothing to worry about,' she'd said, with a smile that didn't go very deep. 'He likes to be at home. Gets anxious even going to the store, or to friends for a drink.' There was a pause. 'The only place he goes willingly and regularly these days is to see Ben.'

Twelve years and more, Hal thought, and sometimes Ben's death still feels like yesterday.

'But he encourages me to get out!' Mary said brightly. 'We all deal with it differently, Hal. Some folk get up, dust themselves off and plough on, some turn inwards and gradually slow down.'

There didn't seem to be anything to add to that. Silently, Hal reached out for her hand.

The next day, Mary said she was taking Sam to a tea dance.

'But I'm recovering from a broken leg!' Sam's face was aghast. Hal smiled to himself. His father loathed dancing.

'Yes, dear, I know,' Mary said serenely. 'But I've seen the fliers, and there's a band, and they're going to play all the numbers you and I grew up with, so you can sit and listen to the music and tap the foot whose shin bone you didn't manage to break while I bat my eyelashes and encourage some handsome fellow to take me onto the floor.' She flashed Sam a saucy smile, in that moment looking so like her son that Hal blinked in surprise.

'But what about Hal?' Sam brought up his final line of defence.

Only to see it dismissed by ruthless logic. 'Hal will be just fine,' Mary pronounced. 'You know as well as I do he's longing for an hour or two on his own.' She turned to him with a smile so affectionate that it took away any criticism he might have sensed in her words.

Hal, rushing into the breach she had opened up for him, said, 'Okay if I borrow your car, Dad?'

And Sam, knowing he was beaten, muttered, 'Suppose so.'

He knew exactly where he was going. He hoped he would remember the route – the roads were small, winding and obscure – but it appeared to have engraved itself into his memory. Half an hour or so after setting out from Sam's house, once again he was standing outside the small house set by itself on the hillside above the ocean.

He opened the gate, walked up the drive. If anything, the place looked more dilapidated than on his previous visit. The leaves were off the broad-leaf trees now, and the pines stood out starkly in the wisps of mist that swirled around.

He went up the steps onto the deck. The wooden boards were slick with moisture and as slippery as an ice rink. They'd need regular power washing, he thought. It's isolated up here, and no place to fall over and incapacitate yourself.

He stood in front of the window staring in at the wide, almost empty room. He imagined a fire in the huge hearth. A chair like his father's drawn up beside it. Music playing, a stack of books beside him.

'It's your fault, Dad,' he said aloud. 'I see your life, I imagine the Christmas Day you'd prefer to be having and I am envious as hell.'

It was the first time he'd uttered the admission. He couldn't decide if he felt a great relief or a sickening guilt. Probably it was fifty–fifty.

He walked on, right round the house. He peered into the two windows at the back, investigated an extension and a couple of outhouses. He went back down the drive to the gate, and kicked through the grass

237

and the winter-dead vegetation. He'd had a hunch he'd find what he was hunting for, and in a while he did. With a grunt of satisfaction he took out a pencil and a small notebook and wrote down an address and a phone number.

The house on the hillside had been on the market for almost seven years. The real estate agent's board had fallen down when the post supporting it had rotted.

'With two bedrooms, one none too generous, it's too small for most people,' the realtor said disarmingly. 'And there's no chance of extending the place. There are more restrictions than you can shake a stick at up there, and you wouldn't even be able to put up a porch.'

'You're very discouraging,' Hal observed. They were in the young man's office, in a small town north of Morro Bay and thirty minutes or so from the house on the hillside. The office's giant window must have been a plus point in good weather but right now did nothing but provide an up-close view of pouring rain.

'I'm realistic,' the young man corrected him. 'The property's been on our books all this time and I've lost count of how many people have come in keen to buy and asking the same questions.' He seemed to realise he was rapidly kissing goodbye to his chances of a commission. 'Well, there must have been five, six, I guess.'

Perhaps, Hal thought with a smile, the young man wasn't too good at counting. 'What's the asking price?'

The young man already had the file for the property on his desk. Glancing down, he pointed to a figure on the front cover, spinning the file round so it was the right way up for Hal.

Hal nodded, opening the file and looking at the photos. They must have been taken soon after the last occupant had left, when the place still looked like a home. An untidy home, but the appeal of it was still there and, if anything, stronger.

'Who lived there?' he asked.

'An elderly woman. She had a dog and it died, and, according to her family, its death led her to make up her mind it was her time too. Oh, nothing dramatic!' he added hurriedly, possibly realising that a suicide might deter this oddly determined client where small size, isolation and dilapidation did not. 'She was found on the sofa by the hearth, dead fire, blanket over her, glass of whisky by her side, smile on her face. So they say. The medic said it was her heart, and that it'd have been peaceful. Like falling asleep.

'Beim Schlafengehen'. Going to sleep. Hal recalled the Richard Strauss song playing in Sam's car on the day when he'd discovered the house on the hillside.

He felt a small tremor somewhere in his chest.

Was it meant to be, then? Did the events of a life play out according to some pattern not fully understood but only grasped in tiny snatches?

I don't believe that, he told himself.

'Much need doing to make it habitable?' he asked.

The realtor shrugged. 'It's sound. I check it out once a year and the last time, this spring, it looked okay.' He held Hal's eyes. 'Want to take a look?'

Hal affected indifference. It didn't do to appear eager. 'Why not?'

He went straight back. He'd tried to disguise his haste by muttering something about limited time but he reckoned the realtor guy wasn't fooled.

He went up to the house. Unlocked the door. It opened without a protest, on hinges that moved so smoothly that they might just have been oiled. He walked slowly into the middle of the room, stopping to turn right round.

His eyes fell on the battered old sofa. A woman died there, he thought. She was old, her dog was gone, she'd maybe had enough. Far from dismaying him, the image of her lying there under her blanket, serene and glad to be dying in her own place, made him feel happy.

He moved to the sofa, touching the thick blanket, smoothing a hand over the cracked leather.

I could restore this, he mused.

He liked the thought of keeping the old woman's sofa. The house had a calm, accepting sort of feel, and he guessed it had emanated from her. She'd understand, maybe, someone else wanting to live there. Someone else appreciating what the place had to offer.

He wandered through the rest of the house. It was pretty basic – kitchen with stove, ancient refrigerator with its door propped open and a walk-in larder in the corner, bathroom with a tub stained green beneath the brass taps, one decent-sized bedroom, one little more than a cupboard – but he didn't see anything that detracted from the house's strong pull.

And even before he'd begun his tour of inspection, he knew he was going to buy it.

He went outside and sat in the car to think about the points he ought to consider before he went ahead. Doing so while still inside the house would weigh the scales so heavily in its favour that it seemed unfair.

One: my father is getting old and it'd be good to have a place where I can spend time over here without crowding him out.

Sam, he'd noticed, always welcomed his son and other family members and close friends, but there was an accompanying sense, with those who had the eyes to see it, that he wasn't a natural space-sharer.

Two: I do not own a house.

Copse Hill House belonged to Jo. She'd lived there when he first met her and she'd purchased it with money that had come to her through Ben's death. He'd carried life insurance, and the company he'd been working for when he was killed had paid a large sum in compensation.

She's never for one moment made me feel it's not my home as much as hers, Hal thought. But it surely makes economic sense to invest some of the money I've earned over the years in property.

Three: Sammie is my son, and California is my home state as much as anywhere is. Sammie loves it, and maybe in the future he might spend a year or two in school here. If so, we'd need a place of our own, because sure as hell we couldn't plan on living with Dad.

Ed's father had also come from California. It was an uncomfortable thought, for reasons Hal didn't want to examine. Well, Ed could come out here too if he wanted. And Jo; yes, sure, so could Jo.

He tried not to dwell on how much she'd loathed living on the west coast the first and only time they'd tried it. Life was different back then, he thought. The kids were much younger, she'd had no time to call her own, it was before she'd gone back to writing. She could surely not resist this house, and she'd enjoy vacations here.

The word pulled him up short.

Vacations.

Was this, then, what he had in the back of his mind? That he'd live here, on his own, and his wife and family would come over when school was out?

No, it wasn't!

It couldn't be.

But he had the uncomfortable feeling that he was following the path whose seductive start he had discovered that day back in October. Or, more honestly – and he felt that, sitting alone in the car outside the house he knew was going to be his, there was a solemn duty on him to be totally honest – a long, long time before that.

Chapter 18

Jo

Jo very much regretted the reason why Hal would not be attending the charity film showing with her, for she loved Sam and hated to think of him having fallen, and being forced to put up with the awkwardness of dealing with the aftermath of a broken leg. But at the same time she had to admit to herself that she was relieved she and the boys would be going on their own.

The film company had hired a function room in a London hotel near the Embankment, and it would be set with forty tables each seating six people. Jo would be at a separate table with the film director and the leading lights of the production; the boys would sit with Jo's parents and her former neighbours, Tom and Laura, who now lived in Sevenoaks.

Even a week before Sammie was hovering on the border of over-excited, thrilled at the prospect of the entire evening but particularly at the thought of meeting Finnegan's Pig. Their song for the film was now heading towards the upper reaches of the charts, there was talk of its being the Christmas number one, and they'd been on 'Top of the Pops'. Sammie's street cred couldn't get a lot higher.

Ed, while clearly as delighted as his brother, had gone quiet as the event approached. Jo, sensing that the whole business was undoubtably reminding him of the father he'd never really known, met him from school one afternoon to give them a chance to talk without Sammie's loud, happy presence.

'Are you looking forward to Friday night?' she asked him as they cleared the Tunbridge Wells congestion and got on the open road.

'Yeah,' Ed said. 'You've worked hard, Mum, you deserve it.'

'Thanks, son. And I've got a gorgeous frock.' It was a dinner jacket do and she had treated herself to an evening dress in violet silk, tight over the waist and hips and flaring into a wide, full skirt that swished as she moved.

She waited a beat. 'But what about you?'

It was his turn to hesitate. 'Honest answer?'

'Always.'

He grinned. 'Do my best,' he muttered. Then: 'I've always liked the book. I can still vaguely remember that day you did the first drawing, and I came into the room and watched you as you were working.'

'Can you?' She was very surprised.

He nodded. 'And I sort of knew it – the picture you were drawing – was my dad, although honestly I can't really remember much about him and I get confused between what I think's in my memory and all the photos I've seen of him.'

'Yes. It would be unusual if you had clear memories, you weren't even two when he died, and …'

'They are clear, the few images I do have.' He paused again, and she waited. 'I can remember paddling in the sea with him, and playing in a little blue plastic pool with whales on it. And then he's reading to me, and being all the different voices. And in the most vivid one I'm standing up on his legs and we're facing each other, and he's holding

244

my hands, and he's just said something funny and both of us are laughing so hard I'm hurting.'

She waited till she could speak without her voice shaking. 'Those are so lovely. But, Ed, you've never told me before?' She couldn't help the slight question in her voice.

He shrugged. Then, as if he knew it wasn't sufficient answer – wasn't any answer – he said, 'I sort of thought you wanted to put it behind you. Losing my dad. Sammie was born – I love Sammie, I'm glad we've got him – and Hal was always around, and we were a new family.' He shrugged again.

'Yes,' she said. 'Yes, you're right. And I suppose I did want to – to move on.' She waited, feeling her fast, distressed heartbeat. She knew she wouldn't be able to keep her voice sounding calm when she went on, but all the same she was determined to do so. 'But that doesn't mean I forgot your dad, Ed. I never have, and I'm sure I never will.'

She forced her concentration onto the road ahead. She felt Ed touch her hand, lightly, just once.

'So, honest answer,' he said after a mile or so. 'Remember? What you were just asking?'

'Yes. Go on, then.'

'Yes, I'm looking forward to the evening and I want to see the film. I hope it'll be dark when they show it so nobody'll be able to look at me. And finally, I'm really glad Hal's not coming.'

'You ...' She was about to jump on the last remark, but some wiser, deeper part of her held her back. In the end, with a laugh to show she wasn't really being serious, she said lightly, 'So am I!'

She'd seen bits and pieces, and an early cut of the whole thing, but the final version of the film was better than she'd imagined it could be.

She'd been secretly afraid that somewhere in the long process from her original drawings and Flavia McGinty's additional material to the final result, what had been so fresh and so precious would be lost. Cheapened. Spoiled. Commercialised.

It wasn't.

As she sat in the room full of people elegant in evening dress – with the lights down, for which she was discovering she was as grateful as Ed – and the images slowly began to materialise on the big screen at the end of the room, and the first notes of Finnegan's Pig's haunting opening theme floated into the silence, she found she was holding her breath.

Then there was Ben, exactly, precisely as she had first drawn him, somehow clad in jeans and a tee shirt while at the same time there was a suggestion of an angel's pale floating garment and a pair of huge, snowy wings. And Ben's blond head turned, Ben's bright blue eyes looked down on the boy playing by himself on the shore, and Ben's striking, beloved face creased in sorrow as he peered through the soft, swirling mist that separated them.

I can see you in the half-light
And it fills me with delight,
It's so long since I've been near you,
Missed so much that you've been through.
You were so small when I died,
Couldn't be there by your side,
And I want so very much to make it right.

The slightly hoarse voice of the lead singer of Finnegan's Pig broke across the scene, and it was almost as if Ben was singing the words. There had been a lot of discussion, tipping over into outright argument, over the lyrics of the song; the director said they were too simplistic, too trite, and that this opening scene was the place for something deep and meaningful, and the intellectual elements in the production team agreed. But the Finnegan's Pig singer said he didn't do deep and meaningful, and Jo said Ben had talked like everybody else and wasn't the poet laureate, and in the end the intellectual elements had been outvoted.

Now, listening, watching, the beautiful colours softening and merging as the tears filled her eyes, Jo was so glad they had.

But the poignant mood soon changed, and as the boy and his father reached out to each other and began to play, to run, to leap in the waves and blossom in the joy of being reunited, humour entered the story and presently the room was echoing with laughter.

The story was winding towards its conclusion now; the film was only forty-five minutes long. Jo had left the ending open to interpretation, wanting to respect those who believed in an afterlife and told themselves they would see their loved ones again; and also those who, like her, believed that memory, and the enduring nature of deep love, were the only immortality. The film did it beautifully; the final scene, of the boy now turning into a man and looking down so tenderly at his father's photograph in his hands, was exactly how she had done it in the story.

But then, as if the producer wanted a last and slightly mischievous word, just for a second the angel was back, his hand hovering just above his son's head, before, with a smile, he slowly disappeared.

The credits began to run, and the final song played.

But nobody heard it, because a storm of appreciation broke out.

Jo was floating on a cloud of exhilaration. She'd sat through a meal for which she was far too excited to have much appetite, drunk a glass and a half of champagne, accepted congratulations from dozens of people, stammered her thanks to a few dozen more, listened to some clever and mercifully brief speeches and said a few halting words herself. The charity people were delighted, having made more money than they'd hoped on ticket sales and with high hopes of the raffle: 'The dear people have been so, so generous!' said the powerful woman in stern slate grey and minimalist silver jewellery who was the charity's director.

Jo had managed to get away from her own table to spend a while with her sons, her parents and her former neighbours at theirs, and seeing how impressed they'd all been in their different ways was perhaps the best reward. She made her apologies to them and left to set off on a round of greetings, but first – for there hadn't been a chance before now – she diverted to the corridor leading to the ladies' cloakroom.

Going in, she bumped into Angela coming out.

Both of them gasped, both of them said simultaneously, 'Sorry!'

Angela was dressed in a tight-fitting dress with a tiered net skirt in a dramatic shade of flame that only a woman with her colouring could wear. Her hair was longer, glossy and in a well-cut bob. She looked gorgeous.

There was a very awkward silence. Jo saw the blush begin, creeping up from Angela's chest.

Then Angela said, 'The film was wonderful. To do that, to have written that … God, if he – Ben, your Ben – somehow knows what you've done, how much you love him, what's he thinking? How happy is he going to be?' Her grey eyes filled with tears. 'Sorry,' she hurried on, 'I'm sorry if I'm upsetting you.'

If Ben knows how much I love him, Jo thought.

In an odd moment that was full of emotion but also sudden clarity, she thought, but he does, of course he does.

And quite a lot of things seemed to nudge themselves into a new pattern.

'You're not upsetting me,' Jo said. 'And I'm very glad you liked it.'

Angela leaned closer. 'I've had a couple of drinks and probably more because I was so nervous,' she said, 'and so I'm speaking where I shouldn't, but I'm really sorry about Hal and I wanted to tell you, and I doubt I'll get another chance like this, when I bump into you and I'm a bit pissed. You and him and your boys are Max's family,' she hurried on, 'and I hope ... well, you know.'

'Yes, I do,' Jo said. 'It's in the past. It hasn't ...' She'd been about to say that it hadn't changed anything, but it had, only of course – and she could see it so clearly right this moment – it hadn't been Hal sleeping with Angela that had changed everything, but that everything had already changed and it was this that had led to Hal sleeping with Angela.

But she knew there was absolutely no chance of putting that lot into words.

'It's the past,' she said again. Angela was still looking at her very intently. 'Shall we start again?' she said softly.

And Angela said fervently, 'Yes.'

'Where's Max?' Jo asked after a moment in which both of them had surreptitiously wiped their eyes. 'I'm doing my lap of honour – that's a joke, actually – and I may as well start with him.'

Angela's face lit up in a huge smile of relief, and she led the way between tables to where Max sat deep in conversation with two men and a rather brittle-looking woman. He stood up in mid-sentence to hurry round and take Jo in his arms. 'Brilliant,' he said in her ear. Then he gave her a smacking kiss. Angela, Jo thought with a grin, wasn't the only one who'd had a couple of drinks.

The careful seating plan was fast going to pot now, and people were mingling, talking, laughing, the noise level already deafening and steadily rising. Jo took Max and Angela over to her family's table, and it wasn't nearly as hard as she'd anticipated because nobody knew what had happened between Angela and Hal and so they all just accepted her as Max's partner. Ed and Sammie greeted Max with hoots and howls; they too appeared to have had at least a sip or two of some sort of alcohol. Paul Daniel got up rather too swiftly to shake hands and had to hold onto the back of his chair, and Jo's mother Elowyn found it rather funny.

'I'm pleased that one Dillon made the effort,' Paul said too loudly.

'Dad!' Jo said. 'You know why Hal's not here.'

She thought he was going to argue with her, but Elowyn grabbed his hand and pulled him back into his chair, leaning over to whisper in his ear. 'But ...' he began.

'Enough.' Jo heard her mother's reply clearly, as, from their expressions, did everyone else round the table.

With easy tact, Max drew up a chair next to Paul and asked him what he'd thought of the film.

Jo had no idea what the time was. She'd just spent ages chatting to Flavia McGinty, resplendent in a boned evening gown dating from the fifties and a feather boa, and Flavia had insisted they each had a large brandy with which to drink to the film's success. Jo's sense of unreality was steadily growing.

Some people were drifting away now, others were dancing, and the film's soundtrack album was playing softly over the music system. The violin player from Finnegan's Pig asked her to take a turn with him, and as they shuffled round the tiny dance floor they sang along together to one of the lesser-known numbers on the soundtrack. Then she returned to the family table, to find that Tom and Laura were just leaving and her parents about to do the same.

'Come on, boys,' Jo said, dropping a hand on each of her sons' shoulders.

'But …' Sammie began.

'But nothing!' Jo's father said, so firmly that Sammie actually flinched.

All of them, except Tom and Laura, had booked rooms in the hotel, and to Jo's surprise, Max said he and Angela had, too. 'Neither of us was prepared not to drink in order to drive,' he said cheerfully, 'so we thought we'd make a night of it.'

His bow tie was untied, his normally smooth hair flopped over his forehead and he had what looked like a piece of shrimp on one black silk lapel. Angela giggled. 'We certainly did that,' she muttered.

They were all heading out towards the foyer, and the bank of lifts in the corridor beyond.

And then, just for a moment, Jo saw someone.

A man, quite tall, strongly built, in an old-fashioned dinner jacket. He turned away even as her eyes fell on him.

She almost ran after him.

I can't, she thought; and emotion – grief, longing – flooded through her.

'Darling, are you all right?' her mother asked anxiously. 'You've gone quite pale!'

'I'm fine, Mum,' Jo said, hoping she had sounded as if she meant it. 'Tired, that's all, and too much fizz!'

'Bedfordshire,' announced her father.

'Bedfordshire?' Sammie echoed in a giggling whisper.

'A spot of Bedfordshire means it's time for bed,' said his grandfather.

251

Two lifts arrived together, their doors pinged open, and Jo and her party went inside.

She looked longingly towards the foyer, but he was long gone.

Nevertheless, the fact that Silas had been there for her big night made her heart sing.

Part Three

Changes
1991-1994

Chapter 19

1991

As January got under way, Silas sat late one night in the living room of his peaceful old house. Outside, it was bitterly cold. There was snow on the ground, ice on the puddles and the island was very quiet. The Christmas and New Year guests had all gone and Old Harbour had drawn in on itself, recovering its strength.

Silas stretched forward and chucked another log on the fire. Then he leaned back into the sofa cushions, his mind far away.

He knew he shouldn't have gone to London. They hadn't put it into words, but he understood, as he was sure she did, that seeing each other would only cause pain. More pain. But he'd seen the charity showing advertised in the bookshop where he'd first seen her photo: a big poster pinned up in the window behind a stack of a new edition of the book with an image on the jacket that presumably had been taken from the film.

He hadn't been able to resist. He'd gone straight into the shop and ordered a ticket. It cost an eye-watering amount, and he'd have to find a dinner jacket from somewhere, but neither factor could put him off. He borrowed Archie's DJ – Helly kindly let down the trouser hems for him – and he didn't notice that it dated from the days when Archie was a young man.

He'd sat in a corner and watched her from afar. She was dressed in violet silk and she looked beautiful. He had tried to guess which of the men at her table was her husband, but none seemed to fit the role. Later on she had spent a lot of time with a group of people, two of which he thought were her parents – she bore a resemblance to each of them in different ways – and the two sons she'd spoken of with such love. The younger boy clearly adored her, holding onto her with a total lack of inhibition or embarrassment; the elder one, who looked very like the man in the film, was much more reserved, but the look he gave his mother shouted out his pride.

And pride was right, Silas thought now. The film was enchanting and he guessed she must be gratified at how faithfully it kept to her story. He'd bought a copy of the book, so he knew.

He had made sure she didn't see him. He watched her circulate, chatting, hugging, full of happiness and, he thought, relief.

Then as the evening came to a close and everyone was leaving, he made a stupid mistake. He'd meant to slip away earlier but he'd been unable to. So he'd been in the foyer when she left.

He was sure she'd seen him.

It had cost him a lot to keep walking.

Two days before Christmas Eve, a padded envelope had arrived for him, addressed care of the big house. It contained a beautifully bound little story, with an image on the front of a small boy struggling to eat an enormous portion of Christmas pudding. The story was silly, funny and light-hearted, and he guessed she had deliberately made it so; made sure it didn't touch the deep things that lay unspoken between them because to do so would be to hurt him and no doubt her too.

She had put her address on the back flap of the envelope.

Spotting it had made him whoop with joy.

He'd got to work straight away. It was so easy, for the images of her were constantly in his mind. It was a small oil painting, eight inches by six, of Lindisfarne seen from the Pilgrims' Path, with two tiny figures sitting on a rock looking out to sea. They were eating a picnic, but you had to have been there at the time to know that.

He didn't get it to her in time for Christmas. The paint had to dry, he had to treat it, he had to wait till the post office opened so that he could buy bubble wrap, paper and string. He wanted it to look like an old-fashioned parcel; a brown paper package tied up with string.

He was aware that he was probably breaking their unspoken agreement. But then, so had she.

It was all they had.

It will be enough, he thought as he watched the parcel disappear behind the post office counter.

It would have to be.

Now, lying on the sofa before the fire, he reached for her story. Read it again. Smiled; it was meant to amuse. Touched the paper that she had touched. Wondered, as he'd so often wondered, how it had come to be that so much had flared up between them so swiftly.

He'd told Archie. Briefly, saying merely 'I fell for her hard, and it was the same for her. She's married – she told me that straight off – and has two children. There are problems in the marriage, but she's trying to make them go away.'

Archie, wise, compassionate, had nodded. 'She is right to do so,' he said.

'I know!' Silas had snapped out the response, immediately apologising. But Archie shook his head and said it didn't matter.

Helly seemed to pick up what had happened without being told: Silas didn't tell her, and he was quite sure Archie hadn't.

'You've known and loved each other in a previous life,' she stated, as matter-of-factly as if she was saying Silas had blue eyes. 'Perhaps as lovers, but it could have been another close relationship – brother and sister, for example.'

'Helly, I'm not sure I believe in reincarnation.'

She put her head on one side. 'It's not exactly that,' she said. 'You do love her?'

'Yes. Almost as soon as I saw her, I sensed I knew her and the love … it seemed to me that the love was already there.'

'Yes. Of course, it would,' Helly said softly.

'I'd seen her photo in the bookshop,' he went on, 'so …'

'That is immaterial,' Helly said. 'You saw a face, you remembered it when you saw her again. That can happen to anybody. But to be overwhelmed with such strong emotion – as both of you were, not just you – points strongly to the fact that you recognised what you'd previously been to each other.'

He looked at her, strong, sturdy, working pony of a woman that she was, and wondered yet again how she knew so much. But her awareness of matters beyond the reach of ordinary people was a comfort. Impulsively he put his arms round her and gave her a hug.

'Don't be too sad,' she said softly. 'I know it hurts, but it's happened. And love by its very nature can never be anything but good.'

As January dragged by and presently turned into February, however, Silas wasn't so sure.

On a sunny morning in late spring, Angela sat on the bed on the bed, silently weeping.

Max had gone to work, but she didn't need to go in until lunchtime. She was now employed in Gus's museum, a small and perfect place with an old-fashjioned air that made no effort to compete with its larger and more famous rivals in the city but was content to wait for people to discover it for themselves and, having done so, fall under its spell, as they invariably did. When Angela had begun working there the cataloguing system was shambolic; as shambolic as dear Gus himself, who was a big, rambling sort of man who loved to dress in linen and trousers with pleats at the front and the elegant clothes of an earlier age, but never quite remembered to hang them up when he took them off at night. Now, thanks to her determined efficiency, nearly every item in the museum had a card with a comprehensive description of what it was, when it was made and when (and usually how) it had come to be in the museum, and each card had a place in the beautiful old set of apothecary's drawers that Angela had made Gus buy. She'd been very afraid that her own efficiency and speed would all too soon put her out of a job, but Gus had recently told her that she was now an intrinsic part of the place and she had no choice but to stay.

So there they were, for all or part of the working week, quite often accompanied by the flamboyant but slightly distracting presence of Kieran Heaney, Max's partner, when he wasn't racing round the British Isles and the nearer countries of the Continent in pursuit of voice-over work. He spoke French with a Dublin accent; and, according to French people who had employed him in the past, this was an accent that was apparently irresistible to the Gallic ear: 'I feel I'm pulling a fast one,' Kieran had once said with a rueful shrug. 'Cheating, somehow. I tell them that a particular camembert knocks the *chaussettes* off every other brand and because it's my voice, they believe me! It's bollocks really, the whole advertising thing, and so is the camembert, but that's the world we live in, Anja, so what can you do?'

She had noticed that both Gus and Kieran had copied Max and called her Anja.

She loved it.

She sat up and dried her eyes.

It's because I love him, she thought, coming back reluctantly to what was making her weep.

She did love Max; of that there was no doubt. He loved her too, and he made it plain in everything he said and did. He allowed her to be the person she really was. He tried all the time to adapt to her, instead of doing what every other man she'd been close to did and trying to make her fit in with them. As she was doing precisely the same thing, their life was harmonious and full of delight.

She heard the front door open. It had a particular sort of rattle, a vibration, as if it was giving itself a shake in recognition of people going in and out.

She sat up straight, wiping her eyes with her sleeve. She hadn't been expecting him home. Had he forgotten something?

'Anja?' he called up the stairs.

'In here!'

She heard him coming up. 'I meant to take the blue file with me this morning and I left it in my study, so ...'

He picked up her distress even as he came into the bedroom. He sat down beside her on the bed, put his arms round her and held her to him. 'What is it, my darling girl?' he said after a moment.

'It's silly!'

'Tell me anyway?' It was a question. It was as if he was saying, I'd like you to explain but I respect your privacy if you don't want to.

'Oh … I thought for a few days that I might be pregnant, but it turns out I'm not.'

After quite a long time he said, 'And that is what's making you sad.' No question this time; he knew it was.

She nodded.

He said tentatively, 'We – I – sort of assumed we were preventing your conceiving.'

'Yes, we were. Assuming, I mean, and I was. Am.'

Then he said, 'Would you like us to have a child?'

And she heard herself say fervently, 'Yes.' Then, hardly daring to speak, 'You?'

He gave a sort of sigh. Then, his voice shaky with emotion, he said, 'I can't think of anything I'd like more.'

Two days later he came home in the afternoon with a bouquet of flowers and told her he'd booked a table for dinner. Before that, he took her to Silver Street bridge and they hired a punt. It was a beautiful spring evening. As they drifted slowly past King's College Chapel he took a little box out of his pocket.

'I had thought I might kneel down to offer you this,' he said, glaring at a party of undergrads in an out-of-control punt, 'but I think I'd better keep poling.' He flipped it to her and she caught it one-handed.

She opened the little box.

A diamond set in a circle of smaller diamonds blinked suddenly as the evening light caught it.

Her head shot up and she stared at him. 'Really?'

'Really.' He smiled at her, the expression full of love. 'If we're going to have a child, I would very much like us to be married.' He did a swift evasive manoeuvre, neatly avoiding the end of the punt full of students. 'Do you mind?' he yelled. 'I've just asked this beautiful woman to marry me and she hasn't answered yet.'

The students started to cheer and shout, and the shouts turned into an impromptu chorus: 'Say yes! *Say yes*!'

Angela, laughing, tears in her eyes, looked straight at him and shouted over the noise of the students 'YES!'

Jo and Hal and the boys travelled by car down to the Basque region. It was August, and the journey down was shared with what Hal said tetchily was the entire population of western France. They were held up several times on the various motorways, and going round Bordeaux they came to a complete standstill and stayed that way for twenty minutes. Jo pointing out that they were in the prime spot for an unexpected delay since they were at the apex of the bridge over the Dordogne did nothing whatsoever to cheer him up, and in the end she hissed at him, 'I'll drive, then you can dive back into that fascinating book you stuffed in your bag and stop being such a grumpy old fart and give us all a break!'

She'd thought she'd spoken too quietly for the boys to hear in the back, especially as Ed had his Walkman and he and Sammie had an ear bud each. But she heard Ed snigger and Sammie said very softly, 'Dad's a grumpy old fart,' so probably she hadn't.

But they all agreed, even the grumpy old fart, that the destination was worth the journey. They were renting a gîte on the outskirts of a town called St-Jean-Pied-de-Port, a shabby old farmhouse with white-painted walls and a red-tiled roof whose steep pitch suggested heavy snow in winter. They were, after all, in the Pyrenees. The house's interior wasn't shabby, having been done up to a standard acceptable to the most discriminating of gîte patrons, and Jo and Hal agreed they'd have been happy with less shining, modern perfection and more original charm.

But the modern gloss meant that the hot water was always plentiful (and gushed out of the taps and particularly the dinner-plate-sized shower head like Old Faithful, as Hal said, having scorched his shoulders going to ease the tensions of the drive), the fridge, freezer and cooker worked with quiet efficiency ('Go on then, Mr I-can-cook-a-casserole, now's your moment in the spotlight,' Jo said to Hal, pointing at the stove) and, best of all from Ed and Sammie's point of view, their bedrooms were up in the roof and reached by a ladder and the pool was large, sapphire blue and had a springboard.

The first few days were wonderful. Jo found herself relaxing, and she thought she could actually see her tense muscles smoothing out, and the little worry line that had appeared between her eyebrows growing shallower. She did twenty or thirty lengths in the pool every morning before everyone else was up, swimming strongly and steadily, her mind far away. Sometimes she took a deep breath and performed her sea spirit routine. It made her feel guilty to be thinking of Silas here, with the family, with Hal being so nice and everyone enjoying themselves, but she couldn't not do so. She tried to keep images of him, and the sense of him that was somehow always with her, buttoned up for most of the time. But this quiet half hour, as the light grew strong and the day woke up around her, was for him.

They thoroughly explored St-Jean the first morning, and on a steep, narrow, cobbled street they ate a rather surprising lunch in a restaurant that appeared to specialise in trout. Specialise was an understatement,

Hal pointed out, since all but one of the list of starters and main courses featured trout in some form or another. Sammie amused himself by speculating on trout puddings, and they voted trout crumble with custard as the favourite.

They found out – actually Jo realised Hal knew already – that St-Jean-Pied-de-Port was a rallying point for pilgrims doing the walk across northern Spain to Santiago de Compostela. Ed said it was probably the town where they stuffed themselves on a good trout meal to get them through the climb up over the Pyrenees. A path with worn old stones led out of the town towards the mountains soaring up to the west, and the four of them hiked along it one morning and had a picnic overlooking a wonderful view, marred slightly by the constant stream of hot, sweaty, complaining modern-day pilgrims toiling along the track.

They went out on the car on most of the ensuing mornings, visiting St-Jean-de-Luz ('Ravel was born here,' Hal informed them), a wonderful beach near Biarritz and a museum of witchcraft at Bayonne. Sammie bought a lethal-looking dagger at the museum, Hal bought a CD of 'The Mother Goose Suite' in St-Jean-de-Luz. They explored some caves with prehistoric wall paintings and amazing stalactites and stalagmites in the deep folds of the mountains. On that trip they came across a dead cat in the road, and Jo, who was driving, stopped at a house close by and they all got out to tell the occupants what had happened, Sammie distressed because he was sure they were bringing tragic news of a beloved family pet. The indifference of the man who came to the door astounded and angered them all, and they were united all the way back to the gîte in their condemnation of French heartlessness.

The afternoons were usually spent at the gîte, where the boys had the run of the surrounding land and, of course, the pool.

Jo was happy. Hal was the old Hal, the wry, affectionate and entertaining man she'd fallen in love with. When they made love in their wonderfully atmospheric bedroom with the window looking out at the mountains, she felt that they had truly found each other again.

Then, in the second week, it changed.

They were having lunch at the gîte after a morning in St-Jean-Pied-de-Port. It was market day, and Hal had bought a fierce local cheese studded with garlic and peppers, Jo a pair of sheepskin slippers, Ed a penknife (he was clearly regretting not having bought a dagger in the witchcraft museum) and Sammie a scarlet beret.

'What's on the agenda for this afternoon?' Hal said casually.

'Pool,' chorused the boys with a rigidity that wasn't going to be gainsaid.

'Sounds good to me,' Jo said, taking a mouthful of iced water in an attempt to put out the flames set off by Hal's cheese. 'I'm two-thirds of the way through my book and I can't wait to get back to it.'

There was a pause.

She knew, even before he spoke, what he was going to say. She silently cried out a quick plea that she was wrong.

She wasn't.

'I reckon I'll take the car and have a drive round,' Hal said with an attempt at cool nonchalance that didn't fool her for a moment. 'There's a few places we've flashed by that I'd like to revisit and take some time over,' he hurried on, 'and if you're all happy here, I may as well.'

She put down her knife and slowly turned to look at him. She held his eyes for a moment, then said, as neutrally as she could manage, 'Thinking of writing a book on the rich and intriguing history of the Basque region, are we?'

265

The flash of annoyance on his face that preceded the guilt that came just before the appeasing smile told her she was spot on.

He wasn't gone long; three or four hours. He came back laden with supermarket bags and cooked them all a delicious supper. They had discovered a local wine called Irouléquy, and he'd bought a couple of bottles to have with the meal, and tubs of the boys' favourite ice creams ('Trout!' Sammie said) for pudding. The evening was cheerful, and Jo was sure the boys hadn't noticed that anything was wrong.

Nothing is wrong, she told herself as she dried the glasses and put them back on the enormous dresser. Hal had washed up, which she thought was good of him since he'd cooked, but she always gave the glasses an extra polish as she like the way they sparkled. No, everything's fine. Hal had an afternoon researching a possible subject for the next book, her thought continued, but that's okay. Isn't it?

But an insistent little voice at the back of her head said, Why didn't he say so? Why didn't he say, when you were talking about where to go on holiday, that he was interested in the Basque area and why not combine an initial visit with our family holiday? I might have been a bit iffy because it'd mean he'd be distracted, she admitted to herself, but I'd have got over it. And I'd have known. Wouldn't have had to face this sense of disappointment when I found out.

Hal came into the kitchen, took the tea towel from her hands and led her into the main room. He sat her down and gave her a coffee and a snifter of brandy. He settled beside her, took her hand.

Later, they made love. But she sensed he wasn't really there.

He was distant the following day, and she knew from long experience that he was working on some idea and wanted nothing more than to be left alone in some quiet corner to write his precious thoughts in his notebook.

She said to the boys, forcing herself to sound cheerful, 'Come on, we'll leave the grumpy old fart to it and go out just the three of us. Where d'you fancy?'

The boys both answered at once and, typically, they wanted different things, so Jo said they'd take the whole day, buy a picnic for lunch and do one activity either side of midday.

Hal was creeping away to his quiet corner even as she went out of the door after the racing boys. But he must have sensed her eyes on him, for he stopped, turned and looked at her.

She said quietly, 'It just doesn't change, does it, Hal?'

Then she left.

At the end of the summer, Max and Angela were preparing for their September wedding. They were to be married in a tiny, ancient chapel in Max's college, and a friend of Gus's was to conduct the ceremony. The lack of space was an advantage, since both bride and groom were short on relatives. Which, as Angela pointed out, made the ones they did have rather more relevant.

Angela had steeled herself and gone down to Cheltenham to visit her mother and stepfather. Max phoned Copse Hill House and Hal answered.

They exchanged fairly reserved greetings. Then Max said, 'Any chance you and I can meet in London? Lunch, maybe?'

'Yeah, if you like,' came the laconic reply. Don't sound so eager, Hal, Max thought. 'Only it'll have to be soon, I'm about to go to California for three weeks.'

They arranged a date – the next day – a time and a venue.

As Max put the phone down, he realised with a surge of relief that Hal would be away on the day of the wedding.

* * *

The venue was a pub in a street off the Strand. It was Hal's choice, and considerably nearer to Charing Cross than to Liverpool Street. Purely coincidental, Max told himself magnanimously, and nothing to do with our relative convenience.

Hal was waiting for him and swiftly got him a drink, handing him a menu. They ordered a ploughman's each, then headed to a table away from the bar, where the noise level was much lower.

'Okay, shoot,' Hal said as they sat down.

'Angela and I are getting married,' Max said. 'We'd like you and Jo to be there.'

Hal nodded. Max, watching him closely, saw some fleeting expression cross his face. Then he said, and the warmth and sincerity in his voice took Max by surprise, 'I'm very pleased for you both. She's a special woman, and I hope you'll both be happy.' He raised his pint in a silent toast.

'Thanks,' Max replied. Then: 'It'd be good if what happened between you and her can be in the past.'

'It is,' Hal said shortly. 'It shouldn't have happened, and I guess I ought to say I'm sorry, but it'd be a lie so I won't.'

'You …'

'It's okay, Max,' Hal interrupted, 'I'm not carrying a torch for her, and I meant it when I said I hoped you'd be happy.' He paused, frowning. 'I loved her, in a way. And that's all I'm going to say.'

Watching him, sensing the conflicts that raged in him, Max reckoned he'd got more than he expected.

'So, will you and Jo be able to come to the wedding?'

'When is it?' Max told him. 'Nope. I'll still be in California.'

'What about Jo?'

Hal hesitated.

'She and Angela have met, Hal,' Max said quietly. 'Seems to me there isn't any animosity between them.'

'She'll have to decide for herself,' Hal said. 'I'll get her to ring you.'

The food arrived, and it seemed natural enough to attend to it and stop talking about weddings, and Jo, and what had happened between Hal and Angela, and pretend that all they were thinking about was eating.

Jo took the train to Cambridge. For one thing, everyone said parking in the town was impossible, and for another, she was going to a wedding, and that meant champagne, and she wasn't about to miss out.

The September day was glorious. The weather was warm and sunny, more like June than September, and as Jo got out of the taxi and went in under the low stone arch opening onto the college – a square of buildings around a green space, a little chapel on the far side – she had the illusion of a burst of colour. It wasn't flowers or bright shrubs, however, but a crowd of people, the men smartly dressed, the women in brilliant summer dresses.

She edged her way through them, politely asking those most intent on their conversations to move. She reached the chapel, and noticed that one of the pair of heavy oak doors was marginally ajar. A face was peering out anxiously.

The two dark eyes in the face lit on her and a man's voice hissed, 'Are you Jo?'

'Yes!'

The door opened a fraction wider and a hand beckoned her inside. The cool interior smelt like joss sticks – it's incense, dummy, she told herself – and candles had been lit on the low wooden partitions enclosing the little box of the choir stalls, their flames protected by narrow glass funnels. The simple altar was decorated with huge displays of flowers in yellow, orange and red on either side of the plain wooden cross. There were only a few short rows of pews, and almost all of them were already full.

'I'm Kieran,' the man said. He held out his hand and Jo took it.

He was not tall, very slim, beautifully dressed in a dark grey suit over a pristine white shirt with a flame-coloured tie. Noticing her eyes on this, he said, 'It's not really my colour, but it's Anja's day, and it definitely is her colour!'

Recalling the brilliant dress at the charity event, Jo said, 'Is it ever!'

Kieran said, 'We have a small problem. The venue, as you will have observed, is small, and Max and Anja were very careful not to invite many people. But word has got out, and now the quad out there's heaving with people, and I'm on strict orders only to admit people who are invited, which is very dodgy because this is a holy place and you're not meant to keep people from entering …' He broke off, his beautiful, sensitive face creasing in a frown.

'I don't think they're going to storm the doors,' Jo said gently. Kieran gave a slightly hysterical snort of suppressed laughter. 'The mood is quite festive, I'd say, and definitely well-meaning. Perhaps they've come along simply because they want to be here and wish the happy couple well?'

Kieran's dark eyes held hers. 'I hadn't thought of that,' he admitted. He risked one more quick glance out through the door. 'I believe you're absolutely right!' he exclaimed, turning back to her. 'Come on, you're the last, let's go and claim our seats.'

He took her hand and led her up the aisle to the second row on the left, where they slid into a pew behind a woman sitting straight-backed and wearing a huge cerise hat set at an angle of forty five degrees, held in place by an almost invisible piece of thin elastic that disappeared into her elaborate coiffure. A hunched man in a grey suit sat beside her.

'Anja's ma and step-father,' Kieran said in her ear.

Jo nodded. Then, for she had been wondering, 'Anja?' He said it *An-yer*.

'It's what Max calls her, and Gus and I picked it up,' he said. Then: 'Gus is my chap. He's Max's best man, and at present they're out the back somewhere with the minister and the organist.'

'Oh, right, so …'

A large man in a very crumbled grey suit appeared, his tie – slightly crooked – identical to Kieran's. 'That's Gus,' Kieran whispered. Gus couldn't have heard, but all the same his eyes had flicked to Kieran, and he gave him a smile. Seeing Jo, he mouthed, 'Jo?' and she put a thumb up in confirmation. He gave her a wave that almost toppled the nearer flower arrangement.

Max emerged after him, dressed in a dark grey three-piece suit whose waistcoat was bedecked with a gold watch and chain. He too had the white shirt and flame-coloured tie combination. He looked, Jo thought, gorgeous. He also looked nervous. Gus whispered something to him, and he turned and saw Jo. He gave her a smile.

Angela's mother was muttering to her husband. Her voice was too carrying for an echoing little chapel. '… met him, holidayed with him, moved in with him in the blink of an eye, as you well know,' she was saying, the upper-class nasal whine in her voice detectable even at relatively low volume, 'and they seem to be making a go of it, but one has no *idea* of his background, and Angela refuses to discuss what he does, or his prospects, and apparently he has no people bar a distant cousin who hasn't even had the decency to turn up, and …'

Kieran leaned forward, edged in under the angle of the ridiculous hat and said, quietly and with frosty politeness, 'Max and Angela are blissfully happy and love each other deeply. Max's background is utterly respectable, he is a renowned professor of psychology with a fine reputation and first-rate prospects, and although his distant cousin indeed cannot be here, his wife is and she's sitting right next to me.'

Jo, unsure whether to be shocked or laugh aloud, watched as a deep flush spread up Angela's mother's neck and across her carefully made-up face.

And just then the priest stepped out and stood before the altar, facing his small congregation with a happy smile, the organist began on an uplifting piece of Bach and a flurry of movement to the rear suggested Angela was on her way in.

Turning round with the rest of them, Jo looked at her. She was alone, and she wore an ivory dress, knee length, with a full skirt held out by layers of net and a neckline that lay across her shoulders. There was a wide, flame-coloured silk sash round her waist. Her hair shone in the candlelight and she looked beautiful. Max turned to smile at her, and her beauty turned into something else.

With a lump in her throat, Jo sat very still and listened to the immortal words of the service.

When it was over, the new husband and wife went with the vicar, the best man and a stout woman sitting in the front row opposite to a small table to sign the register. Kieran, Jo perceived, was tense, as if waiting for something. After a moment, the organist began to play an elaborate but unmistakable version of 'The Way You Look Tonight'.

Kieran breathed a sigh. 'Oh, Max got what he wanted!' he said happily.

'They danced to this the night they got engaged,' he said, leaning close to Jo. 'You wouldn't think a stocky bloke like Max would dance as well as he does, would you?'

Max, Jo thought, was strongly-built and tall. She supposed he would seem stocky to someone as wraith-slim as Kieran, but then everyone else probably did too, including herself.

'That's lovely!' she replied.

'Max was doubtful they'd be allowed to have the song here, but it seems he was more persuasive than he thought.'

They listened to the old tune. Jo watched Max's face, his joy very apparent. Suddenly, she felt very miserable.

Kieran's hand found hers, and he gave it a gentle squeeze. 'Don't be sad,' he said, so quietly she only just heard. 'You're thinking you're not loved, not like Max loves Anja, but you are.' He squeezed her hand again. 'My granny had the sight, and I know things sometimes, just like she did. He's far away, but he's thinking of you right this minute.' With his free hand he pointed to the middle of Jo's chest. 'That's where your heart chakra is,' he whispered, 'and it's glowing.' He smiled. 'Your heart knows someone loves you, even if you don't.'

And, sitting there with this stranger being so kind, the happiness of Max and Angela's wedding day seeming to fill the air with elation, Jo realised that Kieran's words were no surprise.

But I do know, she thought.

And, for the first time in quite a while, she too felt happy.

Chapter 20

1992

Hal finally told Jo about the house on the hillside in the dismal, damp chill of mid-January.

Sam had made it inevitable, although Hal knew it wasn't Sam's fault.

Sam had come for Christmas, and they'd been joined by Paul and Elowyn Daniel. Hal had half-dreaded it, half been very relieved that he, Jo and the boys would have company. In the end, it had been good. More than good.

But then, the day before Sam went home, after Jo's parents had set off back to Cornwall, Sam had said over the breakfast table, 'Son, I forgot to tell you: there were a couple of calls for you after your visit back in September. Some realtor guy with a name I can't bring to mind – Bromwell? Bromham? – said he was acting for you and needed to talk to you, and I said you were no longer at that number, and I told him I couldn't give him your contact details but I'd call you and get you to call him.' Sam looked pleased with himself for having remembered Hal's notorious antipathy to being troubled by phone calls from people he didn't want to talk to, which was pretty much everybody. 'He said not to bother as he had your number in England but had hoped to catch you before you left. Did he get through to you?'

'Yup.'

Sam was peering at him over the top of his spectacles, clearly expecting more. But Hal, aware that Jo standing at the sink with her back to them had gone very still, wasn't going to supply it.

Just as Sam began to say, 'Everything okay?' Hal said loudly and heartily over him, 'Last day, Dad! What do you want to do?'

Jo hadn't said a word.

New Year had come and gone, the boys had returned to school for the new term, and it felt to Hal as if someone had lit a very long fuse on a small but powerful bomb.

So, on that dismal, damp, chilly January morning, he made two cups of coffee and took them up to her writing room, tucked away at the end of the upstairs landing and with a door that she kept locked, so that the only access was from his room immediately below and up a narrow little wooden staircase with a kink in it, which they thought must once have been a priest's means of access up to his raised pulpit in some vast old church.

He stopped on the tiny square of landing outside the door, which was open a crack. 'Can I come in?' he asked. 'I've brought coffee but the kids have eaten all the M and S cookies.'

'Yes, door's open,' she replied.

He went inside, putting her coffee on her desk. Her computer screen was lit up, shining a blueish light on her face. She was writing swiftly, and he moved away to let her finish.

He liked her writing room. He liked it better than his, mainly because it was less accessible, but since he had commandeered the downstairs space before she'd had a chance to and they'd had to make this new room for her by adding an upper floor to the extension, he could hardly say so. He let his eyes wander round.

One wall was full of photographs, different sizes and subjects (although invariably people) and unified by their soft blue mounts and dull gold frames. Her desk was huge, since she also used it as a sewing table, and two ceiling-high bookcases stood either side of it. She had a sofa covered in cushions and a big patchwork throw. He wandered over to the bookcase on her right. The little oil painting of Lindisfarne was propped up at what would be her eye level when she was sitting at her desk.

He knew who had sent it, because she'd told him.

He went to sit on the sofa.

Presently she turned her revolving chair round to face him, picking up her coffee. 'Sorry, I was just working out a tricky end of chapter.'

'It's okay.' He looked down at his coffee mug. 'Jo, I'm buying a house, up on the hills behind and to the north of Morro Bay.'

She didn't say anything for a while. Then: 'Would we be having this conversation if Sam hadn't dropped his little clanger?'

He shrugged. 'Probably not. Not yet,' he amended quickly.

'So when were you going to tell me?'

'Jo, it's no big deal!' He'd told himself the same thing, many times. 'But it makes sense. Sam's getting old, we've suggested he moves here to live with us but he's set against it, and he has a right to say where he spends his final years. It's likely I – we – will need to be over there more frequently and for longer, and neither he nor I like crowding each other in his house, and it's even worse if the boys come too. I don't own a house, and I have money which it makes good sense to invest in property. Sammie …' He stopped short. This last argument made a lot of sense to him but he didn't think it was the moment to raise it with Jo.

'Sammie loves it there,' she finished for him. 'Yes, indeed he does, and it's no surprise since he adores the sea, and the boat, and the sailing, and being with his grandfather, of course, and I ought to have put that first.' Her frown deepened. 'And you could throw in that he's half American, and that it's his right to live in his paternal country if he wants.'

I very nearly did, Hal thought.

Then, in a voice so soft he had to strain to hear, she added, 'Not quite yet, though, hm?'

'I have no intention of …'

'Hal, shall we leave your intentions out of it for now?' she said with acerbity. 'So, how do you envisage us using this house on the hillside? We go over all together in the school holidays, and you use it as a place to live when you go over on your own to visit Sam when we can't go with you?'

It struck him in that instant that he hadn't envisaged it like that at all.

But, 'Yes!' he said, forcing enthusiasm into his voice. 'It's small – one decent bedroom and one small one, but the main room's a generous size.'

She was looking at him intently. For a moment he thought she was about to challenge him: to say, Hal, what's this really about? But she didn't.

'We won't be able to visit it all together for quite a while,' he said into the silence. 'It needs a deal of modernisation, and I'll be pretty much camping out while the work's being done.'

She drank the rest of her coffee and spun round to face her computer again. 'Then I won't hold my breath,' she said.

It was as clear a dismissal as if she'd told him to go.

Jo heard Hal's tread going down the wooden stairs. She got up and pushed the door almost closed.

Then she went back to her desk, staring out of the window to the winter-bare garden and the softly-rolling landscape beyond.

I knew he'd do something like this, she thought dismally.

But then, why not? All the reasons he gave make good sense. Sam is very important to him – to me, to all of us – and Hal and the boys love going there to see him. Well, Sammie does.

She sat deep in the depressing depths of her thoughts for some time. Then she realised why she was sad: it was like the Basque trip all over again. If he'd told her what he had in mind before circumstances forced him to, it would have been very different.

He acts as if he's a single man with only himself to consider, she thought, and the realisation hurt like a fist punched in the chest.

She remembered Kieran, at Max and Angela's wedding, pointing to her heart chakra. Now she seemed to be feeling the painful aspect of that mystical organ, if organ it was, and it was deeply uncomfortable.

She turned to the right, to the Lindisfarne painting, and the pain was alleviated by a single shaft of joy.

He had sent her another one for Christmas. It was of a room full of movement, with a throng of people and sparkles of light set off from jewels, glasses, silverware. In it, to left of centre, was a figure in violet with a pennant of shiny blonde hair. It was in total contrast to the Lindisfarne painting but it was equally beautiful. His name was just visible in the bottom right-hand corner: just Silas, and the second S had a tail that underlined the whole name.

Her story for him this year hadn't been funny or even particularly happy. She hadn't been able to summon either happiness or humour when she'd written it. It was about a boy who had found a dead cat and taken it to the nearest house, very anxious because he was sure he was taking heartbreak along with the little corpse and then devastated to be met with indifference. He had crept out late that night and retrieved the body from where the householder had dumped it and given it a proper funeral and interment, patting down the soft earth like a blanket and putting a circle of stones to mark the place. He was a child who loved cats and had always wanted one, but his parents were too busy working and said dismissively that cats made work and who was going to do it? Him? Don't make them laugh! But then, very early one morning as he came home from his paper round he heard a pitiful little sound coming from behind the dustbin and there was a minute kitten, black and white and with exactly the same markings as the poor little corpse. It was an optimistic ending, even if not a happy one, because the final paragraph had the boy standing on the doorstep with the kitten in his arms vowing that he was going to keep it and his parents would just have to lump it.

For the cover illustration she'd drawn the scene in the Basque country, and her own Sammie bending over the pathetic little body at the side of the road.

She had taken the oil painting of the charity evening out of her desk drawer and now sat looking down at it. 'Thank you, Silas,' she whispered. 'And I hope you liked the story.'

In April Angela was feeling huge, uncomfortable, impatient and apprehensive. Her pregnancy had gone smoothly, and nobody seemed unduly concerned about a woman in her mid – okay, mid to late – thirties having a first baby. She'd felt thoroughly well throughout the months, reassuring Max that it really was all right to go to Denmark over Christmas as they'd long planned to do, and she had gone on feeling well while they were away.

However, the days after the festivities, when they'd got down to following some promising leads concerning Max's great-grandparents, had proved tiring, and he'd made the last trip on his own while she rested. She'd been so sorry afterwards that she hadn't gone with him, because it was the day when he made what they later called The Big Breakthrough:

the day when he'd finally found the little village where Kai Nicolajsen, Cille Jespersen, Aksel and Freja Møller had lived, where Kai believed he'd killed a man, and from where the four of them had fled to Brittany.

It had felt right, somehow, that he'd made the discovery when the family was about to produce a new generation. When they returned to Cambridge Angela had worked hard, writing to Danish genealogists and to an elderly local historian who seemed to have researched the tale of the minister's daughter, and the violent man who had made up his mind to marry her until her true love persuaded him otherwise. Max had written up the full story, incorporating Angela's careful family trees and foot notes, and they planned to conclude it with how they had made their extraordinary discovery in the heart of a Breton forest. That, however, was for the future: for now, they had more urgent concerns.

Max had been a calm, reassuring presence throughout the pregnancy, coming with her to hospital appointments and antenatal classes and listening intently to everything they were told. At home, he had painted the smaller spare room. They had chosen pale apple green and white, having decided that they didn't want to know the child's sex beforehand. Angela had made white curtains, and they'd gone over the top in Mothercare and bought almost as much nursery furniture as would fit in the room.

The baby was due in ten days.

Angela had had to persuade Max quite hard that morning to go off to London as he'd planned. 'I'm fine,' she insisted. 'I'm tired and grumpy, so I'm probably better on my own. I'll have a walk this morning – it's lovely out there and I'll go along the Backs and admire the crocuses yet again – and I'll be sure to have a rest after lunch. Go!' she added, giving him a push towards the door.

'Really?'

She smiled. 'Really.'

Around an hour later, she was halfway across Christ's Pieces when she felt a pain.

Oh.

It eased off again almost immediately, and she walked on. She emerged onto the road by the bus station, heading towards King's.

It happened again and, quite soon afterwards, once more.

She found a bench and sat down.

After some time she got up and rather shakily set off for home.

She lay down on the sofa in the living room and fell asleep.

She was woken violently by a pain like someone tightening a belt round her lower belly. She cried out. It was followed by successive further pains, exactly the same, and she remembered she was meant to time them. She wasn't wearing her watch – oh damn damn damn – and the clock on the mantel was beautiful, and delicate, and antique, and probably worth thousands of pounds, but it had ornate little gold scrolls for hands which made telling the time with any accuracy something of a challenge, especially for a woman in labour.

Which, she had to admit, she appeared to be.

Between contractions she stumbled upstairs and fetched the battery-operated alarm clock from beside the bed. She was stopped halfway down by another contraction, and made it back to the sofa gasping and sweating. Having something to concentrate on besides her womb helped, and she stared at the alarm clock's face as if it was a how-to manual.

The contractions were roughly ten minutes apart.

She thought she ought to phone for an ambulance.

She got almost to the hall, then paused to wait while another pain wracked her. She bent over double, and felt something give between her legs: a rush of water ran down her thighs and over her feet. She thought, what a good thing I'm standing on a wooden floor, and wondered if she should fetch the mop. Suddenly she felt dizzy, and had to slump against the wall.

By the time she felt able to stand without falling over and go on towards the phone, she knew without checking that the interval between contractions was quite a lot shorter.

'I'm having a baby,' she said to the pleasant male voice that answered her call, inspired by his total lack of a sense of urgency to be calm herself. 'It's not due for another ten days, but it seems to have its own ideas.'

The man chuckled. 'They will do that. What's the address, my love?' She told him. 'And how fast are the contractions coming?'

'They were about every ten minutes, but that was some time ago and now they're coming a lot faster, and … AAAAAAAGH!'

The man waited. Then he said, 'That sounded like a biggie. Ambulance is on its way. Is there anyone there with you?'

'No,' she gasped before another one hit her.

'Okay, then. Are you able to get to the door?'

'I'm standing in the hall. The floor's all wet, they'll need to take care they don't slip because- OOOOOOH!'

'You leave them to worry about that. Stay right where you are, they'll be with you very soon, and …'

'Don't go!' she yelled at the top of her voice.

'I won't, I'll be here till they're with you, and you can tell me whenever you feel another contraction.' But she was wailing loudly as he spoke and, when the pain eased, he said ruefully, 'On second thoughts, I'll probably pick it up for myself.'

To her amazement, she actually laughed.

Time passed, and she had no idea how long, then there was a brisk rapping at the door and someone called out, 'Ambulance service!'

She crawled over and let them in.

The ambulance crew was comprised of a smiling young man and a comfortable plump woman, and she felt safe with them as soon as they came in. They helped her back into the living room, and the woman made her lie down so that she could see what was going on. In a voice that held only excitement and encouragement, she took one look and said, 'Ah, yes. This little laddie or lassie wants to be born right here. Where do you keep the towels?'

'Upstairs, airing cupboard next to the bathroom.'

'Freddy, up you go,' the woman said.

Then it was a muddle of piercing pain, kind voices, a thick, soft padding of towels beneath her and a desperate need for something to lean against because suddenly her back was aching worse than any other bit of her, and she was crying, shrieking, and then someone said, 'Darling girl, I'm here, lean against me,' and somehow, Max was there kneeling behind her, his strong body supporting her like a chair back and his knees either side of her wide-spread thighs. It was, she thought in a surreal moment, as if both of them were giving birth.

Then the pain turned to a quite different feeling that didn't hurt nearly as much and she felt her body take over. Listening intently to the woman crouching in front of her, following her clear instructions, it all happened very quickly and she felt something issue out of her in a rush of fluid.

The woman gave a cheer and Freddy, leaning over her shoulder and as deeply involved as the rest of them, yelled, 'It's a boy!'

They took her and her new-born son into hospital, but it was, the woman said reassuringly, just to be on the safe side and there wasn't anything to worry about.

And an hour or so later, Angela was sitting up in bed, Max beside her with his arm supporting her, both of them staring down at the cross little face screwed up around the busily-suckling mouth. Their new son had taken to the practicalities of life with admirable sang-froid; the nurse who was looking after them said he must be an old soul who had been round before and knew the ropes.

Angela said, 'How did you come to be there when I needed you so much? You were meant to be in London.'

'Didn't go,' he said.

'Duh!' she replied.

He grinned. 'I was lurking,' he admitted. 'There was something about you this morning, and I had a feeling it might be today. I came round the corner and saw the ambulance, and – well, you know the rest.'

She reached out a hand. 'I'm glad you were there.'

Which was, she reflected, the understatement of the year.

Darkness fell.

Angela was sleepy, and Max took the baby and held him close. Looking at his expression, Angela didn't think she'd ever seen him happier.

'Don't leave us,' she said drowsily.

'I'm not going anywhere,' he replied. 'Us is the three of us. I'm staying.'

She smiled. 'What shall we call him?'

Max thought for a while. The baby gave a soft little sigh, turning his face towards his father's chest. Otherwise there was a serene silence, as both of them ran through names.

Then Max said, 'Jake.'

And Angela said, 'Perfect.'

* * *

In early June there was a phone call from Jo. She had sent a card, signed by all four of them (although Max strongly suspected she had forged the brief *Hal* scrawled across the corner) and promised to deliver a present when they had settled down a bit. On the phone she said they were planning to come tomorrow if he was sure it was okay ('Yes!') and that she'd bring some lunch so they didn't have to bother ('No need!') and that it'd be just her and Ed, as Hal was working on an article due in two days and Sammie was at school, but Ed had mild concussion from playing after-school baseball and couldn't do anything remotely strenuous.

Putting the phone down with a smile, Max had the distinct impression that Jo was nervous about coming. He went to tell Angela they were expecting guests.

Jo and Ed arrived in the late morning of the following day. Ed had a black eye, a bump on his forehead and carried a quiche: 'I didn't make it,' Jo said disarmingly, 'we stopped at the delicatessen in the village.'

'Bring it through to the kitchen,' Max said, 'I'm just putting some salads out.' Ed followed him along the passage but Jo had heard the wild, distressed wails coming from upstairs; you'd have to be deaf not to, Max reflected.

'Shall I go up? Would she mind? ' Jo whispered, as if Angela could possibly have heard her normal speaking voice over the racket.

'Yes. I imagine she'd be delighted. Come on, Ed, we'll shut the door.'

Angela heard the soft tread of bare feet on the stairs and didn't know whether to be relieved or horrified. Jo tapped gently on the door and said, 'All right if I come in?'

Angela had rarely felt so hideous. She still carried some of the fat laid down in pregnancy, her hair was unkempt, she was wearing track suit bottoms and an old shirt of Max's and two vast patches of leaking milk were spreading across her front. Jake in her arms felt like a heavy, hot, wrestler who appeared to believe she was doing everything but try to make him feel better.

Jo seemed to take it all in at a glance. She made a rueful grimace of sympathy. 'Oh, bloody hell, I'd forgotten how awful it can be,' she said quietly. Then, after a tiny pause, 'Would you like me to take him?'

Before she could even think of saying No thanks I'm fine, Angela breathed 'Yes!' and thrust the wriggling, screaming Jake into Jo's arms.

She held him close, his head to her left side, staring down into his scarlet face. He was staring back up at her with an expression of interest that was almost, but not quite, dispelling the disgruntlement.

'He has Max's light eyes,' Jo murmured. Then, to Jake, 'Crikey, that's a God-awful noise for a small boy, Jake. Care to turn it down a bit?'

He filled his lungs and emitted a couple more screams, but more for form's sake than because it was necessary. Then he gave a quiet little sigh and his eyelids started to droop. He hiccupped once or twice and emitted a few more half-hearted wails.

'I'm dying for a wee,' Angela whispered. 'Okay if I ...?'

'Yes, go on!'

When she returned, Jo was standing by the window looking out over the garden and Jake was fast asleep.

'How did you do that?' Angela said softly. 'He's been fed, burped, changed twice, walked up and down, sung to – I've tried everything!'

Jo looked down at the deeply relaxed child. 'I'm not his mother,' she said simply. 'I didn't like the noise any more than you did, but it wasn't acting on me like insistent torture the way it was on you. Maybe he was picking up your distress, and came out in sympathy.'

'Great way to show it,' Angela muttered.

'Yes, but he's only two months old. It gets better.'

They shared a conspiratorial smile over Jake's coppery head.

'Shall I put him in his cot?' Jo suggested.

'Yes.'

She did so, and both of them crept out of the room.

Angela said, looking down at herself, 'I ought to change.'

'Why?' Jo replied. 'Ed has a black eye and a hole in the knee of his jeans, and I'm wearing my comfy travelling trousers.' She hesitated. 'And we're family, really.'

Angela gave her a steady look. Then she just said, 'Thanks.'

In the kitchen, Max was hearing about the baseball bat that an enthusiastic friend had flung through the air and that had landed on Ed's forehead. The two of them were working efficiently together and the food was almost ready.

Max raised his head. 'Can you hear something?' he asked.

Ed listened. Then, understanding, he grinned. 'That was probably Mum,' he said. 'She's pretty crap at cooking but there are dozens of really useful things she can do.' He paused. 'Like knowing the secret of how to get to the middle of the Hampton Court maze and out again, and how to change a wheel, and remembering a great mnemonic for how to spell diarrhoea.'

'How does it go?' Max asked.

'Do I Ache Really Roughly? Hurry Or Else Accident.'

'Good one.'

'She invented another when we were doing the planets at primary school, for remembering the order they come in: My Very Eager Mouse Jumps Swiftly Under Nuclear Power. She said you have to make a story out of it so that the image stays in your head.'

'She also seems to be able to quieten very noisy infants.'

'Oh, yeah,' Ed said nonchalantly. 'Can we eat as soon as they come down? I'm starving.'

They'd eaten most of the food and the conversation had flowed while they did so. Jo had told Max and Angela some more about Hal's article and they had made noises of polite interest, although neither had asked any supplementary questions. Now it was time for Jo and Ed to leave, and Max saw them to the door. Angela had gone up to tend to Jake, who had just woken up, and called out goodbye as she flew up the stairs.

'Don't you want to wait and see the baby?' Max said to Ed.

'No, you're all right, I …' Ed began hastily, then, seeing Max's expression, grinned.

Max kissed Jo. 'Thank you so much for the blanket,' he said. She'd given them a pale blue cashmere baby blanket, very light but also very warm. 'It'll get him appreciating the exquisite things of life from an early age.'

'You're welcome. Keep in touch?'

'Will do. Safe journey.'

On the way home Ed said, 'Max doesn't like Hal much.'

And Jo just said, 'No.'

Autumn arrived and Ed started on his GCSE year, while Sammie and his class embarked on the eleven plus. They had managed a summer holiday all together, and Hal had made the supreme sacrifice and not even taken a notebook with him for the fortnight in Minorca. They had a place right by the beach and all four of them had done little more than swim, laze, sail, eat, drink and sleep. Then they came home again, immediately before the school term started, and Hal said he was going to see Sam and wasn't sure how long he'd stay away.

Normal service, Jo thought sadly, has been resumed.

Chapter 21

1993

In late summer, Silas was on the overnight train speeding southwards through Italy.

He had spent the past couple of months in an ancient, crumbling house near Cortona, where the equally ancient and crumbling owner had discovered a beautiful painting on the wall of a previously blocked-up passage leading off the cavernous hall. There had been a minor earth tremor back in February, part of the blocking-off wall had collapsed, and a torch poked through the resulting hole revealed the painting. Someone who knew someone who knew about Silas had given his name to the elderly owner, who had written a letter in excellent English on thick cream paper in an elegant hand, asking Silas very courteously if he would consider coming out to give his opinion and, assuming it to be favourable, stay and try to bring the painting alive again.

Silas, heartsore and lonely, had said an instant yes by return of post.

That Christmas he'd sent Jo a painting of his fireplace, with two empty chairs either side of it. It made him sad to work on it, and he was sure she would pick up the emotion. But then her story of last year hadn't been any too cheerful, and its successor, when it arrived, was much the same: like him, he concluded, she was suffering.

So rushing off to Italy seemed a good idea.

Archie drove him to the station. Silas was going by train, ferry and more trains. He didn't fly nowadays, partly because he thought it was terrible for the environment but mainly because he'd had one too many near misses in his previous life.

'How long will you be away?' Archie asked delicately as they approached the drop-off point.

'I don't know,' Silas replied. 'It depends on the state of the painting and whether it's worth restoring. Whether there's anything to restore.'

'That's not really what I meant,' Archie said.

'No. Right.' Silas sighed. 'I'll see. If being away feels better, then I'll stay away.'

'Okay.' Archie indicated and shot into a spot vacated by a taxi. 'I'm not meant to stop here, so you'd better be quick.'

Silas grabbed his bag and got out. 'Bye, Archie, and thanks,' he said, about to close the door.

But Archie called out, 'Silas! What happens if she – if there's post for you?'

So, he knew about the Christmas parcels that contained her stories.

'If I stay away I'll send you an address.'

Then all at once leaving the country, and in particular this place that was his only true connection to her, seemed at the same time a very stupid thing to do yet the only thing he wanted. He knew he had to go, now, before he could change his mind. He gave Archie a curt wave, turned and hurried away.

He had let himself become totally absorbed by the work.

He suspected that the painting on the wall was fifteenth century. It was of the Annunciation, and the scene had been set inside an arch that made it seem as if you were looking between the pillars of a low cloister. The old man said the building had once been a monastery, dating from a long time before the fifteenth century. Silas had an idea that the work could have been by a pupil of Filippo Lippi. There was something about the vibrant pink robe that the butch-looking angel wore over his elaborate garments that seemed familiar.

It was a long, slow job. He had no inclination to hurry, and the old man – whose name was Giovanni di Lucca – wasn't pressing him; seemed, in fact, pleased to have company, even if Silas spent all but the final hour or so of each day down in the hidden passage, cool when everyone else was broiling in the heat of early summer. There were openings in the old stone walls which admitted fresh air and daylight, but not the hot, exhausting sunshine.

Signor di Lucca did not broil either, for his beautiful old house had outdoor places constructed to make the most of any slight breeze, and huge old chestnut and walnut trees that gave generously of their shade. Each evening as Silas was finishing up for the day, Signor di Lucca would put his wrinkled head on its turtle-like neck round the very edge of the door to the secret passage, careful never to look at what Silas was engaged upon, and say, 'Now, a drink, my friend? I have white wine that has the little fizz and is as cold as the inside of the deepest vault.'

Over the days, the weeks and the months, Silas and Giovanni slowly entered into a reserved but genuine friendship.

'You carry sadness with you, my friend,' Giovanni said one evening in August. Silas had told him he had nearly finished and that the Great Unveiling Ceremony could be arranged for the next week; Giovanni had resolutely refused to have even so much as a glimpse of what was unfolding until the work was completed, and he was planning a party with a dozen of his closest friends.

Silas wondered if it was only because he'd be leaving soon that the courteous old man had allowed himself to advance a more intimate remark than those which constituted their usual evening talks.

'I met a woman three years ago. We spent a week together, but it felt as if we'd known each other always. Someone I know said we'd loved each other in a previous life. She was married, and I'd lived on my own for a long time, and we didn't become lovers. We haven't tried to contact each other, although each year she sends me a story and I send her a little painting. I didn't imagine I would forget her and I haven't. I have no idea if I'll ever see her again, but she's here.' He put his hand to his heart. 'And here.' He moved it to his head.

Giovanni didn't speak for some time, although he silently filled up their wine glasses and raised his to Silas, a compassionate expression on his lined old face. Eventually he sighed and said, 'Does she love her husband?'

'I expect so. They have two boys, although the elder one is the son of her first husband, who died. She certainly loves the boys.'

Giovanni nodded. 'And she loves you.'

It was nice of him, Silas thought, to make it a statement and not a question. He said very softly, 'Yes.'

'You do not have a choice, my friend,' Giovanni said. 'It is for her to – ah – to rearrange her life, if that is what she decides. Both of you, for your own reasons, have taken the strong moral decision not to proceed yet, and in this day and age that is rare and I applaud you for it.'

'It may be moral but it fucking well hurts,' Silas muttered, far too quietly for Giovanni's old ears.

But Giovanni's old ears were sharper than Silas had anticipated, for he nodded sagely and said, 'Of course it fucking well does. When, however – and I believe it is when and not if, for I see happiness ahead for you – when you come together, it will be the more precious because you both went through this time of waiting.'

'What if it's all for nothing?' Silas said. It was the dark fear that crept along behind him, all the darker for rarely being acknowledged.

Giovanni shook his head vigorously. 'Do not let yourself even think that it could be,' he said, very sternly. His small, dark eyes fixed on Silas's. 'Believe,' he said.

The Great Unveiling Ceremony was a resounding success. Silas and the electrician grandson of one of Giovanni's friends set up a string of lights, for although Silas had worked by daylight, the ceremony was to be at night. He was nervous, and kept going back to check that the soft lights were working properly and would be bright enough: 'They must be only what there would have been in the fifteenth century!' the electrician grandson insisted. At least, Silas thought that was the gist of it, but the boy didn't speak English and Silas's Italian was limited.

He need not have worried.

When the door to the secret passage was flung open and Giovanni hit the switch, the lights came blazing on like wall torches and everyone present gasped with delight. They spent ages in the secret passage, getting in each other's way, pushing and shoving and exclaiming in fortissimo Italian, and eventually Giovanni clapped his hands and told them it was time for a drink. The party went on till after midnight, and there were several sore heads in the morning.

In the afternoon, Silas took his farewell of Giovanni di Lucca. The old man insisted on driving him to the station and he had tears in his eyes as he took Silas in his arms. 'Goodbye,' he said. 'Be happy.' And he had pressed far too much money into Silas's hand.

'This is much more than we agreed,' Silas said.

'But your work is much better than I envisaged,' Giovanni replied. 'Go! The train will depart without you!'

And he had stood waving a spotless white handkerchief until the train was out of sight.

Silas went to Brindisi, where he got on a ferry that called at Corfu and went on to Piraeus. From there he went in easy steps north and east through Greece, stopping where he felt like it, yet always heading towards the eventual destination.

He arrived at the monastery high in the hills as summer turned to autumn. He said to the monks 'I'm back,' and they said, 'Come in.' There were no more old frescoes for him to work on and so he offered to create a new one, on the end wall of the recently-built and utilitarian refectory. He asked what the subject should be, and the monks said they didn't mind.

'Paint what is within you,' Brother Aidan said. He was almost ninety, or perhaps more than ninety: he couldn't remember, and it didn't seem important. He had left Ireland decades ago and been a resident of the monastery for at least half a century.

'What if whatever's within me isn't right for a monastery refectory?' Silas asked.

'It will be,' Brother Aidan said serenely. Then, more prosaically, 'Anyway, we can always paint over it.'

He was probably joking, but you could never be certain with Brother Aidan.

Silas sat and looked at the big blank space for a while. The raw new refectory was so bland (and so ugly) that it gave no clue as to what might be suitable; not even a colour clue, for the walls and ceiling were stark white and the floor was greyish-beige concrete.

It needed the outdoors, Silas thought. It needed nature. He began to envisage foliage, trees, flowers, above a sloping beach that led to a deep sea. It would be acceptable, he thought, for the prime mover responsible for the natural world could surely not be a million miles away from the god to whom these men had given their lives.

He made some sketches, then threw them aside and went to work on the wall.

The scene developed as if it had a momentum of its own. It emerged pretty much as Silas had first seen it with his inner eye, and the only addition was a faint swirling figure down in the navy-blue of the sea, although you could only see it – her – if you looked in a certain way.

She is there because I love her, Silas thought.

He had an idea the monks wouldn't mind her presence if they detected it.

Autumn turned to winter, and work speeded up on an orphanage the monks were constructing in the foothills beneath the monastery's mountain. Silas replaced his artist's brushes with a hod, a wheelbarrow and then, as one of the monks who could lay bricks took him on as his apprentice, a trowel and a slab for the mortar. Then came cans of white-wash, paint rollers and a wall-banger, and the monks and Silas worked long into the night to get the place ready before the cold weather set in.

The children moved in at the end of November. There were eight girls under the care of three nuns, and ten boys looked after by a priest and a quartet of cheerful young monks. Brother Aidan enlisted Silas to help him teach the children English. It was hard work to begin with, but Brother Aidan's sense of humour soon won the children round, and it was not uncommon for the primitive (and cold) little schoolroom to echo with laughter.

The end of the year loomed.

Silas, as content in the monastery as he was anywhere and with the advantage of sensing he was doing something valuable, decided he would stay a while.

In his spare time he was working on the annual Christmas painting. It was of the monastery, and he had managed to find a viewpoint where the brash new refectory was out of sight. The original buildings were very old, and over the centuries they had blended in with the surroundings. He chose dawn for the time setting, and, facing east, the scene was backlit with rosy pink; he'd become much more of a fan of pink since working so intimately with the Filippo Lippi pupil.

He had intended the painting to be a sort of landscape-with-ancient-buildings, without figures, without even much in the way of human sentiment. But his inner self betrayed him: what was meant to be an image of a beautiful, calm and neutral sort of place turned into one of a desolate, abandoned old ruin where there was nothing to be found but loneliness.

He knew she would detect that emotion the moment she looked at the painting.

He sent it anyway.

A bundle of post arrived for him just after Christmas. There had been a heavy snowfall, and the postman's van didn't make it up the mountainside until just before the new year.

Silas opened his cards first. Archie, Helly and several of the others at Old Harbour had sent cheerful greetings, and some of them asked when he was coming back. Both of his sisters had also remembered him, and there was even a cheap little card from his mother and signed by his two brothers as well.

He opened the big padded envelope last.

He knew even before he opened the story that she was feeling as bleak as he was, for the illustration on the cover was of a figure – a woman – walking alone down a long road that wound away into the distance. The story tried to inject a note of optimism, but it was about loss; about longing; about wanting to mend something that was broken, even while the woman knew it was beyond her power to do so.

Silas went out onto the night-dark mountainside and stared down at the valley. The snow still lay thick, and it was bitterly cold. He could see the lights of the orphanage below. He and several of the monks had gone to help with the Christmas meal, and the day had been a good one. He looked east, then turned in a slow circle through south to west. Finally he looked north, adjusting his position so that, judging by the stars, he was facing roughly north-north-west.

He said softly, 'Jo,' and he sent her his love.

Chapter 22

1994

At the beginning of January, Jo and Hal flew with Ed and Sammie to San Francisco for a five-day visit. Both boys needed to be back for the start of the school term. Sammie had passed the eleven plus the previous year and was a term into his first year at the same school as Ed. Ed's GCSE results had been excellent, and he was now deep into his A levels. He was doing physics, maths and biology, and he wanted to be a marine engineer. But before the boys returned to school, they were all going to see Mary.

Bernard MacAllister had died five weeks before Christmas.

The family had been out to see him the previous summer and found him weak but cheerful, happy to sit in his chair in the sunshine while his family chattered and laughed around him. Jo had spent a quiet hour by his side, holding his hand, watching him watching his daughters and his grandchildren. Sometimes, looking at Ed, he got confused and called him Ben.

Hal and Jo hadn't managed to get to the funeral, since it was during the school term and at short notice as well. But as Mary said on the phone, it had been far more valuable to have been there when Bernard was still alive to enjoy them.

Now, on this visit, all four of them spent most of the day with Mary and then Hal and Sammie set off for Morro Bay, leaving Mary to follow on with Jo and Ed in a couple of days.

In the big house in San Francisco, the three of them were quiet, each deep in their own thoughts. Ed spent quite a long time in the room that had once been his father's, and Mary went upstairs to sit there with him.

'I'm selling this house,' Mary said to them both over supper that evening. 'It's too big for me, and it has been for a long time.' She took a shaky breath. 'It's been a very happy home, but the family isn't here anymore and I don't want to be here on my own. I've only been waiting for …'

She stopped abruptly, her mouth working. But Jo and Ed knew very well what she'd been waiting for; there was no need to put it into words.

Jo waited until she could speak without her voice shaking. 'I think that's very understandable,' she said. 'Will you buy something smaller locally?'

'No. I'm moving to Morro Bay.'

'Oh!' Jo was surprised, then saw the sense of it. 'Sam,' – and Hal's new house, she added silently – 'and Annie and Emily and their families will be quite a lot closer. What a good idea!'

'I'm not planning to cramp Sam's style,' Mary said firmly, 'but I've visited the place many times, going to see Sam, and I like it. There's a development right on the shore and a little out of town and I have my eye on one of the small apartments there.'

You knew this day was coming, Jo said silently to her. You knew dear old Bernard was on the way out, you thought it through and realised you didn't want to live here without him, and you made your plans. Good for you, Mary my love.

She glanced at Ed, who nodded almost imperceptibly and then came up with just the right emotion-defusing remark: 'Cool,' he said. 'You can show us when we go down to Grandpa Sam's., then we'll be able to picture you living there.'

The three of them took flowers to Bernard's grave. He was buried beside Ben, and the headstone lay close by waiting until the ground over the new grave had subsided. Ed took the dead wreaths to the trash, then they distributed the fresh bouquets between Bernard and his son.

They stood deep in their own thoughts for some time. Jo felt as if a circle bound them all together. She said a silent goodbye to Bernard, then spoke inside her head to Ben, and what she had to say went on for a while.

When they turned away and went home, she felt clearer in her mind than she had done for a long time.

They were almost at Morro Bay.

Mary stopped at the place where she was planning to buy her apartment. Jo and Ed both admired it. Ed said she'd be able to hear the sea when she went to sleep. Then they went on to Sam's house.

Mary stayed overnight at Sam's, taking the spare room. Jo had the sofa while Ed slept on the floor. Hal and Sammie were camping out, as Hal referred to it, at the hillside house. Jo said she and Ed would like to have a look, but she sensed he was reluctant to show them. In the end she said, half-amused, half-irritated, 'Hal, we have to see it sometime! It doesn't matter if it's a work in progress, we'll get the general idea.'

The next day he came back to fetch her and Ed and drove them up to the house.

Sammie showed them the tiny bedroom he was busy making his own. Hal flung open the door to the larger bedroom. 'It's short on storage space,' he said.

'It sure is,' Jo muttered. 'Still, it's a holiday home, so we won't need to bring masses of stuff with us.'

It might have been her imagination, but she thought Hal shot her a rather sharp look when she said that.

Ed was prowling round the big main room. He didn't say much, only a brief 'Yeah' when Jo said how terrific the view was.

The next day Mary went home, and Sam took the four of them to the airport.

Hal shut himself away with his work. He was on the final draft of his book on the Basque region and it was due with his agent at the beginning of March. Jo saw little of him. She too was busy. She had written a proposal for a second illustrated book and sent it to the publishers of the angel story, where it had been very well received; the film company, she'd been told, were expressing interest. Encouraged, she was settling down to write and to draw.

Hal delivered his book.

Then, just as Jo was about to suggest the four of them took a short break over the Easter school holidays, he announced he was going to California.

'I have to see what's happening with the house,' he said, in the sort of tone that didn't sound as if he was prepared to argue about it. 'And I need to start on some research for my next project. I'm planning …' Abruptly he stopped.

'Planning what?' Jo asked.

He paused, then said gruffly, 'Something about the Spanish missions.'

'Of course,' she said very softly. But he wasn't meant to hear.

He set off for California.

Jo took Ed and Sammie to stay with her parents in Cornwall. Sammie had a great time. Ed was thoughtful, inclined to be quiet. He spent quite a lot of time with his grandmother. Elowyn said once or twice to Jo, 'Everything all right, darling?' and Jo replied brightly, 'Fine!'

Towards the end of the summer term, she asked her mother to come and stay at Copse Hill House. Elowyn didn't seem at all surprised at the invitation, nor at Jo's explanation that she was flying out to California to see the house on the hillside. 'Of course I'll hold the fort here and look after the boys,' she said. She gave Jo an extra-tight hug as the taxi came to collect her. 'Good luck,' she said very softly.

Jo arrived in San Francisco in the morning. She'd been going to book into a hotel to catch up on some sleep, but she was too tense, too jagged, and knew she wouldn't be able to rest, so instead she hired a car and drove south.

She didn't hurry. It was a long time since she'd driven on the roads of California, and she took it carefully.

She turned off the highway and onto the quieter back roads. She took one or two wrong turns, but then she recognised a couple of landmarks and eventually found the house on the hillside. There was a car parked outside.

She parked out on the road, walked through the open gate and onto the deck. Looking around, she could see evidence of a great deal of work, and the house looked very different from how it had been back in January.

She went inside.

Hal was deeply involved in the history of the Spanish missions. He was sitting at his desk at one end of the big main room, his books and papers arranged to his satisfaction on shelves on three sides. He had the house to himself for the first time in ages: the work was almost all done now, and he was only waiting for one or two final touches in the streamlined new kitchen.

He was vaguely aware of a car outside. Then the noise stopped and he forgot about it.

A few minutes later he heard a voice call out, 'Hal?'

His head jerked up. His heart began to thump. He felt cold, then hot.

Very slowly he pushed his chair back and got up. Walked over to the door.

Jo stood just outside.

He looked at her, and for a while he had no idea what to say.

Then: 'I didn't know you were coming.'

'Nor did I.' There was a pause. 'Can I come in?'

'Sure, of course.' He stood back.

She advanced into the room. 'It's looking great,' she said. 'You've … it's very you.' She smiled faintly.

'Yeah.'

She wandered along to the bedrooms, the big one (his) and the little one, where Sammie had made his mark. There was a poster on the wall: *Jurassic Park*. A row of books filled a shelf with two Tyrannosaurus Rex models as bookends.

She walked back to the big room, and Hal walked behind her.

She turned and said, 'Hal, what are we going to do?'

'I … I need to be here, for a while at least.'

She nodded. 'I know.'

They looked at each other.

'Was it Angela?' he asked huskily.

'No,' she said. 'It wasn't.' She raised her head, staring out through the open door. 'It's …' She hesitated, then said in a rush, 'Hal, I have such a lot to give that you don't really want.'

'But …' He was about to protest, but it hit him with sudden harsh clarity that she was absolutely right.

He tried to speak, cleared his throat and tried again.

'Jo, you once told me that you were shoved into a role you didn't fit. When the boys were little, when you had no choice but to be a housewife and you never had the time to finish a thought.'

'Yes!' she said wonderingly. 'Fancy you remembering. I did say that.'

He paused, thinking. Then: 'I know what you meant. I feel just the same.'

She watched him, and he thought her face had paled. 'You … you've been shoved into a role you don't fit?'

'Yeah.' It was harsh, but he needed to say it.

There was a very long silence.

Then she said very softly, 'You like being here on your own. Working, thinking, arranging your days around what you want, free to come and go without reference to anyone else.' She looked up at him briefly and his heart ached with the pain of it. Then she looked down again. 'Without reference to the boys and me.'

And, again, he said, 'Yeah.'

Slowly she nodded. 'Yes,' she echoed. 'Yes, Hal. I know.'

Part Four

Conclusions
Autumn 1995–Autumn 1997

Chapter 23

It was late September, and Jo and Ed were driving a car full of Ed's stuff towards the city that would be his home for the next four years. He had passed his A levels; done rather more than pass them, in fact, with A stars in maths and physics and A in biology. There had been mutterings at the school about Oxbridge, but Ed knew exactly where he wanted to go and his application had been successful.

They had a long journey ahead. Ed had been out late the night before, enjoying a farewell booze up with his mates from school before they all went their separate ways. He was heavy-eyed, smelled of beer and was taking none too subtle drinks from a large bottle of water. Jo said, 'Why not tip your seat back and have a sleep?'

'Wouldn't you mind? Don't you want to talk?'

'No and no. I'll put some music on.'

'I'll do it.' Ed leaned forward. 'What do you want?'

'I'll have Jacques Loussier.'

He settled back as the cool sounds filed the car. Quite soon he was snoring gently.

Jo smiled. Then, free to think her own thoughts for the first time in what seemed like ages, she allowed her mind to slip back to everything that had happened in the past year.

*   *   *

She wondered occasionally – quite frequently – how she'd got through it. At times it had all but ripped her apart, and often she was shaken to her core by the thought that the future was so terribly uncertain and wasn't it better to stick with the devil she knew? She'd poured it all out to Elowyn: 'How will it be? How will it affect us? Me? I have no idea how to deal with it all, how there can be any chance of happiness if …' But she couldn't go on.

Elowyn had taken her hand, stroking it gently. Then she said with profound wisdom, 'You're not happy now.'

So Jo had ploughed on.

She and Hal had done their utmost. Last year they'd talked, made herculean efforts – well, Hal had been the one attempting to change, and she admired and loved him for how hard he'd tried – and it had seemed at one point that they could have found a way. But then that summer Hal, Jo and Sammie went out to California for a fortnight while Ed was on holiday with a girl called Bella, and Sammie took his grandfather out sailing most days.

And it was during that horribly difficult, profoundly painful time that Jo and Hal at last recognised the truth.

It was a relief, really, to have made the decision. What followed was awful and sometimes agonising, but they slogged on.

And there had been other decisions to make.

Sammie wanted to go ahead with the plan to spend a couple of years or maybe more in a school in California. He had it all arranged: he'd stay with Grandpa Sam in the week, then go to the house on the hillside to be with Hal at weekends. He'd go home to England in the holidays. '*Promise*!' he'd said fervently to Jo.

She didn't really see how she could stand in his way. He'd spent the first thirteen years of his young life in her country, living a thoroughly English life. She would miss him like hell and the thought of his absence was like a dull ache which she didn't dare touch with her fingertips, let alone prod with any force, but it wasn't fair to let him know and make him feel guilty.

She didn't really have any idea how she was going to cope with it. Although Ed was off to university, Sammie was still a child; her child. She wasn't ready to stop being a full-time mother to him, but it was rapidly becoming evident that she didn't have any choice.

I'll always be his mother, she thought now. Whether I'm with him or not, it makes no difference. I'm the only mother he'll ever have, and nothing will change that.

Now, driving with the cool sounds echoing through the car, she sent him her love, did what she could to put a full stop on the pain, and then let her thoughts move gently on.

And they moved, quite naturally, to Ed, snoring beside her.

Ed was excited and very happy. He was doing precisely what he wanted to do; he had achieved his goal. He and Bella – Bella Mackie, it turned out – were still together. They'd met when Ed made his first visit to the university where he was about to take up his place and they'd liked the look of each other. They'd kept in touch, she had come to stay and Ed had made a return visit to her family. She too had a place at the university and she would be reading history. The two of them had travelled round the north of England and up into Scotland over the summer. Jo wasn't sure if they were friends or if it was more than that. It didn't seem to matter. She was glad Ed would have someone he was so close to as he embarked on his new life.

* * *

They were about ten miles short of their destination. Jo pulled into a service area, parked, shook Ed awake and he grunted, sat up and blinked. 'God, are we there?'

'Not quite. I thought you might like to get back in touch with reality before we arrive. Fancy something to eat?'

Ed thought about it. Then he nodded, grinning. 'Yep. I can face food now.'

They were back on the road within half an hour.

Ed got out his file of useful information and directed her efficiently to his hall of residence. She slipped the Discovery in between two other parental cars in the process of being unloaded, and exchanged friendly smiles with other mothers and fathers. She and Ed humped his belongings up the stairs and into his room.

'When's Bella getting here?'

'She's probably here already, since she lives much nearer. I'll get this lot stowed then go and find her.'

'Then I'll leave you to it and get on my way.'

Suddenly her stomach felt as if it had fallen several floors in a high-speed life. Ed, coming with her back out to the car, looked at her. 'You okay, Ma?'

'Yes!' she said brightly.

I'm scared, I'm terribly nervous, I'm full of hope and I have no idea if I'm about to find bitter disappointment or absolute joy, she could have said.

Ed put his arms round her and hugged her very hard. 'You've done the right thing, Mum,' he said softly.

She nodded, gently extracting herself. 'Go on, back to your unpacking.'

He looked slightly sheepish. 'Actually I thought I'd go and meet up with Bella.'

Jo smiled then laughed. 'Ten quid says you'll still be living out of boxes at Christmas.'

He shook her outstretched hand. 'Done. That'll be a tenner you owe me.'

She got into the car. She wound down the window, blew him a kiss.

'Let me know?' he said.

'I will.' Then with a wave she let in the clutch and was gone.

She had roughly eighty miles to go.

It was mid-afternoon, and she hoped she'd got the timing right.

She didn't want to think. Thinking was too dangerous, too liable to tip her into an anxiety so great that she might have to stop driving.

She put more music on. It was Mozart, and it kept her mind off her increasing doubts.

She parked. Got out. Dithered over whether or not to take her bag: on the one hand, it was surely tempting fate, but on the other she knew it was undoubtedly now or never …

She slung the bag over her shoulder.

She had put her heavy boots on, so it didn't matter that she was splashing through shallow water for some of the way.

She reached the end of the path. Walked quickly past the big house, for she wasn't ready to see anyone, talk to anyone, hear the devastating news they might have to break to her.

She hurried on.

She could see the house now. The sun was going down and golden light was reflecting off the windows.

She put down her bag, went in quietly through the half-open door. He had his back to her. He was working on a big canvas and painting a pink sunset. He was concentrating deeply; didn't know she was there.

She stood absolutely still.

Then suddenly he stopped moving. Froze. And spun round to face her.

Her heart gave a huge leap.

He stared at her, his dark blue eyes intent on hers. He had gone pale. Then he said, 'Are you here to stay?'

She nodded. Tried to speak, tried again. 'Yes. I wouldn't have come otherwise.'

He put his brush down. Walked towards her. Raised his hand and very gently touched her hair. 'I can't believe it.'

'It's true.'

'We kept our promise, didn't we?' he said. His hand stroked her hair again. 'Five years, and not a word.'

'Yes. I couldn't come back unless I was no longer married. I'm not.'

He nodded. 'I'm sorry.'

'It was the right thing,' she said. 'We tried. We gave it our best shot. But …' She shrugged.

'Yes,' he said, so quietly that she only just heard.

They stood in the silence, just looking at each other.

Then he said, 'I loved your stories. Especially the last one.' The previous Christmas she'd sent him as modern-day fable, full of hope.

'Loved your oils.' His final painting had been of a glorious sunrise. Now he smiled. It lifted him; filled his face with joy.

He reached out for her again. 'I've put pink paint in your hair.'

'I don't care.'

'I need to clean up.' He looked down at his hands. Then, meeting her eyes again, 'And I need to - to adjust. To realise that you're really here. You know?' Now he looked anxious.

'Yes, I know.' She was trying to drink him in. 'I've had a long time to do it. To adjust. I realise it's not the same for you.'

'It's okay. Jesus, so much more than okay!' He smiled again. 'I'm-' He shrugged, gave up.

'I'll go and see Archie and tell him I'm back,' she said.

He nodded. 'Fifteen minutes, on the shore by the maze?'

'Okay.'

She walked back to the big house, hardly able to feel her feet on the ground.

She heard soft music from the Sea Room. She went in. Straight away she saw the Sea Spirit fresco - a band of vivid colour, an impression of smooth, sinuous movement - but she barely took it in. Now wasn't the moment.

Archie was standing by himself by the big window, looking out. She said softly, 'Archie?'

He turned. He stared at her. His face had lifted at the sight of her but then he frowned. Just as Silas had done, he said, 'You're staying?'

'Yes.'

He nodded. 'I see.'

'We just didn't work anymore, Hal and me,' she said very softly. 'It was painful – both of us felt so much hurt – but we knew it was the right thing for us. He's bought a house in California on a hillside near to his father, he's working, travelling, and he's living the life he's meant to.'

'What about your boys?'

'Sammie's in school over there, living with Hal.' She hurried over that bit, trying to smile, because of the hurt. 'Ed's just started university.' She grinned. 'Durham.'

'Durham,' Archie repeated. Then he moved towards her, taking her hands. 'You're sure?'

'About Silas? Yes. There hasn't been a day I haven't thought about him.'

'It has been the same for him. At least I assume so,' Archie added. He looked at her, frowning. 'He's been away. For a long time – eighteen months, getting on for a couple of years. Italy, then Greece.'

'Yes.' She felt she should explain. 'He's sent me a little painting every Christmas – I've been sending him stories – and the last two packages had foreign stamps.'

Archie said quietly, 'It wasn't the same here without him. He …' Then, abruptly, 'You've seen him? It must have been such a shock to see you. He knows you're staying? He's not-?'

'Yes, yes, and he isn't anything, Archie. He's cleaning his hands and we're meeting on the shore in a few minutes.'

Archie was looking at her hair. He chuckled. 'Too late with the hand-washing,' he observed. 'You have a streak of pink in your hair that's going to be hell to get out.'

Then I won't bother, she thought.

When it fades I'll dye it the same colour, for ever, because it marks the moment I came back to Silas.

'See you later, Archie.'

She was already heading for the door. For the path to the spot above the little beach where the maze was laid out. Archie was saying something but she didn't stop to listen. She'd spent so long trying to make sure everyone else was all right and happy – as happy as they were going to get just now – and now it was her turn.

Hers and Silas's.

She was nearing the shore.

He was waiting for her.

She broke into a run.

* * *

They didn't want to be apart.

They walked until it was dark that night, then went back to his house for a vegetable hotpot he'd made earlier in the day. They got ready for bed, but both of them knew it was too soon to become lovers. So he made up his bed with clean sheets for her and set out a mattress and sleeping bag beside it for himself. The bed was low to the ground, and she could reach out her hand and hold his. They talked long into the night.

The next day and night followed the same pattern.

'We are filling in the years apart,' he said to her. Her heart sang for joy.

And now, as if released by the fact that she had come back, he told her in far greater detail about his life before he came to the island. Things he did because he had to; things he was not proud of; things he had never told anyone before. 'It was a filthy war,' he said, 'and I was in the army so I had to fight it. Worse, I was in a section of the military that involved deceit, and I discovered I was good at it. But it was wrong, so wrong; and decency, honesty, humanity, compassion, love, all were the casualties alongside all the dead and wounded. The soldiers and the ordinary men and women.'

She did a quick calculation and realised which conflict he was referring to.

Yes.

He told her more, much more; sometimes she felt she could see a river of horrors flowing out of him.

'I am sorry to describe such things to you,' he said as they stood on the headland looking out at the sea getting up. It was late in the day, and growing cold. She could feel the sweat from their long walk cooling on her body; they'd gone over to the mainland and walked for miles. 'But you need to know, I think?'

317

He turned it into a question. She replied without even thinking, 'Yes, I think so too.'

We need to know each other's hidden areas, she thought as for a brief moment they were both silent. No – she corrected herself – not know them; we both need to tell each other about them. It's an active thing.

'It's why I went to the monastery. Why I stayed there,' he said eventually.

And she thought she understood.

She told him of her own times of darkness. Losing Ben. Bringing up Ed – Teddy – on her own. Loving him so deeply, desperate for someone else to share the huge responsibility of being a parent. Hal: great love followed by an even greater disillusionment.

Another long night, more hours of talking; of laughing now, for all at once there was an ease and a delight between them. As they started to fall towards sleep in the thinning darkness around dawn, he said, 'It seems to me that I know all about you, and that what I've been telling you isn't news to you. It's as if …' He paused. 'As if there's another life running alongside this one we're in, and that we've been living in it together, all this time and for years before we met.'

'Yes, I feel the same.' For his words had set off an instant echo in her. 'It's just as you said. I know things without being told.'

The next morning they slept late. Or Jo did; Silas woke up before her, and for a while propped himself up and watched her as she slept. Then he got up and, when he heard her stirring, took her a cup of tea.

Later they set out and did the circuit around the island.

'Ed's just started at Durham,' Jo said as they strode along right by the water's edge. 'He's doing engineering.'

'Why Durham?'

She smiled. 'I'm guessing that the fact his friend Bella is going there – it's where they met, in fact, at an introductory session – may be relevant. But he says he really likes this part of Britain.'

'Durham's a beautiful city,' Silas said.

'He's no stranger to the area, since he was travelling round the north east with Bella for a couple of weeks in the summer.'

'Tell me about Bella.'

'She's lovely, she's got very long light brown hair and hazel eyes, and I've no idea if they're really girl and boyfriend or just mates. Not that it matters.'

Silas waited till she'd stopped talking. He really liked just listening to her. She sounded so full of joy, so full of love. But as he realised she wasn't going to add any more, he said, 'What does your son look like?'

'He's tall, quite broad-shouldered with dark blond hair and blue eyes.' She grabbed his hand and hurried him the short remaining distance back to his house. 'I'll show you.'

She fetched her Filofax and took some photos out of the section at the back. 'That's Ed, and that's him with Sammie.'

Silas studied the smiling faces. He pointed to the one she'd said was Ed. 'He came here,' he said. 'With a girl with very long hair. We had an open day back in August and it attracted a lot of visitors. He and the girl asked if they could go and look at the fresco in the Sea Room, and Archie sent Helly to fetch me to talk to them about it.'

'Did he?' She sounded very surprised. 'I'd forgotten he knew about it.'

He started to grin.

'What?' she asked, beginning to smile too.

'I was just thinking it was a good job you kept your clothes on.'

They spent the next night as they had done the first two. In the morning, early, they put on wet suits and went for a long swim. Neither of them felt hungry, so they had marmite toast for lunch. He was sure she remembered, but she wasn't sad now.

He said to her after they'd washed up that he had an idea.

She put away the glass she had in her hand and turned to look at him. 'Oh, yes?'

She knows, he thought. 'We can get across the path very soon because the tide's falling. Shall we set off in my truck and see where we get to? We could go up into Scotland and find a place to stay that's miles from anywhere and where we don't know anyone.' He paused. 'Where it'll be new, and we won't have any memories.'

'I don't want to lose the memories,' she said very quietly.

'Neither do I. But I just think we need to be somewhere else for … for the next day or so.'

She was nodding. She did know. 'Yes.' She was smiling at him, her expression soft, her eyes full of love. 'Okay.'

They headed north, past Berwick and inland past Coldstream and towards Kelso. They kept near to the Tweed, then branched off on a narrow road leading down to a stretch of open water. There was a large Victorian building on the shore, advertising itself as the Sweetwater Country Hotel. Silas headed up the drive, parked – there were about half a dozen other cars there – and they went inside.

An elegantly dressed, straight-backed man in his late sixties stood behind the reception desk. His name badge said he was Eric Prior. Silas carried in their bags while Jo went over to speak to him.

'Have you got a room that looks out over that lovely view, please?' she asked with a smile.

'Indeed, madam.' He reached behind him and ran his hand along the rows of keys on large wooden fobs.

Jo leaned closer, dropping her voice. 'Would it be possible to have one without tartan and dead animals?'

Without a word, he returned the key he had just selected and handed her another one. Silently he put one carefully-manicured finger beside his nose. The he asked, 'Would sir and madam care to reserve a table for dinner?'

She turned to Silas. She was flashing him a message with her eyes, but he wasn't sure what it was. He leaned closer to her. 'What is it?' he asked quietly.

'Oh …' She went on looking at him, then back at the man behind the desk. 'If it's all right, and if it's possible, what I would really love would be to have a picnic served in a wicker basket, on a blanket down there.' She nodded towards the lakeside, to where a path wound off among a thin stand of trees.

'For a woman of such discernment regarding tartan and other overt Caledonian manifestations,' the man said, 'anything is possible. What time would you like to eat?'

Silas, amused, pleased, saw that Jo was looking at him again. 'Half past seven,' he said decisively.

And the man behind the desk said, 'Consider it done.'

The room was simply but tastefully furnished, and the wide windows looked out over the water. The view, as Jo remarked, was adornment enough. Silas unpacked the few things he'd brought with quick efficiency, and he was gratified to see her do the same. He knew she wouldn't be the sort of woman who brought changes of clothes to suit several possible contingencies and a sack full of cosmetics. She went to use the bathroom and came out drying her hands. 'The soap smells of bluebells,' she remarked.

He held out his hand, and she took it. 'Once round the loch before we eat?' he suggested.

'Yes.'

They walked hand in hand. The track was narrow and in places hard to make out, but they had their boots on and neither minded a bit of scrambling. They talked about the view, discussed the wildlife, admired the beauty of the evening sky's deepening blue.

It wasn't the moment for anything else.

Silas could feel the excitement building in him.

They came out of the patch of woodland right by where a large checked blanket with a waterproof backing had been laid on the shore. Beside it stood a wicker hamper, next to that an ice bucket with a bottle of Veuve Clicquot. There was an old-fashioned brown card luggage label tied around its neck: on it was written, 'I believe you may be celebrating so I took the liberty'. It was signed *EP*.

Jo flung herself down with a whoop of joy – 'He's given us a bottle of the Widow! What a lovely man!' – and opened the hamper. While Silas popped the cork and filled the two tall, slim glasses, she set out plates of delicate smoked salmon sandwiches, small quiches still warm from the oven, a variety of salads in little covered bowls and some miniature beefburgers. 'I don't eat meat!' Jo said, eyes wide in dismay.

'Neither do I,' Silas replied. 'Don't worry, I'm sure he won't be offended.

They worked their way through almost all the rest of the food. But then he happened to glance up to find her looking at him. After that he couldn't eat any more.

Jo felt as if she was diving into his eyes.

She said, her voice shaking a little, 'Have you had enough to eat?'

'Yes.'

She began to pack up the bowls, plates and glasses. He put the empty bottle upside down in the ice bucket. Between them they gathered up the blanket and shook it, then folded it. She took the rug and bucket, Silas the hamper, and they walked side by side, not speaking, back to the hotel.

A different, younger man was on duty at reception. 'Is Mr Prior here?' Silas asked. Jo didn't think she could have said a word.

'No, he's gone for his supper,' the young man said. 'Want to leave a message?'

'Yes. Please tell him thank you very much for taking so much trouble, the picnic was perfect and we're sorry but we don't eat meat.'

The young man muttered as he wrote down the words. 'Will do, sir. Goodnight, sir, madam.'

Jo walked ahead towards the wide curve of the stairs. She heard Silas's soft footfalls behind her.

She stood in the bathroom cleaning her teeth. She'd had a quick shower, towelled herself dry in an enormous bath sheet and now stood in one of the mid-thigh-length tee shirts she wore at night. She was trembling.

She went back out into the room. Silas looked at her briefly, then took his turn in the bathroom.

She went to stand by the window.

I want this so much, she thought.

I'd thought there might be awkwardness, difficulties, misunderstandings.

We're together again after five years, and we only had a week the first time.

But it was a week unlike any other.

She wasn't sure where the thought had come from. It was a voice, really, speaking quietly and with great love right into her head. She didn't try to puzzle it out. She just smiled and whispered, 'Thank you.'

Now he was walking towards her. She felt the vibration of his steps on the floorboards.

She turned round.

For a beat or two they simply looked at each other.

Then he said, 'Oh, God, I love you.'

'And I you.'

He opened his arms and she stepped into his warmth.

He kissed her, softly at first and then with growing passion. Breaking away briefly, he said, 'That is only our second kiss,' and she could hardly believe it.

He had his arms around her waist, and now he tightened his grip and lifted her off her feet, walking with her over to the bed. He threw back the duvet and laid her down, kneeling on the crisp white sheet beside her. He dragged off his tee shirt and boxers, she grabbed at the hem of her tee shirt and wriggled out of it. They looked at each other's bodies for the first time.

'You're beautiful,' he said. He ran his hands up her arms, over her ribs and right down the length of her legs. 'You're so strong.' He looked up into her eyes again. 'I know already what you look like in a wet suit – I spent hours drawing you. But this …' Very delicately he brushed his fingers over her stomach. 'You're so soft!'

She was studying his chest, his strong shoulders, his muscled stomach. He had a big tattoo right at the top of his left arm; it was a circle, intricately patterned like a mandala.

'This is lovely,' she said.

He was smiling at her. In that moment he looked almost unreal; as if his joy was making him shine.

He lowered himself down beside her. Then he was kissing her again, his hands running over her, setting her on fire with desire. She felt him hard against her, and then that was not enough. She shifted her position and instantly he did the same; as in so many areas, already they seemed to know each other.

When finally he was inside her and they were making love, she was lost in a wonderful confusion, aware that this was their first time, yet also aware that somehow they had done the same unbelievable act, given each other the same incredible heights of arousal and ecstasy, a thousand times before.

Chapter 24

As they drove back to Old Harbour, they talked about how they were going to arrange their life. Jo was driving; crossing the gravelled drive to the car park he had lobbed the keys to her. 'I put you on the car insurance a few days ago,' he said. 'No greater guarantee of good faith can any man make.'

She laughed, but it hadn't been quite so funny as she got to grips with the pick-up's V8 engine.

Now, half a morning's experience made her feel like an old pro.

'I've got a house in Kent,' she said as they descended a long, steep slope.

'I know. You told me.'

'Come and see it?'

'Right now?'

'Ha.'

'Yes, of course. What do you want to with your house in Kent?'

'Well, if we're living at Old Harbour' – this had been one of their first decisions – 'then we don't need it as a residence. I let it before.' She didn't need to explain to Silas about living for a while in America, hating it, sensing she was losing Hal and following him to Greece, putting their lives right, for a time; she'd already told him. 'I could do so again.'

'You could,' he agreed.

'I don't really want to sell it,' she went on, appreciating that he hadn't even implied she should. 'There have been fraught and distressing times there, but also very happy ones.'

'Pretty much like any house,' he remarked.

'Yes. I could probably get it back with the same letting agent, and there's a chap in the village who would probably decorate it for me just as he did before.'

'I can decorate,' he said.

'I'm sure, but I'm also sure you can't sing the entire score of *South Pacific* all by yourself like Reggie Pickett can.'

'I'm prepared to give it a go. I could be up a ladder beside him and sing the harmonies. He'd have to be Mitzi Gaynor, though.'

'Nothing Reggie Pickett can't handle.'

It was Hal's phrase, she thought. *Nothing I can't handle.* But it didn't hurt; she thought of him and sent him a bubble of love.

Silas waited for a moment, as if he knew she had briefly been absent. Then he said, 'On the subject of living at Old Harbour, we could turn the smaller spare room into an office for you, or you could have one of the guest houses if you want more space.'

'No thank you.' I don't want two walls and a gap between us, even when we're both working, she thought.

'Okay. So, we'll have guests, and there's plenty of room for them. How many visiting friends and relations should we be considering?'

'Um... the boys, to start with. Ed for vacations, Sammie too.' Thinking of Sammie and sending her love wasn't painless. On the contrary, it hurt a lot.

Silas said softly, 'I'm sorry.'

'I'm okay,' she replied. He wasn't saying it as an apology for anything he'd done; it was that he was sorry she was hurting. She knew it, so did he, and there was no need to explain. 'Then,' she went on, 'my parents, my brothers and their wives – I'm not serious about my brothers, I'm quite sure they won't venture this far north, especially not my older brother' and his fatuous wife. They'll want to come and check you out, I expect, but they pretty much live in Switzerland except for brief visits to the ridiculously expensive London flat they bought a year or so back. Oh, and there's Max and Angela, and Jake.'

She'd told him everything there was to say about Angela, too, and how much she now liked her and had always liked Max. 'They live in Cambridge. We could call in on them on the way home from Kent.'

He said, 'I like the way you just said *home*.'

She grinned. 'Thought you might.'

Silas had thought they might have slipped quietly back into Old Harbour and taken up residence together without anyone taking much notice. He was wrong.

As they were sitting over a cup of tea that afternoon, the washing machine churning away and Jo saying she ought to get a new waxed jacket if it was going to go on raining since hers had a leak across the shoulder, there was a tap at the door and Archie put his head round it.

'Busy this evening?' he enquired. He was trying to suppress a smile. 'And don't say yes because I won't believe you.'

'No, then,' Silas replied.

'Come over and eat in the big house?' He made it sound like a casual invitation, but Silas wasn't fooled and he didn't think Jo was either.

'Ye-es,' he said slowly, just as Jo said with a beaming smile, 'We'd love to!'

And it wasn't, of course, a simple supper.

It was a party.

Jo hadn't really appreciated how many people lived and worked at Old Harbour – her time there during her first visit had been filled with Silas – and it was quite a surprise now to discover what a lot there were; an even bigger surprise was that they'd all turned up to welcome her. Not a few of them seemed to have been expecting her.

'Glad you're here at last,' Helly Dunbar said quietly to her as she wrapped her in a hug. 'Welcome home,' said a very thin man who apparently taught a very abstruse form of yoga. Somebody else – an elderly man with a lined face and very clear light grey eyes whose function at Old Harbour she didn't yet know – remarked with a very loving smile that she had begun in the far south west of England and now she had come to the far north east. 'It is time,' he added mysteriously.

He went on looking at her for some time after his pronouncement, smiling gently, and she felt as if his warmth surrounded her. And she knew suddenly that nobody had told him where she'd been born and lived the first part of her life.

'How did you know?' she whispered.

But he just shook his head, still smiling, and drifted away.

The evening wasn't all prophetic pronouncements and enigmatic smiles, however. There was a buffet, a very well-stocked bar and the music got louder as the hours went by. It quickly became apparent to Jo that the people at Old Harbour liked to party, and welcomed a good excuse for a wild evening. Perhaps it was the large amounts of self-control they exercised in their daily work, she reflected vaguely as Archie swung her round in a strange variation on a Scottish reel; perhaps they all needed the chance to let it all out once in a while.

As they finally staggered home, Silas's arm round Jo's waist, he said, 'I had no idea you could do the Mexican Hat Dance on a very small table.'

And she replied, 'Neither did I.'

They made the trip to Kent and stayed at Copse Hill House for a week, in the course of which, with the invaluable Reggie Pickett and his repertoire (to which he had added *My Fair Lady* and one or two highlights from *West Side Story*), they prepared it for tenants.

'We're blanding it down,' Silas said one night as they slumped over the kitchen table eating a scrap supper they were too tired to enjoy.

'Blanding?'

'Making it bland. Covering up your bright colours.'

'I like off-white!' she protested mildly. 'It's what you have at home, and it gives such a sense of space.'

'I know, and I like it too,' he replied. 'And it's looking good here. I just wondered if you minded. It's transforming the house,' he added.

She looked around. He was right. For years the walls had been painted in the autumnal shades she'd chosen when she did up the house before racing off to Greece after Hal. Prior to that it had been pastels and flowers; the colours and fabrics she'd selected pretty much at random when she and her little son had moved to Kent after Ben's death. My house, my refuge, she thought now. First when I was trying to stand up again after Ben, then when I thought I was losing Hal.

Out of nowhere she was back on a ferry that was taking her to a Greek island, where Hal was – somewhat reluctantly – waiting for her to join him. She'd had no idea, really, what her reception would be like. She had comforted her unease by thinking of her house; this house. She'd wondered why the very thought of it made her happy and realised something profound: the house had been her refuge and helped her get over Ben, so she knew that if it had to, it would also get her over Hal.

And then, sitting there in the kitchen with Silas waiting patiently for her answer, another profound realisation came to her.

She let it sit in her mind for a while, testing it.

Yes.

She reached out for his hand. 'Maybe I mind a bit,' she said honestly, answering his implied question. 'It feels rather as if we're painting over the past, which is both a good thing and a poignant one. But we have to do it,' she hurried on. 'I hadn't realised how shabby the dear old place had become. And ...' She stopped abruptly.

'Go on,' he said softly.

'It's not the same anyway, because Hal took his stuff away months ago, and Sammie's got his bedroom treasures in his new room in Hal's house, and Ed's always travelled light anyway. So it's just me here now, really.' She gave him a shaky smile.

He nodded. She knew he understood. He gave the moment the silence it deserved; she loved it that he never tried to jolly her along with trite remarks. He got up, came over to her and crouched down in front of her, pushing her long hair back from her face, his hands like a hairband. He loved her hair; he often slept with his fingers entwined in it, as he'd done that very first night.

'Silas?' she said softly.

'Yes?'

'Let's not let the house.' She paused, and he waited. 'Let's sell it.'

He thought about that. 'You said you didn't want to.'

'Yes. I know. But ...' She stopped, thinking carefully about what she wanted to say. It was important he understood. 'It's to do with what I just said: it's just me here now,' she began. 'It's not home anymore to the family that lived here, because although the constituent parts of that family are doing just fine, it – the family – doesn't exist anymore.'

She stared into his concerned eyes, picking up strength from him because this was so difficult.

'We could do what I thought I wanted to, and keep the house, letting it out to tenants, but … But it would always be part of me. Of us, you and me. And I don't think it ought to be. It's time to thank the old place, do it up so it looks its very best, then say a final goodbye.'

Silas put his hand up to her face and brushed away her tears. She hadn't realised she was crying. After a moment she said, 'What do you think?'

'It's your decision,' he replied instantly.

She smiled. She'd have put money on that being precisely what he'd say. 'But?'

He smiled back. 'But for what it's worth, I think you're right.'

She bent forward until she was leaning against him, her forehead resting on his. There was so much in her head, in her heart, but she reckoned he knew pretty much all of it. So she just said, 'Thank you.'

He straightened up, briefly bending to kiss her. Returning to his chair, he said, 'Then tomorrow we'll get the interior finished while your Reggie does the last bits of the exterior, and …'

'And we'll put it on the market.'

There was a little left in the large bottle of beer they were sharing. Silas divided it between their two glasses and they drank a silent toast.

They went from Kent to Cornwall and stayed a couple of nights with Jo's parents. At the beginning of the year, Elowyn and Paul had greeted the news of Jo's divorce with understanding and kindness: 'I think perhaps both of you will be happier apart,' Elowyn had said, while Paul, giving her a rare, hard hug, muttered, 'You did your best.'

Now she watched as her parents formed their first impressions of Silas.

Silas was exactly himself. There was something reserved about him, Jo thought. Perfectly polite, mannerly; fielding questions, describing life at Old Harbour and what he did there; well aware, she had no doubt, that her parents had a right to ask since their daughter was going to live on the island with him.

But she knew there was so much more to him. She had only just started on the long road to understanding him, for he was deep. She felt a flash of joy, accompanied by humbleness, that he was allowing her in. I won't let you down, she said silently to him.

After Cornwall, they drove as quickly as the truck could manage it back to Old Harbour.

Autumn turned into winter. Jo drove them down to visit Max and Angela, and she observed with interest how Max and Silas sized each other up and both came to a positive conclusion. 'Could have been a stags-locking-horns situation,' Angela murmured to her, 'but it looks as if it's going to be okay.'

Christmas came, and with it first Ed and Bella, fresh from Durham, full of what their inaugural term had been like (Bella was, anyway, Ed as usual a man of few words) and eager to start celebrating the season straight away. Jo asked what accommodation they wanted and unerringly they went for Tern Cottage. It was where she had stayed, it was furthest from the house and it only had one bedroom.

Returning from showing them how the heating and hot water worked, Silas was grinning. He said, 'I think we finally have an answer to the question of whether or not they're just friends.'

Sammie flew in to Teesside airport. Ed and Bella wanted to come with Jo and Silas to meet him, so they took the Discovery. The four of them lined up along the barrier, jostling with other people and everyone full of happiness because loved ones were coming for Christmas. Sammie came bursting through the doors, his one small bag sitting alone on a luggage trolly and a woman in a smart and colourful airline uniform trotting on heels to keep up with him.

'I'm looking for someone called Jo Dillon, or it might be Daniel?' she said in a carrying voice with a West Coast accent, even while Sammie's arms wrapped tightly around his mother made the enquiry superfluous.

'That's me!' Jo said, laughing and crying at the same time.

The woman smiled, perfect Californian teeth set in shiny rose-coloured lipsticked lips. 'You don't say.' She proffered a clip board. 'Couple of signatures, then he's all yours.'

'Has he behaved himself?' Ed asked, punching his brother lightly on the shoulder.

The woman in the uniform turned a suddenly earnest face to him. 'He's been a delight,' she replied. 'Jeez, I wish all my passengers were like him. So long, Sammie,' she said, 'hope we fly together again real soon!'

'Bye, Savannah!' Sammie replied. 'Me too!' Then, as she tripped away on her glossy shoes, he hissed indignantly, 'They referred to me as an unaccompanied minor and I'm *fourteen* next year!'

'This is Silas,' Jo said as they trundled the trolly into quieter waters, 'he's the man I've been telling you about, and …'

'Yeah, Mum, it's cool,' Sammie said. 'Hi, Silas, nice to meet you.' And, quaintly, he put out a hand and Silas shook it.

'Nice to meet you too, Sammie,' he replied solemnly.

'And this is Bella,' Ed said, grabbing his chance and pushing Bella forward.

'Hi, Bella. Mum, can we sail?'

'Er …' Jo looked at Silas.

'Maybe,' Silas said.

He said it with such calm authority that even jet-lagged, hyper and over-excited Sammie didn't question the ambiguous reply.

Sammie settled into the spare room opposite Silas and Jo's room. He seemed to take the fact that they were clearly living together in his stride, and Jo sent Hal a silent thank you for preparing the way. She'd been planning to find a moment for a quiet chat with her younger son, but in the end events seemed to overtake the need for it and she didn't bother.

Paul and Elowyn came by train: Cornwall to London, overnight at Jo's brothers' flat ('They're all there for Christmas and they all send their love,' Elowyn said, which Jo greeted with a largish pinch of salt, especially in the older brother's wife's case), and on north next day. Paul was intrigued by the path to the island, and returned once they were settled in to study the tide table posted up beside it. Archie had put them in the best room in the big house. He'd been looking forward very much to welcoming them, and reckoned, from Jo's description of her father, that one or two choice therapy sessions might be of benefit.

'Good luck with that one,' Jo had muttered under her breath.

Other Christmas guests were arriving at the big house, and there were three more for Jo and Silas: Max, Angela and Jake took up residence in the largest of Silas's cottages, and it was apparent as soon as Angela took off her down jacket that she was pregnant.

On Christmas Day there was a service of celebration at the big house, which seemed to Jo be an amalgam of the timeless Christian story, the return of the god of light, the winter solstice and a few other elements she didn't recognise. The message was clear: simply, it was full of joy.

She watched the faces of the people who were only there because she had met and fallen so deeply in love with Silas: Ed, Sammie, Bella, her mother and her father, Max, Angela and Jake. Not one of them looked remotely as if they regretted having made the journey; quite the contrary, in fact, and her father was actually singing. She caught her mother's eye and Elowyn smiled, raising her eyebrows briefly in exasperated affection. Paul Daniel couldn't carry a tune, but he did sing loudly.

Lunch took up most of the remainder of the day. The hours passed in a flurry of food, drink, laughter, and the weather played its part by producing a very cold but bright day which turned Old Harbour into a painting and heightened its wild beauty.

A week later, with bad weather predicted, the guests made a retreat back to the mainland and their own homes before Old Harbour got cut off. Ed and Bella returned to Durham, and then Jo and Silas took Sammie to the airport for his flight back to California. As Jo handed her younger son over, the pain of seeing him leaving was mitigated by Sammie's excitement and comforted by Silas and his quiet strength beside her.

Tucked up in the house that night, Jo experienced her first midwinter storm.

Safe and warm in Silas's arms, she listened to the wind howling round the sturdy old house. Felt the violence of the pellets of hail hurled against the window. Heard the sea, so close, blasting huge waves onto the shore as if trying to destroy it.

She loved it.

On a day in late March, Jo and Silas had been down by the island's quay servicing the outboard on his boat. They were both filthy and they'd got thoroughly wet when a series of large waves appeared out of nowhere and caught them by surprise. But the job was done, and Silas had a look of quiet satisfaction.

'It was much easier with four hands,' he remarked as they walked home.

'Even when one of those hands dropped a very small screw that took ages to find?'

'But you did find it, so it doesn't count.'

He went on into the kitchen while she was still in the boot room struggling out of her wet overalls. She heard him fill the kettle and slide it onto the hot plate.

As she came in through the door he said, 'Would you like to marry me?' in so precisely the same tone of voice he used for *would you like a cup of tea?* that she had to run the words through her head again to make sure she'd heard him right.

She looked straight into his eyes. 'Yes.'

He was there in front of her in a nanosecond from right over on the other side of the kitchen, and she thought in wonder that it was a little miracle alongside the huge one.

They didn't speak; they didn't even kiss. He just held her.

Later as they sat beside the fire under a blanket – neither of them had any clothes on – he reached into the little salt cupboard set into the side of the fireplace and took out a small box covered in blue velvet. He said, 'Hold out your hand,' and she did so. He put the box into her palm. 'Open it.'

It was a gold ring set with five stones: an indigo sapphire, an ultramarine one, a very bright emerald, an aquamarine and a diamond. It said *sea* as loudly as if it had spoken the word.

He took it gently from her and put it on her finger.

'Was that guesswork?' she asked, indicating the perfect fit.

He smiled. 'No. I borrowed the ring you wear on your right hand one day when you were helping me with yet another filthy job and

337

had left it on the shelf above the sink. I drew round it, and the bloke who made the ring took the size from it, making this one very slightly smaller because you're right handed.'

'Someone made this?' His grin widened. 'Well of course, but I mean, someone you actually know?'

'Yep. His name's Mark, and I knew him in the service.'

Someone else, Jo thought, who almost got crushed by the darkness but managed to emerge again and start making something beautiful.

'I love it,' she said quietly. 'Thank you.'

'My pleasure.'

Thinking that maybe thank you wasn't enough – by rather a long way – she turned into him and began to kiss him.

They set the date for the end of July, for they couldn't get married without Sammie.

Jo took a rare trip to the big city to buy a wedding dress. She had a colour in her head: greyish, blueish, silvery white. She had no idea if they made wedding dresses in that shade. After quite a lot of foot-slogging – which served to remind her that she really didn't like big cities any more, if she had ever done – she found what she was looking for in a little shop set away from the main throng.

The young woman who had been doing her best to help for a good half an hour said shyly, 'What about this one? It's not exactly …'

'Oh, but I think it is,' Jo interrupted. 'You clever girl!'

She went back into the cubicle, handed back the five dresses that weren't right and slipped into the one that was.

It had a tight-fitting bodice in silvery white lace shaded subtly with the colour of the crepe silk underneath, which was a pale grey-blue. The full-length skirt was made up of layers of the same crepe

338

silk, overlapping so that they fell in folds that intertwined. When she moved, they floated around her. It could have been made for her; it was perfect.

The young woman thought so too.

On the day before the ceremony, people started to arrive. Ed and Bella, Paul and Elowyn, bringing Sammie from the airport. Max, Angela, Jake and their new-born son – whose name was Felix – with all the baggage needed for a new baby. Silas's sisters and their children; this was the third time Jo had met them and it was getting a little easier. One of them had brought a card and a present from Silas's mother; the present turned out to be a set of plastic-covered place mats. The guests were escorted to their rooms by what seemed most of Old Harbour, and the mood of excitement affected everyone. The ceremony was to be in the Sea Room, and Archie would be conducting it. All of the downstairs areas of the big house were decorated with foliage and flowers.

Jo was over in her and Silas's bedroom checking for the tenth time that Silas's wedding ring was safe in her knicker drawer when she heard him call out to her.

'Jo, sorry to disturb you but the boat's on its way across and it looks like there are another couple of guests arriving.'

'Oh? I thought everyone was here already. Anyway, the tide's in.' The rhythms of Old Harbour were already becoming ingrained in her.

'Yes, that's why the boat went over,' he said patiently.

She looked questioningly at him. He shrugged. He was smiling gently at her, but she assumed it was just for general happiness.

'We'd better go and meet them, then, whoever they are,' she said.

They walked up past the big house and down to the little harbour. The boat was just drawing alongside, and the skipper hurled the fore rope across to Silas. He made it fast and the skipper did the same at the stern.

Jo stood watching as two figures appeared, coming out of the little cockpit and negotiating the short step down to the quay. They were being careful, because both of them were quite old …

With a great shot of joy, Jo raced to hug them. And Mary MacAllister and Sam Dillon hugged her back, all three of them in a muddle of kisses, arms, laughter and tears.

'I had no idea!' Jo cried. 'How on earth did you get here?'

'Much the same way as everyone else, I guess,' Sam said with a smile.

'Yes, right, but how did you know?'

Mary glanced at Silas. 'You have your man here and your mom and pa to thank,' she smiled. 'They got their heads together, and here we are!'

'But …' She paused, for she had no idea how to go on. How to say somehow that the three of them were so close only because Jo had been married to both their sons, but that Ben had died and she and Hal couldn't make it work, and that now she was marrying someone else.

'Jo, honey, we know,' Sam said gently. 'Okay?'

And, blinking away her tears for she realised she really didn't need them, she said, 'Okay!'

She stood in the doorway of the Sea Room.

Chairs had been set out in rows on either side, leaving a clear aisle up the middle. She could see most of the Old Harbour people on the right, Silas's sisters, nephews and nieces among them, and Silas stood alone at the front. He wasn't having a best man, any more than she was having attendants or someone to give her away. On the left were her family and those as close to her heart as if they too were linked to her by blood. The remaining chairs on that side were filled by more people from Old Harbour.

340

She held a bunch of white flowers: roses, little carnations, a couple of lilies. There was soft music playing: it calmed her.

She started to walk towards Archie, who she was peripherally aware was smiling encouragingly at her; her eyes were on Silas's broad back. He was wearing a suit – a suit! She hadn't realised he possessed one – in an expensive-looking grey fabric with a subtle blue tone and a faint sheen. I bet he's not wearing a tie, she thought.

And then he turned right round to face her.

He was wearing a very pale blue shirt and no, he wasn't wearing a tie.

He was smiling at her, he looked absolutely gorgeous, smarter and better-groomed than she'd ever seen him, and it made her heart flip over that it had mattered so much to him, that he'd taken so much trouble.

As she went to join him it was all she could do to stop herself breaking into a run.

Chapter 25

In the house on the hillside autumn was closing in again, and Hal set about ensuring his wood supply would last him through the winter.

His life in the solitary house suited him so well that at times it made him feel guilty.

His work was progressing solidly; better than ever before. The book on the Basque country had sold well in Europe, less well in the States, but his publisher reassured him that they'd expected precisely that and were not disappointed. 'But maybe something of more interest to us next time, huh?' both his agent and his editor had said in slightly different words.

His lavishly illustrated book about the Spanish Missions appeared to have been pretty much what they'd had in mind. Hal had worked on it on and off throughout the year when he and Jo had finally hit the buffers and quietly agreed to end their marriage, and throwing himself into travelling up and down the south west and into Mexico, taking hundreds of photos, haunting visitor centres and seeking out out-of-the-way one-room museums, following up the hidden trails that led to old men and women with a story to tell, had absorbed him so that sometimes he forgot what was happening.

But mostly he didn't.

It was a time to be endured. He'd been through something similar before, when Magdalena told him she had to marry someone else and he'd taken off to travel, at first aimlessly, through South America. It was different this time, though, because the pain was mitigated by the awareness that he knew he was doing the right thing; that he and Jo both were. The only thing, in truth.

Now his mind was full of the next project and he'd begun on the research for something – he wasn't absolutely sure what just yet – about the history of the First Nation in the areas that were now Washington State and the Pacific coast of Canada. He was planning a trip right up the coast – Nevada, Oregon, Washington, British Columbia and as far north as he could go, perhaps into Alaska and the Yukon – but it was too late in the year to embark on it now and it'd have to wait till spring.

The thought of the trip gave him a constant, quiet pleasure.

He came and went exactly as he pleased. He called in on Sam at least once a week and often included a quick visit to Mary, happily settled in her waterside apartment. Quite often the visit to his father would include Mary anyway; the two of them seemed to derive a quiet pleasure from each other's undemanding company, and the trip they'd made to England for Jo's wedding looked like being the first of more travels. Good for them, Hal thought; they were cheerfully and courageously setting off while they still could, making up for lost time. Mary had been kept at home because in his latter years Bernard didn't want to go anywhere, and Sam had never had anyone to travel with.

Sammie came to stay most weekends. He seemed to like his school well enough, and he adored the house on the hillside. He often invited school pals home and they seemed to like it too. Hal suspected it was more likely his somewhat relaxed attitude over what his son and his friends got up to that they appreciated. He took the view that as long as they didn't smoke or drink in his presence, told him where they were going when they went off exploring and returned without fail at the time he'd specified, there wasn't too much harm they could fall into.

In the school holidays, Sammie went to England to stay with his mother and her new husband and Hal was entirely alone. Sam understood that he both desired and needed the solitude. Well, why wouldn't he, Hal sometimes thought, he's just the same; or at least he used to be, until Mary McAllister breached his defences. Only a little, maybe, but it was good to see. Quite clearly it made both of them happy.

After Sammie's visit the previous summer he had come back full of Jo's wedding, not even suspecting it'd hurt his father to hear every last detail. It didn't; he was pleased for her.

I'm not husband material, he thought now as he swung the axe and the two halves of bisected log fell either side of the block. I've loved women; still love them. But …

He thought of Magdalena. He'd loved her, for sure, and when he'd learned that she'd died in childbirth along with her baby only a year after her marriage, he'd thought to begin with that he wasn't going to recover from the pain. But he did.

He thought of Angela. He reckoned he'd loved her too; her memory had persisted, that was for sure, and he'd gone hurrying to find her as soon as he'd accidentally discovered where she was. She'd had such a hold on him, and it had been a deep pain to walk away.

According to Sammie – blissfully unaware of his father's history – Angela and Max were married now and had two little sons.

Strange, Hal mused as he stood another log on the chopping block, how life works out.

He thought of Jo.

He'd loved her all right.

He was able to look at himself and the women he had loved with clearer eyes now, and he understood that neither Magdalena nor Angela could have endured in his heart like Jo had done; like she does, he admitted honestly. It wouldn't have lasted with either of them even as long as Jo and I did, he thought. We gave it our best shot, and it wasn't her fault. She was asking me for something I didn't possess, that wasn't a part of my nature, and in the end it wore us both out.

Just as with the others, with Magdalena and Angela, he reflected, he was better at loving her when he didn't have to live with her.

There was still a stack of logs to split. He wiped his sweaty forehead and threw himself into the task.

Sometime later he was done. He glanced at his watch. It was later than he thought: he'd have to be quick. He ran inside the house, took a rapid shower and changed into better clothes, then hurried out again.

He got into the car and drove down into Morro Bay. He parked and walked swiftly to the framing place where he and Sam had taken his mother's photograph that day one Christmas – how many years ago? Seven, nearly. He had something to pick up.

The young man behind the counter gave him a smile. 'It's ready,' he said. His tone was a little awe-struck.

He laid a framed oil painting on the top of the counter. It was a portrait, around eighteen inches by two foot. It was of a woman with long fair hair and green eyes, lying back on a deep blue velvet covered chair, a bright turquoise shawl wrapped around her and the baby she held against her chest. It was exquisite.

'Mum says she's probably too old because she's in her mid-forties,'

Sammie had said, 'but both of them want to and the doctors and people say it's not too bad because she's had us already, me and Ed.'

With the painting Silas had sent a letter, written on thick paper in a beautifully artistic hand. Hal knew most of it by heart. 'I love her more than I thought I could love anyone,' he'd said. 'Please know that she is very well, she is happy, she is glowing. I'm sending you this so that you can see for yourself; I don't believe that what I've written is an exaggeration. The baby is a girl and her name is Lillie.' He had signed it simply *Silas*.

Hal came back into the moment, and the realisation that the young assistant was speaking to him.

'… a real name in the best art circles,' he was saying.

'Excuse me?' Hal said.

'Silas Gerritt!' the assistant said. 'The man who painted this!'

'Yeah, I know.'

'He's not widely known in the wider art world, but boy is that ever about to change! They're saying he's entering a new phase where his work's suddenly a good deal brighter and more optimistic, and the smart word is that it's not hard to see why.' He indicated the painting. 'She's a beautiful woman,' he sighed.

'She sure is,' Hal echoed softly.

The young man leaned forward, lowering his voice. 'My boss came down specially to have a look at this painting while we were working on it,' he whispered. 'He said to say he sure hopes you have it insured, and to check that you really are aware how much it's worth.'

'Sure, I am,' Hal assured him. He didn't add that there would be no point insuring it because it was irreplaceable.

He hung it above the fireplace so that Jo would be with him.

He fetched a cold beer and sat back on the old leather sofa where an

346

old woman had died. He had restored it, rubbed a lot of leather food into the cracks, and now it was as good as new. Better, for it had age, character and a long history.

He'd found out about the old woman. Her name was Mabel, she'd lived in the house on the hillside for most of her life and she'd loved it. She'd been married and had children and they'd grown up and moved away. Her husband had died and she'd been almost entirely alone for the last decade of her life. But her solitude was from choice; Hal sensed a kindred spirit. Now, when he sat on Mabel's Sofa – he always referred to it like that and as if it had capital letters, and Sammie did too – he often talked to her. Sometimes he even fancied he heard her answer. Her presence was good; he welcomed it.

'That's my wife, Mabel,' Hal said softly. He took another slug of beer. 'She's not in fact, not now. She's married to someone else, and apparently she's very happy.'

Jo was made for happiness, he reflected.

He wondered if she was finding with this Silas what she'd had with Ben, and suddenly it was as if a voice said in his head, *of course she is, dummy.*

He smiled.

He had an idea whose voice it was, and whether it was real or simply his imagination didn't seem to matter much.

He looked up at the painting.

She was looking straight out of it at the viewer, and her face was full of love. She looked young – younger than in any of the years he'd known her. She'd grown her hair, and what he could see of her body under the baby and the shawl looked strong and muscular. Hard life, is it sweetheart, on that island of yours? he asked her silently. Good food, fresh air and plenty of exercise?

347

He thought her soft smile broadened for an instant. He imagined her saying something faintly dismissive and definitely crude.

It would have been dishonest to say he missed her. He didn't; he knew he was better living alone. He was content, and contentment frequently turned into happiness.

But as he looked up at her – and it was soon to become a habit – and raised his beer bottle to her, he knew that a part of him would love her for the rest of his life.

He finished the beer. Got up, took the empty bottle over to the kitchen and set about preparing his supper.

While he'd been in town he'd picked up a book he'd had on order at the book store. It was about the history of the Cree nation, and he was looking forward to reading it. He'd make a start while he ate.

As he fetched vegetables from the rack and eggs from the fridge, he was humming.